Born near Bern, Switzerlar
internationally known as dr
now, with Max Frisch, the most celebrated German
dramatist of his generation.

The five novels collected here can be described as paradoxical detective stories with a touch of Kafka – unrelenting, bitter, also cruelly funny. They were originally published separately in the fifties and sixties but have long been out of print and appear here for the first time in one volume.

Friedrich Dürrenmatt

His Five Novels

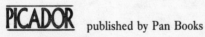 published by Pan Books

The Judge and his Hangman first published as *Der Richter und Sein Henker* in 1952
by Benziger Verlag
© Benziger Verlag 1952
First published in Great Britain 1954 by Jonathan Cape
English translation Copyright Cyrus Books

The Quarry first published as *Der Verdacht* in 1953
by Benziger Verlag
© Benziger Verlag 1953
First published in Great Britain 1962 by Jonathan Cape
English translation © New York Graphic Society 1961

Once a Greek . . . first published as *Grieche Sucht Griechin* in 1955
by Arche Verlag AG
© Peter Schifferli, Verlags AG 1955
First published in Great Britain 1966 by Jonathan Cape
English translation © Alfred A. Knopf, Inc. 1965

A Dangerous Game first published as *Die Panne* in 1956
by Arche Verlag AG
© Peter Schifferli, Verlags AG 1956
First published in Great Britain 1960 by Jonathan Cape
English translation © Alfred A. Knopf, Inc. 1960

The Pledge first published as *Das Versprechen* in 1958
by Arche Verlag AG
© Peter Schifferli, Verlags AG 1958
First published in Great Britain 1959 by Jonathan Cape
English translation © Alfred A. Knopf, Inc. 1959

This edition published 1985 by Pan Books Ltd,
Cavaye Place, London SW10 9PG

© Pan Books Ltd, 1985

9 8 7 6 5 4 3 2 1
ISBN 0 330 29112 2
Phototypeset by Input Typesetting Ltd, London
Printed in Great Britain by
Richard Clay (The Chaucer Press) Ltd, Bungay, Suffolk

Contents

The Judge and his Hangman

Chapter one

On the morning of November 3rd, Alphonse Clenin, constable of the village of Twann, came upon a blue Mercedes car by the roadside, just where the highway from Lamlingen emerges from the woods that surround the gorge of the Twann River. It was one of those foggy mornings of which there are many in the late autumn of the year. Clenin had walked past the car when something caught his eye and made him stop and turn back. In passing he had glanced through the fog-dimmed window and got a blurred impression of the driver collapsed over the wheel. Thinking that the man was drunk, he strode slowly back to the car to arouse the sleeper and offer a few fatherly words of advice. Then, maybe, he would drive the man into Twann and let him sober up over a breakfast of black coffee and porridge in the 'Bear' Hotel. For while it was forbidden to drive a car while under the influence of drink, there was no law against a man quietly sleeping off the effects of drink whilst sitting in a car by the roadside.

Clenin opened the car door and put a rousing hand on the stranger's shoulder. As he did so he realized that the man was dead – a bullet had passed through one temple and out of the other. At the same time Clenin also noticed that the near-side door was unlatched. There was little blood in the car and the dead man's dark grey coat was not even stained. The edge of a yellow note-case showed bright from the overcoat inside pocket, and Clenin drew it out. With no difficulty he established that the dead man was Ulrich Schmied, a lieutenant in the Berne police.

Clenin wondered what to do next. As a village constable, he had never encountered a case of such gravity. He left the car and paced nervously up and down by the roadside until the early morning sun, breaking suddenly through the fog, shone full on the corpse. This was more than Clenin could stand. He went back to the car, picked up the grey felt hat that lay at the dead man's feet and pulled it so far down on the fellow's head that the wound was completely hidden. Then, feeling a little better, he crossed to the side of the road that looks over Twann, and wiped the sweat from his forehead. After some minutes he reached a decision. Returning to the car, he manhandled the corpse on to the passenger seat, and gingerly raised it into an erect sitting posture, securing it in position with a leather strap found in the back of the car. Then he climbed in beside it and took the wheel.

The engine refused to start when he pressed the starter and a brief inspection showed that the tank was empty of fuel. But the car was standing on a steep incline and Clenin had no difficulty in coasting it down the hill into Twann and stopping outside the 'Bear'. There he filled up with petrol without the attendant suspecting that the motionless passenger was a corpse. With petrol in the tank Clenin started up the engine and drove along the lakeside road towards the town of Biel. The fog thickened again, the sun was blotted out and the morning grew as grey as Judgment Day. After a time, Clenin found himself in a long line of cars, bonnet to tail, which for some mysterious reason seemed to move even more slowly than the poor visibility made necessary. Like a funeral procession, Clenin thought grimly. The corpse sat motionless at his side, except that now and then, when they came to a rough bit of road, its head nodded like a wise old Chinaman's, so that Clenin felt less and less inclined to hurry past the cars ahead. As a consequence he reached Biel much later than he had expected.

While the detailed investigation of the Schmied case was entrusted to the Biel police, the officer who took charge of it in Berne was Inspector Barlach, who had been the dead man's superior. Barlach had spent much of his life abroad. He had had a distinguished career in the detection of crime, first in Constantinople and later in Germany, where he had been in charge of the criminal investigation department in Frankfurt-on-Main during the early Nazi days. He had returned to Berne not so much out of love for his birthplace, which he often alluded to as his 'golden grave', but because he had slapped the face of a high official of what was then the new German Government. His action attracted a great deal of attention at the time in Frankfurt. In Berne it was assessed progressively in accordance with the European

political situation: first as disgraceful, later as regrettable but understandable, and finally as the only possible thing a Swiss could have
done.

Barlach's first action in the Schmied case was to order it to be kept
secret, at least for a few days, and he had to exert all his authority to
get the order observed. 'We know too little,' he insisted. 'Besides,
why give the story to the press, anyway? Nothing more superfluous
than newspapers has been invented in the last two thousand years.'

But Barlach's insistence on secrecy was not shared by his chief, Dr
Lucius Lutz, lecturer in criminology at Berne University. Lutz, on
whose mental outlook a childless but wealthy uncle in Basle had
exercised a beneficent influence, had recently returned from a visit to
the police departments of New York and Chicago. What he had seen
there had greatly impressed him so that he was now frankly horrified
– as he admitted to Commissioner Frieberger as they went home
together by tram – at the 'prehistoric inadequacy of the safeguards
against crime in the federal capital of Switzerland'.

The same morning, having had two telephone conversations with the
Biel police, Barlach paid a visit to the Schönlers in Bantiger-strasse,
where Schmied had lodged. As always he went on foot for in his
opinion Berne was too small for riding in 'trams and suchlike'. It cost
him some effort to climb the steep flight of steps which lay in his path
– for he was over sixty and felt it at such times – but eventually he
reached his destination and rang the bell.

The door was opened by Frau Schönler herself, a short, plump,
not undistinguished woman, who knew him and admitted him at once.

'Schmied had to go away on duty last night,' said Barlach. 'He had
to leave unexpectedly and asked me to send him some papers he has
been working on. Kindly take me to his room, Frau Schönler.'

She nodded and led the way down the passage, passing a large
picture in a heavy gilt frame. Barlach glanced at it – it was a painting
of the Dead Islands.

'Where's he gone to?' asked the plump woman, as she opened the
door of her lodger's room.

'Abroad,' said Barlach, looking inscrutably at the ceiling.

The room was on the ground floor and overlooked a small park of
old, brown pine trees, which must have been diseased for the ground
was covered thickly with needles. Barlach guessed it was the best

room in the house. He went over to the writing-table and looked around him. On the divan was one of the dead man's ties.

'Has he gone to the tropics, Herr Barlach?' Frau Schönler asked, full of wonder.

Barlach was a little startled by the question. 'No, not the tropics. The mountains, more likely.'

Frau Schönler's eyes goggled and she raised her hands above her head. 'The mountains! The Himalayas, perhaps?'

'Perhaps!' Barlach agreed. 'You're not far from the truth.' He opened a brief-case that lay on the table and glanced inside. Then he quickly tucked it under his arm.

'Have you found what you wanted to send to Herr Schmied?'

'Indeed I have.'

He took another look round, his eyes avoiding the tie on the divan.

'He's the best lodger we've ever had,' Frau Schönler assured him. 'Never any trouble with ladies and such-like.'

Barlach went to the door. 'I may look in now and then or send a constable round. Schmied has some other documents here, which he may need.'

'Do you think I shall get a postcard from Herr Schmied while he's abroad?' Frau Schönler inquired. 'My son collects stamps.'

Barlach frowned and looked at Frau Schönler with a glance of official disapproval. 'Most unlikely,' he said. 'Police officers never send postcards when travelling on duty. It's forbidden.'

At which Frau Schönler again raised her hands above her head, and cried protestingly, 'Nowadays the police forbid everything!'

Barlach went out, glad to leave the house behind him.

Deep in thought, Barlach lunched in the Café du Théâtre instead of his usual restaurant. As he ate he examined the contents of the brief-case he had brought from Schmied's room, here and there pausing to read absorbedly. Then he left the café and, after a short stroll along the Bundes-strasse, returned to his office at two o'clock where he heard that Schmied's body had been brought in from Biel. He decided not to pay a call on his deceased subordinate, for he had no liking for corpses and gave them a wide berth whenever he could.

He would also have preferred not to call on Lutz, but he had no choice in this and had to make the best of it. Without examining its contents further, he carefully locked Schmied's brief-case in his desk.

Then he lit a cigar and went into Lutz's office, well knowing that Lutz furiously resented the liberty he took by smoking cigars in his 'chief's' room. Once, some years before, Lutz had dared to object, but Barlach had waved aside his objections condescendingly. He had served ten years in Turkey, he said, and had always smoked in his superior's office. It was a statement that was all the more exasperating to Lutz because it could not be disproved.

Dr Lucius Lutz received Barlach with more than his usual irritation, for in his opinion nothing had yet been done in the Schmied case.

'Any news from Biel?' Barlach asked.

'Not yet,' answered Lutz.

'Hm-m!' said Barlach. 'Well, they're working on it.'

He dropped into the comfortable armchair in front of Lutz's desk and threw a quick glance at the pictures by Traffelet that hung on the walls; tinted pen-and-ink drawings of soldiers, sometimes with a general, sometimes without, marching either from right to left or from left to right under a great flowing banner.

'It causes me increasing anxiety', began Lutz, 'that detective criminology in this country is still in its infancy. God knows I'm hardened to most of the ineptitudes that go on in this canton, but the procedure that seems to be regarded as right and proper in the case of Lieutenant Schmied throws an even worse light on the professional competence of our rural constabulary.'

'Come, come, Dr Lutz,' Barlach answered. 'Our village constables are quite as competent in their own way as the Chicago police. We shall find out who killed Schmied. Take my word for it.'

'Have you a lead? Is there anyone you suspect, Inspector Barlach?'

Barlach looked reflectively at Lutz for some time. At last he said, 'Yes, there is someone, Dr Lutz.'

'Who?'

'I can't tell you yet.'

'Well, that's most interesting,' said Lutz sarcastically. 'I know you always prefer to follow your own line of investigation rather than take advantage of modern methods of detection, Inspector, but don't forget that time marches on and has no respect even for the most distinguished of reputations. I've seen crimes handled in New York and Chicago in a way we in Berne have absolutely no conception of. But this time, remember, a lieutenant of police has been murdered and that means trouble for us at Police Headquarters.

We've got to act ruthlessly.'

'Naturally,' said Barlach. 'That's exactly what I'm doing.'

'I am most pleased to hear it,' said Lutz, and coughed.

A clock on the wall went on ticking.

Barlach placed his left hand gingerly on his stomach and with his right hand crushed out his cigar in the ashtray which Lutz had pushed towards him. He told Lutz that for some time he had not been in the best of health. His doctor had pulled a very long face when last he had examined him. He had frequent attacks of abdominal trouble, and would be grateful if Dr Lutz would appoint someone to assist him in the Schmied case, someone who could undertake much of the active work. Such a course would free Barlach to concentrate on the finer details of the case. Lutz agreed.

'Whom do you suggest as assistant?' he asked.

'Chanz,' Barlach replied promptly. 'I understand he's still on leave in the Bernese Oberland, but we can recall him.'

'A good idea,' said Lutz. 'Chanz is a man who works hard to keep abreast of the times.'

Then he deliberately turned his back on Barlach and stared out of the window at the Waisenhausplatz, which was crowded with children. He was conscious of an irresistible desire to quarrel with Barlach on the merits of science in criminal investigation. He spun round to face his visitor again but Barlach was no longer there.

Although it was already nearly five o'clock in the afternoon, Barlach decided to drive out to Twann to take a look at the scene of the crime. He was driven by a big, fat constable named Blatter, who never spoke and for whom, therefore, Barlach had a warm affection. Clenin met them at Twann, looking a little sulky in anticipation of a reprimand. But the Inspector was all amiability, shook the constable's hand and said he was pleased to meet a man who knew how to think for himself. Clenin brightened considerably when he heard this, though he did not quite know to what the Inspector referred.

He led Barlach to the scene of the crime, while Blatter trudged behind, disgruntled at having to walk.

They quickly reached the spot where the road was edged by a wall, below which lay the village of Twann.

'Where was the car, Clenin?'

'Here,' replied the constable, pointing. 'Almost in the middle of the road.' When Barlach scarcely looked in the direction indicated, Clenin went on, 'Ought I to have left the car there with the body untouched inside it?'

'No,' replied Barlach, looking up at the walls of Jura rock above them. 'It's best to get dead bodies out of the way as soon as possible; they have no business here among us. You were quite right to drive Schmied down to Biel.'

He crossed the road and looked down over Twann. There was nothing but vineyards between him and the ancient village. The sun had already set but he could still see the road writhing like a snake between the houses and a long goods train was standing in the station.

'Did no one down there hear anything?' he asked. 'The village is not far away. Someone must have heard the shot.'

'They heard nothing but the engine of the car running. It ran most of the night, but they didn't think anything was wrong.'

'Of course not. Why should they?'

He looked at the vineyards. 'How is the wine this year, Clenin?'

'Good. Would you like to sample it?'

'Yes. I should enjoy a glass of new wine.'

He kicked something metallic with his foot, and bent down to pick it up. When he stood up again he was holding a small, elongated piece of metal, crushed flat at one end, between his lean fingers. Clenin and Blatter looked at the object curiously.

'A pistol bullet,' said Blatter.

'How did you come to find it, Inspector?' asked Clenin in surprised chagrin.

'Just luck,' said Barlach. And they set off down the hill for Twann.

Chapter two

The young wine did not agree with Barlach, for next morning he declared that he had been vomiting all night. Lutz, who ran into the Inspector on the stairs, seemed genuinely worried about the state of his health and advised him to consult his doctor.

'All right, all right,' growled Barlach, adding to himself that he was even less fond of doctors than he was of modern criminology cranks. By the time he reached his office he felt better. He sat down at his desk, unlocked a drawer and brought out the dead man's brief-case.

At ten o'clock, when Chanz called to see him, Barlach was still immersed in its contents. Chanz had returned from his leave later the previous night, and as he entered Barlach gave a start. Chanz was wearing a felt hat and an overcoat very like Schmied's, and for a moment Barlach thought the dead man Schmied had entered the room. Only the face was different: it was plump and good-humoured.

'I'm glad you've come, Chanz,' said Barlach. 'We must have a talk about the Schmied case. You'll have to take over most of the hard work, I'm afraid. I'm not too well.'

'Yes,' said Chanz. 'I heard.'

Chanz drew up a chair and sat down, resting his left arm on Barlach's desk, on which lay Schmied's open brief-case.

Barlach leaned back in his chair. 'I don't mind telling you,' he began, 'that I've come across some thousands of policemen, good, bad, and indifferent, between Constantinople and Berne. Some had little more sense than the poor devils with whom we fill our prisons except that they happened to be on the right side of the law. But I never met one to compare with Schmied. He had brains. By comparison most of us looked pretty small fry. He had a cool head that knew what it wanted and kept what it knew to itself. He never talked except when it was necessary. We must take a leaf out of his book, Chanz. He was a better man than you or me.'

Chanz turned his head slowly from the window through which he had been gazing and looked steadily at Barlach. 'That's possible,' he said, but Barlach saw by his expression that he was not convinced.

'We don't know much about how he died,' went on the Inspector. 'This bullet – that's all.' And he laid the bullet he had found at Twann on the desk. Chanz picked it up and looked at it.

'From an army pistol,' he said, putting it down again.

Barlach was closing the brief-case as he went on: 'We don't yet know what took Schmied to Twann. He didn't visit Lake Biel on duty, I should have known if he had. We know of absolutely nothing that would explain his presence there.'

Chanz seemed to be only half listening. Throwing one leg across the other, he said: 'All we know is that Schmied was murdered and how it was done.'

'What makes you think we know that?' asked the Inspector with some surprise.

'Schmied's car had a left-hand drive and you found the bullet on the left-hand side of the road, looking in the same direction as the car. Schmied must have been stopped by the murderer as he was driving down from Lamlingen to Twann. It's probable that he knew the man who shot him, otherwise he wouldn't have stopped. Schmied opened the near-side door of the car to let the murderer get in and sat back behind the wheel. That's when he was shot. Schmied cannot have had any idea that the man intended to kill him.'

Barlach thought over what Chanz had said. 'I think I'll have a cigar,' he said surprisingly. When he had lit up he went on: 'You're right, Chanz. That's more or less how it must have happened. But it still doesn't explain what Schmied was doing on the road from Twann to Lamlingen.'

'Perhaps the fact that he was wearing evening-dress tails may point to the explanation.'

'I didn't know he was,' said Barlach in surprise.

'But haven't you seen the body?'

'No. I don't like bodies.'

'It's also mentioned in the official report.'

'I don't like official reports either.'

Chanz said nothing.

'If anything, it makes the case even more complex,' Barlach said thoughtfully. 'Why should Schmied wear a tail-suit in the gorge of Twann?'

Chanz answered that this fact might simplify rather than complicate the case. There couldn't be many residents in the Lamlingen district who would throw the sort of party for which the guests put on tails. He produced a small diary from his pocket and held it up for Barlach to see. 'This was Schmied's,' he said.

Barlach nodded. 'I've seen it. There's nothing in it of any importance.'

Chanz was less sure. 'Against Wednesday, November 2nd', he pointed out, 'Schmied has written the letter G. That is the day he was murdered – shortly before midnight, according to the police surgeon. There's another G against Wednesday, October 26th, and again against Tuesday, October 18th.'

'G might mean anything,' said Barlach. 'A girl's initial probably.'

'Hardly a girl's name,' Chanz objected, 'because Schmied's girl was named Anna and Schmied was the steady sort.'

'I know nothing of his girl friends,' the Inspector admitted, and, seeing that Chanz was astonished at his apparent indifference, he added: 'I'm only interested in who killed him.'

'Of course,' said Chanz politely. Then he shook his head and laughed. 'What a man you are, Inspector Barlach.'

'I'm a big, black tom-cat' – Barlach said the words quite seriously – 'and I have an appetite for mice.'

Chanz did not know what to say to that. At last he remarked: 'On the days marked G, Schmied put on his tails and drove off in his Mercedes.'

'How do you know that?'

'From Frau Schönler.'

'Ah-ha,' said Barlach.

Chanz looked keenly into the Inspector's face. He lit a cigarette and said with some hesitation: 'Dr Lutz told me you have a possible suspect in mind.'

'Yes, Chanz, I have.'

'Since I've been appointed to act as your assistant in this case, wouldn't it be better if you told me whom you suspect, Inspector Barlach?'

'Look here, Chanz', answered Barlach, choosing his words carefully, 'what I have in mind is as yet completely without foundation in fact. I have no evidence to justify it. You've just seen how little I really know. All I've got is a hunch as to who the murderer might be; I still have to get the proof.'

'But if I'm to co-operate with you, I must know who it is I have to investigate,' said Chanz civilly.

'Your job is to be objective. Whether my suspicions will be confirmed or not will depend on the results of your investigations. Your job is to put your finger on Schmied's murderer whatever may be my private suspicions. If my hunch is right you will reach the same conclusion though – in contrast to my own methods – you will reach it by unexceptionable scientific means. If I am wrong, you will have succeeded in your task without ever knowing the name of the person I suspected so unjustly.'

Chanz said nothing for a while. Then the older man asked: 'Do you agree to our working on that basis?'

Chanz hesitated for a moment before answering: 'All right, I agree.'

'What do you propose to do now?'

Chanz walked over to the window. 'Schmied had marked a G against today. I'll drive out to Twann and Lamlingen and see what I can find. I shall start at seven o'clock, the time that Schmied always started on these occasions.'

He turned round and asked politely but half jestingly, 'Would you care to come along, Inspector?'

'Yes, I'll come.'

'Right,' said Chanz, a little taken aback, for he had not expected this. 'At seven, then.'

At the door he turned again. 'I hear you went to see Frau Schönler, Inspector Barlach. Did you find anything there?' The old man did not answer at once. He locked the brief-case in a drawer of his desk and put the key in his pocket.

'No,' he said at last. 'I didn't find anything of consequence. I won't keep you any longer, Chanz.'

At seven o'clock Chanz drove to the house overlooking the river where the Inspector had lived for some years. It was raining and the fast police-car skidded as it turned after crossing the bridge over the river. Chanz expertly corrected the skid and drove more slowly along the Altenberg-strasse. It was the first time he had been to Barlach's house, and he peered through the streaming car window at the house numbers, which he had difficulty in deciphering. He found the one he was looking for at last and, repeated hooting producing no sign of life from within, Chanz got out of the car and ran through the rain to the front door. It was too dark to find the doorbell and, after a moment's hesitation, he turned the handle. The door opened and Chanz found himself in a small entrance hall. In front of him was a half-open door, a ray of light shining through the aperture. He knocked on this door and, receiving no answer, pushed it wide open. In front of him was a large room of which the walls were lined with books. Barlach was lying stretched on a divan. He was asleep, but he seemed to have prepared for the drive to Lake Biel for he was wearing a heavy overcoat. He had a book in his hand. Listening to his quiet breathing Chanz felt uneasy and embarrassed. The sight of the sleeping man, surrounded by his shelves of books, was somehow oddly disconcerting. Chanz looked cautiously round the room; it had no windows but there was a door in each wall, leading no doubt to other rooms. A massive writing-desk stood in the middle of the floor and on it lay a large brass snake. Chanz started a little as he caught sight of the reptile.

'I brought it back from Constantinople,' said a quiet voice from the divan. Barlach sat up. 'As you see I have my coat on, Chanz. We can go.'

'I apologize for breaking in,' said Chanz, caught at a disadvantage. 'You were asleep and didn't hear me. I couldn't find the bell at the front door.'

'There is no bell. I don't need one. The door is never locked.'

'Not even when you're out?'

'No. It amuses me to come home and see whether anything has been stolen.'

Chanz laughed and took up the snake to examine it.

'I was nearly killed with that thing once,' remarked the Inspector blandly, and Chanz noticed for the first time that the snake's head formed a handle and its body the blade of a knife. He stared fascinated at the strange decorations that shone on the terrible weapon.

' "Be ye therefore wise as serpents",' said Barlach, standing close beside him and eyeing him quizzically with a long, thoughtful look, ' "and harmless as doves." ' He tapped Chanz lightly on the shoulder. 'I've had some sleep – the first I've had for days. It's this damned stomach of mine.'

'It's as bad as that?'

'It is bad.' The Inspector stated a fact.

'You'd better stay at home, Herr Barlach. It's cold and wet outside.'

Barlach looked at Chanz again and laughed. 'I think you would prefer it if I did stay at home,' he said. 'But that would never do. We've got a murderer to hunt down.'

As they were driving across the Nydegg Bridge, Barlach asked, 'Why aren't we going via the Aagauerstalden? It's quicker than driving through the town.'

'Because it is better not to go through Zollikofen and Biel. The road through Kerzers and Erlach is better.'

'It's not the usual way.'

'It's not at all an unusual way, Inspector.'

They lapsed into silence. The lights of the town glided past them. When they reached the hospital Chanz asked, 'Did you ever drive with Schmied?'

'Often. He was a careful driver.' Barlach looked significantly at the needle of the speedometer which pointed to nearly sixty.

Chanz slowed down a little. 'He drove me once – as slow as hell. I remember he had a strange sort of name for his car, but I can't remember now what it was.'

'He called it "Blue Charon",' replied Barlach.

'That was it. Charon is the name of a character in Greek mythology, isn't it?'

'Charon ferried the dead across to the underworld, Chanz.'

'Schmied's parents were well off. They sent him to a good school. More than my people could afford for me. That's why he knew who Charon was, and why I didn't.'

Barlach thrust his hands in his overcoat pockets, and looked again at the speedometer. 'Yes,' he said. 'Schmied was an educated man. He knew Greek and Latin. With his advantages he had a great career before him. Even so, there's no cause for you to drive at sixty miles an hour all the time.'

The car pulled up sharply at a filling station and a man came out to attend to them.

'Police,' announced Chanz.

Indistinctly they saw an inquisitive and rather startled face framed in the car window.

'Ever had a man stop here who called his car "Blue Charon"? A blue Mercedes.'

The man shook his head in astonishment, and Chanz drove on. 'We'll try the next one.'

At Kerzers the filling station attendant was equally unhelpful.

'Where's the sense in all this?' growled Barlach.

But at Erlach Chanz was lucky. He was informed that the car he sought had called there on Wednesday evening.

'You see,' said Chanz triumphantly, as they joined the Neuchâtel-Biel road. 'We know now that Schmied passed through Kerzers and Erlach last Wednesday night. Proved it beyond doubt.'

'Oh, you've proved it all right, but what good does it do us?' asked Barlach.

'It's something,' answered Chanz. 'Every fact we prove helps us further forward.'

Barlach peered through the window looking for a glimpse of Lake Biel. The rain had stopped. Beyond Neuveville the lake came suddenly into sight through swathes of mist. They passed through Ligerz. Chanz drove slowly, looking out for the turning to Lamlingen. They found the turning and the car began to climb through the vineyards. Barlach opened the window and looked down at the lake. Lights were mirrored in the water and a motor-boat raced across the lake. Late for this time of year, thought Barlach.

They found a bend in the road and drove towards the woods, which they could sense rather than see in the darkness ahead. Chanz was uncertain they were on the right road. He stopped. A man wearing a leather jacket was coming towards them. 'Is this the way to Lamlingen?'

'Straight on. Turn right when you come to a row of white houses in the trees,' the man answered. He whistled to a small, white, black-headed dog which was dancing in the glare of the headlamps.

They left the vineyards behind and were soon in the woods. The pines rushed towards them, an endless row of columns in the beam of the headlights. The road was rough and so narrow that now and then a branch would sweep along the windows of the car. To their right the land dropped away steeply. Chanz drove slowly and through the open window they could hear a stream gushing far below them.

'This is the Twann gorge,' Chanz explained. 'The road into Twann lies on the other side.'

To their left crags towered into the night, flashing out whitely now and then. Otherwise all was dark, for it was the time of the new moon. The road flattened out and the stream they had heard earlier was now rushing beside them. They turned left and crossed a bridge. A broad road lay ahead – the road from Twann to Lamlingen. Chanz pulled up.

He switched off the headlights and they were in complete darkness. 'What now?' asked Barlach.

'We'll wait. It's twenty minutes to eight.'

They sat waiting. When nothing had happened by eight o'clock Barlach observed drily that it was about time Chanz told him what were his plans.

'I've no definite plans, Inspector. I've not yet got far enough to make plans. Even you, with your hunch to work on, are groping in the dark. I'm staking everything on the chance that there'll be a party again tonight at the house Schmied visited on Wednesday. If so, some of the guests are almost certain to drive along this road. It's bound to be a largish party if the guests wear evening dress. You may think it smells of a wild-goose chase, Herr Barlach, but all I've got to go on is the hope that we may pick up a clue somewhere in this neighbourhood.'

'The investigations of our colleagues in Biel, Neuveville, Twann and Lamlingen regarding Schmied's activities have produced precious little in the way of clues,' the Inspector reminded him quietly.

'That's simply because Schmied's murderer is a good deal cleverer than the police of Biel and Neuveville,' returned Chanz. 'If one can use the word "respect" in connection with a killer, I would use it of the man who murdered Schmied.'

Barlach listened without moving, his shoulders hunched up. 'But you're confident you will get him – this man you respect?'

'I hope so, Inspector.'

Again they waited in silence. Suddenly a light gleamed through the trees from the direction of Twann, and a few moments later the headlamps of a car flooded them with garish light. A big closed car sped past towards Lamlingen and disappeared into the night. Chanz started his engine and waited as two more cars passed them, large, dark limousines, each full of people. Chanz let in the clutch and drove in pursuit.

The woods came to an end. The cars passed a restaurant, its sign illuminated by the light from an open doorway, and then a cluster of labourers' cottages. Chanz had eyes only for the rear light of the car in front.

They reached the broad plateau of the Tessenberg. The sky was swept clean, the setting Vega, the rising Capella, Aldebaran and flaming Jupiter burned in the heavens. The road turned northwards and ahead of them stood out the dark outlines of mountain peaks at whose feet lay the few flickering lights of the village of Lamlingen.

Suddenly the cars ahead turned sharply left into a field-track, and Chanz stopped the car to watch. He wound down the window and stuck his head out. Across the field they could see the indistinct mass of a house surrounded by poplars. Its front door was illuminated and the cars they had followed were pulling up in front of it. The sound of voices came across to them as the new arrivals alighted and streamed into the house. Then the light in the doorway went out and all was still. 'No one else expected,' grunted Chanz.

Barlach got out and inhaled deep breaths of the cold night air. He felt the better for it and waited while Chanz parked the car on the grass verge at the side of the road, for the Lamlingen road was a narrow one. Chanz got out and walked across to the Inspector. Together, they went down the field-track towards the house. The ground was clayey and there were puddles everywhere, left over from the rain.

They came to a wall with a gate set in it, its rusty iron framework rising high above the level of the wall. They tried the gate, it was not locked. They looked across the bare garden at the house. The cars lay like great beasts among the poplars. Not a light was to be seen anywhere; it was as though the place was deserted and desolate.

Despite the darkness they managed to make out a plate affixed to the centre bars of the gate. A screw had come loose and the plate was hanging drunkenly sideways. Chanz switched on the flash-lamp he had brought from the car: in the centre of the plate was a big letter G.

They were in darkness again. 'You see,' said Chanz, triumphantly. 'I was right. A chance shot that hit, the bull's eye. I should like a cigar, Inspector, if you have one to spare. I think I deserve it,' he added complacently.

Barlach handed him a cigar. 'The next step is to find out what G stands for.'

'No problem about that,' said Chanz. 'It stands for Gastmann.'

'How do you know?'

'From the local telephone-directory. There are only two G's in Lamlingen.'

Barlach laughed in surprise. 'Mightn't it be the other G?'

'No, that's the gendarmerie. Unless you think a gendarme had something to do with the murder?'

'Anything's possible, Chanz.'

Chanz struck a match. But a fresh breeze had sprung up and was shaking the poplars in fury. He found it hard to light his cigar.

Chapter three

Barlach could not for the life of him understand how the police of Lamlingen had come to overlook Gastmann. His house lay in open country, easily visible from Lamlingen; it would be difficult, if not impossible, to give a party there without it being seen and noted by everybody in the village. Indeed such an event would be most conspicuous. He mentioned these points to Chanz, but his subordinate had no explanation to offer.

They decided to make a complete circuit of the house, going separately in opposite directions. Barlach watched Chanz disappear in the darkness, before setting off himself. He turned up his coat collar, for he was shivering, and was again tormented by the stabbing pain in his stomach that brought a cold sweat to his forehead. He walked along beside the wall, following it closely as it bent to the right. The house still lay in utter darkness.

After a while he stopped and leaned against the wall. He could see the lights of Lamlingen coming down to the edge of the wood. He walked on. The wall changed direction and the back of the house came into view. It was ablaze with light. Light poured from a row of windows on the first floor. He stopped as he heard the notes of a piano; listening intently he recognized that it was Bach that was being played.

He walked on. According to his reckoning he should soon be meeting Chanz again. He strained his eyes to see across the light-flooded stretch of lawn and as he did so he caught sight of a great dog only a few steps away as it moved silently out of the shadow. Barlach knew a good deal about dogs, but he had never seen one so huge as this. He could not distinguish his breed; all he could see was a silhouette that stood out against the lighter surface of the ground, but it was so big and threatening that Barlach could not stir. He saw the brute slowly turn its head, and look at him. Its round eyes were bright, blank orbs.

The suddenness of the encounter, the huge size of the animal and the strangeness of its appearance seemed to paralyse him. He forgot the need for action, but stared stupidly at the beast, unafraid but spell-bound.

Suddenly the dog leapt at him. Its gigantic bulk hurtled through the air, an unleashed mass of power and fury. The weight of the beast as it struck him threw the Inspector to the ground, but as he fell he threw up an arm to protect his throat. The beast was almost on top of him, its jaws about his forearm, when Barlach heard the whipcrack of a shot. A sudden convulsion ran through the dog's massive body and Barlach felt his hand become sticky with warm blood. The hound was dead.

The weight of the beast lay heavy upon him. Barlach passed his hand over its smooth sweaty fell and heaved the carcase to one side. He scrambled to his feet, trembling, and cleaned his hand in the thin grass. Chanz was there, pushing an automatic pistol back into his coat pocket as he came up.

'Are you all right, Inspector?' he asked, looking with concern at Barlach's torn sleeve.

'Perfectly. The brute's teeth didn't reach my arm.'

Chanz bent down and turned the creature's head: the light fell dully on its lifeless eyes.

'Teeth like a wolf's,' he said. 'The brute would have torn you to pieces, Inspector.'

'You saved my life, Chanz.'

'Don't you ever carry a pistol?' Chanz asked.

Barlach prodded the motionless mass with his toe. 'Not often,' he answered.

The dead hound lay on the bare, muddy ground, and both men looked down at it in silence. The blood that had welled from the creature's throat like a dark lava-stream had spread out to form a black pool at their feet.

When they looked up again the scene at the house had changed. The music had stopped, the lighted windows had been thrown open and men and women in evening dress were leaning out. Barlach and Chanz looked at each other. It was embarrassing to stand there as though before a crowded grandstand.

In the mid-most of the five windows was standing a solitary man, apparently isolated from the rest. He called out in a deep, clear voice, 'Who is there and what do you want?'

'We are police officers,' answered Barlach, quietly. 'We wish to speak to Herr Gastmann.'

In heavy scorn the man answered that he found it an extraordinary circumstance that they should need to shoot a dog in order to speak to Herr Gastmann. For himself he had only the desire to listen to Bach. With that he closed the window, giving the action a quality of unhurried finality, as unemotional and indifferent to outside disturbances as the timbre of his voice.

From the other windows came a babel of exclamations: 'Disgraceful!' 'Scandalous!' 'What boors these policemen are!' Then the heads were withdrawn: the windows closed one by one, and all was silent again.

The two policemen had no choice but to retrace their steps. At the main gate in front of the house, a solitary figure was awaiting them, pacing nervously up and down.

'Flash your light on him,' whispered Barlach. The sudden beam of Chanz's flash-lamp revealed above the starched collar and white tie a square, bloated face, not undistinguished yet of limited intelligence. A large stone sparkled on the finger of one hand. At Barlach's whisper the light was switched off again.

'Who the devil are you?' growled the stout man.

'Inspector Barlach. Are you Herr Gastmann?'

'My name is von Schwendi, Colonel and member of the National Council. Good God in Heaven, man, what do you mean by letting off your guns around here?'

'We are making some inquiries and desire to speak to Herr Gastmann, Councillor,' answered Barlach imperturbably.

The Councillor was not to be easily mollified. 'A Separatist, eh!' he thundered.

Barlach decided to address him by his alternative title. 'You are mistaken, Colonel,' he answered. 'We're not concerned in the political affairs of – '

But before Barlach could go on, the Colonel had become even more furious than the Councillor had been. 'A Communist!' he roared. 'Hell and damnation! As an officer and a gentleman I will not have people letting off guns in the middle of a private concert. It's an offence against decent civilization.'

The Councillor was obviously getting beyond himself. Barlach saw that it was time to take the situation firmly in hand.

'Don't put the Councillor's remarks in your report, Chanz,' he said in official tones.

The Councillor magically became comparatively calm.

'What report?' he demanded.

'As Inspector in the Criminal Investigation Department of the Berne Police,' returned Barlach, 'I am making inquiries into the murder of Police-Lieutenant Schmied.' He went on to explain that it was his duty to include in his report the answers made by all persons whom it was found necessary to question. But since – he hesitated for a moment over the title – since the Colonel had evidently misjudged the situation, he would not put the Councillor's words in his report.

The Colonel was disconcerted.

'You're policemen?' he said. 'That's a different matter. You should have explained yourselves right away.'

He begged their pardon and went on to give a parrot-like account of his day's activities: how in the morning he had attended a special meeting of his political party, how he had lunched at the Turkish Embassy, and from there had gone to a meeting of an association of Army officers of which he had been elected president. Afterwards, he had celebrated his election with a glass or two at his club. Finally, he had come to this reception of Gastmann's in honour of a world-famous pianist. He was dog-tired.

When he had finished Barlach again patiently inquired whether he might speak to Herr Gastmann.

'But what do you want with him?' demanded von Schwendi. 'What possible connection can there be between Gastmann and the death of a lieutenant of police?'

'The lieutenant was at Gastmann's party last Wednesday night and was murdered on his way home.'

'What else can one expect?' the Councillor sneered. 'Gastmann invites such a mixed crowd to his soirées that something was bound to happen sooner or later.'

He stood in silence, apparently thinking deeply.

'I'm Gastmann's lawyer,' he went on at last. 'Why did you have to call on him unannounced – tonight of all nights? You could at least have telephoned.'

Barlach explained that they had only just discovered that Schmied and Gastmann had been associated.

'And his dead dog? What am I to say to him about that?'

'The dog attacked me, and Chanz had to shoot.'

'Well, I'm sorry,' said von Schwendi, in more amicable but quite definite tones. 'You can't possibly see Gastmann tonight. Even the police must have some sense of social obligations. I'll find time for a word with Gastmann later on and will come to your office in the morning. By the way, do you happen to have a picture of Schmied with you?'

Barlach took a photograph from his wallet and passed it to him.

'Thank you,' said the Councillor.

Then with a nod he went into the house.

Barlach and Chanz found themselves once more in front of the rusty bars of the gate. The front of the house was as dark as it had been before.

'There's not much you can do against a member of the National Council,' said Barlach. 'And when he's a colonel and a lawyer into the bargain you have three kinds of devil to deal with at once. So here we are with a murder on our hands and nothing we can do about it.'

Chanz was silent and seemingly deep in thought. 'It's nine o'clock, Inspector,' he said at last. 'The best thing we can do is drive into Lamlingen and find out what the constable can tell us about this Gastmann.'

'Right,' answered Barlach. 'You talk to him. Find out why nothing is known in Lamlingen about Schmied's visits to Gastmann. I shall go to that little restaurant at the entrance to the gorge. I must take something for my stomach. I'll wait for you there.'

They walked back along the track to the car and Chanz drove off. It only took him a few minutes to reach Lamlingen.

He found the constable with Clenin, who had walked over from Twann, sitting at a table in the inn. The Lamlingen constable was red-haired, short and stout. His name was Jean Pierre Charnel. They sat apart from the farmhands, importantly aware of having official business to discuss.

Chanz sat down with them and soon managed to dissipate the suspicion they felt for their colleague from Berne. But Charnel was uncomfortable because he had to speak German instead of his customary French and it was a language he had never properly mastered. They drank white wine and Chanz ate bread and cheese with it. He made no mention of the fact that he had just come from Gastmann's. He asked whether they had brought to light any clues.

'*Non*,' said Charnel. '*On n'a rien trouvé*. Nothing.' He then went on to say that there was only one person in the district about whom the authorities knew very little – Herr Gastmann. He had bought a place called the Maison Rollier and he entertained there on a big scale. He had given a large party only the previous Wednesday, but Shmied had not been present. Gastmann had known nothing of Schmied, hadn't even recognized his name. It was not possible that Schmied had been a guest of Gastmann.

Chanz listened to Charnel's theorizing, and suggested that inquiries would have to be made of others who had been present at Gastmann's house that night.

'I've done that,' Clenin announced. 'There's an author fellow who lives at Schernelz. He knows Gastmann well and often goes to his house. He was there last Wednesday. But he'd never heard of Schmied, didn't know the name and said he didn't believe Gastmann would ever have had a policeman in his house.'

'An author, you say?' asked Chanz, and frowned.

'Maybe I'll tackle that customer myself some time. Writers are shady characters,' he added lugubriously, 'but I know how to handle them. Meanwhile, what sort of person is this Gastmann?'

'*Très riche*,' Charnel answered enthusiastically. 'Spends money like water, and most generous. He gives my fiancée tips' – he pointed proudly to the waitress – '*comme un roi*, but not because he wants anything from her, you understand. *Jamais*.'

'What's his business?'

'*Philosophe*.'

'What do you mean by that?'

'A man who thinks much but does nothing.'

'How does he earn his money?'

Charnel shook his head. 'He does not earn money, he has money. He pays the taxes for all in the village of Lamlingen. That's good enough for us. Gastmann is the best man in the whole canton.'

'That's as may be,' Chanz replied. 'But even so there are some pretty searching questions we have to put to Herr Gastmann. I'll come out tomorrow and have a talk to him.'

'Then watch out for his dog,' warned Charnel. '*Un chien très dangereux.*'

Chanz stood up and patted the Lamlingen constable reassuringly on the shoulder. 'I'll watch out for his dog all right.'

It was ten o'clock when Chanz left Clenin and Charnel to drive to the restaurant at which Barlach was to await him. When he reached the spot where the field-track branched off to Gastmann's house, he stopped the car and, getting out, walked slowly to the front gate and then along beside the wall. The house was just as it had been earlier, dark and solitary, surrounded by huge poplars swaying in the wind, the cars still parked outside. Chanz did not go right round the back of the house, but stopped at a corner from which he could survey the lighted rear windows.

From time to time the figures of men and women were silhouetted against the yellow panes. Keeping close to the wall to avoid being seen, Chanz looked across the grass to where the hound had been lying on the bare ground. There was no sign of it now except the pool of blood which still gleamed dark in the light of the windows. Someone must have taken the body away. Chanz returned to the car.

Barlach was not in the restaurant when he got there. The landlady said that he had taken a glass of Schweppes and had left for Twann about half an hour ago. He had not been in the restaurant more than five minutes.

As he drove off, Chanz asked himself what the old man had been up to, but gave up his speculations when the narrowing road called for all his attention. He drove very fast, past the bridge where they had waited and down into the wood. The jet darkness of the place gave him an uncanny feeling down his spine, a sensation which was suddenly heightened as he caught sight of the lake gleaming below him, a nocturnal mirror edged by white crags. With something of a shock he realized he had reached the scene of the murder, and his heart gave a faster beat as a dark figure detached itself from the wall of rock and signalled to the car to stop.

Without knowing why he did so, Chanz pulled up and opened the near-side door. The next moment he regretted his action as he remembered in a flash that this was precisely what Schmied had done a few seconds before he was shot. Chanz's hand flew to his coat pocket and his fingers closed round the pistol. The cold metal reassured him.

The figure came closer, and Chanz saw that it was Barlach. Even so his tension did not immediately relax; he was pale with a horror he was unable to explain to himself. Barlach leaned forward and they looked into each other's faces. Those few seconds seemed to last for hours. Neither spoke and their eyes were like stones. Then Barlach got into the car, and Chanz's fingers released their grip on the pistol in his pocket.

'Drive on, Chanz,' said Barlach, and Chanz thought he detected a hint of veiled contempt in his voice that made him wince. Furthermore, it seemed to him that thenceforward the sneering note was always present in the Inspector's voice whenever he spoke to him.

They had passed through Biel before Barlach broke the silence, asking what information Chanz had gained in Lamlingen. Chanz reported that both Charnel and Clenin thought it quite impossible that Schmied could have been a guest of Gastmann's. Barlach said nothing to this, but when Chanz mentioned the author who lived in Schernelz, the Inspector said he would interview the fellow himself.

Chanz gave his report less ponderously than was his usual custom; it was as though he was deliberately trying to conceal the fear he had felt. But before they reached Schüpfen they had again relapsed into silence.

Shortly after eleven the car drew up at Barlach's house in Altenberg and the Inspector got out.

'Thanks again, Chanz,' he said, and shook his hand. 'It's embarrassing to speak of, but you saved my life.'

He stood on the pavement and watched the car drive rapidly away till the rear light was lost in the distance. 'Now he can drive as fast as he likes,' he said to himself.

He entered his house by the unlocked door. Standing in his booklined room, he put his hand in his coat pocket and brought out an object which he laid carefully on the desk beside the brass snakeknife. It was a large, heavy automatic pistol.

Then he slowly removed his overcoat and jacket, revealing his left arm thickly wrapped in bandages. The bandages were loosely wound and bulky, such as men use to protect themselves when training dogs to attack intruders.

Chapter four

The Inspector knew from experience that some unpleasantness (for so he described the ever-present friction between himself and Lutz) was to be expected next morning. 'All Saturdays are alike,' he said to himself, as he walked across the Altenberg Bridge. 'A guilty conscience sets us on edge because we've done nothing useful all the week.'

He was wearing formal black for Schmied's funeral which was to take place at ten o'clock. He could not decently stay away from the ceremony and this was the real cause of his irritability.

Von Schwendi called early at police headquarters. He by-passed Barlach and asked to see Lutz, to whom Chanz had just reported the happenings of the previous night.

Von Schwendi belonged to the same political party as Lutz and had played some part in Lutz's advancement. After the last party dinner, which had followed a meeting of the central committee, he had even called Lutz by his Christian name, despite the fact that Lutz had not been elected to the Council. Von Schwendi waggishly explained Lutz's non-election to the fact that in Berne it was just a sheer impossibility for any public figure to prosper under the name of Lucius.

'You'd never believe, my dear Lucius,' he began, as his stout figure appeared in the doorway of Lutz's office, 'how these Berne policemen of yours behave. They actually shot my client Gastmann's dog, a rare and valuable specimen from South America, and completely ruined Anatol Kraushaar-Raffaeli's piano recital. Your men have no manners, no breadth of vision and no culture. Three years of compulsory military training would do them all a world of good.'

Lutz, who found the intervention of his political colleague embarrassing and was apprehensive lest he embark on one of his usual, endless tirades, offered von Schwendi a chair.

'You must understand', he began deprecatingly, intimidated despite himself, 'that we are involved in a tricky investigation. The young police officer who is mainly responsible for its conduct is, by Swiss standards at least, an able man and a shrewd detective, although the Inspector who was with him last night is, I must admit, more than ready for the junk heap. I deeply regret the death of the your client's hound, particularly so because I am a dog-owner and a dog-lover myself. But you can trust me to have this incident properly investigated.'

'The trouble is', he went on confidently, 'that our police methods are lamentably behind the times. When I recall what I saw of scientific detection in Chicago, I am forced to admit our present organization is quite hopeless.'

He paused for a moment, embarrassed by von Schwendi's silence and by the unwinking stare the other had fixed on him. His self-assurance was oozing from him as he went on: 'You surely ought to know whether Schmied was a guest of your client last Wednesday night. The police have some grounds for assuming that he was.'

'My dear Lucius,' interposed the Colonel. 'Why all this humbug? The police knew all about Schmied's visits to Gastmann, so why do you pretend otherwise?'

'What do you mean by that, Councillor?' Lutz demanded, bewilderment making him involuntarily relapse into formality. He never found it easy to be informal with von Schwendi.

The Councillor leaned back and folded his hands under his chin.

'I'd give a lot to know why you're trying to connect this Schmied affair with my friend Gastmann,' he said. 'Schmied was a guest at Gastmann's house but the entertainment that is offered at a private house has nothing whatever to do with the police. We're still some way from having a Gestapo in this country, you know.'

Momentarily, Lutz felt himself on safer ground. 'Why should you say we are trying to connect Schmied's murder with Gastmann?' he asked. 'As yet, we know nothing about him. Moreover, I must remind you that murder is the concern of the police wherever it is committed.'

'Do you mean to tell me,' von Schwendi persisted, ignoring the interruption, 'that you did not know that Schmied went to Gastmann's parties and that he went under the name of Dr Prantl, lecturer in American Cultural History at Munich University? If not, you and the whole police force should resign as criminally incompetent.' Von Schwendi drummed impatiently on Lutz's desk with the fingers of his right hand.

'We knew absolutely nothing of it, Oscar,' said Lutz, relieved at having at last remembered the Councillor's christian name, for which he had been racking his brains since the interview began. 'I confess what you tell me is news to me.'

'Ah!' von Schwendi exclaimed drily.

In the moments of silence that followed Lutz became more and more uncomfortably conscious of a growing sense of inferiority. He knew that he would have to give way to the Colonel step by step at every point. To cover his discomfort, he stared hard at Traffelet's pictures, at the marching soldiers and their waving Swiss flags. The Councillor noted Lutz's embarrassment with satisfaction.

'So, it's news to the police, is it?' he said. 'The police knew nothing of it?'

Unpleasant as the admission was, and intolerable as was von Schwendi's overbearing behaviour, Lutz had again to admit that Schmied's visits to Gastmann and his repeated presence in Lamlingen had been unknown to the police. He blustered a little when he pointed out that Schmied, when off-duty, was entitled to behave in a private capacity as he thought fit, though it was a complete mystery why he should have chosen to assume a false name.

Von Schwendi leaned forward and looked at Lutz with heavy, bloodshot eyes. 'There can, then, only be one explanation. Schmied was spying for a foreign power.'

'My dear fellow!' Lutz was genuinely shocked.

'From now on', the Councillor persisted, 'the primary duty of the police is to find out Schmied's reason for going to Gastmann's.'

'In that case the police must first know a great deal more about Gastmann, my dear Oscar,' Lutz objected.

'Gastmann does not enter into it,' von Schwendi answered. 'Neither the police nor anyone else need concern themselves with him. He has had no hand in this affair and has no desire to be mixed up in it. That's his wish, he's my client, and my job is to see that his wishes are respected.'

Lutz was so nonplussed by this impertinent reply that at first he could find nothing to say. He lit a cigarette, forgetting to offer his case to von Schwendi. Then he sat back in his chair.

'Unfortunately the fact that Schmied went to Gastmann's compels us to give your client a measure of our attention, my dear Oscar.'

Von Schwendi was not to be diverted. 'It also compels you to give me a little of your attention,' he said. 'I'm not here merely to help Gastmann – I'm ready to help you, too. Admittedly, the case is embarrassing for my client, but I think it must be even more embarrassing for you. The police have not advanced very far, have they, and it seems unlikely they will get any further.'

'The police,' answered Lutz, 'are almost always successful in murder cases. That is a matter of statistics. I admit that we have encountered unforeseen difficulties in the present instance, but we have also' – he hesitated a second – 'made substantial progress. How else do you think we got on the trail of Gastmann? But for that, Gastmann would never have sent you here. It's Gastmann who faces embarrassment, not us, and it's up to him to put his cards on the table. Schmied was a visitor at his house and that fact compels the police to interest themselves in him. Gastmann must be made to talk, either personally or through you. Are you prepared to tell us honestly and completely why Schmied went to Gastmann's house under a false name, not once but on several different occasions?'

'Very well,' said von Schwendi. 'Let's have the cards on the table. You'll soon see that it's not so much a question of my explaining Gastmann as of your explaining Schmied. Maybe, you will then agree that it's you, my dear Lucius, who are in the dock, not we.'

With these words he produced a large, white sheet of paper, which he unfolded and placed on Lutz's desk. 'Here are the names of the persons who have been guests at Gastmann's house,' he said. 'The list is complete. I have divided it into three sections. The first section we can ignore because it consists only of artists. It comprises the names of only small-time home-bred artists – the sort that write plays about the Battle of Morgarten or paint pictures of mountains. It does not, of course, include the names of such great performers as Kraushaar-Raffaeli who, anyway, are foreigners. The second section consists of big-business men. You will recognize their names; they are men of high position, men whom I regard as the backbone of Swiss society. I make no secret of that opinion though I myself come of peasant stock.'

'And the third section?' asked Lutz, when the Councillor suddenly stopped speaking. Von Schwendi's pause was deliberate, intended to build up Lutz's nervous tension.

'The third section', he went on at last, 'represents the major complication of the Schmied case, both from your point of view and from ours. It makes it necessary for me to speak of matters which would have better kept secret even from the police. But since your Berne constabulary felt it necessary to search out Gastmann, and since, unfortunately, it has come to light that Schmied was at Lamlingen, I have no option but to give the police such information as is necessary to clear up the case. It is a matter of some embarrassment to us as it means we shall have to reveal important political activities we should have preferred to keep secret. But it may well be embarrassing to you as the people named in the third section are people over whom you, as a policeman, have no authority or jurisdiction.'

'I don't understand,' Lutz interjected, frowning.

'That's because you have no knowledge of international affairs, my dear Lucius,' von Schwendi answered suavely. 'The third section contains the names of members of the staff of a foreign embassy, and the embassy concerned considers it desirable that its staff should not be associated in the public mind with certain of the industrialists whose names appear on my second list.'

At last, Lutz began to understand what lay behind von Schwendi's words and there was a long silence. The telephone rang and Lutz took up the receiver merely to snap into it: 'In conference.' Whereupon the silence was re-established. At last he said:

'Am I to understand that official negotiations are going on with this power for a new trade agreement?'

'Precisely. Negotiations are conducted officially and at high level because otherwise the diplomats would have nothing to do. But there are also unofficial negotiations, and in Lamlingen the talks are private and off the record. In modern industry there are some affairs in which the State may not interfere.'

'Of course,' agreed Lutz, nervously but without understanding.

'Of course,' repeated von Schwendi. 'And unfortunately, your deceased subordinate, Lieutenant Schmied, insinuated himself into these secret negotiations under a false name.'

Von Schwendi saw by the awkward silence which again intervened that he had calculated rightly. Lutz was now so utterly at a loss that the Councillor could do with him as he liked. He was so put out by the unexpected developments in the Schmied case that he was ready to be driven to almost any concession, even though it might seriously prejudice further legitimate investigation. Nevertheless, Lutz made an effort to pretend he had the situation under control.

'My dear Oscar,' he said. 'Are we not taking this too seriously? Swiss industrialists have every right to negotiate privately with whomever they like, including foreign governments. That is big business and the police don't interfere in such matters. I have already told you that Schmied went to Gastmann's as a private individual, not as a policeman. Doubtless it was wrong of him to masquerade under a false name and pretend he was a lecturer at Munich University, and I am prepared to offer an official apology, but he was not there alone; there were all those artists you talked about.'

'The necessary framework to cloak our affairs. The negotiations had to be secret and secrets are safest in a crowd of Bohemians. All dine together, good food, wine, cigars, women, conversation. Then the artistic ones get bored, gather in little groups, drink, and fail to notice that the people who really matter have also drifted together. They don't notice it because it doesn't interest them. Artists are only interested in art and themselves. But not so a policeman who has come to pry.'

'I can only repeat,' answered Lutz, 'that we have no knowledge of why Schmied visited Gastmann.'

'If the police did not send him there, someone else did,' returned von Schwendi. 'Other governments, my dear Lucius, are vastly interested in what has been going on at Lamlingen.'

'Schmied was not a spy.'

'We have every reason to assume that he was. At least, it is better for the honour of Switzerland that he should have been spying for a foreign power than as an agent of the Swiss police.'

'Well, he's dead now,' sighed Lutz, who would have given a great deal at that moment to be able to put a few questions to Schmied himself.

'But we had no hand in it,' said the Colonel. 'I don't want to go about spreading rumours, but it is a fact that the people who insisted on the secrecy of the negotiations at Lamlingen were the representatives of the foreign power concerned. With us such deals are no more than a matter of money, with them it's a political creed. Let's face it. If these people are behind Schmied's death it's going to be very difficult for you fellows to take positive action.'

Lutz rose from his chair and walked over to the window. 'I still don't see where Gastmann comes into all this,' he said slowly.

Von Schwendi fanned himself with the sheet of paper. 'Gastmann put his house at the disposal of the parties concerned. That is all.'

'But why Gastmann?'

'My respected client', growled the Colonel, 'happens to be the man with the necessary background and qualifications. As a former member of the Argentine Diplomatic, he enjoys the trust of foreign diplomats, while big business has confidence in him for his work as President of the Tin Trust. Besides, he happens to live in Lamlingen.'

'What difference does that make?'

Von Schwendi smiled patronizingly. 'Had you ever heard of Lamlingen before Schmied was murdered?'

'Almost not.'

'That's the reason: because nobody has ever heard of the place. We needed obscurity and Lamlingen provided it. That's all there is to it, so you can safely leave Gastmann in peace. He wants no dealings with the police and doesn't want them sniffing around with their everlasting questions and investigations. That technique is all very well when you are dealing with crooks and criminals who've got themselves into a mess, but not for a man who refused election to the French Academy. Besides, your policemen put themselves hopelessly in the wrong when they shot his dog and interrupted the Bach prelude. Not that Gastmann feels aggrieved about it. He really doesn't care a rap. You could shoot his house to pieces and he wouldn't bat an eyelid. He's like that. Take my tip and accept the fact that behind this murder there are forces which have nothing to do with big business nor with Gastmann.'

Lutz walked up and down in front of the window. 'We shall have to concentrate on probing into Schmied's private life,' he observed. 'As for the foreign power of which you speak, that is a matter for the Federal Attorney. To what extent he will want to take up the case, I cannot yet say. But he will hand over most of the work to us, you can be sure of that. Meanwhile, you can count on our sparing Gastmann as much as possible. Should it be necessary to question him later, I will ask you to arrange the meeting and will invite you to be present. In this way we may be able to dispose of the formalities in an informal way.'

The Councillor rose to his feet and the two men stood facing each other. Von Schwendi tapped Lutz on the shoulder.

'So that's agreed,' he said. 'You will leave Gastmann alone, Lucius – I have your word for it. I'll leave this paper – the list is accurate and complete. Its compilation meant telephoning most of the night. The important speculation now is whether our foreign friends will want to pursue negotiations when they are informed of the Schmied murder. Millions are at stake, Lucius, millions! I wish you luck with the Schmied case. You'll need it.'

With these words von Schwendi stumped out of the room.

Chapter five

Lutz had just had time to glance through the Councillor's list and note with a groan the celebrity of many of the names it contained, when Barlach came in. He entered, as usual, without knocking. He had come to ask for authority to visit Gastmann at Lamlingen, but Lutz put off the discussion till the afternoon. It was time, he said, they set off for the funeral.

Barlach raised no objection and the two men left the room together. With each passing moment Lutz became more aware of the foolishness of his half-promise to leave Gastmann in peace, and he knew how vigorously Barlach would oppose the decision. They reached the street in silence, both in black coats. They turned up their collars. It was raining heavily, but it was not worth while to put up their umbrellas for the few steps to the car. Blatter was driving. The rain was cascading down, lashing slantwise against the windows. Lutz and Barlach sat motionless, each in his corner. I must tell him soon, thought Lutz, and looked at Barlach's calm profile. Barlach put his hand to his stomach as he had done so often in recent months.

'Are you in pain?' asked Lutz.

'Always,' answered Barlach.

They fell silent again, and Lutz thought, 'I'll tell him this afternoon.' Blatter drove slowly. The surrounding buildings disappeared behind an opaque veil, the rain was so heavy. Trams and motor-cars moved somehow through the monstrous oceans of descending water. Lutz did not know where they were; the dripping panes defeated all efforts to see through them. Inside the car it grew darker and darker. Lutz lit a cigarette, blew out the smoke, and determined to avoid any discussion with Barlach on the Gastmann case except on broad general lines. He said:

'The newspapers are reporting the murder. We couldn't hold it back any longer.'

'No need to,' answered Barlach. 'We're on the track of something now.'

'There never was any need,' said Lutz, crushing out his cigarette.

Barlach did not answer. Lutz would have liked to quarrel with him, but peered instead through the window. The rain began to subside a little. They had already reached the avenue leading to the Schosshalden Cemetery, which now came towards them between the steaming tree-trunks as a dripping grey mass of masonry. Blatter drove into the courtyard and stopped. They got out, put up their umbrellas and set off on foot between the lines of graves. They had not long to seek. The gravestones and crosses receded, and it seemed to the two men that they had stumbled across a building site. The ground was dotted with freshly dug graves, over which planks had been laid. The moisture from the wet grass penetrated their shoes and the muddy earth clung to them. In the middle of this open space, among the still-unoccupied graves in the depths of which the rain had collected in dirty pools, a group of people was standing round a grave. A little way away was a forest of provisional wooden crosses and mounds of earth, thickly covered with rotting flowers and wreaths.

Schmied's coffin had not yet been lowered. The priest was reading from the Bible and beside him, holding an umbrella over both their heads, the gravedigger, wearing a ridiculous garment that resembled a frock-coat, was standing first on one frozen foot, then on the other. Barlach and Lutz stopped at the grave-side. Someone was crying. It was Frau Schönler, round and shapeless under the unceasing rain. At her side was Chanz; he had no umbrella, but the collar of his raincoat was turned up. He was wearing a black bowler hat. Beside him was a girl, pale, hatless, her fair hair hanging down in dripping strands – Anna, thought Barlach. Chanz bowed to them; Lutz nodded in return but the Inspector gave no sign of recognition. He looked across at the other figures round the grave – all policemen, all in mufti, all with the same raincoats, the same black bowler hats, holding umbrellas aloft like sabres – fantastic mourners come from God knew where, unfitting to the occasion.

Behind them in orderly ranks stood the municipal band in their black and red uniforms, trying desperately to keep their brass instruments under their coats. Such was the group round the coffin, a wooden box without a wreath, without flowers, and yet it was somehow the only warm, homely thing in the ceaseless rain.

The priest had stopped speaking for some time. No one noticed. Only the rain was there and they heard nothing else. The priest coughed. Once. Then several times. Suddenly there was a blare of trombones, French horns, cornets and bassoons, the instruments proud and impressive like yellow lightning flashes in the floods of rain. Then they too subsided and died into silence. Everyone shrank back under umbrellas and raincoats. The storm grew more violent, shoes sank into the mud, water poured into the empty grave. Lutz bowed and stepped forward. He looked down at the wet coffin and bowed again.

'Men' – his voice was almost inaudible through the sheets of rain – 'men, our comrade Schmied is no more.' Suddenly his graveside oration was interrupted by the wild bawling of a song:

The devil goes round,
The devil goes round,
And beats us black and blue . . .

Two men in black frock-coats came staggering across the cemetery. Without overcoats or umbrellas they ran unprotected from the rain. Both wore tophats on their heads, from which the water streamed over their faces. They carried between them a huge laurel wreath, from which a ribbon hung down, trailing along the ground. They were great loutish fellows, so drunk that they were always on the point of falling, but since they contrived not to stumble both at the same moment they steadied themselves alternately on the laurel wreath they clutched tightly between them. Now they struck up a fresh song:

The miller's wife, she killed her man,
And she's alive, alive-o!
The miller's wife, she whored all night,
And she's alive, alive-o!

They ran for the group of mourners, and plunged right through them, even between Frau Schönler and Chanz. No one hindered them, everyone watching as though petrified. Then they were stumbling away through the wet grass, holding each other up, clinging to each other, falling over graves and overthrowing crosses in the violence of their intoxication. Their song died away in the rain, and the last glimpse of them was gone.

Everything passes over,
Everything passes by . . .

was the last that was heard of them. Only the wreath remained,
carelessly tossed on to the coffin, bearing the words in smeared ink
on the muddy ribbon: 'To our dear Dr Prantl.'

By the time that the people round the grave had recovered their
wits and were beginning to express their disgust at what had happened,
and the Municipal Band was desperately trying to retrieve the situation, the storm suddenly increased to such fury that everyone was
forced to dash for shelter. Only the gravediggers, black scarecrows in
the howling wind and rain, were left to lower the coffin into the grave.

When Barlach and Lutz were back in the car and Blatter was driving
along an avenue overrun by fleeing police and municipal bandsmen,
Lutz gave vent to his indignation.

'What a swine that fellow Gastmann must be!'

'Why do you say that?' asked Barlach.

'Schmied went to Gastmann's parties under the name of Prantl.'

'Then that little exhibition was meant as a warning,' returned
Barlach, but without asking for further information.

They drove towards the quarter where Lutz lived. Now was the
moment, thought Lutz, to speak to the old man about Gastmann and
tell him he was to be left alone. But he said nothing. At the Burgernziel
he got out of the car, leaving Barlach alone.

'Shall I take you into town, Inspector?' asked Blatter.

'No, take me home.'

Blatter put on speed. It was raining less heavily now. Indeed, when
they reached the Muristalden, Barlach was bathed for a few seconds
in dazzling light as the sun burst through the clouds, vanished again,
and came back a second time – all part of the wild game of the
elements. Monster clouds came hurtling from the west, banked up
against the mountain-sides, throwing fantastic shadows across the
town which lay by the river between forest and mountain. Barlach
passed a tired hand over his wet overcoat; his narrow eyes sparkled
as he avidly drank in the spectacle. The world was so beautiful.

The service car stopped. Barlach thanked Blatter and got out. The
rain had now ceased, but the wind was still high – a wet, cold wind.
The old man stood waiting while Blatter turned the big car, then he

saluted as the constable drove off. He walked across to the river-bank. The water was high and dirty brown. An old rusty perambulator swam past, branches of trees, a young pine; then a little paper boat came dancing by. Barlach stood for some time looking at his beloved Aare. Then he passed through his garden to the house.

Barlach removed his wet shoes before entering the house. At the doorway to his sitting-room he stopped short. A man was sitting at his writing-table, turning over the papers from Schmied's brief-case. With his right hand he was playing with Barlach's Turkish knife.

'So it's you,' said the old man.

'Yes, it's me,' said the other.

Barlach closed the door and sat down in his armchair, facing the desk. He watched in silence as the other went on calmly turning over the papers from Schmied's brief-case, an almost rustic figure, calm and reserved, with short hair and deep-set eyes in a full, large-boned face.

'So you call yourself Gastmann now,' said the old man at last.

The other took out his pipe and filled it, keeping his eyes all the time on Barlach. He lit his pipe and then tapped Schmied's brief-case with his forefinger:

'You've known that for some time. You set that young fellow on my track. These notes are yours.'

He shut the brief-case. Barlach glanced at his writing-table, his automatic was still there, the butt towards him. He had only to put out his hand. He said:

'I shall never stop hunting you. One day I shall get you.'

'You'll have to hurry, Barlach,' answered the other. 'You haven't much time left. The doctors give you another year and only then if you let them operate at once.'

'True,' said the old man. 'Twelve more months. but I can't let them operate now. The time has come to act. It's my last chance.'

'Your last chance,' confirmed the other. Then they were silent again, sitting there as though they would never move or speak again.

'It's over forty years,' began the other at last, 'since we first met in that decaying Jewish wine shop on the Bosporus. A moon like a slice of Gruyère cheese hung between the clouds, and its light fell on our heads through the rotting rafters. I remember it so clearly. You, Barlach, were a young Swiss policeman working for the Turks, who had come to the Bosporus to institute some sort of reform, and I – I was a foot-loose adventurer. I still am; still greedy to find out the meaning of my own unique existence, and of this mysterious world. We liked each other at first sight, sitting opposite each other among Jews in kaftans and unwashed Greeks. But presently the local schnapps of fermented dates and fiery potions from the cornfields of Odessa began to work on us. Our eyes shone like red-hot coals and our tongues became fiery and impetuous. I love to think of that hour – it determined the courses of your life and mine.'

He laughed.

Barlach sat watching him in silence.

'You have one more year to live,' went on the other. 'And you've spent forty stubbornly tracking me down. That's how the account stands. Do you remember what we talked about that night, Barlach, in that stinking wine shop with its atmosphere made thick by clouds of Turkish cigarette smoke? You were the champion of law and order; the wrong-doer, you said, must always pay for his crimes. Why? Because no crime is perfect; because no man can foresee with certainty how another will act, and because no man can calculate exactly and on every occasion the ever-present element of chance. In other words, crime is the game of fools because it is impossible to foresee the moves of men and women as one can foresee the moves on a chessboard. I, on the other hand, maintained – more for the sake of argument than because I believed it at the time – that it is just this chaos in human relationships that makes it possible to commit crime and get away with it. That it is because of this that so many crimes not only are not solved but are incapable of solution because the world never even knows they have been committed.

'So we went on arguing, stimulated by the raw schnapps the Jewish landlord brought us and by the ardour of youth. Much later that night we made a wager, a bet with the satanic appeal of an impious joke that blasphemes the divinity.'

'Yes,' said Barlach quietly. 'We made that wager.'

'But you never thought,' laughed the other, 'when we woke with a hangover in that filthy wine shop next morning – you on a rotting bench and I under a table still wet with schnapps – you never thought I would see it through.'

'I never thought that any man would do as you did.'

'That's because you've never known the meaning of temptation. But I have, and to me it was a challenge that could not be resisted. I accepted it gladly and proved, as I had promised, that I could commit a major crime actually in your presence without your being able to convict me of it.'

'Three days later,' said Barlach softly, immersed in his memories, 'we were walking across the Mahmud Bridge with a German shopkeeper and I saw you push him into the water.'

'The poor devil couldn't swim and you were not much of a swimmer yourself, for when you tried to save him they had to drag you half-drowned out of the muddy waters of the Golden Horn,' went on the other unmoved. 'On a fine summer day with a pleasant breeze from the sea, I openly committed murder on a bridge crowded with courting couples from the European colony, Mussulmans and local beggars. Yet you couldn't prove it was murder. You had me arrested, had me put through hours of cross-examination, but to no purpose. The court accepted my story that the German had killed himself.'

'You won because you proved that the German was on the point of bankruptcy and had tried unsuccessfully to save the situation by defrauding his creditors,' said Barlach, bitterly.

'Naturally, I chose my victim carefully, my friend,' laughed the other.

'And that is how you first became a criminal,' said the Inspector.

The other played absent-mindedly with the Turkish knife.

'I can't deny', he said at last in a casual tone, 'that I have found crime intensely interesting. As the years went by I grew to be a better and better criminal and you became a better and better policeman. But I was always a jump ahead of you, and you've never been able to catch up. I've crossed your path again and again, committing crimes under your very nose, bolder, madder, badder crimes, and each time you have failed to convict me. You have triumphed over fools, but never over me.'

His expression as he smiled at Barlach was a mixture of contempt and amusement. 'So we have lived our lives – you at the beck and call of superior officers, working in police stations and musty offices, a worthy fellow, climbing rung by rung the ladder of modest achievement, and pitting yourself against thieves, forgers and miserable little murderers, all of them poor devils who never really learned how to live. How different has my life been. Sometimes underground in the jungles of great cities, sometimes in the splendour of high position with a breastful of decorations. Sometimes when I was in the mood practising virtue for the fun of it and sometimes, when the mood changed, loving evil. How opposed have been our lives. Your life-long object has been to destroy me, and mine to exist in spite of you. That one night on the Bosporus chained us to each other for ever!'

The man at Barlach's writing-table clapped his hands in a single, violent concussion. 'Now we are reaching the end of our careers,' he said. 'You have come back to Berne, a semi-failure in a pleasant sleepy town where no one can distinguish between life and death. And I have come back to Lamlingen, as a matter of caprice. It's nice to round things off: I was born in that God-forsaken village. A woman, long since dead, bore me without thought or purpose. Then, one rainy night when I was thirteen, I ran away. And now, after the years between, we both are back where we started from. Give up your crusade, my friend. Death won't wait that long.'

With a movement so fast it was almost imperceptible, he threw the knife he had been playing with. He threw it hard and accurately. It grazed Barlach's cheek and buried its point deep in the back of the chair. The old man did not flinch: the other laughed.

'So you think it was I who killed Schmied?'

'My job is to investigate the case,' answered the Inspector.

The other stood up, the brief-case in his hand.

'I'll take this with me.'

'This time I shall bring you to justice,' said Barlach doggedly. 'It must be this time for it is my last chance.'

'This brief-case contains the only evidence – and not much of it. Schmied collected it for you in Lamlingen. You can do nothing without it. I know you well enough to know you have made no copies or photostats.'

'No,' admitted the Inspector. 'I have nothing of that kind.'

'Why don't you stop me with that pistol?' asked Gastmann with a sneer.

'Because you've taken out the cartridges,' answered Barlach, unmoving.

'True,' said the other. He patted Barlach on the shoulder and walked past him. The door opened and closed. Outside, a second door opened and closed. Barlach still sat in his armchair, the steel blade of the knife cold against his cheek. Suddenly he picked up the automatic and opened it. It was still loaded. Pistol in hand he jumped up, ran into the vestibule and tore open the outer door.

There was no one in the street.

Then came the pain, the throbbing, stabbing pain, like a sun rising inside him. It threw him on the sofa and convulsed him, scalding him with feverish heat. For some minutes he crawled around the floor on hands and knees like an animal; then he threw himself full-length across the rug and lay still, bathed in cold sweat.

Chapter six

Barlach felt better after the attack. It was a long time since last he had been free from pain. He drank mulled wine in little cautious sips. That was his only food and drink. But he did not fail to take his usual walk through the town and along the Bundes-strasse. Though utterly weary, every step in the rain-washed air did him good.

Shortly afterwards he was sitting in Lutz's office. Lutz noticed nothing amiss. Perhaps he was too much occupied with his own guilty conscience. He decided he must tell Barlach at once of his talk with von Schwendi. He settled himself in his chair, assuming a cold impersonal attitude with his chest thrown out, like the general in Traffelet's picture on the wall above him, and addressed the Inspector in abrupt, telegraphic phrases. To his immeasurable surprise and relief the Inspector raised no objection; he approved of everything; he agreed that it was better to wait for Government instructions and to concentrate the investigations on Schmied's private life. Lutz was so surprised that he dropped his pose, and became quite cheerful and talkative.

'Of course, I have found out a good deal about Gastmann,' he said. 'Enough to be sure that he could not possibly he regarded as a suspect.'

'Of course,' agreed the old man.

Lutz, who had received some oddments of information from Biel during the lunch-hour, assumed an air of great assurance.

'Born at Pockau in Saxony, son of a wholesale dealer in leather goods, he appears first as an Argentinian – was once Argentine minister in China. Must have emigrated to South America as a young man. He next occurs as a Frenchman, generally travelling about the world – wears the cross of the Legion of Honour, and is the author of several publications on biology. Characteristic of the man is the fact that he refused to be elected to the French Academy. I find that impressive.'

'An interesting point,' agreed Barlach.

'We're still making inquiries about his two men-servants. They have French passports but appear to come from Emmental. It was they who behaved so disgracefully at the funeral. A joke in the worst possible taste.'

'Gastmann seems to be in the habit of making jokes,' observed the Inspector, drily.

'Perhaps he was upset over the death of his dog. We've got to be careful how we handle the case where Gastmann is concerned. We've put ourselves in a false position once. It's lucky I happen to be a friend of von Schwendi's. He tells me Gastmann's a thorough cosmopolitan and the leaders of Swiss industry have every confidence in him.'

'Then he must be all right,' said Barlach.

'Quite beyond suspicion.'

'Definitely,' the old man nodded.

'Unfortunately, we can't say the same about Schmied,' added Lutz. He picked up the telephone and asked the switchboard operator to connect him with a government department.

As Lutz sat waiting for the call, the Inspector, who had got up to leave, said suddenly:

'I wish to apply for a week's sick leave, Dr Lutz.'

'Very well,' answered Lutz, his hand over the receiver, for the call has just come through. 'Take a rest'.

Chanz was waiting in Barlach's office. He got up when the old man came in. He looked calm but the Inspector sensed his nervousness.

'Let's drive out to Gastmann's,' said Chanz. 'It's getting late.'

'We'll go to the writer fellow's instead,' answered Barlach, putting on his overcoat.

'Why must we work in such a roundabout way?' protested Chanz, as he followed Barlach down the stairs.

The Inspector stopped as they reached the door.

'There's Schmied's blue Mercedes.'

Chanz explained that it was now his, that he had brought it and was paying for it by hire-purchase. He got into the driver's seat.

Barlach took the seat beside him and they drove across the Bahnhof-
platz towards the hospital.

'Going via Ins again?' asked Barlach.

'I like that route.'

Barlach looked across the rain-washed fields. Everything was bathed
in bright, tranquil light. A warm, mild sun hung in the sky and was
already beginning to decline towards the west. The two men were
silent, only once did Chanz speak. That was between Kerzers and
Müntschemier.

'Frau Schönler tells me you took a brief-case from Schmied's
room,' he said.

'Nothing official, Chanz. Just private papers.'

Chanz made no reply and asked no more questions. When the
speedometer needle pointed to eighty Barlach tapped its glass face.

'Not so fast, Chanz, not so fast! Not that I'm really nervous; it's
just my stomach is out of order. I'm getting an old man.'

The man of letters received them in his study. It was an old room,
very low, and both visitors had to stoop to pass through the door. A
little white dog with a black head was still barking outside, and somewhere in the house a child was crying. Their host, dressed in jeans
and brown leather jacket, sat by the Gothic window. Without rising
from his paper-strewn desk, he turned sideways in his chair to face
his visitors. He nodded slightly and asked what they wanted of him.

He has no manners, thought Barlach. And he doesn't like the
police. His sort never do like the police. He resolved to tread warily.
Chanz did not find their task much to his liking. We mustn't let him
study us, he thought with childlike distrust. Otherwise he'll put us in
a book. Their host pointed to two comfortable armchairs and when
they were seated they found to their annoyance that they were facing
the light from the window. They themselves could scarcely see his
face, so confusing was the reflected light in this little green room with
its rows of books.

'We're making inquiries into the death of Police-Lieutenant
Schmied,' began the Inspector. 'He was the man who was found dead
on the hill above Twann.'

'I know. Dr Prantl, the man who was spying on Gastmann,' said
the dark figure between them and the window. 'Gastmann told me
about it.' He lit a cigarette. For a few short moments his face was lit

up. The two policemen saw it twist into a grin. 'Do you want my alibi?'

'No,' said Barlach.

'You don't think me capable of murder?' asked the novelist, disappointed.

'No,' answered Barlach, drily. 'Not you.'

The writer groaned. 'Oh, dear, writers are shockingly under-valued in this country!'

Barlach laughed. 'If you really want to know, we've already got your alibi. At half-past twelve on the night of the murder you met a forester between Lamlingen and Schernelz and the two of you walked home together. The forester said you were quite merry.'

'I know. The village constable from Twann has twice questioned the forester about me. And so have most other people about here. Even my mother-in-law. But you did suspect me ... success of a sort, I suppose.'

Barlach thought, It's just the vanity of the dreamer anxious to be taken for a man of action. All three fell silent. Chanz tried hard to catch a clear glimpse of the writer's face, but it was quite impossible in that light.

'What else do you want?' asked the novelist at last.

'How often do you go to Gastmann's?'

'If this is to be a cross-examination,' the man said, edging farther into the shadow, 'I'm busy.'

'I must ask you to be a little more obliging,' said the Inspector. 'We want to talk a little.' The writer grunted, and Barlach began again. 'How often do you go to Gastmann's?'

'Occasionally.'

'Why?'

Barlach expected another grudging answer, but the writer laughed, blew a thick cloud of smoke towards them, and said:

'An interesting chap, Gastmann. A man of his kind attracts a novelist as honey attracts bees. And he's a magnificent cook. Did you know that?'

He began to enlarge on Gastmann's culinary skill, describing one dish after another. The two policemen listened for five minutes, then another five minutes. When their host had talked for a solid quarter of an hour about Gastmann's cooking, Chanz got up. 'I'm sorry', he said, 'but we didn't come here to discuss gastronomy.'

But Barlach, apparently invigorated by the talk, contradicted him, protesting profound interest. He himself took up the theme, growing enthusiastic as he talked of the culinary masterpieces of the Turks, Rumanians, Bulgarians, Yugoslavs, Czechs. He and the writer threw dishes at each other like tennis balls. Bored, Chanz cursed inwardly, but nothing could distract the other two men from their subject. Three-quarters of an hour had passed before they stopped, as replete as if they had partaken of a gargantuan meal. There was silence. The author lit a cigar. In the next room the child began to cry again and the dog barked outside. Chanz took the opportunity to snap out the words: 'Did Gastmann kill Schmied?'

The crudity of the question made Barlach shake his head. The dark figure by the window laughed and said: 'You don't beat about the bush, do you?'

'Answer me, please,' said Chanz stolidly. He leaned forward trying hard to see the novelist's face but the features were indistinguishable.

Barlach waited, curious to see how their man would react. The writer was quite unruffled.

'At what time was the policeman killed?' he asked.

'Shortly before midnight,' answered Chanz.

'I do not know whether the rules of logic are valid for the police,' the writer said. 'Personally I doubt it. But, as the local police have already ascertained, I met the forester on the Schernelz road at half past twelve, which means that I must have left Gastmann not earlier than twenty past. Gastmann, therefore, obviously could not have committed the murder.'

Chanz asked whether any other guests had remained at Gastmann's after the writer had left.

'No.'

'Schmied left with the others?'

'Dr Prantl was invariably the last but one to leave,' answered the writer, in a faintly mocking tone.

'Who was the last?'

'I'.

Chanz was not to be beaten. 'Were the menservants present?'

'I don't know.'

'Why can't you give a straight answer?' Chanz demanded abruptly.

'I thought I had,' snapped the novelist. 'I don't generally concern myself with what other people's servants are doing.'

With a lack of restraint that caused the Inspector some embarrass-ment, Chanz boldly demanded to know their host's opinion of Gastmann, was he an honest man or a rogue? Only a miracle can prevent him putting Chanz in his next novel, Barlach thought with amusement.

In reply the author blew a cloud of smoke into Chanz's face so that the police officer began to cough. Then followed a long silence throughout the house; even the child had ceased to cry.

'Gastmann is a bad man,' pronounced the writer at last.

'And yet you often visit him? You're interested in nothing but his cooking?' sneered Chanz, disbelieving, after a fresh fit of coughing.

The novelist laughed. 'I'm a kind of policeman, too', he said, 'even though I have no authority or ceremonial, no law or prison system behind me. Yet it is my job, as it is yours, to study human nature.'

His answer left Chanz confused and at a loss for words. Barlach took up the thread. 'Of course. We understand that,' he said. The streaming sunlight suddenly faded from the window as he spoke. 'I am afraid that the zeal of my assistant sometimes runs away with him and on such occasions nobody emerges without a few scratches. But there is something to be said for the brashness of youth, and it seems that in this instance the ox in his impulsiveness has trampled a path for us.' (At these words Chanz turned red with fury.) 'So let us pursue a little further the questions he put and the answers you gave. Suppose you give us your personal views on this business. What do you think? Is Gastmann capable of committing murder?'

The overclouding of the sun had made the room almost dark, but the writer made no move to switch on the light. Instead he crossed to the window-seat and faced the police officers who looked back at him like two prisoners in a cell.

'I would say that Gastmann is capable of any crime under the sun.' His voice was brutal in its judgment, with a hint of malice in it. 'But I am certain that he did not murder Schmied.'

'You think you know him pretty well?'

'I've a good idea of the type of man he is.'

'Albeit a personal idea, no more', Barlach amended coolly, speaking straight at the dark figure silhouetted in the window frame.

'What fascinates me about him', said the writer, 'apart from his cooking – though these days I find it difficult to raise much enthusiasm for anything else – is that here is a man who is a genuine nihilist. It always gives me a thrill to meet an iconoclast in the flesh. Yet for all I know, Gastmann may have done more good in his life than the three of us put together. When I say he is bad I mean that if ever he does good it is out of pure caprice, on the spur of the moment, in the same way that I am sure he would commit any of the crimes of which I believe him capable. He is not the man to do evil for the sake of gain, as other people commit crimes, for money, women or power. He will do it for no reason at all. The alternative paths of right and wrong, good and evil are open to him and it's a matter of chance which he chooses. But the ordinary criminal is a very different man. He is a criminal because his outlook on life is warped and evil; he will follow the path of crime just as determinedly as another man pursues the good.'

'Well, that's as may be,' remarked the Inspector. 'But perhaps we had better get back to Gastmann. He's more important to me at the moment.'

'As you wish,' said the novelist. 'Gastmann, Inspector, represents the negative pole of evil. For him evil is not the expression of a philosophy or an instinct, but of freedom – the freedom of the nihilist.'

'I wouldn't give a penny for such freedom,' answered the old man.

'You are not asked to give a penny for it,' returned the other. 'But one could devote one's life to the study of such a man and his conceptions.'

'The whole of one's life,' Barlach agreed.

The novelist was silent. He seemed to have come to the end of what he had to say.

'Meanwhile, I have to deal with Gastmann as he is,' said Barlach at last. 'With the man who lives at Lamlingen, and gives parties, one of which cost a police lieutenant his life. I want to know whether the person you have described to me is the real Gastmann or a figment of your imagination.'

'*Our* imaginations,' corrected the writer.

The Inspector said nothing.

'I don't know,' said the other abruptly, and came forward to show them out. He shook hands only with Barlach.

'I never bother about living people. It's up to the police to keep an eye on them.'

Chapter seven

Barlach and Chanz went back to the car, the little white dog following at their heels, barking furiously. Chanz took the wheel.

'I don't care for that fellow,' he said. Barlach buttoned his coat before he got in. The dog had jumped up on a wall, whence it continued to bark.

'Now for Gastmann,' said Chanz as he started the engine. But Barlach shook his head.

'Back to Berne.'

As they drove towards Ligerz the landscape opened out in vast depths ahead. There, unfolded before them, were the elements – stone, earth and water. The road was in shadow, for the sun had sunk behind the Tessenberg, but it was still shining on the lake, the island, the hills, the outliers of the mountains, the glaciers away on the horizon and the cloud monsters piled in tiers and floating away in the blue oceans of the sky.

But Barlach was not concerned with the constant changes of the late autumn weather.

Always the same, he thought. However much it changes, it's always the same. At a sharp turn of the road the convex shield of the lake appeared perpendicularly below them. Chanz then stopped the car.

'I must talk to you, Inspector,' he said in a determined voice.

'What about?' asked Barlach, staring down the precipitous rock-face.

'Gastmann. We must talk to Gastmann. It's the only way to make progress. It's the logical thing to do. And especially must we talk to those servants of his.'

Barlach leaned back in his seat. A grey-haired well-groomed figure. His cold eyes in their narrow slits observed the young man at his side.

'Unfortunately, Chanz, we can't always do the logical thing. Lutz insists that we leave Gastmann alone. And it's not unreasonable now that he's had to surrender the case to Government ruling. We have to wait on their instructions. That's what happens when you're up against a bunch of tricky foreigners.' Barlach's equable tone seemed to enrage Chanz.

'That's all nonsense,' he protested. 'Lutz is sabotaging the case for political reasons. He's a friend of von Schwendi, Gastmann's lawyer. Can't you see what he's up to?'

Barlach's expression did not change. 'It's a good thing we're alone, Chanz. That's a serious charge. Lutz acted hastily perhaps, but he had sound reasons. Schmied is our problem, not Gastmann.'

But Chanz was not to be put off. 'We want the truth,' he contradicted, flinging the words dramatically at the great banks of cloud that were drifting towards them. 'The truth and nothing but the truth! We want the man who murdered Schmied!'

'True enough,' agreed Barlach, coldly, unemotionally. 'The truth – the man who murdered Schmied.'

Chanz put his hand on Barlach's left shoulder and peered earnestly into his face.

'Therefore we must make use of every means in our power against Gastmann. One can't leave great gaps in the evidence in a case. You say we can't always do the logical thing, but in this case we *must* do it. It's impossible to leave Gastmann out.'

'Gastmann is not the murderer,' said Barlach firmly.

'But the murder could have been committed on his orders. What about those menservants of his?' returned Chanz.

'I cannot see the slightest reason why Gastmann should have wished to kill Schmied,' said Barlach. 'We must look for a man who had some motive for killing Schmied. Perhaps we'll get a lead from Government sources.'

'The author thinks Gastmann is the murderer whatever he may have said to the contrary,' cried Chanz.

'And do you think he is?' asked Barlach warily.

'Yes, I do, Inspector.'

'Then you're the only one who does. That novelist only regards him as being capable of the crime, and that is something quite different. He told us nothing of what Gastmann had done, only of what he's capable of doing.'

His companion suddenly lost patience. He gripped the older man by the shoulders, and cried passionately:

'For years I've been kept in the background, Inspector. I've always been passed over, looked down on, kicked around and treated like a superior sort of postman!'

'I don't deny it, Chanz,' said Barlach, looking unmoved into the young man's contorted face. 'For years you've played second fiddle to a man who now has been murdered.'

'Simply because he'd had a better education. Because he knew Latin and things like that.'

'You're not being fair to him,' answered Barlach. 'Schmied was the best policeman I have ever known.'

'And now', cried Chanz, disregarding Barlach's words, 'now at last I have a chance of promotion it's to be snatched away from me and lost because of some idiotic game of diplomacy. You're the only one who can change that, Inspector. Speak to Lutz. You're the only one who can persuade him to let me go to Gastmann.'

'No, Chanz, I can't,' said Barlach.

Chanz shook him as though he were a child, held him between clenched hands, shouting: 'Speak to Lutz! You must speak to Lutz!'

But Barlach was not to be persuaded. 'It's no good, Chanz,' he said. 'I can't struggle against things any more. I'm old and sick, and I need peace. You must look after yourself.'

'Very well,' said Chanz. Suddenly he released Barlach, and took hold of the wheel, though he was still trembling and deadly pale. 'Very well. You won't help me.'

That evening Barlach called to see his doctor, Dr Basler, who lived at Bären-platz. The street-lamps were already lighted and night was rapidly falling. Barlach looked down from Basler's window on to the surging crowds of people in the square while the doctor packed up his instruments. The two men had known each other most of their lives, and had been at school together.

'Your heart is sound, thank goodness,' said Basler.

'Have you kept notes on the progress of my case?' Barlach answered.

'Naturally. A whole folder full of them,' answered the doctor, pointing to a pile of papers on his desk.

'You've never talked to anyone about it, Basler?' inquired the old man.

'My dear Hans,' returned the other, shocked. 'There is such a thing as professional secrecy.'

Out in the square a blue Mercedes drove up and stopped between other parked cars. Barlach's glance became more intent. Chanz got out of the car. He had a girl with him in a white raincoat; her hair flowed down to her shoulders in a blonde cascade.

'Ever had burglars, Fritz?' asked the Inspector.

'What makes you ask?'

'I just wondered.'

'Not burglars, but I once found my desk had been ransacked,' admitted Basler. 'But no money was taken, though there was a substantial sum in the desk.'

'Why didn't you report it to the police?'

The doctor scratched his head. 'As I said, no money was taken. Even so, I did intend to report it. I suppose I forgot all about it.'

'I see,' said Barlach. 'You forgot. Burglars evidently have a good time in these parts.' So that, he thought, is how Gastmann got to know about me. He looked down into the square again. Chanz and the girl were just entering an Italian restaurant.

On the day of Schmied's funeral, thought Barlach, and turned his back to the window. He watched Basler who was sitting at the desk, writing.

'Well, what's the verdict?'

'Do you have much pain?'

Barlach told him of his recent seizure.

'That's bad, Hans,' said Basler. 'We've only a few days in which to operate. It's your only chance.'

'But I feel as well as ever now.'

'In three or four days you'll have another attack, Hans,' said the doctor, 'and you will not survive it.'

'But meanwhile I still have at least two days. Two days. You can operate on the morning of the eighth, Fritz. On Tuesday morning.'

'On Tuesday morning,' said Basler.

'After that I shall have one more year to live, shan't I, Fritz?' said Barlach, looking with his usual air of inscrutability at his school-friend. Basler got up quickly and paced across the room.

'Who told you that nonsense?'

'The man who read my case-history.'

'Did you break in here yourself?' demanded the doctor.

Barlach shook his head. 'No, no. But it's true, Fritz, isn't it? Twelve more months.'

'Yes, it's true,' Basler admitted. He sat down on a chair by the wall and looked helplessly at Barlach, who was standing in the middle of the room. There was something cold, remote and solitary about him, something humble and yet immovable, and the doctor averted his eyes from the forlorn look in his friend's face.

Chapter eight

Barlach awoke suddenly nearly three hours after midnight. On Basler's advice he had gone to bed early and taken a sleeping pill. It was the first time he had done so, and for a moment he attributed his sudden waking to this unaccustomed measure. Then he knew he had been awakened by a noise. His sight and hearing were abnormally clear, as often happens when one wakes with a start. It took him some seconds to remember where he was. He was not in the room where he usually slept but in his library. Expecting a bad night, he had intended – he remembered it now – to read. He must have fallen into a sudden, profound sleep.

He passed his hands over his body and found he was still in his day clothes and had merely covered himself with a woollen rug. He listened. Something fell to the floor – it was the book he had begun to read. The blackness of the windowless room was profound but not complete: a faint light came through the open door of the bedroom, it was the grey shimmer of the stormy night. He heard the wind howling in the distance. Presently he managed to make out through the gloom a bookcase, a chair, then the edge of the table, on which he recalled his automatic pistol was lying.

Suddenly he was conscious of a draught of air; a window rattled in the bedroom, then the door shut with a loud bang. Immediately afterwards the old man heard a soft sound in the passage. Now he knew. Someone had opened the outer door and entered the passage, forgetting that by so doing he would cause a draught of air. Barlach rose to his feet and switched on the standard lamp.

He snatched up the automatic pistol and released the safety catch. The intruder switched on the passage light so that Barlach could see the shining bulb through the half-open door. This action of his unknown visitor surprised Barlach for he could see no sense in it. He understood when it was too late. He saw the silhouette of an arm and hand as it snatched at the lamp. Then a blue flame blazed out and there was darkness both in the passage and in the library. The unknown had torn out the bulb and blown the fuse. Barlach stood in complete darkness. The intruder had laid down the conditions of the fight and issue was about to be joined. Barlach was to fight in the dark.

Gripping his automatic, the old man cautiously opened the door to the bedroom and went in. A dim light seeped through the window, hardly perceptible at first, though it grew stronger as the eyes became accustomed to it. Barlach leaned against the wall between the bed and the window which faced on to the river. The other window was to his right and over-looked the next house. Thus he stood in impenetrable shadow. The drawback of his position was the impossibility of retreat, but he hoped that his invisibility outweighed it. The door to the library was faintly lighted by the windows. He would be bound to see the outline of anyone coming through the door.

Suddenly he saw the thin beam of a flash-lamp in the library. It glided, searching over the books, across the floor, over the armchair and finally reached the desk. Its ray lit up the snake-knife. Again Barlach saw the hand through the open door in front of him. It was cased in a brown leather glove; it groped across the desk and closed round the handle of the snake-knife. Barlach raised his pistol and took aim. The flashlamp went out. The old man lowered his weapon without firing and waited. From where he stood he could look out through the window at the dark mass of the unresting river, the piled-up town beyond, the cathedral stabbing the sky with its arrow-like spire, and over all the drifting clouds. He stood motionless, waiting for the enemy who had come to kill him. His eyes bored into the vague opening of the door. He waited. All was still and lifeless.

Then the clock struck in the corridor – three. He listened. In the distance he could hear the soft tick of the clock. Not far away a car hooted, and then drove past. People coming home from a night-club. Once he thought he heard breathing, but decided he must have been mistaken. He waited. Somewhere in his house an enemy was standing, and between them was the night, the patient, cruel night, that hid beneath its black mantle the deadly snake-knife that sought his heart.

The old man scarcely breathed. He stood clasping his pistol, scarcely aware of the cold sweat that ran down the back of his neck. He thought of nothing – not of Gastmann, not of Lutz, not even of the disease that gnawed at him hour by hour, that was about to destroy the life he was defending, defending with such lust to live. He was but an eye that searched the night, an ear that examined the faintest sound, a hand closed round the cool steel of an automatic pistol.

When at last he became conscious of the approaching attacker it was in an unexpected way: he felt a vague chill on his cheek, a slight change in the air. It was a long time before he could explain it, then he guessed that the door between the bedroom and the dining-room had been opened. The assassin had acted unexpectedly: he had reached the bedroom by a roundabout route, remaining invisible, inaudible, irresistible, with the snake-knife in his hand.

Barlach decided he must act first, that he must take the initiative and begin the fight. He, a mortally sick man, must begin the fight for a life that at best could only last a year, and only then if Basler used his knife expertly.

Barlach aimed at the window overlooking the river. He fired, fired again, three times in rapid succession, through the splintering glass out towards the river. Then he dropped to the floor and as he did so something hissed above his head. It was the knife, quivering now in the wall. But the old man had done what he wanted: light shone up in the neighbouring windows. The people in the next house were leaning from their open windows, staring, startled and confused, into the night. Barlach rose to his feet. The light from the next house flooded the bedroom: he caught a vague glimpse of a figure in the dining-room doorway, then the outer door slammed, and after it slammed the library door in the sudden draught of air, then the dining-room door – crash after crash. Then the window slammed and there was silence.

The occupants of the neighbouring house were still staring out into the darkness. The old man stood there by the wall, his hand still holding the pistol. He stayed there, unmoving, as though he had lost count of time. The neighbours withdrew, the lights went out. In the darkness Barlach stood by the wall, one with it, alone in the house.

Half an hour passed before he went into the corridor and looked for his electric torch. He telephoned Chanz and asked him to come round. Then he changed the blown fuse for a new one, and the light went on again. Barlach seated himself in his armchair and listened to the sounds of the night. Outside a car drove up and braked sharply. Suddenly the front door opened and he heard a step. Chanz entered the room.

'Someone's been trying to kill me,' said the Inspector. Chanz was hatless and pale. His hair hung in disorder over his forehead and his pyjamas showed under his overcoat. Together they went into the bedroom. Chanz pulled the knife out of the wall. It cost him an effort, for it had buried itself deep in the panelling.

'With this?' he asked.

'With that.'

The young policeman looked at the splintered window-pane. 'Did you fire through the window, Inspector?' he asked in surprise.

Barlach told him the whole story.

'You couldn't have done better.'

They went into the passage and Chanz picked up the bulb from the floor.

'Cunning,' he said, not without admiration, and laid it down. Then they went back into the library. Barlach lay down on the divan and drew the rug over him. He lay there, helpless, and suddenly looked very old and frail. Chanz still had the snake-knife in his hand.

'You couldn't see who it was?'

'No. He was cautious and kept to the darkest shadow. All I saw was that he was wearing brown leather gloves.

'That's not much to identify him by.'

'Nothing at all. But though I didn't see him, scarcely even heard him breathe, I know who it was. I know.'

The old man spoke almost inaudibly. Chanz weighed the knife in his hand, looked at the grey outstretched figure, at the tired old man, at the hands lying beside the frail body like faded flowers beside a corpse. Then he caught Barlach's eyes. They were fixed on him, calm, inscrutable and clear. Chanz put the knife back on the desk.

'You must get away to Grindelwald tomorrow. You're ill. Or would you rather not go after all? Maybe mountain air is not what you need. It is winter up there.'

'I shall go.'

'Then you must get some sleep now. Shall I stay and keep watch?'

'No, you go, Chanz,' said the Inspector.

'Good night,' said Chanz, and went slowly out. The old man did not answer him; he seemed to be already asleep.

Chanz opened the outer door, went out and closed it behind him. Slowly he walked the few steps to the street and closed the open garden gate. Then he stopped and looked back towards the house. The night was still dark. Everything was lost in the darkness, even the neighbouring houses. There was no light anywhere except a street-lamp some way off – a lost star in the sinister night that was filled with sadness and the swirl of the river. Chanz stood still and suddenly cursed softly to himself. He kicked open the garden gate again and strode resolutely up the garden path to the front door, retracing his former steps. He seized the door handle and turned it. But the door was locked.

Barlach got up at six after a sleepless night. It was Sunday. The old man washed and put on clean clothes. Then he telephoned for a taxi, intending to breakfast on the train. He got into his thick winter overcoat and went out into the grey morning light. He took no luggage with him. The sky was clear. A drunken student staggered past, reeking of beer. He wished Barlach good morning. 'Probably just failed his first M.B. for the second time, poor devil,' Barlach conjectured to himself. 'Spent the night drowning his sorrows.' The taxi drove up and stopped. It was a big American car. The driver's collar was turned up so that only his eyes were visible. He opened the car door.

'The station,' said Barlach, getting in. The car moved off.

'Well,' said a voice at his side. 'How are you this morning? Have a good night?'

Barlach looked round. At the far end of the seat was Gastmann. He was wearing a light raincoat and his arms were folded: on his hands were leather gloves. He sat there sneering like an old peasant. The driver turned his head and grinned; he had turned his coat collar down again. He was one of Gastmann's menservants.

'What do you want of me now?' Barlach asked.

'You are still at my heels. Yesterday you went to see that novelist fellow,' said the man in the corner; his voice was threatening.

'It's my job.'

Gastmann kept his eyes on him. 'No one meddles with my affairs without coming to a bad end, Barlach.'

The man at the wheel of the car was driving fast up the Aargauerstalden.

'I'm still alive,' answered the Inspector, calmly. 'And I've meddled quite a lot in your affairs.'

Both were silent for a while.

The car was hurtling towards Viktoria-platz. An old man hobbled across the street, and only just managed to avoid being run over.

'Steady there!' cried Barlach angrily.

'Drive faster,' said Gastmann sharply, and gave the old man a mocking glance. 'I love the speed of machines.'

The Inspector shivered. He hated being shut up in a stuffy vehicle. They raced on to the bridge, passed a tram and, with the silver ribbon of the Aare far below them, sped into the town which seemed to open welcoming streets before them. The narrow roads were still empty and deserted; the sky above the town was as clear as glass.

'Take my advice and throw your hand in. It's time to admit defeat,' said Gastmann, filling his pipe.

The old man looked at the dark arches of the porticoes past which they were speeding and at the shadowy figures of two constables, standing in front of Lang's bookshop.

'Geiss and Steger,' he thought.

'Our game', he said at last, 'yours and mine, is something neither of us can give up. We are both guilty, Gastmann; you because you proposed a wager, and I because I accepted it.'

They drove past the Parliament buildings.

'Do you still believe I killed Schmied?' asked the other.

'I have never believed it for a moment,' answered Barlach. Watching unconcernedly as Gastmann lit his pipe, he went on: 'I did not succeed in convicting you of the crime I know you committed; so now I shall get you convicted of a crime I know you have not committed.'

Gastmann looked inquiringly at the Inspector.

'That is a possibility I had not thought of,' he said. 'I must take care.'

The Inspector did not answer.

'Perhaps you are more dangerous than I took you for,' said Gastmann, reflectively, from his corner.

The car slowed down and stopped. They had reached the station.

'The next time we meet I shall not talk to you, Barlach,' said Gastmann. 'The next time I shall kill you. That is, of course, if you survive your operation.'

'You are mistaken,' said Barlach, standing shivering a little in the morning freshness of the square. 'You will not kill me. I'm the only man who knows you, and am therefore the only man who can judge you. I *have* judged you, Gastmann, and I've sentenced you to death. Today the sentence will be carried out. Today the executioner will come to kill you. For in the name of God it is time that deed were done.'

Gastmann stared at the old man speculatively as Barlach turned and entered the station, his hands deep in his coat pockets. Without looking back, he vanished into the dark building, which was slowly beginning to fill with people.

'You fool!' Gastmann suddenly called after him, so loudly that the passers-by turned to look at him. 'You fool!' But Barlach was already out of earshot.

Chapter nine

The day was coming up clear and hot. The sun, an immaculate orb, threw long, hard shadows which gradually shortened as it mounted higher. The town lay like a white shell, drinking in the light, sucking it into narrow streets which would give it back again the form of a thousand lamps when night fell.

Chanz waited for an hour, his face pale in the sunlight reflected from the walls. He walked restlessly up and down under the trees in front of the cathedral, looking up occasionally at the gargoyles that drained the roof, grotesquely grimacing masks staring into the street when the sunlight lay.

At last the great door opened. A dense stream of people, who had come to listen to a celebrated preacher, poured out. Chanz quickly made out the white raincoat for which he had been waiting.

Anna came up to him. She gave him her hand and said she was glad to see him. They went up the Kessler-gasse, surrounded by the swarm of church-goers, young and old: a professor, a baker's wife in her Sunday best, two students with a girl, officials and teachers, all neat, well-washed, hungry, all looking forward to their Sunday lunch. Chanz and Anna reached the Kasino-platz, crossed it and went down into the Marzili. They stopped on the bridge.

'Anna,' said Chanz. 'Today I'm going to tackle Ulrich's murderer.'

'Do you know who he is?' she asked, surprised.

He looked at her. She stood facing him, pale and slim. 'I believe so,' he said. 'When I have dealt with him, will you be to me what—' he hesitated a moment and then went on, 'what you were to – Ulrich?'

Anna did not answer immediately. She drew her coat round her as though she were cold. A light breeze came up, disarranging her blonde hair. Then she said:

'Yes. I promise you.'

They shook hands and Anna walked on across the bridge. He watched her go. Her white raincoat gleamed between the beech trunks, lost itself among passers-by, reappeared and finally was gone for good. He walked back to the station, where he had left his car, and drove out towards Ligerz.

It was almost noon before he got there, for he had driven slowly, stopping now and then to walk into the fields and smoke, before returning to the car and driving on. At Ligerz he parked the car outside the station, and climbed the steps beside the church. He was calm now. The lake was deep blue, the last leaves had fallen from the vines and the earth between them was brown and friable. But Chanz neither saw nor cared. He went on, steadily, without pausing or hesitating or turning back. The path led steeply uphill, between white walls, past vineyard after vineyard.

Chanz climbed higher and higher, calm, slow, unhesitating, his right hand in his coat pocket. Several times lizards darted across his path, buzzards flew up, the land shimmered in the blaze of the sun as though it were summer. He went on unrestingly. Presently he left the vineyards behind and plunged into the woodland. It was cooler there. The white Jura rocks gleamed between the tree-trunks. He climbed still higher, always at the same steady pace, and came to open country, pasture and arable land. The path rose more gently now. He walked past a rectangular cemetery, enclosed by a grey wall. The gate was wide open. Women in black were moving along the paths between the graves; an old man with bent back stopped and watched Chanz go by, his right hand still in his coat pocket.

He reached Prêles, and took the turning towards Lamlingen. The air on the high plateau was still. There was no mist; even the most distant landmarks stood out with abnormal clarity. Only the ridge of the Chasseral was sprinkled with snow; all else shone light brown, broken by the white walls, the red roofs, and the broad, black ribbons of ploughed land.

Chanz strode on steadily. The sun shone on his back and threw his shadow forward. The path began to drop downwards, and he turned to the right so that the sun was now on his right hand. He went on, unthinking, unseeing, impelled by a single purpose, governed by a single passion. Somewhere a dog barked. The little animal ran up, sniffed at him as he passed, and ran away. Chanz walked on, keeping to the right-hand side of the road, never hastening, never slackening his pace, making for the house set in the brown background of the fields and surrounded by leafless poplars which were just coming into sight.

Chanz left the path and made his way across country. His feet sank into the warm earth of an unploughed field. He went on till he reached the gate. The gate was open and he went through it. An American car was standing in the forecourt. Chanz made straight for the front door. This too was open. He entered the lobby, opened a second door and found himself in a great hall that took up the whole of the ground floor. There he stopped. Bright light was pouring in through the windows opposite, and facing him, not five steps away, was Gastmann. At his side ranged the powerful figures of his two menservants, motionless and menacing, like two huge butchers. All three were wearing overcoats; trunks and cases were piled up close by. All was ready for instant depature.

Chanz did not move.

'So it's you.' said Gastmann. He looked with faint surprise at the policeman's calm, pale face and at the still-open door behind him.

Then he began to laugh. 'So that's what the old man meant! Not bad, not bad at all!'

Gastmann's eyes were wide open and a spectral merriment shone in them.

Quietly, deliberately and without a word, one of the thugs took a pistol from his pocket and fired. Chanz felt the bullet strike him in the left shoulder. Then he drew his right hand from his pocket and dodged aside. He fired three times into Gastmann's laughing face, and his laughter died away in empty infinite space.

Summoned by a telephone call from Chanz, Charnel went with all speed from Lamlingen, Clenin from Twann, and the flying squad from Biel. They found Chanz bleeding profusely near three dead bodies. The fight must have been short, yet each of the three men who now lay dead had found time to fire, and a second bullet had struck Chanz in the left forearm. Each of his adversaries had used an automatic pistol; one of the menservants still held his weapon in his hand.

Chanz was in no state to follow what happened after Charnel's arrival. He fainted twice while the doctor from Neuveville was dressing his wounds, but the injuries proved not to be dangerous. Villagers, peasants, workmen, women, came to stare. The courtyard was soon crowded and the police closed the doors into the house. But one girl managed to force her way into the great hall and threw herself screaming on to Gastmann's body. It was the waitress, Charnel's fiancée. He looked on, red with fury.

Then they made a way through the crowd in the courtyard and carried Chanz to a car.

'There they are – all three,' said Lutz next morning, with a gesture towards the bodies, but there was no exultation in his voice, it sounded sad and tired.

Von Schwendi nodded. The Colonel had not yet recovered from his shock. He had driven over to Biel with Lutz. The two men were in the room where the bodies lay, and despite their overcoats they were shivering. A diagonal beam of light fell through the little barred window. Lutz's eyes were red and tired. He had spent the whole night reading Gastmann's diaries which were written in an almost illegible shorthand.

Lutz thrust his hands deeper into his pockets. 'We surround ourselves with policemen, soldiers, and public opinion for protection from men like these, and what good does it do?' He grimaced, his eyes bulging, and laughed a hollow, mirthless laugh that re-echoed in the cold, little room. 'A fool at the head of a great nation, Councillor, and it is overwhelmed; a Gastmann in a community and our cordons are pierced, and outposts turned.'

'What about Schmied's murder?' inquired the Councillor, anxious to break away from Lutz's highflown imagery.

'We found a brief-case of Schmied's in Gastmann's house. It contained a full story of Gastmann's career and evidence on his crimes. Schmied was out to bring Gastmann to book and he was doing it as a private individual. It was a mistake for which he paid with his life, for we have proof that Gastmann was responsible for Schmied's murder. Schmied was killed with the same pistol that one of the servants was clasping when Chanz shot him. Gastmann killed him because he knew that Schmied was ready to expose him. Schmied should have taken us into his confidence, but he was young and ambitious, and doubtless wanted to claim all the credit.'

Barlach came into the mortuary. At the sight of him, the look of melancholy again came over Lutz's face and he buried his hands ever deeper in his pockets.

'Well, Inspector', he said, putting his weight first on one foot, then on the other, 'I'm glad to see you here. You've wasted no time in getting back from your leave. The Councillor and I got here as quickly as we could. The bodies are laid out for inspection.

'We've often quarrelled, Barlach. In police matters, I've always favoured a stream-lined, scientific organization while you have advocated what seemed to me to be a rustic gendarmerie of trustworthy granddads. Let us now bury the hatchet. We were both wrong. Chanz has confuted us both with his pistol. I don't really care how he did it. We can take his word that it was in self-defence and there's no reason to believe otherwise. The end justified the means; the men he shot deserved death a thousand times over. It looks as if he will now have to be promoted, while you and I are shown up as a couple of dolts. But at least, it marks the end of the Schmied case.'

Lutz looked away, embarrassed by the Inspector's enigmatic silence. He seemed to shrink into himself as he suddenly became again the meticulous, correct official. He cleared his throat and, suddenly becoming aware of von Schwendi standing at his side, blushed. Then, accompanied by the Colonel, he went out into the gloom of the corridor, leaving Barlach alone.

The bodies lay on stretchers, covered over with black sheets. Barlach went up to the middle stretcher and uncovered the body. It was Gastmann's. Barlach stood over him, leaning slightly forward, holding the black sheet in his left hand. He looked down in silence at the waxen face of the dead. The expression on the lips was almost insolently gay, though the eye-sockets were deeper, and there was no longer anything terrible in their depths. Thus they faced each other for the last time. The hunter and the hunted.

Barlach knew that his life, too, was played out. Once more his mind sped back through the years; once more he retraced the mysterious paths of the labyrinth that was the lives of both men. There was nothing left between them now but the infinitude of death, a judge whose verdict is silence.

As Barlach stood there, the dim light of the mortuary fell on his face and hands and played over the corpse, the same for both, created for both, reconciling them. The silence of death fell on the old man, crept into him, but it did not bring him the peace it had brought the other. The dead are always right.

Barlach slowly covered Gastmann's face. He had seen him for the last time; from now on this man belonged to the grave. For years Barlach had been obsessed by only one thought – to destroy the man now lying at his feet in this bare, grey room, sprinkled with the falling plaster as with fine, sparse snow. Nothing was left to the old man now but wearily to cover the face, and humbly to say a prayer for forgetfulness, the one mercy that can soothe a heart consumed by raging fire.

Chapter ten

Punctually at eight o'clock that evening Chanz arrived at Barlach's house in Altenberg. He had received an urgent invitation to be there at that hour. To his surprise he was admitted by a young servant-girl in a white apron, and when he entered the passage he could hear from the kitchen the spitting of roasting meat and the clatter of plates and dishes. The maid slipped his overcoat from his shoulders, for his left was was in a sling, and then opened the door to the dining-room. Chanz stopped spellbound on the threshold. The table was formally laid for two people. Lighted candles shone in the candlesticks and Barlach was seated in an easy chair at one end of the table, his face ruddy in the quiet candle-glow, the picture of unruffled calm.

'Sit down, Chanz,' the old man called to his guest, waving his hand to a second chair drawn up to the table. Chanz sat down.

'I didn't know I was to come to dinner,' he said at last.

'We must celebrate your triumph,' answered the Inspector quietly, and pushed the candlesticks a little to one side, so that they could look each other full in the face. Then he clapped his hands. The door opened, and a portly woman bore in a dish overflowing with sardines, crayfish, and gherkins, as well as tomato and green-pea salads. Mountains of eggs and mayonnaise garnished cold meats, cold chicken and salmon. The old man helped himself to everything. Chanz watched him pile his plate and was so astonished that he took nothing but a little potato salad.

'What shall we drink?' inquired Barlach. 'Ligerzer?'

'Ligerzer is excellent,' returned Chanz as though in a dream.

The maid came and filled their glass. Barlach began to eat, helped himself to bread, and avidly devoured the salmon, sardines, crayfish, cold meats, salads and mayonnaise. He clapped his hands and called for more. Chanz, benumbed, had not yet finished his potato salad.

Barlach had his glass refilled for the second time.

'Now the pies and the red Neuenburger,' he called out.

The plates were changed. Barlach was served with three pies containing goose-liver, pork and truffles.

'I thought you were seriously ill, Inspector,' said Chanz incredulously.

'Not today, Chanz, not today. I'm celebrating. I've got my hands on Schmied's murderer at last.'

He emptied his second glass of red wine and began on his third pie, never pausing, greedily consuming the good things of this world, crunching them between his jaws like a demon intent on satisfying a boundless hunger. His figure threw a grotesque and enormous shadow on the wall behind him. The vigorous movements of his arms, the rise and fall of his head resembled the dance of some triumphant negro chieftain. Chanz watched with a feeling of horror the sinister drama which the sick man was enacting for him. He sat there unmoving, eating nothing nor drinking even a mouthful of wine from his glass.

Barlach called aloud for veal cutlets, rice, *pommes frites* and green salad. He ordered champagne. Chanz could not believe his ears.

'You've been shamming,' he said in a low voice. 'You're not ill.'

For a while the Inspector did not answer. He just laughed, and gave all his attention to the salad, enjoying each leaf separately.

'Yes, Chanz,' said Barlach at last, and there was a wild gleam in his eyes. 'I've been shamming. I've not been ill at all.' He crammed a chunk of roast veal into his mouth, and went on eating, unpausing, insatiable.

Then in a flash Chanz guessed the truth and saw that the way to escape was barred. A cold sweat broke out on his skin. Panic seized him with overpowering arms.

'So you know, Inspector?' he said in a whisper.

'I know, Chanz,' said Barlach, firmly and calmly, without raising his voice; it was as though he was speaking of some quite everyday matter. 'You murdered Schmied.' He took up his glass of champagne and emptied it at one draught.

'I often felt that you knew.' Chanz spoke almost inaudibly.

The old man's expression did not change. He seemed to be interested in nothing but his food. He recklessly heaped his plate with a second helping of rice, poured gravy over it and placed a veal cutlet on top. Chanz tried to defend himself against this devilish gourmand.

'The bullet that killed Schmied was fired from the manservant's pistol. The same gun was in the man's hand when Charnel found him,' he stated defiantly, but there was a note of apprehension in his voice.

Barlach's narrowed eyes flashed with contempt. 'Nonsense. You know well enough that it was *your* pistol the servant was holding in his hand. You put it there yourself after you had shot him. But for Gastmann's criminal record your story would certainly have been investigated and easily disproved.'

'You'll never be able to prove it against me,' said Chanz, in defiance.

The old man sat back in his chair, no longer frail and sick, but strong and masterful, the picture of unchallengeable superiority, a cat playing with its prey. He finished the rest of the champagne in the bottle, and the servant, who had been running in and out the whole time, brought the cheese. He ate with it radishes, pickled gherkins and spring onions. He still went on eating, as though he was tasting for the last time the good things earth has to offer.

'Haven't you realized, Chanz,' he went on at last, 'that you betrayed yourself long ago? It was your pistol. The bullet that killed Gastmann's hound and saved my life came from the same gun that killed Schmied. Yours, Chanz. You yourself provided all the proof I needed.'

'So that's why I couldn't find the body of the dog,' answered Chanz mechanically. 'Did you know that Gastmann owned that hound?'

'Certainly. Before we set out I took the precaution of protecting my arm with bandages.

'So even in that you laid a trap for me.'

'Even in that. But you provided the first proof when you took the Ins road to Ligerz on the Friday, and treated me to the farce about "Blue Charon". On the Wednesday Schmied took the road through Zollikofen. I knew that because he stopped at the garage in Lyss.'

'How could you know that?' asked Chanz.

'Simply by telephoning. Whoever drove through Ins and Erlach that night was the murderer – you, Chanz. You came from Grindelwald. The Pension Eiger in Grindelwald has a blue Mercedes for hire. You had watched Schmied for weeks, observed every step he took; you were jealous of his ability, his success, his education, even his girl. You knew that he was after Gastmann; you knew when he visited him, but you didn't know why. Then by chance the briefcase on his desk containing the documents fell into your hands. You determined to take over the Gastmann case, to kill Schmied, and for once to have a success yourself. You were right in believing it would be easy to pin a murder on to Gastmann. When you saw the blue Mercedes in Grindelwald you knew what to do. You hired the car for Wednesday night. I went to Grindelwald in order to confirm the fact. The rest is quite simple; you drove through Ligerz to Schernelz and left the car in the woods by the Twann River; you took a short cut through the wood by following the gorge, which brought you to the Twann-Lamlingen road. You waited by the cliffs for Schmied. He was surprised to see you and stopped. He opened the door, and you killed him. You told me the story yourself. And now you've got what you wanted – his success, his job, his car and his girl.'

Chanz listened. In the course of this horrifying meal this pitiless chess-player had mated him. The candles were burning less steadily; their light flickered over the faces of the two men and the shadows darkened. A deadly silence reigned. The serving-women had withdrawn. The old man sat motionless, seeming hardly to breathe.

'You played a cat-and-mouse game with me,' said Chanz slowly.

'I played a game with you,' returned Barlach gravely. 'There was nothing else I could do. You killed Schmied and I had to get you for it.'

'In order to kill Gastmann,' added Chanz, suddenly realizing the whole truth.

'As you say. I've spent two-thirds of my life trying to corner Gastmann, and Schmied was my last hope. I unleashed him on the most evil man I ever knew – a thoroughbred hound against a raging wild beast. Then you came, Chanz, with your petty ambition and snatched my chance away. So I took you – the murderer – and used you for my purpose. That part was easy for you were driven on by the desperation of the criminal who has to throw his guilt upon another. I forced you to make my aim and object your own.'

'I've been through hell,' said Chanz.

'We've both been through hell,' went on the old man calmly. 'Von Schwendi's intervention provided the final straw that made it imperative that you should establish Gastmann's guilt. Any deviation from the trail that led towards Gastmann might lead back to you. Schmied's brief-case was the only thing that could help you. You knew it had been in my possession, but you did not know that Gastmann had removed it. That is why you attacked me here on Saturday night – that, and your uneasiness about my visit to Grindelwald.'

'You knew it was I who attacked you?' asked Chanz tonelessly.

'Right from the first moment. Every move I made was made with the intention of driving you to desperation. And when you could bear it no longer you went to Lamlingen to force a decision with Gastmann, one way or another.'

'It was Gastmann's thugs who shot first,' said Chanz.

'They were ready for you. On Saturday morning I told Gastmann I was sending an executioner to kill him.'

An icy shiver ran through Chanz and he reeled in his chair. 'You set us on each other like dogs.'

'Two wild beasts,' came the pitiless reply.

'You appointed yourself the judge and me the executioner.'

'Precisely.'

'And I, who only did your will whether I wanted to or not, am a criminal fit only to be hunted down!'

Chanz got up, steadying himself on the table with his uninjured right hand. All the candles but one had gone out. Chanz's burning eyes tried to make out the outlines of the old man's figure in the gloom, but all he could see was an unreal, black shadow. He made a quick, groping movement towards his hip pocket.

'Stop that,' he heard the old man rap out. 'That won't help you. Lutz knows you are here and the two women are still in the house.'

'I see,' said Chanz softly.

'The Schmied case is settled,' Barlach announced through the darkness of the room. 'I will keep your secret. But go! Anywhere! Only never let me see you again! To judge one man is enough. Now go.'

Chanz went slowly out with lowered head, quickly merging into the blackness of the night. The door closed behind him, and a little later, a car drove off from outside the house. As it did so, the last candle flared up and went out, throwing its final garish flicker across the face of the old man who sat silent with eyes closed.

Barlach spent the night in his armchair, without once leaving it. The immense energy that had risen within him earlier in the evening had subsided and now threatened to die out completely. He had dared all in one last, audacious throw. Yet in only one respect had he lied to Chanz.

Early next morning, as dawn was breaking, Lutz came storming into the room to report breathlessly that Chanz had been found dead – that a train had run into his car at the level crossing between Ligerz and Twann. Lutz found the Inspector mortally ill. With an effort Barlach asked him to remind Basler that it was Tuesday. 'Tell him, I'm ready for him,' he said.

Then the old man sat and stared out of the window into the glass-clear morning. 'Twelve more months,' Lutz heard him say. 'Just one year.'

The Quarry

In the beginning of November, 1948, Commissioner Barlach had been committed to the Salem – the hospital from which one looks down on the old city of Berne and its town hall. A heart attack had delayed the urgent operation for two weeks. When the difficult task was finally undertaken, it was performed successfully, but the pathological report showed the hopeless disease the doctors had suspected. Things looked grim for the Commissioner. His boss, Dr Lutz, had twice now expected his death, and had twice been given new hope, when, finally, shortly before Christmas, improvement set in. The old man slept through the holidays, but on the twenty-seventh, a Monday, he was awake and looking at old issues of *Life* magazine from the year 1945.

'They were beasts, Samuel,' he said that evening, when Dr Hungertobel entered the room to make his visit. 'They were beasts,' and he handed him the magazine. 'You as a doctor can fully comprehend it. Look at this picture from the Stutthof concentration camp! The camp doctor Nehle is performing a stomach operation on an inmate without anaesthesia, and somebody photographed him.'

'The Nazis did that sometimes,' said the doctor, and looked at the picture. He turned pale just as he was about to throw it aside.

'What's the matter?' the sick man asked, surprised.

Hungertobel did not reply immediately. He dropped the open magazine on Barlach's bed, reached in the right upper pocket of his white coat, and pulled out a pair of horn-rimmed glasses. The Commissioner noticed that his hands shook when he put them on. Then he looked at the picture a second time.

Why is he so nervous? thought Barlach.

'Nonsense!' Hungertobel finally said angrily, and put the magazine on the table with the others. 'Come, let me have your hand. We want to check your pulse.'

There was silence for a minute. Then the doctor let go of his friend's arm and looked at the chart over the bed.

'You're doing fine, Hans.'

'One more year?' Barlach asked.

Hungertobel was embarrassed. 'We won't talk about that now,' he said. 'You'll have to be careful and come in for checkups.'

'I'm always careful,' scoffed the old man.

'That's fine,' said Hungertobel, and bade him goodby.

'Give me that *Life*,' the sick man said, in a seemingly bored tone. Hungertobel gave him a magazine from the pile on the night table.

'Not that one,' said the Commissioner, and looked scornfully at the doctor. 'I want the one you took away from me. I'm not that easily diverted from a concentration camp.'

Hungertobel hesitated for a moment, blushed when he saw Barlach's inquisitive glance, and handed him the magazine. Then he left quickly, as if there was something that distressed him. A nurse entered. The Commissioner had the other magazines removed.

'How about this one?' asked the nurse, and pointed to the magazine lying on Barlach's blanket.

'No, not this one,' said the old man. After the nurse had left, he scrutinized the picture again. The doctor who was conducting the ghastly experiment appeared in his calm like a terrible god. Most of his face was hidden under the surgical mask.

The Commissioner carefully put the magazine into the drawer of the table and folded his arms behind his head. His eyes were wide open, and he watched the night which more and more filled the room. He did not turn on the light.

Later the nurse came with food. It was still not much and still part of a diet – oatmeal soup. He did not touch the lime-blossom tea, which he loathed. After he had finished the soup, he turned out the lights and looked again into the darkness, into the impenetrable shadows.

He loved to watch the lights of the city fall through the window.

When the nurse came to prepare the Commissioner for the night, he was already asleep.

Around ten o'clock in the morning, Hungertobel came.

Barlach was lying in bed, hands behind his head, and on the blanket was the magazine – opened. His eyes searched the doctor. Hungertobel saw that it was the picture from the concentration camp the old man had in front of him.

'Won't you tell me why you turned pale as death when I showed you this picture in *Life?*' the sick man asked.

Hungertobel stepped to the bed, took down the chart, studied it more carefully than usual, and hung it back in its place. 'It was a ridiculous error, Hans,' he said, 'not worth mentioning.'

'Do you know this Doctor Nehle?' Barlach's voice sounded strangely aroused.

'No,' answered Hungertobel. 'I don't know him. He just reminded me of somebody.'

'The resemblance must be great,' said the Commissioner.

The doctor admitted that the resemblance was great, and again looked at the picture. And again he was upset, as Barlach could clearly observe. But the photograph only showed half the face. 'All doctors look alike when they operate,' Hungertobel said.

'Whom does that beast remind you of?' the old man insisted without pity.

'But it doesn't make sense,' answered Hungertobel. 'I've already told you it must be a mistake.'

'Nevertheless – you'd swear it was he, wouldn't you, Samuel?'

'Well, yes,' replied the doctor. He would swear to it were it not for the fact that it could not be the man he suspected. They were better off leaving well enough alone. It was not a particularly good idea to thumb through old *Lifes* right after an operation which had been a matter of life and death.

'That doctor there,' he continued after a pause, looking at the picture again as if hypnotized, 'could not be the one I knew, because the doctor I knew was in Chile during the war. So the whole thing is nonsense, anybody can see that.'

'In Chile, in Chile,' said Barlach. 'When did he return, this doctor of yours who could not possibly be Nehle?'

'In forty-five.'

'In Chile, in Chile,' Barlach repeated. 'And you don't want to tell me who this picture reminds you of?'

Hungertobel hesitated. The whole affair was very painful to the old doctor.

'If I tell you the name, Hans,' he finally volunteered, 'you'll become suspicious of the man.'

'I *am* suspicious of him,' answered the Commissioner.

Hungertobel sighed. 'You see, Hans,' he said, 'that's what I was afraid of. I don't want it, do you understand? I'm an old doctor and I don't wish to harm anybody. Your suspicion is sheer insanity. You can't just suspect somebody on account of a mere photograph, especially if it shows so little of his face. And besides, he was in Chile. That's a fact.'

'What was he doing there?' the Commissioner interrupted.

'He directed a clinic in Santiago,' said Hungertobel.

'In Chile, in Chile,' Barlach repeated again. 'That's a fascinating refrain and a difficult fact to check. You're right, Samuel, suspicion is something terrible and comes from the devil. Nothing makes man as evil as suspicion,' he continued. 'I know it, and I've often cursed my profession for it. A man shouldn't ever have to think like that. But now I do have a suspicion, and you gave it to me. I'd like to give it back to you, old friend, if you were able to forget it yourself. But you're the one who can't shake it off.'

Hungertobel sat down on the bed. Helplessly he looked at the Commissioner. The sun fell through the window. It was a beautiful day outside, as so often in this mild winter.

'I cannot,' the doctor finally said into the silence of the sickroom. 'I cannot. God help me, I cannot get rid of the suspicion. I know him too well. I studied with him, and twice he took over my practice for me. It's him in the picture – even the scar above the temple from the operation is there. I know it, I operated on Emmenberger myself.'

Hungertobel took off his glasses and put them in his right upper pocket. Then he wiped the perspiration off his forehead.

'Emmenberger?' the Commissioner asked calmly after a while. 'Is that his name?'

'Now I've said it,' Hungertobel answered distressed, 'Fritz Emmenberger.'

'A medical doctor?'

'A medical doctor.'

'And he lives in Switzerland?'

'He owns the clinic Sonnenstein on the Zurich mountain,' answered the doctor. 'In thirty-two he emigrated to Germany and then to Chile. In forty-five he returned and took over the clinic. One of the most expensive clinics in Switzerland,' he added in a low voice.

'Only for the rich?'

'Only for the very rich.'

'Is he a good scientist, Samuel?' asked the Commissioner.

Hungertobel hesitated. Finally he said that it was difficult to answer that question. 'At one time he was a good scientist, only we don't really know whether he remained one. His methods appear questionable to us. As yet, we still know dishearteningly little about the hormones in which he specializes. All kinds of people are invading his field, as in any about to be conquered by science. Scientists and quacks – often combine in one person. But then, what do you want, Hans? Emmenberger is liked by his patients, and they believe in him as they do in God. To me, that seems the most important point for such wealthy clients who want even their illnesses to be a luxury. Nothing can be accomplished without faith – least of all when it involves hormones. So he has success, is loved, and makes money. After all, why else would we call him the "heir apparent"?'

Hungertobel suddenly stopped talking, as if he regretted having uttered Emmenberger's nickname.

'The heir apparent. Why that nickname?' asked Barlach.

'The clinic has inherited the fortunes of many patients,' answered Hungertobel, obviously plagued by a bad conscience. 'Willing one's estate to it seems to be the fashionable thing to do there.'

'So you doctors noticed this?' said the Commissioner.

The two did not speak. The silence bore something unspoken, of which Hungertobel was afraid.

'You mustn't think what you're thinking,' he suddenly exclaimed, horrified.

'I'm only thinking your thoughts,' answered the Commissioner calmly. 'We want to be precise. What we're thinking may be criminal – yet, we ought not to be afraid of our thoughts. Only if we admit them to our consciousness can we test them and – if we're wrong – overcome them. What *are* we thinking now, Samuel? We're thinking that Emmenberger forces his patients to leave him their fortunes. He forces them by methods he learned in the Stutthof concentration camp. And later he kills them.'

'No!' Hungertobel cried with feverish eyes. 'No!' Helplessly he stared at Barlach. 'We mustn't think that! We're not beasts!' he called again, and jumped up to pace around the room, from the wall to the window, from the window to the bed.

'My God,' groaned the doctor. 'This is one of the most terrible hours of my life.'

'Suspicion,' said the old man in the bed, and then once more, mercilessly, 'suspicion.'

Hungertobel stopped at Barlach's bed. 'Let's forget this talk, Hans,' he pleaded. 'We went too far. Naturally, we all like to play around with possibilities at times. But it's bad. Let's drop Emmenberger. The more I see the photograph, the less it looks like him – honestly, I'm not making up an excuse. He was in Chile and not in Stutthof, and so our suspicion is senseless.'

'In Chile, in Chile,' said Barlach, and his eyes sparkled greedily for a new adventure. He stretched his body, then he lay motionless and relaxed, hands behind his head.

'You must go to your patients now, Samuel,' he said after a while. 'They're waiting for you. I don't wish to detain you any longer. Let's forget our talk. You're right, it's best this way.'

When Hungertobel, on his way out, suspiciously turned toward the sick man, the Commissioner was already asleep.

The alibi

The next morning at seven-thirty Hungertobel found the old man studying the *City Gazette*. He was surprised, for the doctor had come earlier than usual and Barlach was usually asleep again at this hour or at least dozing, his hands behind his head. Also, it seemed to the doctor that the Commissioner was friskier, and the old vitality seemed to gleam in his eyes.

'How're you doing?' Hungertobel greeted the sick man.

He was sniffing the morning air, was the evasive answer.

'I came earlier than usual, and I'm not really here officially,' said Hungertobel and stepped to the bed. 'I'm just bringing a heap of medical journals. The *Swiss Medical Weekly*, a French one and, since you understand English, too, a number of issues of *Lancet*, the famous British medical journal.'

'It's ever so nice of you to assume I'm interested in this stuff,' answered Barlach, without looking up from the *Gazette*, 'but I don't know that it's quite the proper literature for me. You know perfectly well I'm no friend of medicine.'

Hungertobel laughed. 'And that from somebody we've helped.'

'Well,' said Barlach, 'that doesn't make it any less of a nuisance.'

Hungertobel asked him what he was reading in the *Gazette*.

'Advertisements for stamps,' answered the old man.

The doctor shook his head. 'Nevertheless, you'll look at these journals, even though you generally won't have anything to do with us doctors. I'm determined to prove that our talk yesterday was folly, Hans. You're a criminologist and I feel you're capable of having our fashionable doctor and all his hormones arrested out of a clear blue sky. I can't understand how I could have forgotten it. It's easy enough to prove that Emmenberger was in Santiago. He published articles from there in various medical journals, including British and American ones, mostly concerning questions of internal secretion, and made a name for himself. Even as a student he had distinguished himself as a writer with a witty and brilliant style. As you can see, he was a competent and conscientious scientist. His present leaning toward the fashionable, if I may call it that, is all the more regrettable; for what he's doing now is distinctly questionable, any way you look at it. The last article appeared in *Lancet* in January of forty-five, a few months before his return to Switzerland. That's certainly evidence that our suspicion was regular idiocy. I promise you solemnly never again to play criminologist. The man in the picture cannot be Emmenberger, or the photograph is forged.'

'That would be an alibi,' said Barlach, and folded the newspaper. 'You may leave those journals.'

When Hungertobel returned around ten for his regular visit, the old man was lying in bed, diligently reading the journals.

'Medicine does seem to interest you all of a sudden,' the doctor said, surprised, and checked Barlach's pulse.

The Commissioner said that Hungertobel was right. The articles did come from Chile.

Hungertobel was happy and relieved.

'You see! And we already had Emmenberger a mass murderer!'

'Mankind has made the most astonishing advances in that art today,' Barlach answered dryly. 'Progress, my friend, progress. I don't need the English journals, but leave the Swiss ones here.'

'But Emmenberger's articles in *Lancet* are much more important,' contradicted Hungertobel, convinced that his friend really was interested in medicine. 'They're the ones you must read.'

'But in the *Swiss Medical Weekly* Emmenberger writes in German,' Barlach retorted rather ironically.

'And?' asked the doctor, who understood nothing.

'I mean that I'm occupied with his style, Samuel, the style of a doctor who once wrote with elegance and now writes in a most awkward manner,' said the old man cautiously.

And what did that indicate, asked Hungertobel, still unsuspecting, busy with the chart above the bed.

'It's not that easy to furnish an alibi,' said the Commissioner.

'What are you driving at?' the doctor asked, thunderstruck. 'You mean you still haven't gotten over your suspicion?'

Thoughtfully Barlach looked into the face of his dismayed friend

– into this old, noble, wrinkled doctor's face. He was a doctor who had never in his life taken his patients lightly, yet knew nothing about human beings. And then he said: 'You're still smoking your "Little Rose of Sumatra," Samuel, aren't you? It would be nice if you offered me one. I imagine it would be very pleasant to light one after my boring oatmeal soup.'

The discharge

But before lunch was served, the sick man, who had been reading
Emmenberger's article about the pancreas over and over, received his
first visitor since the operation. It was the 'boss', who came in around
eleven o'clock and nervously sat down by the bed, without taking off
his overcoat, holding his hat in his hand. Barlach knew exactly the
meaning of this visit, and the boss knew exactly how things were going
for the Commissioner.

'Well, Commissioner,' Lutz began, 'how are you? For a while there
we had to expect the worst.'

'It's coming along slowly,' answered Barlach, and clasped his hands
behind his neck.

'What are you reading?' Lutz asked. He disliked coming to the
point of his visit and was looking for a diversion. 'Well, what do you
know, medical journals.'

The old man was not embarrassed. 'It reads like a detective story,'
he said. 'You try to widen your horizon when you're sick and look for
new fields.'

Lutz wanted to know how long, in the doctors' opinion, Barlach
would be bedridden.

'Two months,' the Commissioner answered, 'I'm supposed to stay
put for two months.'

Whether he wanted to or not, the boss had to tackle it now. 'The
age limit,' he stuttered. 'The age limit, Commissioner. You understand. We can't get around it, you know, we have to obey the laws.'

'I understand,' answered the sick man. His face was expressionless.

'What has to be done, has to be done,' said Lutz. 'You will have
to take it easy, Commissioner, and that's another reason.'

'And my attitude about "modern scientific criminology", where one
finds the criminal as if he were a jar of name-brand marmalade – that

has nothing to do with it?' said Barlach, correcting Lutz. Who was to be his successor, he wanted to know.

'Rothlisberger,' answered the boss. 'He's substituting for you now.'

Barlach nodded. 'Rothlisberger. Well, with his five children, he'll be glad of the higher salary,' he said. 'Starting at the New Year?'

'Starting at the New Year,' acknowledged Lutz.

'Till Friday then,' said Barlach. 'And from then on I'll be the ex-Police Commissioner.' He was glad to be through with serving the state. Not because he would have more time now to read Molière and Balzac, though that would be wonderful. No, the main reason remained the fact that something was wrong with the nice, simple, homely order of the world. He knew, he had found out. People were always the same, whether they went to the Hagia Sophia in Istanbul or the Cathedral in Berne on Sundays. The big criminals were running free while the small ones were stuck in jails. And anyway, there were all kinds of crimes nobody paid any attention to, only because they were more aesthetic than some sensational murder which gets into the headlines. But actually they were both the same, provided you looked at the facts and had the imagination.

Imagination, there was the crux of the matter, imagination! Out of sheer lack of imagination a good, upstanding businessman will – between his *apéritif* and lunch – commit a crime by closing some shrewd deal. A crime of which nobody has a notion, least of all the businessman, because nobody has the imagination to see all its consequences. The world was bad out of slovenliness, and well on the way to going to the devil out of slovenliness. This was a danger bigger than Stalin and all the other Joes taken together. The civil service was no longer the place for an old hunting-dog like him. Too much petty stuff, too much snooping. But the worthwhile game, the game that should be hunted, the really big beasts, were under the protection of the state, like beasts in a zoological garden.

Dr Lutz looked angry when he heard this sermon. He found it most objectionable, and actually he thought it improper not to protest against such immoral attitudes. But after all, the old man was sick and would very soon retire. Thank God. Unfortunately, he had to go now, he said, swallowing his anger, he was due at a meeting of the Public Welfare Office at eleven-thirty.

The Public Welfare Office was another place that had more to do with the police than the Finance Department, commented the

Commissioner. A lot was wrong there, too. Lutz prepared himself for the worst, but to his relief Barlach switched to something else. 'You can do me a favour now that I'm sick and no longer useful.'

'Gladly,' promised Lutz.

'You see, I'd like some information. I'm curious by nature, and I'm amusing myself in my bed here with criminological combinations. An old cat just cannot give up chasing mice. In this issue of *Life* I found a picture of an SS camp doctor in Stutthof by the name of Nehle. Try to find out whether he is still in jail or what became of him. We have the international service for these cases, and it won't cost us anything since the SS has been declared a criminal organization.'

Lutz wrote everything down. He would inquire, he promised, surprised at the old man's request. Then he said goodbye.

'Good luck, and get well,' he said, shaking the Commissioner's hand. 'I'll have the information for you by tonight. Then you can speculate to your heart's delight. By the way, Blatter's here, and would like to say hello. I'll wait in the car.'

So the big fat Blatter came in and Lutz disappeared.

'Greetings, Blatter,' said Barlach to the policeman who had so often been his chauffeur. 'I'm glad to see you.'

'So am I, so am I,' said Blatter. 'We miss you, Commissioner. We miss you very much.'

'Well, Blatter, now Rothlisberger will take my place and change the tune, I suppose,' answered the old man.

'Pity,' said the policeman. 'Well, I don't mean him any harm, and I guess he'll do. If only you get well again.'

Barlach asked whether Blatter knew the old bookstore in the Matte, the one that was owned by the Jew with the white beard, Feitelbach?

Blatter nodded. 'The one with the display of stamps that never changes in the window.'

'Please drop by there this afternoon and tell Feitelbach to send me *Gulliver's Travels*. It's the last service I'll ask of you.'

'The book about the dwarfs and the giants?' wondered the policeman.

Barlach laughed, 'Well, you see, Blatter, I adore fairy tales.'

Something in this laugh struck the policeman as sinister, but he dared not ask questions.

The hut

By evening Lutz had already called. Hungertobel had just sat down beside his friend's bed. He had ordered a cup of coffee, for he had to operate later and he wanted to take this opportunity of having his friend 'for himself'. Now the phone rang and interrupted their conversation.

Barlach picked it up and listened intently. After a while he said, 'that's good enough, send me the material,' and hung up. 'Nehle's dead,' he explained.

'Thank God!' Hungertobel exclaimed. 'Come on, let's celebrate,' and he lit a 'Little Rose of Sumatra'. 'I hope the nurse won't come just now.'

'She certainly didn't like it at noon,' Barlach said. 'I had to say you gave me permission to smoke, and she said that sounded just like you.'

'When did Nehle die?' asked the doctor.

'In forty-five, on the tenth of August. He committed suicide in a hotel in Hamburg, with poison.'

'You see' – Hungertobel nodded – 'now the rest of your suspicion has gone up in smoke.'

Barlach blinked at the smoke clouds which Hungertobel delightedly puffed in rings and spirals. Nothing was as resistant to going up in smoke as suspicion, because nothing kept materializing again as quickly, he answered finally.

'You're incorrigible.' Hungertobel laughed; he now looked on the whole affair as a harmless joke.

'The first virtue of a criminologist,' replied the old man. And then he asked, 'Samuel, were you a friend of Emmenberger's?'

'No,' answered Hungertobel, 'I wasn't, and as far as I remember, none of us who studied with him was. I've thought about this whole thing – the picture in *Life* and so on – again and again, Hans. I'll tell you how it happened that I thought this monster of an SS doctor might be Emmenberger – undoubtedly you've wondered. After all, one can't tell much from the picture, and my mistake must stem from something different besides a mere resemblance, even though that exists. I hadn't thought about the story for a long time, not only because it lies far back, but even more because it was horrible. And we all like to forget experiences that frightened us. I was present once, Hans, when Emmenberger performed an operation without anaesthesia, and for me it was a scene from hell, if there is such a place.'

'There is,' Barlach answered quietly. 'In other words, Emmenberger did do something like this once – something like what we suspected him of?'

'You see,' said the doctor, 'there was no alternative at the time. The poor devil who was operated on is still alive. If you ask him about it, he'll swear by all that's holy that Emmenberger is a devil. And that's unjust, for without Emmenberger he'd be dead. But to tell you the truth, I can understand him. It was horrible.'

'How did it happen?' Barlach asked.

Hungertobel drank the last drop from his cup and lit his 'Little Rose' again. 'Frankly, it was no magic. There's no room for magic in medicine. It didn't take more than a pocketknife and courage, and, of course, knowledge of anatomy. But who of us young students had the necessary presence of mind?

'Five of us, all medical students, had climbed from Kienvalley into the Blümlisalp region. I don't remember where we were going. I've never been a great mountain climber, and I'm an even worse geographer. I suppose it was some time in nineteen eight, probably July. And it was a hot summer, that I recall. We stayed overnight in a hut on one of the Alps. It's strange that I should recall that hut so vividly. Sometimes I dream of it, and I wake up, bathed in perspiration. Yet it was probably no different from any other such hut, and the horror attached to it for me exists only in my fantasy. That this must be so, I realize when I remember that I always visualize it covered with damp moss, and in reality you don't find moss on mountain huts. I've sometimes read of knackers' huts without really knowing what was meant. Well, when I see the words 'a knacker's hut', I imagine something like this one. It was surrounded by fir trees and had a well not

far from the door. It was of wood, not black, but white and rotten –
but that, too, I may have imagined afterwards. So many years lie
between today and this occurrence that dream and reality are insepar-
ably woven together.

'But I recall very clearly the nebulous fear that struck me when we
approached the hut, crossing a stony meadow. I'm convinced this fear
gripped all of us, except Emmenberger, perhaps. Our talk died down.
The evening sun, which sank before we reached the hut, made the
scene all the more frightful, since a strange deep-red light settled for
an almost unbearable length of time on this empty world of ice and
stone. It was a deathly illumination, tinting our faces and hands, an
illumination appropriate for a planet that revolves around the sun at
a far greater distance than ours.

'Like hunted animals we stormed into the hut. Its door was
unlocked. The inside was poor and bare, furnished with nothing more
than a few bunks. But in the faint light we saw some straw under the
roof. A black crooked ladder, covered with a year's dirt, led up to it.
Emmenberger fetched water from the well with a strange haste, as if
he knew what was going to happen. Needless to say, that's impossible.
We started a fire on the primitive stove; there was even a kettle. And
then, in this weird atmosphere of fear and fatigue which had overcome
us, one of us met with an accident. It was a fat boy from Lucerne,
the son of an innkeeper – nobody really knew why he was studying
medicine. A year later he took over his father's hotel. He was an
awkward fellow. He had climbed the ladder to reach the straw under
the roof. When the ladder suddenly collapsed, he fell clumsily, hitting
his neck against a protruding beam, and lay moaning on the floor. It
was a bad fall! At first we thought he'd broken something, but soon
he started to gasp for breath. We had carried him outside to a bench,
and he lay there in the strange light of the sinking sun which shone
down from towering cloud banks. The sight of the hurt boy was
frightening. His throat bore bloody scratches and was swollen, he held
his head back, while the larynx seemed to convulse. Horrified, we
noticed his face turn darker and darker, almost black in the infernal
shimmer from the horizon, and his wide-open eyes gleamed like two
wet white pebbles.

'We struggled desperately with cold compresses. In vain. His throat
swelled more and more internally, and he threatened to choke. At
first he had been filled with a feverish tension, but now he was

apathetic. His breath hissed, he could no longer speak. We knew that his life was in extreme danger; we were helpless. We lacked experience and probably knowledge. We knew that there was an emergency operation which would help but nobody dared to think about it. Only Emmenberger understood and did not hesitate to act. He examined the Lucerner, disinfected his pocketknife in the boiling water on the stove, and then performed a cut we call a tracheotomy, which in emergencies sometimes has to be performed; it involves making a cut above the larynx in order to get an air passage. The operation wasn't what was so terrifying, Hans – it had to be done with a pocketknife. No, the horror was in something different – something that took place between those two, in their faces. Though the injured boy was almost unconscious from lack of air, his eyes were open, very wide open, and so he had to observe all that happened, even though maybe as if in a dream. And when Emmenberger made that cut, my God, Hans, his eyes were wide open, too, and his face distorted. All of a sudden it seemed as if something satanic broke out of those eyes, a kind of overwhelming joy of torture – or whatever you want to call it. For a second I felt a paralyzing fright, but only for a second – then it was over. But I believe I was the only one to feel it – the others did not dare to watch. I believe, too, that part of what I experienced is in my imagination only, that the sinister hut and the uncanny light contributed to the illusion.

'The strange thing about the incident is, though, that the Lucerner whose life Emmenberger had saved never spoke to him again. He hardly thanked him, which a lot of people resented. Emmenberger, on the other hand became quite a celebrity. His career was strange. We had all thought he would make a name for himself, but fame did not attract him. He studied a lot and in a wild fashion. Physics, mathematics – nothing seemed to satisfy him. He was even seen in lectures on philosophy and theology. He passed his examinations brilliantly, but never practised. He worked as a substitute – for me, among others – and I must admit, patients were enthusiastic about him – with the exception of a few who did not like him. He led a restless and lonely life, until he finally emigrated. He published strange articles, for instance one about the justification for astrology, one of the most sophistical things I ever read. As far as I know, he hardly ever saw anybody and became a cynical, unreliable character, all the more unpleasant because nobody felt capable of handling his sarcasm.

What surprised us was the great change in Chile, that he did such sober and scientific work – it must have been the climate or the surroundings. Of course, once he returned to Switzerland, he became exactly what he had been before.'

'I hope you saved the article on astrology,' said Barlach when Hungertobel had finished.

The doctor answered that he could bring it to him tomorrow.

'So this is the story,' the Commissioner went on thoughtfully.

'As you can see,' said Hungertobel, 'maybe I did spend too much of my life dreaming after all.'

'Dreams don't lie,' replied Barlach.

'Dreams lie most of all,' said Hungertobel. 'But you'll have to excuse me, I have to operate.' And he rose from his chair.

Barlach gave him his hand. 'Not a tracheotomy, I hope, or whatever you call it.'

Hungertobel laughed. 'A ruptured groin, Hans. I like that better even though it is more difficult. But you must rest now. What you need most is twelve hours of sleep.'

Gulliver

But around midnight the old man awakened when a soft noise came from the window and the cold night air rushed in.

The Commissioner did not turn on the lights at once. Instead, he pondered what was happening. He guessed that the shutters were slowly being pushed up. The darkness that surrounded him lifted; phantomlike, the curtains fluttered in the uncertain light. Then he heard the shutters being cautiously pulled down. Again the impenetrable darkness of midnight surrounded him, but he sensed that a figure was moving toward him from the window.

Finally Barlach said, 'There you are, Gulliver,' and turned on his night lamp.

In the room stood a gigantic Jew in an old spotty and torn caftan, the red glow of the lamp falling on him.

The old man settled down again in his pillows. 'I half-expected you to come tonight. I had an idea that you were an accomplished second-storey man.'

'You are my friend,' said the intruder, 'so I came.'

His head was bold and huge, his hands, noble, but everything was covered with terrible scars, bearing witness to inhuman tortures. Yet nothing had succeeded in destroying the majesty of this face and this human being. The giant stood motionless in the room, slightly bent, his hands on his thighs. His shadow played, ghostlike, on the walls and the curtains, his brilliant eyes rested with imperturbable clarity on the old man.

'How could you know that I found to be present in Berne necessary?' It came out of the beaten, almost lipless mouth, in an awkward, too careful mode of expression, as if from one at home in so many languages that he now does not immediately find his way around in German. However, his speech was without accent. 'Gulliver leaves no trace,' he said after a short silence. 'I work invisibly.'

'Everybody leaves a trace,' replied the Commissioner. 'I'll tell you yours: Whenever you're in Berne, Feitelbach, who hides you, puts an advertisement in the *Gazette* that he is selling old books and stamps. At such times Feitelbach has some money, I think.'

The Jew laughed. 'The great art of Commissar Barlach lies in discovering the obvious.'

'Now you know your trace,' said the old man. 'And there is nothing worse than a criminologist who tells his secrets.'

'I shall not cover my tracks for Commissar Barlach. Feitelbach is a poor Jew. He will never understand how to make money in business.'

With these words the huge ghost sat down next to the bed. He reached into his caftan and pulled out a big dusty bottle and two little glasses. 'Vodka,' said the giant. 'We shall drink together, Commissar; we have always drunk together.'

Barlach sniffed the glass. He liked to drink at times, but he had a bad conscience. He thought to himself that Dr Hungertobel would be rather taken aback were he to see all this: the liquor, the Jew, and the midnight, in which one should be asleep. 'A fine patient!' Hungertobel would thunder and make a big fuss.

'Where did you get the vodka?' he asked after he had taken the first sip. 'It's very good.'

'From Russia.' Gulliver laughed. 'I brought it from the Soviets.'

'Have you been in Russia again?'

'None of your business, Commissar.'

'Commissioner,' Barlach corrected him. 'In Berne there are only commissioners. And not even in the Soviet paradise did you take off your awful caftan?'

'I am a Jew and I wear my caftan – as I have sworn. I like the traditional dress of my poor people.'

'Give me another vodka,' said Barlach. The Jew filled both glasses.

'I hope the cat-burgling was not too difficult,' Barlach said with wrinkled brows. 'Something illegal – what you've done tonight.'

Gulliver answered shortly that it was important that he was not seen.

'But it is quite dark around eight o'clock and I'm sure they would have let you in. There are no police here.'

'Then I may just as well climb the wall,' replied the giant, and laughed. 'It was childishly simple, Commissar. Up the wall and down a ledge.'

'It's just as well that I'm being retired.' Barlach shook his head. 'I won't have to worry about you any more. I ought to have put you behind bars a long time ago. It would have been a catch all Europe would have appreciated.'

'You won't do it because you know what I am fighting for,' answered the Jew, unmoved.

'You really should get yourself some sort of papers,' the old man suggested. 'I don't think much of these rules and regulations myself, but for God's sake, there has to be some kind of order.'

'I'm dead,' said the Jew. 'The Nazis shot me.'

Barlach was silent. He knew what the giant was driving at. The light of the lamp surrounded the men with a quieting glow. From somewhere bells rang midnight. The Jew poured vodka. His eyes gleamed with a gaiety of a special kind.

'It was a beautiful day in May forty-five – we had the pleasantest weather, how well I remember a little white cloud – when our friends from the Storm Troopers left me by accident in a miserable lime pit among fifty men of my people they had shot. And when after some hours I was able to crawl, covered with blood, under a lilac bush blooming not far away, the command that shovelled earth on top of the whole thing overlooked me. I swore then that from that moment I would lead the existence of a defiled and beaten animal – since it seems to suit God that we so often have to live like animals in this century. From then on I have lived in the darkness of graves, and stayed in cellars and the like. Only the night has seen my face, only the stars and the moon shone on this pitiful torn caftan. This is the way it should be. The Germans have killed me – I even saw my death certificate. My wife, an Aryan, had it – she is dead now, and she ought to be. She received it through the *Reichspost*. It was filled out neatly and was a credit to the good schools in which the German people are educated to civilization. Dead is dead, for Jews and Christians alike – excuse the order of enumeration, Commissar. For a dead man there are no papers and no borders, you have to admit that. He comes into every country where there are still persecuted and tortured Jews. *Prosit*, Commissar, I am drinking your health.'

The two men emptied their glasses. The man in the caftan poured new vodka and said, as his eyes formed two sparkling slits: 'What do you want from me, Commissar Barlach?'

'Commissioner,' corrected the old man.

'Commissar,' maintained the Jew.

'I want some information from you,' said Barlach.

'Information.' The giant laughed. 'Reliable information is worth gold. Gulliver knows more than the police.'

'We shall see. You were in all the concentration camps. You mentioned it to me once, though usually you don't talk much about those days.'

The Jew filled the glasses. 'At one time they considered me so terribly important that I was dragged from one hell to the next – and there were more than the nine of which Dante sings, who himself was in none. From each one I have brought the proper scars in this life after death that I lead.' He held out his left hand. It was crippled.

'Maybe you knew an SS doctor named Nehle?' Barlach asked intently.

The Jew looked thoughtfully at the Commissioner for a while. 'Do you mean the one from Stutthof?' he asked then.

'Yes.'

The giant looked at the old man with a condescending smile. 'He committed suicide on the tenth of August, nineteen forty-five, in Hamburg, in a run-down hotel,' he said after a while.

Barlach thought – a little disappointed, The hell Gulliver knows more than the police! Aloud he said: 'Did you in your career – or whatever one should call it – encounter Nehle?'

The Jew looked at the Commissioner searchingly, and his scar-covered face twisted into a grimace. 'Why do you ask after this inhuman beast?' he retorted.

Barlach pondered how much he should tell, but decided to remain silent and to keep to himself the suspicion he had of Emmenberger.

'I saw his picture,' he said accordingly, 'and it interests me to know what became of someone like that. I'm a sick man, Gulliver, and I'll have to stay in bed a long time. One can't always read Molière, and so one lets one's thoughts wander. It occupies me to speculate about what kind of a human being a mass murderer is.'

'All human beings are alike. Nehle was a human being. Consequently, Nehle was like all human beings. That is a treacherous syllogism, but a law we cannot alter,' answered the giant, without taking his eyes off Barlach. Nothing in his mighty face betrayed his thoughts.

'I suppose you saw Nehle's picture in *Life*, Commissar,' continued the Jew. 'It's the only picture that exists of him. You could search this beautiful world forever and never find another. That's all the more annoying since the famous picture doesn't show much of this mystical torturer.'

'Only one picture,' Barlach said thoughtfully. 'How so?'

'The devil takes better care of the select members of his congregation than heaven does of its, and arranged the proper circumstances,' the Jew replied sardonically. 'Nehle's name was not in the membership list of the SS, displayed in Nuremberg for the use of criminology. His name is on no other list either – very likely he was not a member. The official reports from Stutthof to the SS headquarters never mention his name, and he was not carried in the personnel rosters. This man – who had so many victims on his quiet conscience – has an aura of legend and irregularity – as if even the Nazis were ashamed of him. And yet Nehle lived and nobody ever doubted his existence, not even hard-boiled atheists; for we all believe easily in a god that concocts the most hellish tortures. We used to talk about him in the concentration camps that were no better than Stutthof. But we talked of him as of a rumour, as of one of the meanest and cruellest angels in this paradise of judges and hangmen. And it remained that way, even after it was all over. From the camp itself nobody was left whom we could have questioned. Stutthof is near Danzig. The few inmates that survived the tortures were trampled to death by the Storm Troopers when the Russians came, who meted out justice to the guards and hung them. Nehle, however, was not among them, Commissar. He must have left the camp before.'

'But they were looking for him,' said Barlach.

The Jew laughed. 'And for whom were they not looking, Barlach? The whole German population had turned into a criminal affair. But nobody remembered Nehle, for there was nobody that could remember. His crimes would have remained unknown if *Life* hadn't carried the picture of a skilful and masterly operation, with the little flaw that it was executed without anaesthesia. Humanity felt properly enraged, and so they started to look. Otherwise Nehle could have retired into private life, unmolested, to turn into a harmless country doctor – or the director of an expensive clinic.'

'How did *Life* get the picture?' Barlach asked innocently.

'Very simple,' the giant answered matter-of-factly, 'I gave it to them.'

Barlach shot up and stared, surprised, into the Jew's face. Gulliver does know more than the police, he thought, shaken. The adventurous life led by this shaggy giant to whom countless Jews owed their lives took place in areas where the trails of crimes and monstrous vices ran together. A judge with his own laws sat before Barlach, a judge who arbitrated according to his discretion, acquitted and condemned independent of the statutes and criminal codes of the glorious fatherlands of this earth.

'Let us drink vodka,' said the Jew. 'A drink is always good. You have to cling to alcohol, otherwise you might lose all sweet illusions on this Godforsaken planet.'

And he filled the glasses and cried, 'Long live humanity!' Then he poured down the drink and added, 'But how? That is often quite difficult.'

'You shouldn't cry out like that,' said the Commissioner. 'The night nurse will come. This is a decent hospital.'

'Christianity, Christianity,' said the Jew. 'It produced good nurses and just as competent murderers.'

For a moment the old man thought that he had had enough vodka, but finally he, too, drank.

The room spun around for a moment, Gulliver reminded him of a giant bat. Then the room stood still again, only it was a little bit crooked. But that he could take in his stride.

'You knew Nehle,' said Barlach.

The giant replied, 'I had dealings with him occasionally,' and occupied himself with his vodka. Then he started to talk, but now no longer in his former cold, clear voice, but in a strangely singing tone, which became more marked when what he said was ironic or sarcastic, but which was sometimes nevertheless soft and tempered. And Barlach understood that everything, the wild and the sarcastic, was only the expression of an immeasurable sadness over the incomprehensible fall of a once beautiful world. And so it happened on that midnight that this gigantic Ahasuerus sat with him, the old Commissioner, lying desperately ill in his bed and listening to the words of this man of sorrows, whom the history of our epoch had made into a gloomy, frightening angel of death.

'It was in December of forty-four,' said Gulliver in his sing-song, his pain spreading on its waves like a dark and oily spot, 'and then in January of the next year, when the glassy sun of hope rose on the horizons from Stalingrad to Africa. And yet those were cursed moments, Commissar, and for the first time I swore by all our honourable scholars and their grey beards that I would not survive them. That I did, nevertheless, is due to Nehle, about whose life you are so eager to learn. Of this disciple of medicine I can report to you that he saved my life. He did it by throwing me into darkest hell and tearing me out by the roots of my hair, a method which, according to my knowledge, only one person survived, namely myself, who am damned to survive anything. And out of my colossal gratitude I did not hesitate to betray him by photographing him. In this perverse world there are good deeds one can only repay with villainies.'

'I don't understand what you're trying to tell me,' replied the Commissioner, who was not quite sure whether this was the vodka's fault or not.

The giant laughed and pulled a second bottle out of his caftan. 'Forgive me,' he said, 'I'm making a long speech, but my tortures were even longer. What I want to tell you is simple – Nehle operated on me. Without anaesthesia. This incredible honour was shown me. Forgive me again, Commissar, but I have to drink vodka and drink it like water when I think of it, for it was nasty.'

'My God!' cried Barlach, and then again, into the silence of the hospital, 'my God!' He was sitting up, and mechanically he offered his glass to the monster by his bedside.

'The story takes only a little nerve to hear, but far more than that to live through,' continued the Jew in the old caftan in a singing tone. 'One should finally forget these things, they say – and not just in Germany. Supposedly there are cruelties taking place in Russia, and sadists exist everywhere.

'But I do not want to forget anything, and not only because I am a Jew – the Germans have killed six million of my people, six million! – no, because I am still a human being, even though I live in my underground holes with the rats. I refuse to make a distinction between peoples and speak of good and bad nations; but a distinction between human beings I have to make. That was beaten into me, and from the first blow that cut into my flesh, I have distinguished between torturers and tortured. I don't deduct the new cruelties of new guards in different countries from the bill I present to the Nazis, I add them to it. I take the liberty of not distinguishing between those that torture. They all have the same eyes. If there is a God, Commissar, and my defiled heart hopes for nothing more, He will recognize not nations but only individuals, and He will judge each one by the measure of his crimes and acquit each one by the measure of his own justice.

'Christian, Christian, listen to what a Jew has to say to you, whose people crucified your Saviour and who now has been crucified with his people by the Christians. There I rotted in the misery of my flesh and my soul in the Stutthof concentration camp, an extermination camp, as they called it, near the old proud city of Danzig, on whose account this criminal war had broken out. And no holds were barred there. Jehovah was far, occupied with other universes, or perhaps studying some theological problem that captivated his lofty spirit. And all the more wantonly his people were driven into death, gassed or shot as suited the Storm Troopers' whim and the weather conditions. With the east wind Jews were hanged and with the south wind dogs hunted down Judah.

'And then there was this Doctor Nehle, whose fate fascinates you so, you man of a well-mannered world. He was one of the doctors that grew like tumours in every camp. Blowflies who dedicated themselves with scientific eagerness to mass murder, who injected hundreds of inmates to death with air, phenol, acid, and whatever else was at their disposal between heaven and earth for this infernal entertainment. Or who performed their experiments on humans without anaesthesia – out of sheer necessity, as they assured themselves, since the fat Reichsmarschall Goering had forbidden vivisections on animals. Nehle was therefore not alone. Now I must speak of him.

'I have in the course of my travels through the various camps taken a close look at the torturers, and I know the types. Nehle was quite outstanding in his field. He did not participate in the brutalities of the others. I must admit that he helped the prisoners as much as this was possible – and as far as help could have a purpose in a camp the only purpose of which was extermination. He was terrifying in a different sense than the other doctors, Commissar. His experiments were not outstanding for their heightened torture. With the others, too, the skillfully chained Jews died bellowing under the knives, not due to the medical art but to the shock brought on by the pain. His devilry was that he did all this with the consent of his victims. As improbable as it sounds, Nehle operated only on Jews who volunteered, who knew exactly what awaited them and who even – this was his condition – had to watch other operations to see the full horror of the tortures before they could give their consent to suffer through the same thing.'

'How was that possible?' asked Barlach breathlessly.

'Hope.' The giant laughed, and his breast rose and sank. 'Hope, Christian.' His eyes gleamed with an abysmal, brutish ferocity. The scars in his face stood out prominently, his hands were like paws on Barlach's blanket. His broken mouth, that greedily sucked new quantities of vodka into his tortured body, groaned in remote sadness: ' " . . . Faith, hope, charity, these three," as it says so nicely in the First Epistle to the Corinthians, thirteen. But hope is the toughest of them all, that is written into my, the Jew Gulliver's, flesh with red letters. Faith and charity, *they* went to the devil in Stutthof; but hope – that remained, and with it *you* went to the devil. Hope, hope! Nehle had it in his pocket, ready-made, and he offered it to everybody that wanted it – and many wanted it.

'It is incredible, Commissar, but hundreds had themselves operated on by Nehle – after they had stood, shaking and pale as death, and watched their predecessors die like dogs on the operating table and could still say No – and all of it for the mere hope of gaining the freedom Nehle promised. Freedom! How man must love it that he is willing to suffer anything to gain it! So much so that in Stutthof he went voluntarily into flaming hell, only to embrace the pitiful bastard of freedom offered to him there. Freedom is sometimes a whore and sometimes a saint, meaning something different to each person – to a worker something different than to a priest, to a banker something else, and to a poor Jew in an extermination camp like Auschwitz, Lublin, Maidanek, Natzweiler, and Stutthof, something else again! There freedom was everything that was outside the camp, but not God's beautiful world, oh no! In our unlimited modesty we hoped only to be brought back to such a pleasant place as Buchenwald or Dachau, which *now* represented golden freedom, where you ran no danger of being gassed, but only of being beaten to death. Where there was a thousandth of a thousandth of a hope of being saved by some improbable act of chance, against the absolute certainty of death in the extermination camps. My God, Commissar, let us fight for having freedom mean the same to everybody, so that nobody has to be ashamed of his kind of freedom. It is laughable. The hope of getting into a different concentration camp drove people in heaps to Nehle's flaying place. It is laughable' (and here the Jew actually broke out into a laugh of scorn, desperation, and rage).

'And I, too, Christian, lay down on the bloody trestle, saw Nehle's knives and pliers in the beam of the spotlight, shadowlike above me, and then sank into the infinitely graded range of pain, into those gleaming mirror-cases of torture! I too went to him in the hope of escaping once more, of getting out of this Godforsaken camp. For since this accomplished psychologist Nehle had proven himself helpful and dependable, we believed his promises, and you always believe in a miracle when the need is greatest. When I, the only one, survived a senseless stomach resection, he had me nursed back to health and sent me back to Buchenwald in the first days of February. But after endless journeying I was not destined to reach it. For there came, in the vicinity of the town of Eisleben, that beautiful May Day with the blooming lilac bush under which I crawled.

'These are the deeds of the man sitting in front of you at your bedside, Commissar, his sufferings and his travels through the bloody nonsense of this era. And still the wreck of my body and my soul is drifting through the whirls of our time, which is devouring millions and millions, innocent and guilty alike. But now the second bottle of vodka is empty and it is necessary that Ahasuerus take the royal road across the window ledge and down the wall to the damp cellar in Feitelbach's house.'

Gulliver had risen, and his shadow cast darkness in the room. But the old man did not let him go yet.

'What kind of a person was Nehle?' he asked, and his voice was hardly more than a whisper.

'Christian,' said the Jew, who had hidden the bottles and the glasses again in his dirty caftan, 'who can answer your question? Nehle is dead. He took his own life, his secret is with God who reigns over heaven and hell. And God does not share His secrets, not even with the theologians. It is deadly to investigate where there is only death. How often have I tried to sneak behind the mask of this doctor, with whom no conversation was possible, who spoke to none of the SS guards or the other doctors, let alone to an inmate! How often have I tried to penetrate what went on behind those glittering eye-glasses! What was a poor Jew like me to do if he never saw his torturer other than with a half-hidden face and in a white coat? For the way in which I photographed him, endangering my life – nothing was more dangerous than to photograph in a concentration camp – was the way he appeared always. A bony figure, clad in white, slightly bent and silent, as if afraid to contaminate himself, he walked around those barracks with their gruesome want and misery. I believe he wanted to be cautious. Very likely he felt that one fine day the whole infernal apparition of concentration camps would disappear – to break out again from the depth of man's instincts like a pestilence with different torturers and different political systems. Through all this time he must have prepared his flight into private life – he was only temporarily employed in hell. According to this I calculated my blow, Commissar, and I aimed well. When the picture appeared in *Life*, Nehle killed himself. It was enough that the world knew his name, Commissar, for he who is cautious hides his name.' These were the last words the old man heard from Gulliver. They were like the dull beat of a bronze bell, echoing terribly in the sick man's ear. 'His name!'

Now the vodka took its effect. The sick man thought he saw the curtains over there by the window swell like the sails of a disappearing boat, heard the clatter of a shutter. Then, still less clear, a gigantic body dipped into the night.

But then, when the countless stars broke through the gaping wound of the open window, an unruly defiance rose in the old man, to survive in *this* world and to fight for a different, a better, one, to fight with this his pitiful body on which the cancer was gnawing, greedy and uncontrollable, a body that had been given another year, not more.

When the vodka started to burn in his intestines like fire, he began to bawl the 'Berner March' drunkenly into the silence of the hospital, awakening the other patients. He could not think of anything stronger to sing. But when the disconcerted night nurse rushed in, he was already asleep.

The speculation

The next morning Barlach awoke, as was to be expected, around twelve, shortly before lunch was served. His head was a little bit heavy, but otherwise he felt better than he had for a long time, and thought that every once in a while there was nothing like a good swig of schnapps, especially when you are bedridden and not supposed to drink. On his table was the mail; Lutz had sent the report on Nehle. Nowadays the organization of the police was really beyond reproach, particularly if you were going to retire, as was the case with him day after tomorrow, thank God. In Istanbul you had to wait for months for information. But before the old man could start reading, the nurse brought lunch. It was Nurse Lina, whom he liked very much, but she seemed rather cool, not at all as she had been. The Commissioner felt concerned. Somehow they must have found out about last night, he suspected. Incredible. Of course, it seemed to him as if he had sung the "Berner March" at the end, after Gulliver had left. But this must be a deception, he was not the least bit patriotic. Damn, he thought, if I could only remember.

The old man looked suspiciously around the room while he ate his oatmeal soup. (Always oatmeal soup!) On the table stood a few bottles and pills that had not been there before. Now what did that mean? The whole thing was not to be trusted. And furthermore, a different nurse appeared every ten minutes, to bring something, to look, to straighten something – one of them giggled out in the corridor, he heard it clearly. He did not dare ask after Hungertobel. It was quite all right with him that he would come toward evening. He had his practice in town during noon hours.

Gloomily the old man swallowed his thick grits with apple sauce (this, too, was no variation), but was astonished when for dessert he got strong coffee with sugar – upon special order of Dr Hungertobel, as the nurse explained reproachfully. That had never happened before. The coffee tasted good and made him feel gay. Then he dug into the dossier, which seemed the safest thing to do under the present circumstances.

But to his surprise Dr Hungertobel entered the room shortly after one. His face was serious – as the old man ascertained with an unnoticeable movement of his eyes, otherwise seemingly absorbed in his papers.

'Hans,' said Hungertobel, and resolutely stepped up to the bed, 'what on earth happened? I'm ready to swear – and with me every nurse in this place – that you were completely soused.'

'Oh,' said the old man, and looked up from his dossier. And then he said, 'Well!'

'Yes,' answered Hungertobel, 'everything pointed to that. I tried in vain all morning to wake you up.'

He was ever so sorry, regretted the Commissioner.

'It's practically impossible that you drank alcohol, unless you swallowed the bottle, too!' the doctor cried in desperation.

'I quite agree.' The old man grinned.

Hungertobel admitted he was completely baffled, and polished his glasses. He always did that when he was excited.

'Dear Samuel,' said the Commissioner. He readily admitted that it wasn't always easy to give shelter to a criminologist, and he, Barlach, would have to bear the suspicion of being a clandestine alcoholic. He would only like to ask him to call the clinic Sonnenstein in Zurich and to request a bed for Barlach under the name of Blaise Kramer. He should describe him as a freshly operated, bedridden, but rich patient.

'You want to go to Emmenberger?' Hungertobel asked, shocked, and sat down.

'Of course,' answered Barlach.

'Hans,' said Hungertobel, 'I don't understand you. Nehle is dead.'

'One Nehle is dead,' corrected the old man. 'Now we have to find out which one.'

'For heaven's sake,' cried the doctor in astonishment, 'are there two Nehles?'

Barlach reached for his dossier. 'Let us look at the case together,' he continued calmly, 'and examine whatever is striking. You will see, our art consists of some mathematics and a lot of imagination.'

'I understand nothing,' moaned Hungertobel. All morning long he had understood nothing.

'I am now reading the physical description,' the Commissioner continued. 'Tall, slim figure, grey hair, formerly brownish-red, eyes a greenish-grey, prominent ears, face slim and pale, bags under his eyes, teeth healthy. Special marks: scar on right eyebrow.'

'That's him,' said Hungertobel.

'Who?' asked the Commissioner.

'Emmenberger,' replied the doctor. He had recognized him from the description.

'But this is the description of the dead Nehle in Hamburg, as set down in the police record.'

'All the more natural that I mistook the man in the picture,' Hungertobel said. 'Anybody can resemble a murderer. My mistake has found the simplest solution in the world. Don't you agree?'

'That's one conclusion. But there are other conclusions that can be drawn. At first glance they may not seem as compelling; nevertheless, they will have to be examined as "after all possible". Another conclusion could be: It wasn't Emmenberger who was in Chile, but Nehle under his name, while Emmenberger was in Stutthof under Nehle's name.'

'That seems a most unlikely conclusion,' wondered Hungertobel.

'Of course,' answered Barlach, 'but a permissible one. We have to account for all possibilities.'

'But for God's sake, where would that lead us?' protested the doctor. 'So Emmenberger killed himself in Hamburg, and the doctor who is now directing the clinic is Nehle? Really!'

'Have you seen Emmenberger since his return from Chile?' the old man interrupted.

'Only a couple of times,' Hungertobel answered, surprised at the question. He had finally put his glasses on again.

'You see, this possibility exists,' the Commissioner continued. 'There is another solution possible; the dead man in Hamburg was Nehle, returned from Chile, and Emmenberger returned from Stutthof, where he went under the name Nehle, to Switzerland.'

'But you have to assume a crime,' said Hungertobel, shaking his head, 'in order to defend this odd theory.'

'Right, Samuel,' nodded the Commissioner. 'We would have to assume that Nehle was killed by Emmenberger.'

'With the same right we could assume the opposite: Nehle killed Emmenberger. Apparently your imagination doesn't have the slightest inhibitions.'

'This theory is also possible; it, too, we can accept, at least in the present state of our speculations.'

'This is all nonsense,' said the old doctor angrily.

'Possibly,' Barlach answered stoically.

Hungertobel protested vigorously. The primitive manner in which the Commissioner was dealing with reality could easily be used to prove whatever one wanted to prove.

'A criminologist has the obligation to question reality,' answered the old man. 'That's the way it is. In this regard we have to proceed like philosophers, of whom they say that first they doubt everything. Then, of course, they dig into their wisdom and come up with the most beautiful speculations about the art of dying and life after death. Only quite likely we are even more useless than they. You and I have developed a number of hypotheses. All are possible. This is the first step. The second one will be to differentiate from the possible hypotheses the probable ones. The possible and the probable are not the same. So we have to examine the degree of probability in our theses. We have two people, two doctors: on the one hand Nehle, a criminal, and on the other, your former acquaintance, Emmenberger, the director of the clinic Sonnenstein in Zurich. We have two main hypotheses; both are possible. The degree of their probability is different at first glance. One hypothesis states that there is no connection between Emmenberger and Nehle, and is probable; the second one presupposes a connection and is improbable.'

And that was what he had been saying all along, Hungertobel interrupted.

'Dear Samuel,' answered Barlach, 'unfortunately, I am a criminologist and obligated to find the criminal aspects of human relationships. The first hypothesis – the one that sets no connection between Nehle and Emmenberger, does not interest me. Nehle is dead and there is nothing on record against Emmenberger. But my profession forces me to examine more closely the second, improbable hypothesis. What is probable about it? It states that Nehle and Emmenberger exchanged roles, that Emmenberger, alias Nehle, was in Stutthof. Further, that Nehle, in Emmenberger's role, stayed in Chile and from there published articles in medical journals. Let's forget for the moment

about the rest: Nehle's death in Hamburg and Emmenberger's residence in Zurich. We can admit quite openly that this hypothesis is
fantastic.

'It is probable insofar as both Emmenberger and Nehle are doctors
and resemble each other. Here is the point from which we can start.
It is the first fact that appears in this jungle of possibilities and
probabilities. Let's examine this fact. How do the two resemble each
other? Resemblances occur often, great resemblances are rarer, and
rarest of all are resemblances that correspond even in the accidental
detail, in distinguishing marks that do not stem from nature but from
specific incidents. Here we have a case like that. Both of them not
only have the same colour hair and eyes, similar facial features and
the same build and so on, but the same peculiar scar on their right
eyebrows.'

'Well, that's chance,' said the doctor.

'Or skill,' complemented the old man. Hungertobel had operated
on Emmenberger's eyebrow. What was wrong with him?

'The scar came from an operation necessitated by a dangerously
inflamed sinusitis,' answered Hungertobel. 'The cut is in the eyebrow
to make the scar less visible. I really didn't do a good job on Emmenberger. It was partly bad luck – I usually operate quite skilfully. The
scar became more prominent than was pardonable for a surgeon, and
besides, part of his eyebrow was later missing,' he said.

Was this operation frequent, the Commissioner wanted to know.

'Well, not exactly,' answered Hungertobel. 'Most people don't allow
a sinusitis to progress to a point where one has to operate.'

'You see!' said Barlach. 'And the peculiarity of which I spoke lies
in the following: this not-too-frequent operation was performed on
Nehle; he, too, had part of his eyebrow missing, in the same spot –
it says this in the police record. The corpse in Hamburg was carefully
examined. Did Emmenberger have a scald mark on his lower left arm,
about a hand wide?'

'What makes you ask?' Hungertobel was surprised. 'Emmenberger
once had an accident in a chemistry experiment.'

'Because the corpse in Hamburg bore this scar,' Barlach said,
satisfied. He went on to ask if Emmenberger still had those scars
today? It would be important to know – and Hungertobel had seen
him.

'Last summer in Ascona,' answered the doctor. 'He still had both scars, I noticed it at once. Emmenberger was his same old self. He made a few spiteful remarks and otherwise hardly recognized me.'

'Aha,' said the Commissioner, 'he hardly recognized you. You see, the similarity is so great that we no longer know who is who. Either we have to believe in a rare and strange kind of chance or a skilful trick. Probably the similarity between the two is not as great as we believe now. What appears as resemblance in passports and official papers is not sufficient to get the two mixed up. But when the similarity reaches such accidental things, the chances become greater that one can substitute for the other. The trick of a fake operation and an artificially induced accident would then have the purpose of changing mere similarity into identity. But we can only voice assumptions at this point in the investigation. However, you will have to admit that this kind of similarity makes our second hypothesis more probable.'

'Is there no other picture of Nehle, aside from the one in *Life*?' asked Hungertobel.

'Three pictures from the Hamburg criminal police,' answered the Commissioner. He took the pictures out of the folder and gave them to his friend. 'They show a dead man.'

'Not much left to recognize,' said Hungertobel in a disappointed tone after a while. His voice shook. 'A strong resemblance may exist, yes; I can imagine that Emmenberger might look like this in death. How did Nehle kill himself?'

The old man looked thoughtfully at the doctor who so helplessly sat by the bed in his white coat and had forgotten everything. Barlach's drunkenness and the waiting patients.

'With cyanide,' the Commissioner answered finally. 'Like most Nazis.'

'In what way?'

'He bit on a capsule and swallowed its contents.'

'On an empty stomach?'

'So they ascertained.'

'Then it took effect immediately,' said Hungertobel, 'yet from the pictures it seems as if Nehle saw something horrible before his death.' The two were silent.

Finally the Commissioner said, 'Let's continue, even though Nehle's death may have its puzzles. We have to examine other suspicious points.'

'I can't see how you can speak of further suspicious points,' Hungertobel said, surprised and depressed at the same time. 'That's rather
exaggerated.'

'Oh, no,' said Barlach. 'First of all, there is your experience as a
student. I will touch on it only briefly. It helps me because it gives
me a psychological clue as to *why* Emmenberger was possibly capable
of the acts he committed *if* he was in Stutthof. But now I come to
another, more important point: I am in the possession of the *curriculum
vitae* of the man we know as Nehle. His background is grim. He was
born in eighteen ninety, which makes him three years younger than
Emmenberger. He is from Berlin. His father is unknown, his mother
was a housekeeper who left the illegitimate child with the grand-
parents, led a vagabond life, wound up in a house of correction, and
finally vanished. The grandfather worked with Borsig Corporation;
himself illegitimate, he had come to Berlin from Bavaria in his youth.
The grandmother was Polish. Nehle went to public school and entered
the army at fourteen, was in the infantry for a year, and was then
transferred into the medical corps as a sanitary orderly. This was done
upon request of a medical officer. Here an irresistible desire for a
medical career seems to have awakened in him. He was decorated
with the Iron Cross for having successfully performed emergency
operations. After the war, he worked as an attendant in mental and
general hospitals, and prepared himself in his spare time for college-
entrance examinations so that he could study medicine. But he flunked
twice. He failed in Greek and Latin and in mathematics. Apparently
the man was talented only for medicine. Then he became a nature-
cure and miracle doctor with a booming practice. He got into conflict
with the law, and was punished with a not-too-great fine because, as
the court stated, "his medical knowledge is surprising". People wrote
petitions, the newspapers pleaded for him, but in vain. Then the noise
about the case subsided. Since he kept getting into the same trouble
again and again, the courts finally decided to "overlook" his activities.
In the thirties, Nehle doctored his way around Silesia, Westphalia,
Bavaria, and Greater Hesse. Then, after twenty years, the big turning
point – in nineteen thirty-eight he passes the examinations. (In thirty-
seven Emmenberger emigrated from Germany to Chile!) His papers
in Greek, Latin, and Mathematics were brilliant. The university passes
a decree relieving him of the actual study and he receives his degree
after again passing his examinations brilliantly. However, to every-

body's surprise, he disappears into the concentration camps as camp doctor.'

'My God,' said Hungertobel. 'What do you want to deduce from all this?'

'That's simple,' answered Barlach, not without scorn. 'Now let's look at the articles by Emmenberger which appeared in the *Swiss Medical Weekly*, and were written in Chile. They, too, are facts we cannot deny, and need to examine. These articles are claimed to be scientifically important. I believe that. But what I cannot believe is that they were written by a man who stood out for his literary style, as you claim Emmenberger did. One could hardly express oneself in a more awkward manner.'

'A scientific treatise is no poem,' protested the doctor. 'After all, Kant wrote a rather complicated style.'

'Leave Kant alone,' grumbled the old man. 'He wrote in a difficult manner, but not poorly. The author of these articles from Chile writes not only awkwardly, but ungrammatically. The man obviously never knew when to use the dative and when the accusative. As you know, this has always been a characteristic of many Berliners. It is also strange that he often refers to Greek as Latin, as if he had not the slightest notion of either language; for instance, in Number Fifteen from the year forty-two, the word *gastrotomy*.'

There was a deadly silence in the room.

For minutes.

Then Hungertobel lit a 'Little Rose of Sumatra'.

'In other words, you believe that Nehle wrote these articles?' he asked finally.

The Commissioner answered calmly that he thought it probable.

'I have nothing left to say,' the doctor said grimly. 'You proved the truth to me.'

'We mustn't exaggerate now,' said the old man, and closed the folder on his bed. 'I have proven to you only the probability of my thesis. But probability still is not reality. If I say that it will probably rain tomorrow, it need not rain tomorrow. In this world, idea and reality are not identical. Otherwise it would be a lot easier, Samuel. Between idea and reality still lies the adventure of this existence, and we should in heaven's name leave it like that.'

'It makes no sense.' Hungertobel groaned and looked helplessly at his friend, who – motionless as always, hands behind his head – was lying in his bed. 'You're running a horrible risk if your speculation is correct, for Emmenberger is then a monster.'

'I know.' The Commissioner nodded.

'It makes no sense,' the doctor said once more, in a low voice, almost a whisper.

'Justice always makes sense,' Barlach persisted in his undertaking. 'Introduce me to Emmenberger. I want to go tomorrow.'

'New Year's Eve!' Hungertobel was aghast.

'Yes,' answered the old man. 'New Year's Eve.' And then his eyes gleamed ironically. 'Did you bring me Emmenberger's treatise on astrology?'

'Of course,' answered the doctor.

Barlach laughed. 'Then give it to me. I'm curious to see whether it contains anything about *my* star. Maybe I have a chance after all.'

Another visit

The terrifying old man spent the rest of the afternoon painfully scribbling full a long sheet of paper and telephoning his bank and a notary.
This idol-like, impenetrable sick man to whom the nurses came with
more and more reluctance, spun his threads with unshakable calm,
like a huge spider, unerringly fitting one conclusion to the next. In
the evening, shortly after Hungertobel had informed him he could
enter Sonnenstein on New Year's Eve, he received another visitor, of
whom one could not know whether he came voluntarily or whether
he had been summoned by the Commissioner. The visitor was a
small, skinny fellow with a long neck. He wore an open raincoat, its
pockets stuffed full of newspapers. Around his dirty neck wound a
lemon-yellow spotty silk scarf. A beret was stuck on his bald head.
The eyes flashed from underneath bushy brows; the strong hooked
nose seemed much too big for the little man, and below it was a
sunken mouth with no teeth. He was talking to himself in verse
form, it seemed, and, in between verses, separate words appeared like
islands, *trolley bus, traffic police*; two things which seemed to irritate
him beyond reason. His shabby clothes were in strange contrast to
the elegant but old-fashioned black walking stick with a silver grip,
which belonged to a different century and which he swung around in
a wild fashion. At the main entrance he ran into a nurse, bowed,
stammered a flowery excuse, got hopelessly lost in the maternity ward,
nearly burst into the delivery room, filled with busy mothers-to-be,
got chased away by a doctor, and tripped over one of the vases filled
with carnations which stood in front of all the doors. Finally he was
led into the new wing (they had caught him like a frightened animal).
However, before he entered the old man's room, his walking stick got
between his legs and he slid down the corridor and crashed against
a door, behind which a very sick man was lying.

'These traffic policemen!' he cried when he at long last stood in front of Barlach's bed. (Thank God! thought the student nurse who had accompanied him.) 'They are everywhere. A whole city full of traffic policemen.'

'Except,' answered the Commissioner, who felt it best to respond to the excited visitor, 'that we need traffic police, you know, Fortschig. There must be law and order in traffic, otherwise even more people would get killed than there are already.'

'Law and order in traffic!' Fortschig called with his squeaking voice. 'All right, all right. But for that one does not need a special traffic police, for that one needs mostly more faith in the decency of people. All Berne has turned into one big traffic policemen's camp. No wonder that all pedestrians are going wild. But that's what Berne has always been – a desolate police village. A wretched tyranny has always nested in this city! Lessing wanted to write a tragedy about Berne when they told him of Henzi's pitiful death! Fifty years I have now lived in this hick town of a capital, and I won't describe to you what it means for a writer to vegetate and to starve in this sleepy, fat town. Terrible, simply terrible! For fifty years I closed my eyes when I walked through the streets – I did that even in my perambulator. I didn't want to see this unholy city in which my father rotted away. And now, when I open my eyes, what do I see? Traffic policemen, everywhere.'

'Fortschig,' said the old man, quite determined to interrupt, 'we have other things to talk about than the traffic police,' and he looked disapprovingly at the rundown, disreputable figure with big eyes like an owl, sitting in the chair and rocking pitifully back and forth.

'I really don't know what's the matter with you,' the old man continued. 'For God's sake, Fortschig, you are talented, you were a good fellow and the *Apfelschuss* you published was a good newspaper even though it was small. But now you fill its pages with indifferent junk about traffic police, trolley buses, dogs, stamp collectors, ballpoint pens, radio programmes, theatre gossip, streetcar tickets, movie ads, senators, and restaurants. The energy and pathos with which you tear these things down – you always make everything sound like Schiller's *Wilhelm Tell* – is worthy of better things, heaven knows.'

'Commissioner,' cried the visitor, 'Commissioner! Do not sin against a poet, a writer who has the infinite bad luck to have to live in Switzerland and, what is ten times worse, to live on Switzerland.'

'Well, well.' Barlach tried to appease; but Fortschig became wilder and wilder.

'Well, well,' he screamed, and jumped off his chair, ran to the window and then to the door, and so on, like a pendulum. '*Well, well* – that's said so easily. What is excused by that *Well, well*? Nothing! By God, nothing! All right, I have become a ridiculous figure, almost one of those Theobalds, Eustaches, and Mustaches, or whatever they claim to be called – who fill the columns of our dear boring dailies with the adventures they have to endure with their collar buttons, wives, and razors – under a by-line, of course. But who did not fall to this level in this country, where they still make verses about the whispering of the soul when all around the world is crashing down about our ears! Commissioner, Commissioner, what *haven't* I tried in order to create a decent existence for myself with my typewriter. But I didn't even reach the income of a public charge. One attempt after the other had to be given up, one hope after another, the best dramas, the fieriest poetry, the most elevated stories! Houses of cards, nothing more! Switzerland made me into a fool, a whirligig, a Don Quixote who fights against windmills and herds of sheep. Here one is supposed to stand up for freedom and justice and all those other articles the fatherland has for sale, and to respect a society which forces one to lead the existence of a tramp and beggar if one dedicates oneself to the intellect instead of to business. They want to enjoy life, but not share one thousandth of this pleasure, not a penny! Once, in the thousand-year Reich, they uncocked their revolvers as soon as they heard the word *culture* – here they hide their purses.'

'Fortschig,' Barlach said sternly, 'it's very good that you bring up Don Quixote – he happens to be one of my favourite subjects. We all ought to be Don Quixotes, if we have an open heart and a bit of brains under our skull. But it's not windmills we have to fight against like the shabby old knight in his tinny armour, my friend. We have to fight against dangerous giants, sometimes against monsters of brutality and shrewdness, and then again, against huge saurians with brains like sparrows. All of them monsters who exist, not in fairy tales or our fantasy, but in reality. That's our task, to fight against inhumanity in any form and under any circumstances. But it's important *how* we fight and that we do it a bit cleverly. The fight against evil must not be like a game with fire.

'But you, Fortschig, are playing with fire, because you lead a worthy fight so foolishly, like a fireman who pours oil instead of water. If one reads the newspaper you publish, this pitiful little paper, one thinks at once all of Switzerland ought to be abolished. Much – very much – is not as it should be in this country. I can testify to that, and I lost quite a few hairs over it. But to throw everything into the fire, as if this were Sodom and Gomorrah, is wrong and indecent. You almost act as if you are ashamed to love this country still. I don't like that, Fortschig. One ought not to be ashamed of one's love, and love of one's country is still a good love – only it has to be stern and critical, otherwise it turns into blind partiality. And so one should start sweeping and scrubbing if one discovers dirty spots; but to tear the whole house down right away is senseless and ignorant. For it is difficult to build a new house in this poor hurt world. It takes more than a generation, and when it is finally built, it won't be better than the old one. It's important that one can tell the truth and that one can fight for it – without landing in jail. That's possible in Switzerland. We ought to acknowledge it and be thankful for it. We need not be afraid of senators and government councillors, or whatever their titles are. Admittedly, too many have to walk around in rags and try merely to survive from one day to the next. This is bad. But a true Don Quixote is proud of his poor armour. The fight against the stupidity and egotism of people has always been difficult and costly and brought with it neediness and humiliation. But it's a holy struggle which must not be fought with wails but with dignity. You, however, thunder and curse into our Berners' ears what an unjust fate you are suffering among them and wish for the tail of a comet to sweep our old town away. Fortschig, Fortschig, you are subverting the battle with petty motives. You have to be above any suspicion of only being concerned about your bread-basket if you want to talk about justice. Leave off this talk about your own misery and the torn pants you have to wear, leave off this petty war about worthless things. God knows there are other things to fight in this world than the traffic police.'

Fortschig's pitiful figure crawled back into the chair, and pulled up its little legs. The beret fell down, and the lemon-yellow scarf hung sadly on the little man's breast.

Commissioner,' he said in a whiny voice. 'You are stern with me like Moses or Isaiah with the people of Israel, and I know how right you are. But for four days I haven't eaten anything warm and don't even have money to smoke.'

Was he no longer eating with the Leibundguts, asked the old man, suddenly a little bit embarrassed.

'I had a fight with Mrs Leibundgut about Goethe's *Faust*. She is for the second part and I am against it. So she did not ask me back. The second part of *Faust* was holy to his wife, Mr Leibundgut wrote me, and he could no longer do anything for me,' lamented the writer.

Barlach felt sorry for the poor wretch. He thought he had perhaps been too harsh with him, and finally asked grumblingly what on earth the wife of a chocolate firm president had to do with Goethe.

'Whom are they inviting now?' he finally demanded to know. 'The tennis pro?'

'Botzinger, the musician,' Fortschig answered meekly.

'Well, at least he has something decent to eat every third day for a few months,' said the old man, feeling somewhat reconciled. 'A good musician. Of course, nobody can listen to his compositions, not even I, and I am certainly used to terrible noises from my time in Istanbul. But that is beside the point. Anyway, I suppose he will soon disagree with Mrs President about Beethoven's Ninth. And then she'll take the tennis pro back – they are much easier to dominate intellectually. I will recommend you to Grollbachs, the Grollbachs of the clothing store. They cook well, though a little bit on the greasy side. I think that may work out better. Grollbach is not literary and has no interest either in *Faust* or in Goethe.'

'And the wife?' Fortschig asked, frightened.

'Stone deaf,' the Commissioner calmed him. 'A stroke of luck for you. And take that "Little Rose" Doctor Hungertobel left, you may smoke it in here.'

Ceremoniously Fortschig lit the cigar.

'Do you want to go to Paris for ten days?' the old man asked as if in passing.

'To Paris?' called the little man, and jumped off his chair. 'Do I want to go to Paris? I, who worship French literature like nobody else? By the next train!' Fortschig gasped for breath in his surprise and excitement.

'My attorney Butz in the Bundesgasse has five hundred francs and a ticket,' Barlach said calmly. 'The trip will do you good. Paris is a beautiful city, the most beautiful city I know, aside from Istanbul. And the Frenchmen – I don't know, Fortschig, but the Frenchmen are still the nicest and most cultivated people. Not even a real

Turk can hold a candle to them.'

'To Paris, to Paris,' stammered the poor devil.

'But first I need you for an affair that bothers me quite a bit,' said Barlach, fixing his glance on the little man. 'It's an unholy affair.'

'A crime?' Fortschig was shaking.

'The point is to expose someone,' answered the Commissioner.

Very slowly Fortschig put the 'Little Rose' in the ashtray next to him. 'Is it dangerous, what I will have to do?' he asked in a whisper.

'No,' said the old man. 'It's not dangerous. And in order to remove all possibility of danger, I'm sending you to Paris. But you must obey me. When will the next issue of your paper appear?'

'I don't know. When I have money.'

'When could you send out an issue?' asked the Commissioner.

'At once,' replied Fortschig.

Did he put out the *Apfelschuss* by himself, Barlach wanted to know.

'Alone. With a typewriter and an old duplicating machine,' answered the editor.

'In how many copies?'

'In forty-five. It's a very small newspaper,' came the whispered reply. 'There were never more than fifteen subscriptions.'

The Commissioner thought for a while. 'The next edition of the *Apfelschuss* has to appear in a large number – three hundred copies. I'll pay for everything. I ask of you only that you write a certain article for it. What else the paper will carry is your business. This article (he handed him a big sheet of paper) will contain what I have written down here. But in your language, Fortschig, I want it in your language as in your best times. You need not know more than the information I am giving you, not even who the doctor is against whom this pamphlet is directed. My statements must not irritate you; they are true, take my word for it. In this article which you will send to certain hospitals will be only *one* lie, namely that you hold the proof of your statements in your hands and know the name of the doctor. That is the dangerous point. That is why you will have to go to Paris as soon as you have mailed the *Apfelschuss*. That same night.'

'I will write and I will go,' promised the writer, holding the sheet of paper the old man had given him. He looked completely different and was dancing around the room.

'You won't talk to a soul about your trip,' commanded Barlach.

'Not to a soul. Not to a single solitary soul,' swore Fortschig.

'How much will it cost for the three hundred copies?' asked the old man.

'Four hundred francs,' demanded the little man, with shining eyes. He was proud to get into some money finally.

The Commissioner nodded 'You may pick up the money from my good old Butz. If you hurry up, he will give it to you today. I've already talked to him on the phone. You will take off as soon as the edition is out,' he ordered once more, filled by an invincible mistrust.

'At once,' swore the little fellow, and raised his right hand. 'That same night. To Paris.'

But the old man was no calmer after Fortschig had left. The writer appeared more unreliable than ever before. He wondered whether or not to ask Lutz to have him guarded. 'Nonsense,' he said then. 'They retired me – I shall handle the Emmenberger case myself. Fortschig will write the article against Emmenberger, and since he will go away, there is no danger. Not even Hungertobel needs to know about it. I wish he would come now. I could use a "Little Rose" '.

Second part

The abyss

When the night set in on Friday – the last day of the year – the Commissioner reached the city of Zurich. Hungertobel was driving the car himself and, because he was worried about his friend, he drove even slower than he usually did. The city was illuminated by cascades of lights. Hungertobel got into droves of cars, gliding into the lights from all sides, disappearing into side streets and opening their intestines to let out men, women, all greedy for this night, for the end of the year, all ready to start a new one and to live on. The old man sat motionless in the back of the car, lost in the darkness of the small curved space. He asked Hungertobel not to take the most direct route. He stared at all this untiring activity.

Barlach held no great love for Zurich; he felt that four hundred thousand Swiss all in one place was overdoing it. He hated the main street they were driving along now. But during this sinister trip to an uncertain and threatening goal (this trip to reality, as he had said to Hungertobel), the city fascinated him.

Out of the black, dull sky it started to rain, then to snow, finally to rain again – silver threads in the lights. People, people! More and more masses pushed down on both sides of the street, behind the curtains of snow and rain. The trams were crowded, ghostlike faces became visible behind the windows, hands clutching newspapers, all fantastic in the silvery light, passing by, disappearing. For the first time since his illness Barlach felt like somebody whose time had passed, who had lost the struggle with death, the irrevocable struggle. The reason that irresistibly drove him to Zurich, this suspicion into which he had put so much of his energetic mind and yet which was merely a dream borne on the waves of his illness, seemed useless and worthless. Why should he fight? For what: to what purpose? He longed to give up, for an endless, dreamless sleep. Hungertobel cursed inwardly, he felt the resignation of the old man and reproached himself for not having put a stop to this undertaking. The uncertain nightly waves of the lake washed toward them, the car glided slowly across the bridge. A traffic policeman appeared, an automaton who mechanically moved arms and legs. Fleetingly Barlach thought of Fortschig, of the desolate Fortschig who now in Berne, in a dirty attic room, was feverishly writing the pamphlet. Then he lost this anchor, too. He leaned back and closed his eyes. The tiredness in him grew, became sinister and gigantic.

You will die, he thought. You will die one day, in a year, as the cities, the nations, and the continents will die one day. 'Kick off,' he thought, that's the word – 'kick off' – and the earth will still revolve around the sun, in the same undiscernibly wavering course, rigid and without mercy, fast and yet so quiet, all the time, all the time. What does it matter whether this city here is alive or whether the grey, watery, lifeless plain covers it all – the houses, the towers, the lights, the people – was it the lead waves of the Dead Sea I saw shimmer through the darkness of rain and snow when we drove across the bridge?

He felt cold. The coldness of the universe, an ominous, large, stony coldness enveloped him for the fleeting trace of a second, for an eternity.

He opened his eyes and stared out again. The theatre building appeared, was swallowed by the darkness. The old man looked at his friend in the front of the car. The calmness of the doctor, a benevolent calmness, did him good (he perceived nothing of Hungertobel's anxiety). Touched by the breath of the big Nothing, he became awake again and courageous. They turned left at the university, the road climbed, got darker, one curve followed another, and the old man drifted, keen, observant, and unerring.

The dwarf

Hungertobel stopped in a park whose firs bordered on the forest, so Barlach assumed. For he could only guess at the edge of the forest against the horizon. Up here it snowed now in large clean flakes. Through the falling snow the old man glimpsed the front of the hospital. The car stood near the front entrance, which was set back into the wall and flanked by two carefully barred windows – from which one could watch the entrance, thought the Commissioner. Hungertobel lit a 'Little Rose', without speaking a word, left the car, and disappeared into the entrance. The old man was alone. He leaned forward and scrutinized the building, as far as that was possible in the darkness. Sonnenstein, he thought, reality. The snow fell harder, none of the many windows was illuminated. Only once in a while a vague shimmer flickered through the white masses of snow. The white modern complex of buildings – mostly built of glass – lay before him like a cemetery. The old man became restless; Hungertobel did not seem to want to return. He looked at his watch – but hardly a minute had passed. I'm nervous, he thought, and leaned back, intending to close his eyes.

At that moment Barlach's glance fell through the car windows. The melting snow ran down in wide tracks, and he saw a figure hanging from the bars of the window to the left of the entrance. At first he thought he was seeing an ape, but then he recognized, surprised, that it was a dwarf, like one of those you sometimes find in a circus for the entertainment of the spectators. The little hands and feet were naked and gripped the bars as a monkey's would, while the huge head turned towards the Commissioner. It was a wrinkled stone-old face of a beastly ugliness, with deep cracks and creases, defiled by nature herself. It ogled at the old man with big dark eyes, motionless, like a weather-beaten mossy stone. The Commissioner bent forward and pressed his face against the wet window to see better, but the dwarf had already disappeared into the room with a catlike jump. The window was empty and dark. Now Hungertobel came, and behind him two nurses, looking all the more white in the incessant snowfall. The doctor opened the car door and was shocked to see Barlach's pale face.

'What's the matter?' he whispered.

'Nothing,' the old man answered. 'I just have to get used to this modern building. Reality is always a little bit different from what one expects.'

Hungertobel sensed that the old man was not telling the truth and looked at him suspiciously. 'Well,' he replied, under his breath as before, 'here we go.'

Had he seen Emmenberger, whispered the Commissioner.

He had talked to him, reported Hungertobel. 'There is no doubt possible, Hans, that it is he. I was not mistaken in Ascona.'

The two were silent. The nurses waited, already impatient.

We are chasing a phantom, thought Hungertobel. Emmenberger is a harmless doctor and this hospital like any other one, only more expensive.

In the back of the car, in the now almost impenetrable shadow, sat the Commissioner, and he knew exactly what was on Hungertobel's mind.

'When will he examine me?' he asked.

'Now,' replied Hungertobel.

The doctor felt how the old man perked up. 'Then say goodbye now, Samuel,' said Barlach. 'You're incapable of putting on an act and nobody must know that we are friends. Much will depend on this first interrogation.'

'Interrogation?' wondered Hungertobel.

'What else?' answered the Commissioner in an ironic voie. 'Emmenberger will examine me and I will interrogate him.'

They shook hands.

The nurses came. Now there were four of them. The old man was lifted on to a stretcher of gleaming metal. Sinking back, he saw Hungertobel hand out the suitcase. Then the old man looked into the black, empty space from which the flakes fell softly in quiet, incomprehensible whirls, dancing, sinking, gleaming in the light, touching his face for a moment, wet and cold. The snow won't last long, he thought. The stretcher was pushed through the entrance, he heard Hungertobel's car drive off. He's leaving, he's leaving, he said quietly to himself. A white glittering ceiling curved above him, with large mirrors in which he saw himself, stretched out and helpless. The stretcher glided noiselessly through mysterious corridors; not even the steps of the nurses could be heard. Black numbers stuck to the gleaming walls on both sides; the doors were almost invisible, having been blended into the general white. In a corner shimmered the naked firm body of a statue. Again the soft and yet cruel world of a hospital surrounded Barlach.

And behind him the red fat face of a nurse, pushing the stretcher.

The old man had crossed his hands behind his neck.

'Is there a dwarf around here?' he asked in High German, for he had had Hungertobel describe him as a Swiss living abroad.

The nurse laughed. 'But Mr Kramer,' she said, 'what gives you such an idea?'

She spoke German with a Swiss accent, from which he concluded that she was from Berne. He saw something positive in that, as much as her answer made him suspicious. At least he was among Berners.

And he asked, 'What's your name, Nurse?'

'I am Nurse Clari.'

'From Berne, aren't you?'

'Yes, Mr Kramer.'

I'll work on her, thought the Commissioner.

The interrogation

Barlach, who was pushed into a room almost entirely of glass, opening with a blinding light in front of him, saw two figures, one of them slightly bent and slim, a gentleman even in his professional coat, with thickly rimmed glasses which nevertheless could not cover the scar on the right eyebrow. Dr Fritz Emmenberger. The old man cast only a fleeting glance at the doctor for the time being. He occupied himself more with the woman, who stood next to the man he suspected. Women made him curious. He looked at her distrustfully. As a good Swiss citizen he found professional women somewhat uncanny. The woman was beautiful, he had to admit, and as an old bachelor he had a special weakness for that. She was a lady, he could tell that at first glance. In her white coat she stood, elegant and yet reserved, next to Emmenberger (who could, after all, be a mass murderer). But in Barlach's opinion she looked a little bit too noble.

You could very well put her on a pedestal, he thought bitterly.

'Greetings,' he said, dropping the High German he had just spoken with Nurse Clari. He was happy to meet such a famous doctor.

'You are speaking Berner German,' answered the doctor, also in dialect.

Living abroad did not mean he had to forget that, grumbled the old man.

Yes, so he could see, laughed Emmenberger.

Hungertobel is right, thought Barlach. He is not Nehle. A Berliner could never learn this dialect.

He looked at the lady again.

'My assistant, Doctor Marlok,' the doctor introduced her.

'Well,' said the old man dryly, glad to meet her. And then he asked abruptly, turning his head a little toward the doctor: 'You were in Germany, weren't you, Dr Emmenberger?'

'Years ago,' answered the doctor. 'I was there once, but mostly in Santiago de Chile,' but nothing betrayed what he was thinking or whether the question bothered him.

'In Chile, in Chile,' said the old man, and then once more, 'in Chile, in Chile.'

Emmenberger lit a cigarette and flipped a switch. The room was now in semi-darkness, sparsely lit by the little blue lamp above the Commissioner. Only the operating table was visible and the faces of the two white figures in front of him; the old man recognized further that the room was closed off by a window through which broke a few distant lights. The red point of the cigarette, which Emmenberger was smoking, moved up and down.

Nobody smokes in rooms like these. The thought struck the Commissioner. I've already made him a little bit uneasy.

The doctor asked where Hungertobel was.

'I sent him away,' replied Barlach. 'I want you to examine me in his absence.'

The doctor pushed up his eyeglasses. 'I think that we can have faith in Doctor Hungertobel.'

'Of course,' answered Barlach.

'You're a sick man,' Emmenberger continued. 'The operation was dangerous and is not always successful. Hungertobel tells me that you are aware of this. That is good. We doctors need courageous patients, to whom we can tell the truth. But I would have welcomed Hungertobel's presence during the examination and I'm sorry to hear that he complied with your wishes. We doctors have to cooperate, that is a postulate of science.'

As a colleague he could well understand that, answered the Commissioner.

Emmenberger was astonished. What did he mean? he asked. To his knowledge Mr Kramer was not a doctor.

'That is simple.' The old man laughed. 'You hunt diseases and I hunt war criminals.'

Emmenberger lit another cigarette. 'Hardly a safe occupation for a private citizen,' he said nonchalantly.

'Exactly,' answered Barlach. 'And now I've become ill in the midst of my hunt and come to you. I call that bad luck, to be here in Sonnenstein – or is it good luck?'

He could not yet give a prognosis, replied Emmenberger. Hungertobel did not seem terribly confident.

'But then you've not examined me yet,' said the old man. 'And that's the reason I didn't wish our good Doctor Hungertobel to be present. We must be unprejudiced if we want to make headway in a case. And we want to make headway, you and I, I think. There is nothing worse than forming an opinion about a criminal or a disease without studying the suspicious matter in its environment and observing its habits.'

The doctor replied that he was right. It seemed logical to him, though he as a doctor understood nothing of criminology. Well, he hoped Mr Kramer would recover somewhat from his profession here in Sonnenstein.

Then he lit a third cigarette and said, 'I think the war criminals will leave you alone here.'

Emmenberger's answer made the old man suspicious for a moment. Who is interrogating whom? he thought, and looked into Emmenberger's face. It appeared mask-like in the light of the one lamp, with blinking glasses, the eyes behind them overly big and sarcastic.

'Dear doctor,' he said, 'you certainly don't want to maintain that there is no cancer in this country.'

'Is that supposed to mean there *are* war criminals in Switzerland?' Emmenberger laughed, amused.

The old man scrutinized the doctor. 'What happened in Germany, happens in every country if certain conditions occur. These conditions may differ. No person, no nation, is an exception. From a Jew, Doctor Emmenberger, who was operated on without anaesthesia in a concentration camp, I learned that there is only one difference between human beings – that between torturers and tourtured. But I believe there is also the difference between the tempted and the untouched. We Swiss, you and I, belong to the untouched. It is a blessing and not a mistake, as many say. For we are supposed to pray, "Lead us not into temptation". I came to Switzerland, not to look for war criminals in general, but to find a *particular* one, of whom I know no more than an obscure picture. But now I am sick, Doctor Emmenberger, and the hunt collapsed overnight, so that the hunted man does not even known how close I was on his track. A ridiculous spectacle.'

Then he hardly had a chance left to find his man, the doctor answered indifferently, and blew out the cigarette smoke, which formed a fine milky-blue ring above the old man's head. Barlach saw how he gave a sign to the woman with his eyes. She handed him a syringe. Emmenberger disappeared for a moment into the darkness of the room; then, when he became visible again, he held a vial.

'Your chances are small,' he said again, filling the syringe with a colourless liquid.

But the Commissioner contradicted him.

'I have yet another weapon,' he said. 'Let's take your method, Doctor. On this last dreary day of the year, after coming to your hospital through snow and rain, you receive me in the operating room for my first examination. Why do you do that? It's unusual to be so quickly whisked into a room which fills a patient with horror. You do it because you want to frighten me. You can only be my doctor if you control me, and I am a stubborn man – Hungertobel must have told you that. So you decided to give this demonstration. You want to dominate me in order to cure me, and fear is one of the means you have to utilize. It's the same in my dreadful profession. Our methods are alike. I have only fear left to utilize against the one I am looking for.'

The syringe in Emmenberger's hand was pointing toward the old man. 'You are a shrewd psychologist.' The doctor laughed. 'It's true, I did want to impress you with this room. Fear is a necessary means. But before I begin with *my* art, let's hear more about yours. How do you want to proceed? I'm curious. The hunted man does not know that you're hunting him, at least these are your own words.'

'He senses it without being sure, and that's more dangerous for him,' answered Barlach. 'He knows that I'm in Switzerland and that I'm looking for a war criminal. He'll calm his fears and tell himself over and over that I'm looking for someone else, not him. For by means of a masterly trick he has escaped into Switzerland from the world of unlimited crime, leaving his identity behind. A big secret! But in the darkest corner of his heart he will sense that I'm looking for *him*, and nobody else, only him – always. And he will feel fear, greater and greater fear – the more improbable it seems to his intelligence that I am looking for him. And I, Doctor, am in this hospital in bed, with my disease, my impotence.' He was silent.

Emmenberger looked at him strangely, almost with pity. The syringe was in his hand.

'I doubt your success,' he said matter-of-factly. 'But I wish you luck.'

'His fear will kill him,' answered the old man, motionless.

Emmenberger slowly put the syringe on the little table of glass and metal which stood next to the stretcher. There it was, a vicious sharp thing. Emmenberger stood slightly bent forward.

'Do you think so?' he said finally. 'Do you think so?' His eyes behind the glasses narrowed. 'It's astonishing to find such a hopeful optimist in these times. Your thoughts are bold; let's hope that reality will not let you down one of these days. It would be sad if you reached disheartening results.' He said it softly, a little bit surprised. Then he went slowly back into the darkness of the room. It became light again. The operating room lay in a glaring light. Emmenberger stood next to the light switches.

'I'll examine you later, Mr Kramer,' he said, and smiled. 'Your illness is serious. You know this. The suspicion has not been removed that your life is endangered. Unfortunately, this is my impression after our talk. Honesty deserves honesty. The examination will not be easy. It requires a certain amount of surgery. And we'd rather do that after New Year, wouldn't we? One ought not to disrupt a beautiful holiday. The main thing is that I have you under my care now.'

Barlach did not answer.

Emmenberger put out his cigarette. 'For goodness sake, Doctor,' he said to the woman, 'here I am, smoking in the operating room. Mr Kramer is an exciting visitor. You should calm us both down, him and me.'

'What are these?' asked the old man when the woman doctor handed him two reddish pills.

'Just a sedative,' she said. But he drank the water she gave him with even greater misgivings.

'Call the nurse,' ordered Emmenberger.

Nurse Clari appeared in the door. To the Commissioner she looked like a soulful hangman. Hangmen are always soulful, he thought.

'What room did you prepare for our Mr Kramer?' asked Emmenberger.

'Number seventy-two, Doctor Emmenberger,' answered the nurse.

'Let's give him room fifteen,' said Emmenberger. 'We've better control over him there.'

The tiredness that he had already felt in Hungertobel's car, over-came Barlach again.

When the nurse rolled the old man into the corridor, the stretcher made a sharp turn. Tearing himself out of his drowsiness, Barlach saw Emmenberger's face.

The doctor was observing him carefully, smiling and amused.

Gripped by a shivering fit, Barlach fell back.

The room

When he woke up (it was still night, around ten-thirty; he must have slept about three hours, he thought), he found himself in a room which he regarded with surprise and not without concern. Yet he felt a certain satisfaction. He hated hospital rooms, and he liked the fact that this room bore more resemblance to a studio, a technical room, cold and impersonal, as far as he could tell by the blue shimmer of the night lamp burning at his left. The bed in which he was lying – in pajamas and well covered – was still the same stretcher on which he had been brought in. He recognized it at once, though with a few hand grips it had been changed into a bed. 'They're practical here,' said the old man into the stillness. He let the light from the revolving lamp fall into the room. A curtain appeared; behind it he suspected the window. It was embroidered with strange plants and animals. It's plain, I'm on a hunt, he said to himself.

He leaned back in the pillows and thought over what he had accomplished. It was little enough. He had followed through with his plan. Now it was necessary to continue, to spin the threads of his mesh tighter. It was necessary to act, but he did not know how to act and where to start. He pushed a button on the little table. Nurse Clari came in.

'Well, well, our nurse from Berne,' the old man greeted her.

'Yes, Mr Kramer, what is it? Finally awakened?' she said, her hands on her hips.

The old man looked at his wrist watch again. 'It's only ten-thirty.'

'Are you hungry?' she asked. 'No? Shall I call the lady doctor? You've met her. She can give you another injection.'

'Nonsense,' growled the old man. 'I haven't had an injection. Turn on the ceiling light. I want to look at this room. After all, one likes to know where one is.'

He was quite angry.

A white, but not glaring, light shone. It was diffuse and one did not quite know where it came from. In this new light, the room was clear and sharp. Above the old man, the ceiling was a single big mirror. It annoyed him; it seemed sinister to have yourself over your head all the time. Mirrors everywhere, he thought, it could drive you crazy. He was secretly horrified by the skeleton that stared down at him whenever he looked up. That mirror lies, he thought. There are such mirrors that distort everything. I couldn't look that bony.

He looked around the room again, forgetting the nurse who waited, without moving. At his left was a wall made of glass against a grey background. Naked figures were carved into it, dancing men and women, linear and yet three-dimensional. From the right, greyish-green wall, between door and curtain, hung like a wing Rembrandt's 'Anatomy', seemingly senseless and yet calculated, a combination that gave the room a somewhat frivolous air – all the more so since a black crude wooden cross hung over the door in which the nurse stood.

'Well, Nurse,' he said, still surprised that the room had changed so much with the light. He had only noticed the curtains before, and had not seen the dancing men and women, the 'Anatomy', and the cross. He was filled with the apprehension these unknown surroundings communicated. 'Well, Nurse, this is a strange room for a hospital, a place that's supposed to make people well, not drive them insane.'

'We're in Sonnenstein,' answered Nurse Clari, and folded her hands across her stomach. 'We comply with all wishes,' she babbled on, gleaming with probity, 'with the most pious ones and others. Really, if you don't like the "Anatomy", you can have the "Birth of Venus" by Botticelli or a Picasso.'

'Then I'd rather have "Knight, Death and Devil",' said the Commissioner.

Nurse Clari pulled out a notebook. ' "Knight, Death and Devil",' she wrote down. 'You'll have it tomorrow. A nice picture for a death chamber. I congratulate you. The gentleman has good taste.'

'I think,' answered the old man, flabbergasted by the crudeness of the nurse, 'I think it hasn't gone that far yet with me.'

Nurse Clari slowly wagged her red fleshy head. 'Oh yes,' she said firmly. 'Only the dying are put here. Exclusively. I've never seen anybody leave Ward Three. And you *are* on Ward Three, that's all there is to it. We all have to die sometime. Read what I've written about it. It was published by Liechti in Waalkingen.'

The nurse pulled out of her bosom a little pamphlet and put it on the bed. *Clari Glauber: Death, Goal and Purpose of Our Life. A practical guide.*

Should she get the doctor now? she asked triumphantly.

'No,' answered the Commissioner, still holding *The Goal and Purpose of Our Life* in his hands. 'I don't need her. But pull the curtains and open the window.'

The curtains were pulled aside, the light went out. The old man turned out the night lamp, too.

The massive figure of Nurse Clari disappeared in the rectangle of the door, but before it closed, he asked, 'Nurse! You answer all questions so openly, you'll answer this one truthfully. Is there a dwarf in this house?'

'Of course' – it came brutally from the rectangle. 'You saw him yourself, didn't you?'

Then the door closed.

Nonsense, he thought. *I* will leave Ward Three. Nothing to it. I'll call Hungertobel – I'm too sick to do anything against Emmenberger. Tomorrow I'll return to the Salem.

He was frightened and not ashamed to admit it.

Outside it was night, and around him was the bleakness of the room. The old man lay on his bed, hardly breathing.

The bells will have to start, he thought, the bells of Zurich, ringing in the New Year.

From somewhere a clock struck twelve.

The old man waited.

Again a clock struck from somewhere, then again – twelve merciless strokes. Stroke after stroke, like hammer blows on a gate of iron.

No bells, not even the distant cry of a happy crowd.

The New Year came in silence.

The world is dead, thought the Commissioner, and again and again, the world is dead. The world is dead.

On his forehead he felt cold sweat that slowly rolled down his temples. His eyes were wide open. He was lying motionless, resigned.

Once again he heard twelve distant strokes, fading away over a desolate city. Then he felt as if he was sinking into a shoreless ocean, into an unknown gloom.

He woke up at dawn, in the twilight of the new day.

The room was more threatening than ever. For a long time he stared into the growing light, into the rising green-grey shadows, until he understood:

The window was barred.

Doctor Marlok

'So he woke up,' said a voice from the door to the Commissioner, who stared at the barred window. Into the room, which filled more and more with a foggy phantom-like morning, stepped an old woman in a white coat. Her features were wrinkled and bloated, and Barlach recognized only with difficulty and horror the face of the doctor he had seen with Emmenberger in the operating room. He stared at her, tired and shaken by disgust. Without paying any attention to the Commissioner, she pulled up her skirt and pushed a syringe through the stocking into her thigh. Then, after she had made the injection, she straightened up, pulled out a mirror, and applied make-up. Fascinated, the old man watched her. He did not seem to exist for this woman. Her features lost all vulgarity and once more gained the freshness and clarity he had noticed. Leaning motionless against the doorframe was now the woman whose beauty had struck him at the time of his arrival.

'I understand,' said the old man, slowly awakening from his numbness, but still exhausted and confused. 'Morphine.'

'Certainly,' she said. 'One needs that in this world – Commissioner Barlach.'

The old man stared into the morning. It grew darker, for now rain was pouring down outside into the snow which must still be there from the night. And then he said in a low voice, as if in passing: 'You know who I am.'

Then he stared outside again.

'We know who you are,' said the doctor, still leaning against the door, both hands buried in the pockets of her white coat.

He asked her how they had found out, although actually he was not at all curious to know.

She threw a newspaper on the bed.

It was the *Bund.*

On the front page was his picture, as the old man noticed right away, a photograph taken in the spring when he still smoked Brazils, and the caption read: *The Commissioner of the City Police of Berne, Hans Barlach, retired.*

'Of course,' muttered the Commissioner. Then, when he looked at it for a second time – angry and disconcerted – he saw the date.

It was the first time he lost his restraint.

'The date!' he screamed in a hoarse voice. 'The date, Doctor! The date of the paper!'

'Well?' she asked, without a muscle moving in her face.

'It's the fifth of January,' gasped the Commissioner desperately. Now he understood the absence of the New Year's bells this whole horrible past night.

'Did you expect a different date?' she asked in a sarcastic tone, obviously curious, lifting her eyebrows a bit.

He screamed, 'What did you do to me?' and tried to sit up, but weakly fell back into the bed.

His arm flapped in the air a few more times, then he lay motionless again.

The doctor pulled out a cigarette case and took out a cigarette.

Nothing of all this seemed to touch her.

'I do not wish you to smoke in my room,' Barlach said in a low voice but firmly.

'The window is barred,' answered the doctor, and nodded with her head in the direction where the rain ran down behind the iron bars. 'I don't think you have anything to say around here.' Then she turned toward the old man and stood in front of his bed, her hands in the pockets of her coat.

'Insulin,' she said, looking down at him. 'The boss has given you an insulin treatment. His speciality.' She laughed. 'And you really want to arrest that man?'

'Emmenberger has murdered a German doctor named Nehle and operated without anaesthesia,' Barlach said cold-bloodedly. He felt that he had to win this woman over to his side. He was determined to risk everything.

'He has done much more, our doctor,' replied the woman.

'You know it!'

'Of course.'

'You admit that Emmenberger was camp doctor in Stutthof under the name of Nehle?' he asked feverishly.

'Of course.'

'You admit Nehle's murder, too?'

'Why not?'

With one stroke Barlach saw his suspicion confirmed, this monstrous, obtuse suspicion, built up from Hungertobel's reaction to an old photograph, the suspicion he had dragged around with him through these endless days like a gigantic burden. Exhausted, he looked out the window. Small silvery drops of water rolled down the bars. He had longed for this moment of knowledge as for a moment of peace.

'If you know everything,' he said, 'then you, too, are guilty.'

The woman looked at him with such a strange glance that her silence disturbed him. She pushed up her right sleeve. On her lower arm, deeply burned into the flesh, was a number, like a cattle brand. 'Do I have to show you my back, too?' she asked.

'You were in a concentration camp?' Barlach cried, dumbfounded, and stared at her. He lifted himself painfully, resting on his right arm.

'Edith Marlok, inmate Four-four-six-six in extermination camp Stutthof near Danzig.' Her voice was cold and dead.

The old man fell back into the pillows. He cursed his illness, his weakness, his helplessness.

'I was a Communist,' she said, and pulled down the sleeve.

'And how could you survive the camp?'

'That's simple,' she answered, and stood his gaze as indifferently as if nothing in this world could ever move her again, no human feelings and no human fate, be it ever so terrible.

'I became Emmenberger's mistress.'

'But that's impossible.' It escaped the Commissioner.

She looked at him in astonishment.

'A torturer had mercy on a dying dog,' she said finally. 'Only a few of the women in Stutthof had the chance to become the mistress of an SS doctor. Any way of saving oneself is good. Aren't you trying everything possible to get out of here?'

Feverish and shaking, he tried for a third time to sit up.

'Are you still his mistress?'

'Of course. Why not?'

'But you can't be! Emmenberger is a monster!' Barlach screamed.

'You were a Communist – you must have your convictions!'

'Yes, I had my convictions,' she said calmly. 'I was convinced that you must love this sad thing of stone and mud that revolves around the sun, this earth; that it's our duty to help humanity in the name of common sense to get rid of poverty and exploitation. My belief was no mere phrase. And when the house-painter with the ridiculous mustache and the silly curl on his forehead 'seized power', the technically correct phrase for all the crimes he committed, I fled to the country in which I – like all Communists – had believed, to our all-mother, to the Soviet Union. Oh, I had my beliefs, and staked them against the world. I was determined like you, Commissioner, to fight against evil till the end of my unholy life.'

'We must never give up this fight,' replied Barlach softly, leaning back in the pillows and shaking with cold.

'May I ask you to look in the mirror above you?'

'I've already seen myself,' he answered, anxiously avoiding a glance upward.

She laughed. 'A beautiful skeleton grins at you – the Commissioner of the City of Berne. Our dogma of the struggle against evil which must never be given up, whatever the circumstances and the conditions, is correct in a vacuum or, what amounts to the same thing, behind a desk. But not on this planet on which we race through the universe like witches on a broom. My faith was great, so great that I did not despair when I was swallowed by the misery of the Russian masses, by the despair of that mighty land, which could be ennobled only by freedom of the spirit, not by violence. When the Russians buried me in their jails, without a hearing or a conviction, and pushed me from one camp to the next without my knowing why, I did not doubt that this, too, had its place in the grand scheme of history. When the splendid pact came about, which Mr Stalin closed with Mr Hitler, I saw its necessity, for was it not aimed at saving the great Communist fatherland? But one morning, deep in the winter of nineteen forty, after an endless journey from Siberia in a cattle train, Russian soldiers drove me across a miserable wooden bridge, in the midst of a crowd of ragged figures. A dirty river lazily made its way underneath, carrying ice and wood. And on the other shore the black figures of the Storm Troopers appeared out of the morning mist. At that moment I understood the betrayal, not only of us Godforsaken poor devils who tottered toward Stutthof, but of the idea of Communism itself, which only makes sense if it is one with the idea of brotherly love and humanity. But now I have crossed that bridge, Commissioner, I have crossed for ever that black, trembling bridge. I know now what human beings are like. You can do anything with them, anything that a tyrant or an Emmenberger ever thought of to give them pleasure or to demonstrate their theories. You can force any confession out of a man's mouth, for his will is limited but the number of tortures is legion. 'Abandon hope all ye who enter here.' I abandoned hope. It's nonsense to fight and struggle for a better world. Man himself wishes for his hell, prepares it in his mind and brings it about by his deeds. It's the same everywhere, there in Stutthof and here in Sonnenstein, the same gruesome melody, rising in sinister harmonies from the abyss of the human soul. The camp near Danzig was the hell of the Jews, the Christians, and the Communists. This hospital here, in the midst of the respectable city of Zurich, is the hell of the rich.'

'What do you mean by that? These are strange words,' said Barlach, listening fixedly to the doctor, who fascinated and frightened him in equal measure.

'You're curious,' she said, 'and seem to be proud of it. You dared to come into the lion's den from which there is no escape. Don't count on me. Human beings leave me indifferent, even Emmenberger who is my lover.'

The hell of the rich

She began talking again. 'Why, for the sake of this lost world, Commissioner, were you not satisfied with your daily petty thefts? Why did you force your way in here, where there is nothing for you to seek? But I suppose a police dog that has served its time yearns for something "higher".' The doctor laughed.

'Injustice has to be sought where it can be found,' answered the old man. 'The law is the law.'

'I see, you like mathematics,' she replied, and lit another cigarette. She still stood by his bed, not hesitant and careful, as one approaches a sickbed, but as one stands next to a criminal who is already chained to a trestle and whose death one has recognized as necessary and desirable; a practical procedure which will extinguish a useless existence. 'I thought from the first that you are the type of fool who swears by mathematics. The law is the law: x equals x. The most monstrous phrase ever to rise to the eternally bloody sky that hangs above us.' She laughed again.

'As if there existed a destiny for man that is valid regardless of the amount of power he possesses. The law is not the law, but the power. This dogma is written down in the bloody valleys in which we were destroyed. Nothing is itself in this world, all is a lie. When we say *law*, we mean power; when we say *power*, we think of wealth; and when we say *wealth*, we hope to enjoy the vices of this world. The law is vice, the law is wealth, the law is the cannons, the trusts, the parties. Whatever we say, it is never illogical, except for the sentence that the law is the law, which alone is a lie. Mathematics lies, common sense, intellect, the arts – they all lie.

'What do you want, Commissioner? We are born on some brittle clod, without being asked, without knowing why. We stare into a universe, into gigantic emptiness and plenty, a senseless waste – and so we drift to the distant cataracts which we will have to encounter – the only thing of which we are certain. We live in order to die, we breathe and talk, we love and have children and grandchildren. And together with them, whom we love and bore, we are turned into carcasses, to disintegrate into the indifferent, dead elements of which we are composed. The cards were mixed, dealt, and gathered together; *c'est ça*. We have nothing else but this drifting piece of dirt and ice to which we cling. And so we wish that this our only life – this fleeting moment in the face of the rainbow that spans the abyss of foam and steam – should be a happy one. We wish the plenty of the earth to be ours for the short time that she carries us, she who is the only mercy bestowed upon us. But this is not so and will never be. And the crime, Commissioner, is not that it is not so, that there is poverty and misery, but that there are rich *and* poor, that the ship with which we all sink still has cabins for the powerful and rich next to the mass quarters of the poor.

'We all have to die, they say, so it does not matter. Dying is dying. Oh, this farcical logic! The dying of the poor is one thing and the dying of the rich and mighty, another. There are worlds between the bloody tragicomedy of the weak and that of the powerful. The poor man dies in the same way in which he lived – on a sack in a cellar, on a torn mattress, or on the bloody field of honour. But the rich man dies differently. He has lived in luxury and wants to die in luxury. He is cultivated and applauds his own departure. Bravo, my friends, the performance is over! Life was a farce, dying a phrase, the funeral an advertisement, and the whole thing a business deal. *C'est ça*.

'If I could show you through this hospital, Commissioner, which has made me what I am, neither man or woman, only flesh that needs always bigger doses of morphine to make the jokes about this world it deserves – I'd show you *how* the rich die. I'd unlock the fantastic sickrooms for you, the gaudy, cunning rooms in which they rot, the gleaming cells of lust and torture, caprice and crime.'

Barlach did not answer. He lay there, sick and motionless, his face turned away. The woman bent over him.

'I'd tell you,' she continued without mercy, 'the names of those who've died here, and *are* dying here – the politicians, bankers, industralists, the mistresses, and the widows – all with famous names. And those unknown criminals who with one big deal that costs them nothing earn the millions that cost us everything. They die here in this hospital. Sometimes they make blasphemous jokes about their rotting bodies, sometimes they rear up and utter wild curses against their fate, that they have so much and yet must die. Sometimes they blubber the most disgusting prayers in their brocade-and-silk-filled rooms, prayers that they may not have to exchange the bliss up here for the bliss of paradise. Emmenberger grants them everything and greedily they take everything he offers. But they need more, they need hope. This, too, he grants them. But the trust they place in him is trust in the devil, and the hope he gives them is hell. They have left God and found a new god. Voluntarily these sick people undergo tortures, so that they may live a few days, a few minutes more, so that they will not be snatched away from the things they love more than heaven and hell, more than salvation and damnation – their power and the earth which gave them this power. Here, too, the boss operates without anaesthesia. Everything Emmenberger did in Stutthof, he does here, in the middle of Switzerland, in the middle of Zurich, unmolested by the police and the laws of this country. Yes, he even does it in the name of science and humanity. Unerringly he gives what people want of him – tortures, nothing but tortures.'

'No!' screamed Barlach. 'No! He must be destroyed!'

'Then mankind must be destroyed,' she answered.

Again he screamed his hoarse, desperate *no* and painfully sat up.

'No, no,' it came out of his mouth, but he could only whisper.

Indifferently, the doctor pushed his shoulder, and he fell back helplessly.

'No, no!' he groaned from the pillows.

'You fool.' She laughed. 'What do you want with your *no, no*? In the black mining town from which I came, I, too, said my *no, no* to this world full of misery and exploitation, and I began to work. In the Party, in evening courses, in the university, and more and more determinedly in the Party. I studied and worked for my *no, no*. But now, Commissioner, now standing next to you in my white coat on this misty morning of rain and snow, I know that this *no, no* has become senseless. The world is too old to become a *yes, yes*. Good and bad were too tightly intertwined on the night of that Godforsaken wedding between heaven and hell which produced mankind ever to be separated again, ever to permit such statements as, "This is well done and that is evil; this will lead to good and that, to bad." Too late! We no longer know what we are doing, what actions will result from our obedience or our rebellion, what exploitation, what crime sticks to the fruit we eat, to the bread and milk we give our children. We kill without seeing the victim, without the murderer knowing it. Too late!

'The temptation of this existence was too great and the human being too small, for the mercy which consists of living and not being Nothing. Now we are deadly ill, eaten by the cancer of our deeds. The world is foul, Commissioner, rotting like a badly-stored fruit. What do we still want! The infernal stream of lava we conjured up in the days of our victories, our fame, and our wealth, the stream which now lights our night, can no longer be restricted to the tunnels through which it rose. Only in our dreams can we win back what we have lost, in the burning pictures of ardent longing morphine gives us. So I, Edith Marlok, commit the crimes demanded of me for the colourless liquid I inject under my skin, which bestows upon me during the day the courage to jeer and during the night my dreams, so that I possess in a fleeting illusion what no longer exists – the world as God created it. Emmenberger, your compatriot, knows people and knows what they are useful for. He puts his merciless levers where we are weakest, in the deadly consciousness of our eternal damnation.'

'Go,' he whispered. 'Go now!'

The doctor laughed. Then she stood up, beautiful, proud, distant.

'You want to fight evil and are afraid of my *c'est ça*,' she said, putting on make-up again, leaning on the door with its senseless and lonely old wooden cross. 'You shudder already before a low and defiled servant of this world. How will you stand up to him, the Prince of Hell himself, Emmenberger?'

And then she threw a newspaper and a brown envelope on his bed.

'Read your mail, sir. I've a feeling you'll be surprised at what you accomplished with your good will.'

Knight, death and devil

After the doctor had left the old man, he stayed motionless for a long time. His suspicion had been confirmed, but what should have given him satisfaction only filled him with horror. He sensed that he had calculated correctly but acted foolishly. Only too well he recognized the helplessness of his body. He had lost six days, six dreadful days of which he knew nothing. Emmenberger knew who was after him and had attacked.

Then, finally, when Nurse Clari came with coffee and rolls, he sat up and ate, suspicious but obstinate, determined to overcome his weakness and to counter-attack.

'Nurse Clari,' he said, 'I'm from the police. Maybe it's better we talk openly with each other.'

'I know, Commissioner Barlach,' answered the nurse, threatening and huge next to his bed.

'You know my name and are therefore informed,' Barlach continued. He was puzzled. 'Do you know, too, why I'm here?'

'You want to arrest our boss,' she said, looking down at him.

'Yes, the boss.' The Commissioner nodded. 'And do you know that your boss killed many people in the Stutthof concentration camp in Germany?'

'My boss has been converted,' Nurse Clari Glauber from Bern answered proudly. 'His sins are forgiven.'

'How so?' Barlach asked, flabbergasted, staring at this monster of probity that stood by his bed, her hands folded over her stomach, beaming and convinced.

'He read my brochure,' she said.

The Goal and Purpose of Our Life?

'That's right.'

But that was nonsense, the sick man cried angrily. Emmenberger was still killing people.

'Before he killed out of hatred, now out of love,' the nurse replied gaily. 'He kills as a doctor, because people secretly long for death. Just read my brochure. Man must go through death to his higher possibilities.'

'Emmenberger is a criminal,' gasped the Commissioner, helpless in the face of such bigotry. These god-damned sectarians, he thought desperately.

'The meaning and purpose of our life cannot be a crime.' Nurse Clari shook her head disapprovingly and cleared away the dishes.

'I'll turn you over to the police as an accomplice,' threatened the Commissioner, reaching for his cheapest weapon, as he well knew.

'You're on Ward Three,' said Nurse Clari, sad over this stubborn man, and walked out.

Angrily the old man reached for the mail. He recognized the envelope. It was one of those in which Fortschig usually mailed out his *Apfelschuss*. He opened it, and the newspaper fell out. It had been written, as always during the last twenty-five years, with a rusty, rattling typewriter, with a bad *l* and *r*. '*Der Apfelschuss*, Swiss Protestpaper for the Inland and Surroundings, published by Ulrich Friedrich Fortschig,' was the printed title, and underneath, typed with the typewriter:

SS Torturer as Clinic Director

If I did not have the evidence [wrote Fortschig], this terrible, clear, and irrefutable evidence, that neither a criminologist nor a poet but reality alone can conjure up, I would be forced to describe as the diabolical scheme of a pathological fantasy what truth now forces me to write down.

Truth shall have the floor – even if it makes us turn pale, even if it forever shakes the trust we put – to this day and in spite of everything – in mankind. That a human being, a Berner, under a strange name, went about his bloody trade in an extermination camp near Danzig – I dare not describe in more detail with what bestiality – horrifies us. But that he can direct a clinic in Switzerland is a disgrace for which we can find no words and an indication that we, too, are reaching the end of the road. May these words initiate legal action, which – though terrible and embarrassing for our country – has to be undertaken. For our honour is at stake, and the harmless rumour that we are struggling honestly through the jungle of these times (though we sometimes earn rather a lot of money with watches, cheese, and a few not-so-important weapons).

In this spirit I shall take action. We will lose everything if we gamble with justice. Justice must not be toyed with! This criminal however, a doctor in Zurich whom we shall not pardon, for he never pardoned, whom we blackmail, for he blackmailed, and whom we will finally kill, for he killed countless numbers – we know it is a death sentence we are writing down for him [Barlach had to read this sentence twice]. That director of a private clinic – to be blunt – is asked to give himself up to the Zurich criminal police. Mankind, which is capable of everything and which in an even higher degree understands murder as it understands no other art, this mankind of which we here in Switzerland are part – for we carry the same seeds of the misfortune, the same tendency to regard morality as unremunerative and the remunerative as moral – should finally learn from the example of this beast of a mass murderer that the sadly disregarded force of the spirit breaks open even closed mouths and has them bring about their own destruction.'

As much as this bombastic text complied with Barlach's original plan, which quite simply had been intended to frighten Emmenberger (the rest would somehow follow, he had thought, with the negligent self-confidence of an old criminologist), he realized now clearly that he had made a mistake. The doctor could certainly not be regarded as a man who allowed himself to be threatened. Fortschig's life was in danger, sensed the Commissioner, but he hoped that the writer was already in Paris and therefore safe.

Then, unexpectedly, there seemed to be a possibility for Barlach to establish contact with the outside world.

A workman had entered the room, an enlarged reproduction of Dürer's 'Knight, Death and Devil' under his arm. The Commissioner looked at the man. He seemed to be a good-natured though slightly run-down-looking person of about fifty years, clad in blue overalls. He immediately began to take down the 'Anatomy'.

'Hey,' called the Commissioner. 'Come over here.' The man continued with his work. Once he dropped a pair of pliers, then a screwdriver, and bent down awkwardly to pick them up.

'You!' Barlach called impatiently, since the workman paid not the slightest attention to him. 'I'm Police Commissioner Barlach. Do you understand? My life is in danger. Leave this house after you have finished your work and contact Inspector Lutz – every child will tell you how. Or go to any police station and have them call Lutz. Do you understand? I need this man. He must come at once.'

The labourer still paid no attention to the old man, who painfully formulated the words – more and more he had difficulty speaking. The 'Anatomy' was taken down and now the man examined the Dürer, first from close up, then holding it away from himself with both arms. Through the window fell a milky light. For a moment it seemed to the old man that he could spot a lustreless ball swimming behind the white fog. It had stopped raining. The workman shook his head a few times; the painting seemed to frighten him. He turned to Barlach and said in a strange, too clearly formulated manner, very slowly: 'There is no devil.'

'Yes!' screamed Barlach hoarsely. 'There is a devil! Here in this hospital. Why don't you listen! They probably told you I'm crazy and babble nonsense, but my life is in danger, don't you understand? – my life is in danger. That's the truth, man, the truth, nothing but the truth!'

The workman had put up the painting now and turned to Barlach. He grinned and pointed to the knight who sat so motionless on his horse. He made a few inarticulate, gurgling sounds which Barlach did not understand right away, but which finally made sense: 'Knight *kaputt*' – it came slowly and clearly out of the twisted mouth of the man with the blue overalls – 'knight *kaputt*, knight *kaputt*!'

Only after he had left the room and clumsily slammed the door did the old man understand that he had talked to a deaf-mute.

He reached for the newspaper. It was the *Berner Bund* he unfolded.

Fortschig's face was the first thing he saw, and the caption read: 'Ulrich Friedrich Fortschig, and next to it – a cross.

Fortschig

The unhappy existence of the more infamous than famous writer Fortschig came to an end during Tuesday night in a manner as yet unclear [read Barlach, who felt as if he was being choked]. This man [continued the unctuous reporter of the *Berner Bund*] upon whom nature bestowed such beautiful talents, did not understand how to make the most of his gifts. He began with expressionistic plays which created a stir among the boulevard literati. But he was less and less capable of giving form to his creative powers [But at least they were creative powers, the old man thought, in a bitter mood]. Finally he succumbed to the unfortunate idea of publishing his own newspaper, which appeared irregularly enough in editions of about fifty typewritten copies. All those who ever saw the content of this example of the gutter press know enough. It consisted of attacks directed not only against everything that is holy to us but against well-known and generally esteemed personalities as well. He sank lower and lower, and was often seen completely drunk, staggering from one inn to the next, with his famous yellow scarf – he was nicknamed Lemon throughout the city – accompanied by a few students who celebrated him as a genius.

About his death the following is known. Since New Year Fortschig has been continually drunk. Financed by some good-natured private source, he had published his *Apfelschuss* once more. It was a particularly sad piece of work, containing an attack against an unnamed, very likely nonexistent doctor, for the sole purpose of creating a scandal. The attack, by the way, has been rejected as absurd by the members of the Medical Association. An indication of just how much of this article was pure fantasy is to be seen in the fact that Fortschig blabbered to one and all about his intention of spending ten days in Paris – while at the same time the article demanded with a great deal of pathos that the unknown doctor give himself up to the Zurich police.

However, he was not destined to reach Paris. He had already put off his journey by one day, and on Tuesday evening, gave a dinner in his shabby apartment. He had invited the musician Botzinger and the students Fiedling and Sturler. Around four o'clock in the morning, Fortschig – who was very drunk – went into the bathroom, which is situated across the corridor from his room. He left the door to his study open, to clear the air of tobacco smoke. The door of the bathroom was therefore visible to his companions, who continued to feast at the table without noticing anything unusual. When he had not returned after half an hour, they grew concerned and, since there was no answer to their calling and knocking, they rattled the locked door, but were unable to open it. Finally they called the policeman Gerber and the night-watchman Brenneisen, who broke the door down. The unfortunate writer was crumpled on the floor – dead.

Nobody knows how the tragedy occurred. However, there is no question of a crime, as the Chief of Police, Dr Lutz, informed the press in today's interview. Though the investigation pointed to some hard object having hit Fortschig from above, the physical layout makes this impossible. The light shaft into which the window opens (the bathroom is on the top floor) is narrow, and it would be impossible for a person to climb up or down there. Appropriate experiments by the police proved this beyond doubt. Furthermore, the door was locked from the inside, and the well-known tricks by which this can be feigned are out of the question. The door has no keyhole and is closed by means of a heavy bolt. No other explanation remains than that the writer took an unfortunate tumble, all the more possible since he was – as has been established – intoxicated to the point of senselessness.

As soon as the old man had read this, he dropped the newspaper. His hand clutched the blanket.

'The dwarf! The dwarf!' he screamed into the room, for all at once he had understood how Fortschig had met his death.

'Yes, the dwarf,' answered a quiet, deliberate voice from the door, which had opened without his noticing it.

'You'll admit, Commissioner, that I've availed myself of an executioner whom it will hardly be easy to find.'

In the door stood Emmenberger.

The clock

The doctor closed the door.

He was not in a white coat, as the Commissioner had first seen him, but in a dark striped suit with a white tie on a silver-grey shirt, a careful appearance, almost flashy, all the more so since he wore heavy yellow gloves, as if he was afraid to soil himself.

'So now we Berners are among ourselves,' said Emmenberger, and made a slight, more polite than ironical, obeisance toward the helpless skeleton that was Barlach. Then he took a chair from behind the curtain and sat down next to the old man's bed, turning the back of the chair toward the Commissioner so that he could press it against his chest and put his arms on it.

The old man had regained his composure.

'You had the poor devil killed,' said Barlach.

'It seems to me that if someone writes a death sentence with so much pathos, he needs his ears boxed,' the other answered in an equally matter-of-fact voice. 'Even writing has become a dangerous profession today, which can only further it.'

'What do you want from me?' asked the Commissioner.

Emmenberger laughed. 'Is it not rather up to me to ask what you want from me?'

'You know that perfectly well,' replied the Commissioner.

'Of course,' answered the doctor. 'I know that perfectly well. And so you know perfectly well what I want from you.'

Emmenberger stood up and walked to the wall, looking at it for a moment, his back toward the Commissioner. Somewhere he must have pushed a button or a lever, for the wall with the dancing men and women opened noiselessly, like a folding door. Behind it, a wide room became visible, with glass cupboards containing surgical instruments, gleaming knives and scissors in metal containers; bottles and a thin red leather mask – all spotless and all neatly arranged. In the middle of the room stood an operating table. At the same time – slowly and threateningly – a heavy metal screen lowered itself across the window panes. The room lit up. The old man noticed for the first time that neon tubes had been fitted into the ceiling, between the mirrors. Above the cupboards hung in the blue light a big, round, greenish, gleaming disk – a clock.

'You intend to operate on me without anaesthesia,' whispered the old man.

Emmenberger did not answer.

'Since I am an old weak man, I am afraid I will scream,' the Commissioner continued. 'I do not believe that you will find me a brave victim.'

This, too, Emmenberger did not answer.

'Do you see the clock?' he asked instead.

'I do,' said Barlach.

'It is now ten-thirty,' said the other man, and compared it with his wrist watch. 'I will operate on you at seven o'clock.'

'In eight-and-a-half hours.'

'In eight-and-a-half hours,' confirmed the doctor. 'But now we still have to talk about something else, I think, my friend. We cannot avoid it; then I won't disturb you any more. They say one likes to be alone with oneself for the last hours. All right. But you are creating an inordinate amount of trouble for me.' He sat down on the chair again, its back pressed against his chest.

'I thought you were used to that,' replied the old man.

For a moment Emmenberger was startled. 'I'm glad,' he said finally, shaking his head, 'that you've not lost your sense of humour. First of all, there is Fortschig. He was condemned to death and executed. My dwarf did good work. It was not easy for Tom Thumb to climb up the light shaft – after a strenuous promenade across the wet roofs, surrounded by purring cats – and to strike such a really energetic and fatal blow with my keys. I was actually curious, as I waited for the little monkey in my car next to the Jewish cemetery, whether he could do it. But such a devil, hardly three and a half feet high, works noiselessly and, most important, invisibly. Two hours later he came hopping along in the shadow of the trees. You, Commissioner, I will have to take on myself. That won't be difficult. But let us spare ourselves conversation which could only be painful for you. But what, in the name of heaven, shall we do with our mutual acquaintance, with our dear old friend Doctor Samuel Hungertobel?'

'What makes you think of him?' asked the old man guardedly.

'He brought you here.'

'I have nothing to do with him,' the Commissioner said quickly.

'He telephones twice a day and asks how his old friend Mr Kramer is coming along and wants to talk to you,' Emmenberger said. He seemed grieved.

Involuntarily, Barlach looked at the clock over the cupboards.

'Yes, it's a quarter to eleven,' said the doctor, and regarded the old man in a thoughtful, but not hostile, manner. 'Let's get back to Hungertobel.'

'He was kind to me, tried to help me get well, but he has nothing to do with us two,' the Commissioner replied stubbornly.

'Did you read the article under your picture in the *Bund*?'

Barlach thought for a moment, trying to figure out what Emmenberger was driving at with this question.

'I don't read newspapers.'

'It stated that in you a famous local personality had retired,' said Emmenberger, 'and yet Hungertobel admitted you here under the name of Blaise Kramer.'

The Commissioner revealed nothing. He had gone to Hungertobel under that name, he said. 'Even if he had seen me at one time or another, he could hardly have recognized me. My illness has changed me.'

The doctor laughed. 'Are you trying to say you became ill in order to look for me here in Sonnenstein?'

Barlach did not answer.

Emmenberger directed at the old man a look full of sorrow. 'My dear Commissioner,' he continued, with a hint of reproach in his voice, 'you really are most unco-operative in this interrogation.'

'I'm the one to interrogate you, not the other way around,' replied the Commissioner.

'You're breathing hard,' Emmenberger said with concern.

Barlach no longer answered. Only the ticking of the clock could be heard, for the first time the old man was aware of it. Now I'll hear it again and again, he thought.

'Don't you think it's time to concede your defeat?' the doctor asked in a friendly manner.

'I don't have much choice,' answered Barlach, dead-tired, putting his hands on the blanket. 'The clock, if only it weren't for the clock.'

'If only it weren't for the clock,' the doctor repeated the old man's words. 'Let's stop going around in circles. At seven o'clock I will kill you. That simplifies the case for you insofar as you can take with me an unbiased look at the case of Emmenberger versus Barlach. We're both scientists with opposing goals, chess players sitting in front of the same board. You made your move, now it's my turn. But this game has *one* peculiarity – either one of us will lose it or both. You've already lost your game. Now I'm curious to see whether I will have to lose mine.'

'You will lose it,' Barlach said softly.

Emmenberger laughed. 'That's possible. I'd be a poor chess player if I didn't consider that possibility. But shall we take a closer look? You haven't got a chance – at seven I will come with my knives, and if, by luck, you do not die then, you will die in another year of your disease. But my chances – how do they look? Very bad, I admit. After all, you're already on my trail.'

The doctor roared with laughter.

'You seem to be amused,' the old man said, with surprise. The doctor seemed stranger and stranger all the time.

'I admit it amuses me to see myself fidget in your net like a fly, especially since you are simultaneously hanging in mine. But let us proceed. Who put you on my trail?'

The old man maintained that he had found it himself.

Emmenberger shook his head. 'Let's talk about more credible things,' he said. 'One does not just sort of accidentally stumble upon my "crimes" – to use this popular expression. And particularly not if one is a Commissioner of the City Police of Berne – as if I had stolen a bicycle or performed an abortion. Let's look at my case. You, who no longer have a chance, may hear the truth – the privilege of all who are condemned.

'I was cautious, meticulous, and thorough – I did a good job in this respect – but in spite of all caution there are, of course, certain circumstances that speak against me. A crime without some sort of circumstantial evidence is impossible in this world of chance. Let's enumerate. Where could Commissioner Hans Barlach enter in? There is, first of all, the picture in *Life*. I don't know who had the foolhardiness to take it in those days, but it is bad enough that it exists.

However, we ought not to exaggerate. Millions have seen this famous picture, among them surely many who know me. And yet nobody has recognized me so far – the picture shows too little of my face. Who, then, could recognize me? Is it somebody who saw me in Stutthof and knows me here? An unlikely possibility. I have complete control over the people I took with me from there. But, as with any possibility, this one cannot be rejected outright. Or is it somebody who remembers me from my life in Switzerland before nineteen thirty-two? During that time I had a certain experience as a young student in a mountain hut – oh, I remember it very well – it happened under a red evening sky. Hungertobel was one of the five who were present then. It can therefore be assumed that Hungertobel was the one who recognized me.'

'Nonsense,' retorted the old man firmly. That was an unjustified conclusion, he went on, an empty speculation, nothing else. He sensed that his friend was threatened, yes, very much endangered, if he did not succeed in diverting all suspicion from him, though he could not quite imagine what this danger could be.

Emmenberger continued, his chin resting on his folded arms. 'Let's not condemn poor old Doctor Hungertobel to death too fast. Instead, let's examine other possible circumstantial evidence against me; we shall try to get him off the hook. The affair with Nehle, for example. That too you found out, Commissioner. My congratulations! Doctor Marlok told me. Shall we admit it? I myself operated on Nehle to put the scar on his right eyebrow and the scald mark on his left forearm in order to make us identical, to make one out of two. I sent him to Chile under my name. And then I forced him, in a desolate, decrepit hotel room in Hamburg, to swallow a capsule of cyanide when he, the naïve nature boy who never did learn Latin and Greek, this amazing talent in the limitless field of medicine, returned – according to our agreement. *C'est ça*, as my beautiful mistress would say. Nehle was a gentleman. He submitted to his fate – a few determined blows on my part are hardly worth mentioning – and simulated the nicest suicide one could imagine. Let's not talk any more of this scene amidst whores and sailors, in the grey morning fog of a half-charred and rotten city, with the melancholy sound of lost ships in the background. This was a risky business which could still play extremely poor jokes on me. For what did I know about this talented dilettante's doings in Santiago, about the friendships he had there and who may suddenly appear here in Zurich to visit Nehle? But we want to stick to the facts.

'What evidence is there against me in the event somebody came upon this trail? There is, first of all, Nehle's ambitious idea of writing medical articles for *Lancet* and the *Swiss Medical Weekly*. They could prove to be fatal, provided somebody had the idea of undertaking stylistic comparisons with my own earlier articles. Nehle really wrote a much too uninhibited Berliner argot. But in order to do that, somebody would have to read the articles, which again points to a doctor. As you can see, things look grim for our friend. Of course, he is unsuspecting. We shall note that down in his favour. But when a criminologist allies with him – as I'm forced to assume – I can no longer give any guarantees for the old boy.'

'I'm here on order of the police,' the Commissioner stated calmly. 'The German police have become suspicious of you and have asked the Berner police to investigate your case. You'll not operate on me tomorrow, for my death would convict you. Hungertobel, too, you will leave alone.'

'Two after eleven,' said the doctor.

'I can see,' answered Barlach.

'The police – the police,' continued Emmenberger, and looked at the sick man thoughtfully. 'It is, of course, possible that even the police might find what is behind my life. However, in this case it seems to me to be most improbable because it would be by far the most favourable solution for you. The German police order the City Police of Berne to look for a criminal in Zurich! No, that does not seem logical to me. Maybe I would believe it if you were not sick, if it were not a matter of life and death with you. Your operation and your illness are not simulated, that I am in a position to decide as a doctor. Nor is your retirement from your office which the papers report. After all, what kind of a person are you? Most of all, a tough and stubborn old man, who dislikes giving up and dislikes stepping down, too. The possibility exists that you followed the call to arms privately, without any support, without the police – armed with your stretcher, so to speak, pursuing a vague suspicion you gained in a talk with Hungertobel, without any real proof. Maybe you were even too proud to tell anybody else besides Hungertobel your secret. Even he seems to be most uncertain of his case. All that mattered to you was to prove that even as a sick man you understood more than those who retired you. I believe all this to be more probable than the possibility that the police will push a desperately sick man into such an unholy undertaking – especially since the police up to this hour have not hit the right trail in Fortschig's case, which they should have if they suspected me already. You were alone and you are proceeding against me alone, Commissioner. Even that vagabond writer was without any real notion of the facts, I believe.'

'Why did you kill him?' cried the old man.

'Out of caution,' the doctor replied indifferently. 'Ten after eleven. Time flies, my friend, time flies. Out of caution I will have to kill Hungertobel, too.'

'You want to kill him?' screamed the Commissioner, and tried to sit up.

'Lie down,' Emmenberger ordered so firmly that the sick man obeyed. 'Today is Thursday,' he said. 'All we doctors take a free afternoon on Thursday, don't we? So I decided to do Hungertobel and you and me a favour and asked him to visit us. He will come from Berne by car.'

'What will happen?'

'Tom Thumb will sit in the back of his car,' replied Emmenberger.

'The dwarf,' moaned the Commissioner.

'The dwarf.' The doctor nodded. 'The dwarf again. A useful tool I brought home with me from Stutthof. It used to get between my feet, this silly thing, when I operated. According to Herr Heinrich Himmler's federal laws I should have killed the little fellow as "unworthy to live" – as if there were ever an Aryan giant worthier to live. I've always loved curiosities, and a deformed human being makes a most dependable tool. Because the little monkey sensed that he owed me his life, he let himself be trained most usefully.'

The clock showed eleven-fourteen.

The Commissioner was so tired that his eyes closed for minutes at a time. And always when he opened them, he saw the clock, always the big round clock. He understood now that there was no escape for him. Emmenberger has seen through him. He was lost, and Hungertobel, too, was lost.

'You are a nihilist,' he said softly, almost in a whisper, into the quiet room in which only the clock ticked. All the time.

'You're trying to say that I believe in nothing?' Emmenberger asked, and his voice betrayed no bitterness.

'I can't imagine that my words could have any other meaning,' answered the old man in his bed, his hands helplessly on the blanket.

'In what do *you* believe, Commissioner?' asked the doctor. He did not move, but looked at the old man, curiously and tensely.

Barlach was silent.

In the background ticked the clock, without pause, the clock, steady, with merciless hands, which pushed toward their goals.

'You are silent,' Emmenberger said, and his voice had now lost the elegant, playful quality, and sounded clear and light. 'You are silent. People of our time do not like to answer the question, "What do you believe?" It's become bad taste to pose that question. One doesn't like to use big words, people say modestly. And least of all to give a definite answer – as for instance: I believe in God the Father, God the Son, and God the Holy Ghost, as the Christians once answered, proud that they could answer. One likes to be silent today when one is asked – like a girl to whom an embarrassing question has been put. Of course, one doesn't quite know either in what one actually does believe. It's by no means nothing. Good God no. One believes in something – even though it's quite vague, as if an uncertain fog hung over it all. One believes in something like humanity, Christianity, tolerance, justice, socialism, and love for one's neighbours – things that sound a little bit empty. People admit it, too, but they also think the words don't matter. What matters is to live decently and according to one's best conscience. And that they all try to do – partly by struggling for it, partly by just drifting. Everything we do, deeds and misdeeds, happens by chance. Good and evil fall into our lap like lottery tickets. By chance you become good and by chance you become evil. But they're always ready with the big word *nihilist*. It's thrown – with much pathos and even more conviction – at those whom they fear.

'I know them, these people; they're convinced it's their right to maintain one plus one makes three, four, or ninety-nine, and that it would be unjust to demand of them the answer that one plus one is two. Anything clear appears narrow-minded to them, for clarity demands character. They have no notion that a determined Communist – to use a somewhat unusual example, for most Communists are Communists like most Christians are Christians, out of a misunderstanding – they have no notion, I say, that such a man who believes with his whole soul in the necessity of revolution and in the fact that only this road – though it may leave in its wake millions of corpses –

will ultimately lead to salvation, to a better world, is much less of a nihilist than they. Than some Mr Miller or Mr Hoffman – who neither believes in a God nor disbelieves in one, but only in his right to make money – a belief which he is too cowardly to postulate as his credo. So they live like worms, with a foggy perception of something that is good and right and true – as if these things could exist in such a sticky mess.'

'I had no idea that a hangman is capable of such a flood of words,' said Barlach. 'I had thought your kind to be rather tight-lipped.'

'Bravo!' Emmenberger laughed. 'You seem to be regaining your courage. Bravo! I need courageous people for my experiments in my laboratory. And it's a pity that my object lessons always end with the death of the pupil. All right, let's see what kind of a belief I have and put it on a pair of scales, and then let's see which of us has the greater faith, when we put yours on the other side. I, the nihilist – since you call me that – or you, the Christian. You came to me in the name of humanity or whatever other ideals, in order to destroy me. I think you can hardly reject my curiosity.'

'I understand,' answered the Commissioner. He tried to keep down the fear that rose in him – more and more threatening, more and more gigantic – with each movement of the hands of the clock. 'Now you want to grind out your credo. Strange that even mass murderers have one.'

'It is after eleven o'clock,' replied Emmenberger.

'How kind of you to remind me,' groaned the old man, shaking with rage and helplessness.

'Man – what is man?' The doctor laughed. 'I'm not ashamed to have a credo, I'm not silent as you were silent. Like the Christians, who believe in three things which are only one thing – the Trinity – I believe in two things which are one and the same, namely that something is and that I am. I believe in matter, which is *simultaneously* energy and mass, an incomprehensible universe and a globe, around which we can walk and which we can feel is like a child's ball, on which we live and drift through the adventurous emptiness of space. I believe in matter (how shabby and empty it is by comparison to say, "I believe in a god") – matter that is seizable as animal, as plant, or as coal, and not seizable, hardly calculable, as atom. It needs no God or whatever else is invented for it. Its only incomprehensible mystery is its being. And I believe that I am, a particle of this matter, atom, energy, mass, molecule – as you are – and that my existence gives me the right to do what I want. As a particle, I constitute only a moment, a mere incident, just as life in this gigantic world is only one of matter's immeasurable possibilities, as much chance as I am – if the earth were a little closer to the sun, there would be no life – and my purpose consists of *only* being a moment. Oh, the tremendous night when I understood this! Nothing is holy but matter: man, animal, plant, the moon, the Milky Way, whatever I see, are accidental groupings, nonessentials, as the form of the waves of the water are something nonessential. It is indifferent whether things are or are not. They are interchangeable. If they are not, something else exists. When life on this planet dies out, it will appear somewhere in the universe on another planet. It is ridiculous to attribute permanence to man, for it will always be only the illusion of permanence. It is ridiculous to invent systems of power in order to vegetate for a few years as the head of some state or some church. It is senseless to strive for the welfare of man in a world structured like a lottery – as if it would make sense to have each ticket win a penny, as if there existed another yearning but this one – *for once* to be the singular, sole, unjust man who wins the whole lottery. It is nonsense to believe in matter and *at the same time* in humanism. One can only believe in matter and the I. There is no justice. How could matter be just? There is only freedom, which cannot be earned – for then there would have to be a justice; which cannot be given – for who could give it? – which can only be taken. Freedom is the courage to commit crime, for freedom itself is a crime.'

'I understand,' cried the Commissioner, shaking, a dying animal, lying on his white sheet as if on the edge of an endless, indifferent road. 'You believe in nothing but the right to torture man.'

'Bravo!' answered the doctor, and clapped his hands. 'Bravo! I call him a good pupil who dares to deduce the law under which I live. Bravo, bravo!' (And again he clapped his hands.) 'I dared to be myself and nothing, nothing else. I devoted myself to that which made me free – murder and torture. For when I kill another human being – and I will do it again at seven – when I put myself outside all the order of this world, erected by our weakness – I become free, I become nothing but a moment. But what a moment! In intensity as gigantic, as powerful, as unjustified as matter. And the screams and the pain which flood toward me from glassy eyes and open mouths, the convulsing, impotent white flesh under my knife, reflect my triumph and my freedom and nothing else.'

He fell silent. Slowly he rose and sat down on the operating table.

Above him the clock showed three minutes to twelve, two minutes to twelve, twelve.

'Seven hours,' Barlach whispered, almost inaudibly, from the bed.

'Now show me your belief,' said Emmenberger. His voice was calm again and without emotion, no longer passionate and hard, as it had been toward the end of his long speech.

Barlach answered nothing.

'You are silent,' said the doctor. 'Again and again you are silent.'

The sick man gave no answer.

'You are silent and silent,' stated the doctor, and put both hands on the operating table. 'Unconditionally I put everything on one card. I was powerful because I was never afraid, because it made no difference to me whether I was discovered or not. I am even now prepared to gamble. I shall concede my defeat if you, Commissioner, can prove to me that you have a faith as great, as unconditional as mine.'

The old man was silent.

'Say something,' Emmenberger continued after a pause while he looked tensely and greedily at the sick man. 'Give me an answer. You're a Christian. You were baptized. Say, "I believe with a certainty, with a power that overshadows the belief of a shameless murderer in matter, like a sun of light overshadows a pitiful winter moon." Or say at least, "I believe with a power that equals his, in Christ, who is God's Son".'

The clock ticked in the background.

'Maybe this belief is too difficult,' said Emmenberger, for still Barlach was silent, and he stepped to the old man's bed. 'Maybe you have an easier, more popular belief. Say, "I believe in justice and in the humanity this justice is to serve. For its sake, and *only* for its sake have I, old and sick, taken it upon me to come here – without giving a thought to fame and triumph of my person over others." Say it, it is an easy, decent belief, which we can still demand of today's mankind, say it and you are free. I will be satisfied with your belief, and when you say it, I will think that you have a belief as great as mine.'

The old man was silent.

'Maybe you don't believe that I will let you go?' asked Emmenberger.

No answer.

'Say it anyway,' the doctor ordered the old man. 'Confess your belief even if you do not trust my words. Maybe you can only be saved if you have a belief. Maybe now is your *last chance*, the chance not only to save yourself but Hungertobel as well. There is still time to phone him. You have found me and I, you. Someday my game will be over, somewhere the accounts won't balance. Why should I not be the one to lose? I can kill you – I can let you go, which means my death. I have reached a point from which I can deal with myself as with a strange person. I destroy myself – I save myself.'

He stopped and looked at the Commissioner. 'It does not matter what I do,' he said, 'a more powerful position cannot be attained. To conquer this Point of Archimedes is the highest that man can win for himself. It is his only sense in the nonsense of this world, in the mystery of this dead matter, which again and again creates out of itself life and death, like a carrion. But I bind – that is my malice – your escape to a silly joke, a childishly simple condition, that you can show me a faith as great as mine. Show it! The belief in goodness ought to be as strong in man as the belief in evil! Show it! Nothing will amuse me more than to watch my own ride to hell.'

Only the clock could be heard.

'Then say it for the cause,' Emmenberger continued after some while, 'for the belief in God's Son, the belief in justice.'

The clock, nothing but the clock.

'Your faith!' screamed the doctor. 'Show me your faith!'

The old man was lying there, his hands clutching the blankets.

'Your faith! Your faith!' Emmenberger's voice was like bronze, like trumpet blasts, breaking through an endless grey sky.

The old man was silent.

Then Emmenberger's face – which had been greedy for an answer – became cold and relaxed. Only the scar above the right eye was reddened. It was as if disgust shook him when he turned away from the sick man, tired and indifferent. He walked through the door, which closed softly, so that the Commissioner was enveloped by the gleaming blue of the room, in which only the round disk of the clock continued to tick as if it were the old man's heart.

A nursery rhyme

And so Barlach lay there and waited for death. Time passed, the hands of the clock turned round, covered each other, separated again. Then it was twelve-thirty, one, five after one, twenty to two, two o'clock, ten after two, two-thirty. The room seemed suspended, motionless, dead space in the shadowless blue light, the cupboards full of strange instruments behind the glass which vaguely reflected Barlach's face and hands. Everything was there, the white operating table, Dürer's painting with the mighty, rigid horse, the metal plate across the window, the empty chair with its back toward the old man – nothing alive except the mechanical *tick-tock* of the clock. Now it was three o'clock, then four. No noise, no moans, no talk, no screams, no steps, penetrated to the old man, who lay there on a metal bed, who did not move, whose body hardly rose and fell. There was no longer an outside world, no earth that revolved, no sun, and no city. There was nothing but a greenish round disk with hands that moved, overtook each other, covered each other, tore away from each other. It was four-thirty, twenty-five to five, thirteen to five, five, one after five, two after five, three after five, four after five, six after five. Barlach had painfully managed to sit up. He rang the bell once, twice, a few times. He waited. Maybe he could yet talk to Nurse Clari. Maybe an accident could save him. Five-thirty.

Carefully he twisted his body around. Then he fell. For a long time he stayed in front of the bed on a red carpet, and above him, some-where above the glass cupboards, the clock ticked, the hands pushed on – thirteen to six, twelve to six, eleven to six. Then he crawled slowly toward the door, reached it, tried to get up, to clutch the knob, fell back, stayed on the floor, tried it once more, a third time, a fifth time. In vain. He scratched on the door, for he was too weak to hammer at it with his fists. Like a rat, he thought. Then he stayed motionless again, crawled back into the room, looked at the clock. Ten after six. 'Another fifty minutes,' he said, loud and clear in the silence, so that it frightened him. 'Fifty minutes.'

He wanted to crawl back into bed, but he felt that he no longer had the power. So he stayed on the floor, in front of the operating table, and waited. Around him were the room, the cupboards, the knives, the bed, the clock – again and again the clock, a burned sun in a blue rotting universe, a ticking idol, a face without a mouth, or eyes, or nose – but with two wrinkles that pulled together became one – twenty-five to seven, twenty-two to seven – that did not seem to separate any more, that separated now after all – twenty-one to seven, twenty to seven, nineteen to seven. Time passed, marched on, in the impartial rhythm of the clock. Ten to seven.

Barlach sat up, leaned against the operating table – an old sick man, alone and helpless. He grew calm. Behind him was the clock and in front of him the door. He stared at it, resigned and humble, this rectangle through which *he* must come, *he* who would kill him, slowly and methodically like a clock, skilfully cutting with the gleaming knives. And so he sat. Now he himself had become time, he was the ticking – he needed no longer to look at the clock, now he knew that he only had to wait for minutes, for three, for two – now he counted the seconds, which were one with the beating of his heart, a hundred yet, sixty yet, thirty yet. So he counted, babbling with white bloodless lips; so he stared, a living clock, at the door, which opened now, at seven, all at once, offering him the vision of a black hell, an opened gorge. In its middle he sensed vaguely a gigantic dark figure, but it was not Emmenberger, as the old man believed. For out of the gaping abyss roared sarcastically and hoarsely an old children's tune.

Little Hans
Went alone
Into the big black forest!

sang a screechy voice. Filling the doorframe, mighty and powerful, in a black caftan hanging, torn, from huge limbs, stood the Jew Gulliver.

'Greetings, Commissar,' said the giant, and closed the door. 'So here I find you again, you sad knight *sans peur et sans reproche*, who went out to slay the evil dragon with the force of his spirit, sitting in front of a trestle similar to the one on to which I was once chained in the pretty village of Stutthof near Danzig.' And he lifted the old man so that he rested against his chest like a child, and put him to bed.

'Greetings.' He laughed when the Commissioner still could not find words, but rested there, pale as death; then he pulled a bottle and two glasses out of the tatters of his caftan.

'I don't have vodka any more,' said the Jew as he filled the glasses and sat down on the bed. 'But in a run-down farmhouse somewhere in the Emmenvalley, a hole full of darkness and snow, I stole a few dusty bottles of this valiant potato brandy. It will do. One has to be lenient with a dead man, right, Commissar? When a corpse like myself – a firewater corpse, so to speak – fetches its tribute from the living in night and fog before crawling back into its cellar, it is perfectly in order. Here, Commissar, drink.'

He put the glass to Barlach's lips, and the old man drank. It felt good, even though he thought it was hardly the proper medicine.

'Gulliver,' he whispered, and groped for the other's hand. 'How could you know that I was in this cursed mousetrap?'

The giant laughed. 'Christian,' he answered, and the hard eyes in his scar-covered naked skull gleamed (he had drunk a few glasses meanwhile), 'why else did you call me into the Salem? I knew right away that you had a suspicion, that maybe the inestimable possibility existed of finding this Nehle still among the living. I did not believe for a moment it was only psychological interest which made you ask after Nehle, as you maintained in that night full of vodka. Should I have let you go down the road to ruin alone? Today we no longer can fight evil alone, like the knights used to once upon a time with some dragon or other. The times are past where it is enough to be a little bit sharp in order to catch the criminals we are dealing with. You fool of a detective! Time itself has led you *ad absurdum*. From then on I never let you out of my sight again, and last night I appeared to the good Doctor Hungertobel in person. I really had to work to get him out of his fainting spell, he was so afraid. But then I knew what I wanted to know, and now I am here to get things back into their old order. For you the mice of Berne, for me the rats of Stutthof. That is the division of the world.'

'How did you get here?' Barlach asked in a whisper.

The giant's face broke into a grin. 'Not hidden under some seat of the Swiss Railroads, as you are thinking,' he replied, 'but in Hungertobel's car.'

'He's alive?' asked the old man, who had finally regained his composure and stared breathlessly at the Jew.

'He'll take you back to the old familiar Salem in a few minutes,' said the Jew, and drank the potato schnapps in huge gulps. 'He's waiting outside in the car.'

'The dwarf,' Barlach screamed, pale as death, at his sudden recognition that the Jew could know nothing of this danger. 'The dwarf! He will kill him!'

'Yes, the dwarf.' The giant laughed, still drinking, frightening in his wild raggedness, and he whistled through the fingers of his right hand, shrill and piercing, as one whistles a dog. Then the metal plate across the window was pushed up. Like a monkey a little black shadow somersaulted into the room, uttering unintelligible gurgling sounds, glided fast as lightning toward Gulliver, and jumped up on his lap, pressing the ugly, old dwarfed face against the Jew's torn chest and clutching with his little crippled arms Gulliver's mighty head.

'There you are, my monkey, my little animal, my little monster,' the Jew fondled the dwarf with a singing voice. 'My poor Minotaur, my tortured little puppy, you who so often whined yourself to sleep in my arms, you only companion of my poor soul during those blood-filled nights in Stutthof. You my son, my mandrake root. My crippled Argos, on his endless wanderings Odysseus has come back to you. Oh, I thought that you were the one who sent the poor drunk Fortschig into another life, that you glided into his light shaft. Did not the evil witchmaster Nehle or Emmenberger or whatever his name train you for such feats in our torture camp? Here, bite into my finger, my puppy. And as I am in the car, sitting next to Hungertobel, I hear a happy whining behind me, like that of a mangy cat. It was my poor little friend, Commissar, whom my fist pulled out from under the seat. What do we want to do with this little animal now, this animal that is nevertheless a human being, this little fellow that was degraded to an animal, this little murderer who alone of us all is innocent and who reflects in his sad brown eyes the misery of all living creatures?'

The old man had sat up in his bed and looked at the ghostlike pair, at this tortured Jew and at the dwarf, whom the giant let dance on his knees like a child.

'And Emmenberger?' he asked. 'What about Emmenberger?' for a moment, the giant's face became like a grey primeval stone, into which the scars had been hammered as with a chisel. He flung the empty bottle with a swing of his huge arms toward the cupboards, splintering their glass – so that the dwarf, squealing like a frightened rat, hid with one jump under the operating table.

'Why do you ask, Commissar?' hissed the Jew, but at once he controlled himself – only the terrible slits of his eyes gleamed dangerously – and slowly he pulled a second bottle from his caftan and began to drink again in wild gulps. 'It makes one thirsty to live in a hell. Love your enemies as thyself, someone said on the stony hill of Golgotha, and had himself nailed to the cross, hanging on its rotten wood, a piece of cloth flapping around his hips. Pray for Emmenberger's poor soul, Christian, Jehovah likes only the daring prayers. Pray! He is no longer – he after whom you ask. My trade is bloody, Commissar, I must not think of theological studies when I pursue my work. I was just according to the laws of Moses, just according to my God, Commissar. I have killed him, as Nehle was killed once in some damp hotel room, and the police will just as infallibly conclude a suicide now as they concluded then. What shall I tell you? My hand led his; clutched in my arms, he pressed the fatal capsule between his teeth. Ahasuerus's mouth is taciturn and his bloodless lips will remain closed. What went on between us, between the Jew and his torturer, and how the roles had to be reversed according to the law of justice, how I became the torturer and he the victim shall – aside from us two – be known only to God, who allowed it all to happen. We must bid farewell, Commissar.'

The giant rose.

'What will happen now?' whispered Barlach.

'Nothing will happen,' answered the Jew. He grabbed the old man by the shoulders and jerked him forward, so that their faces were close together, one's eyes reflecting the other's. 'Nothing will happen, nothing,' whispered the giant once more. 'Nobody – except you and Hungertobel – knows that I was here; inaudibly I glided, a shadow, through the corridors, to Emmenberger, to you – nobody knows that I exist, only the poor devils that I save, a handful of Jews, a handful of Christians. Let the world bury Emmenberger and let the newspapers write the eulogistic obituaries with which they will commemorate this dead man. The Nazis wanted Stutthof, the millionaires, this clinic. Others will want other things. We as individuals cannot save this world, that would be so hopeless a task as that of poor Sisyphus. It was not given into our hands, and not into those of a mighty person or a people or of the devil – even though he is the most powerful of us all – but into God's hands, who makes His decisions alone. We can help only in single instances, not in the whole – the limitation of the poor Jew Gulliver, the limitation of all people. Therefore, we ought not to try to save the world but to get through it – the only true adventure that remains for us at this late hour.' And carefully, like a father with a child, the giant lowered the old man into his bed.

'Come on, my monkey,' Gulliver called, and whistled. With one mighty jump, squealing and babbling, the dwarf shot up and settled on the Jew's left shoulder.

'That's right, my little murderer,' the giant praised him. 'We two will stay together. After all, we are both cast out of human company – you by nature and I because I belong to the dead. Farewell, Commissar, we are off to a nocturnal visit in the wide Russian plain, off to dare a new sinister descent into the catacombs of this world, into the lost holes of those who are persecuted by the mighty ones.'

Once again the Jew waved to the old man, then he reached with both hands into the bars, bent them apart, and lowered himself out of the window.

'Farewell, Commissar.' He laughed once more with his strangely singing voice. Only his shoulders and the huge naked head were visible, against his left cheek the dwarf's old face, while the almost full moon appeared on the other side of his majestic head, so that it seemed as if the Jew carried on his shoulders the whole universe, earth and humanity. 'Farewell, my knight *sans peur et sans reproche*, my Barlach,' he said. 'Gulliver moves on to the giants and dwarfs, to other countries, other worlds, evermore, always. Farewell, Commissar, farewell,' and with the last farewell, he had disappeared.

The old man closed his eyes. A feeling of peace surged through him. Especially since he knew that Hungertobel was now standing in the softly opening door – to bring him back to Berne.

Once a Greek ...

It had been raining all day, all night, for weeks. The streets, the avenues, the boulevards, gleamed with wetness. Rivulets, brooks, little streams, flowed along the curbs. Automobiles splashed through water; people walked under umbrellas, shrouded in raincoats, their shoes soggy, their socks permanently damp. The atlantes, putti, and caryatids that supported the balconies of mansions and hotels, the sculptures that clung to the façades, trickled and dripped; thin streams of water ran down them, dissolving the bird droppings; and the pigeons sought shelter under the Greek gables of the Chamber of Deputies and between the legs and breasts of patriotic statuary. It was a miserable January. Then came the fog, and it too went on for days and weeks. It was accompanied by an epidemic of grippe, not especially dangerous for respectable people of substance, but it did carry off a few old uncles and aunts, to the delight of their heirs, as well as several venerable statesmen. Otherwise the only victims were the clochards who slept under the bridges by the river. And the fogs were succeeded by more rain. And still more.

His name was Arnolph Archilochos, and Madame Bieler behind her counter would say: 'The poor boy. Such an impossible name. Auguste, bring him another glass of milk.' And on Sundays she said: 'Bring him another Perrier.'

She addressed her husband, thin as a rail, winner of a legendary Tour de Suisse and runner-up in an even more legendary Tour de France, who served his customers in his cyclist's getup, a yellow jersey. (His café was the centre for a small group of cycling fans.) But Auguste did not agree. 'Georgette,' he would say in the morning when he got up, or in bed, or behind the stove after everyone had left and he could warm his thin, hairy legs, 'I don't understand your fondness for Monsieur Archilochos. He's not a man, he's all bottled up. A fellow can't go on drinking nothing but milk and mineral water all his life!'

'That's all you drank once upon a time,' Georgette replied in her deep voice, placing her arms akimbo, or, if she were in bed, folding them over her mountainous bosom.

'I grant it,' Auguste Bieler admitted after long reflection, during which he vigorously massaged his legs. 'But that was when I was training for the Tour de Suisse, and I won it in spite of those high passes, and nearly won the Tour de France too. When it's something like that, abstinence has some point to it. But for Monsieur Archilochos? Why, he's never even slept with a woman. And the man is forty-five.'

This matter also bothered Madame Bieler, and she always became embarrassed when Auguste began to speak of it, whether in bed or fully clothed in his cyclist's getup. As a matter of fact, there was no denying that Monsieur Arnolph, as she called Archilochos, had certain principles. For example, he did not smoke either. Swearing was even more out of character. Moreover, Georgette could not even imagine him in a nightshirt, let alone naked – so correct was his manner, so completely dressed the impression he made, although he also seemed very poor.

His world was fixed, punctual, ethical, hierarchic. At the top, at the summit of his world order, his ethical cosmos, the President of the country sat enthroned.

'Believe me, Madame Bieler,' Archilochos would say, gazing reverently at the portrait of the President in its carved frame, which hung above the orderly array of brandy and liqueur bottles behind the counter, 'believe me, our President is a sober man, a philosopher, almost a saint. He does not smoke, does not drink, has been a widower for thirty years, has no children. You can read it in the newspapers.'

Madame Bieler did not dare to take issue with this directly. She, too, like everyone in the country, had some respect for the President. He was, after all, the only fixed point in the passing parade of governments. On the other hand, such a paragon made her nervous. She preferred not to believe it.

'You say it's in the newspapers,' Georgette therefore replied hesitantly. 'All right. But who knows what the real truth is? Everyone says the newspapers are full of lies.'

That was a common fallacy, Archilochos replied; at bottom the world was ethical. Solemnly, deliberately, he sipped his Perrier as if it were champagne, and added: 'Auguste also believes the newspapers.'

'No,' Georgette said. 'I know better. Auguste doesn't believe a word he reads in the newspapers.'

'Why, doesn't he believe the scores on the sports pages?'

Madame Bieler could think of no reply to that.

'Virtue is something apparent,' Archilochos continued, cleaning his rimless, slightly crooked glasses. 'It shines in this face, as it shines in the face of my Bishop.'

Whereupon he turned towards the portrait that hung over the door.

'The Bishop is a little too fat,' Madame Bieler protested. 'He can't be all that virtuous.'

Archilochos' faith was unshakable.

'That is his nature,' he replied. 'If he did not live virtuously, philosophically, he would be even fatter. Now look at Fahrcks, on the other hand. How excitable, how intemperate, how arrogant. Sinful in every respect. And conceited.'

He jerked his thumb over his right shoulder at the portrait of the notorious revolutionary.

Madame Bieler stuck to her guns. 'You certainly can't call him conceited,' she declared. 'Not with that snout and that mop of hair. And with his love of the masses.'

'That is only a particular kind of conceit,' Arnolph maintained. 'I can't see why you have that demagogue's picture hanging here. Why, he's just come out of jail.'

'Oh, you can never tell,' Madame Bieler replied, downing a whole glass of Campari. 'You can never tell. You have to be careful in politics.'

The Bishop – let us turn back to him; the portrait of Fahrcks hung on the opposite wall – the Bishop was Number Two in Monsieur Archilochos' hierarchic world. He was not a Catholic bishop, although Madame Bieler was a good Catholic after her fashion, who went to church – when she went – in order to weep fervently (but she wept just as fervently at the movies). Nor was he a Protestant bishop. Auguste Bieler, an immigrant from German Switzerland, 'the fastest thing on two wheels Switzerland has produced' (*Sports*, 9/9/29), could not possibly recognize any but a Zwinglian bishop (though also after his own fashion; he had no idea that he was a Zwinglian). No, the Bishop was head of the Old New Presbyterians of the Penultimate Christians, a somewhat peculiar and amorphous sect imported from America. He was hanging over the door only because Archilochos had entered the bar, portrait under his arm, and introduced himself to Georgette.

That had been nine months ago. In May. When there were great splashes of sunshine on the street outside, slanting rays of sunlight inside, Auguste's yellow jersey and his sad cyclist's legs, under a hazy shimmer of hair, shining like molten gold.

'Madame,' Archilochos had said timidly, 'I am here because I notice the portrait of our President in your restaurant. Hanging over the counter, in a prominent place. As a patriot, I am reassured. I am seeking a place in which to take my meals. A home. But I must always have the same table, preferably in a corner. I am alone, a bookkeeper, live righteously, and am a strict teetotaller. I do not smoke either. Bad language is also against my principles.'

Then they had settled on a price.

'Madame,' he had then said, handing her the portrait and looking at her woefully through his small, smudged glasses, 'may I ask you to hang this Bishop of the Old New Presbyterians of the Penultimate Christians. Preferably next to the President. I can no longer eat in a room where he is not present. That is why I have just left the Salvation Army restaurant, where I used to have my meals. I revere my Bishop. He is an example to us all, an absolutely sober, Christian person.'

And so Georgette hung up the picture of the Bishop of the Penultimate Christians, though only over the door, where he remained mum and content, a man of honour, although sometimes denied twice and thrice by Auguste. For if people happened to ask who the old gent was, Auguste used to answer: 'A patron of cycling.'

Three weeks later Archilochos appeared with another picture. This time it was a photo, autographed, of Petit-Paysan, owner of the Petit-Paysan Engineering Works. It would give him great pleasure, Archilochos said, if Madame Georgette would also hang this picture of Petit-Paysan. Perhaps in place of Fahrcks. It seemed that the owner of the Engineering Works occupied the third place in Archilochos' ethical cosmos.

Madame Georgette bridled.

'Petit-Paysan manufactures machine guns,' she said.

'What of it?'

'Tanks.'

'What of it?'

'Atomic cannon.'

'You forget the Petit-Paysan razor and the Petit-Paysan obstetrical forceps, Madame Bieler. Purely humanitarian products.'

'Monsieur Archilochos,' Georgette said solemnly, 'I warn you against having anything more to do with Petit-Paysan.'

'He is my employer,' Arnolph replied.

Georgette laughed. 'Then it doesn't do you a mite of good,' she said, 'to drink milk and mineral water, do without meat' (Archilochos was a vegetarian), 'and keep away from women. Petit-Paysan supplies the army, and if the army builds up its armaments, there will be war. It has always been that way.'

Archilochos did not agree.

'Not in our country!' he cried. 'Not with our President!'

'Oh, him!'

Evidently she did not know about Petit-Paysan's Shelter for Expectant Mothers, Archilochos continued unabashed, and his Home for Disabled Workmen. Petit-Paysan was a highly ethical, truly Christian man.

But Madame Bieler refused to be swayed. The result was that his first two heroes shared a place on the wall with the man who stood lowest in Arnolph's ethical cosmos: the negative principle, Fahrcks, the Communist, who had instigated the *coup d'état* in San Salvador and the revolution in Borneo. Pale, shy, rather plump, Archilochos sat in his corner among the cycling fans with the portraits of only the first two of his exemplars on the wall. For he hadn't been able to persuade Georgette to hang Number Four in his cosmos either.

She might want to hang the picture underneath Fahrcks's, he had said, handing her a reproduction – a cheap one, incidentally.

'What artist painted that?' Georgette had asked, staring in bafflement at the triangular rectangles and the twisted circles in the reproduction.

'Passap.'

It appeared that Monsieur Arnolph worshipped the world-famous painter. But what the picture was supposed to represent remained a mystery to Georgette.

'The right way of life,' Archilochos told her.

'But it says *Chaos* down there,' Georgette exclaimed, pointing to the lower right-hand corner of the painting.

Archilochos shook his head. 'Great artists create unconsciously,' he said. 'I simply know that this picture represents the right way of life.'

But Georgette was adamant. Archilochos was so offended that he did not turn up for three days. Then he began coming for his meals again, and in time Madame Bieler found out about the life of Monsieur Arnolph, insofar as it could be called a life, for it was all so punctual, well ordered, and screwy. Thus, for example, there was room in Archilochos' cosmos for Numbers Five to Eight.

Number Five was Bob Forster-Monroe, the American Ambassador. Though not an Old New Presbyterian of the Penultimate Christians, he was an Old Presbyterian of the Penultimate Christians – a painful but not hopeless difference which Archilochos, who was quite broad-minded where religion was concerned, could discuss for hours at a time. (Aside from other churches, the only sect he resolutely rejected was the New Presbyterians of the Penultimate Christians.)

Number Six in the cosmos was Maître Dutour.

Number Seven was Hercule Wagner, Rector magnificus of the University.

Dutour had been the defence attorney for a sex murderer, eventually sentenced to be guillotined, who had been a curate of the Old New Presbyterians. This curate had sinned only in the flesh; his soul remained above the battle, uncontaminated, redeemed. The Rector magnificus, on the other hand, had visited the students' dormitory of the Penultimate Christians and chatted five minutes with Number Two in the cosmos (the Bishop).

Number Eight was Bibi Archilochos, Arnolph's brother – a good man, Arnolph maintained; he was unemployed, which surprised Georgette, for thanks to Petit-Paysan the country was booming.

Archilochos lived in a garret quite close to Chez Auguste, as the cycling star's little restaurant was called. It took him more than an hour to reach his place of work in the white twenty-storey, Corbusier-designed administrative building of the Petit-Paysan Engineering Works, Inc. As for the garret: it was up five flights of stairs, a mal-odorous hallway, small, slanting ceiling, wallpaper of indeterminate design, a chair, a table, a bed, a Bible. In a curtained-off nook hung his Sunday suit. On the wall: first, President; second, Bishop; third, Petit-Paysan; fourth, reproduction of a painting by Passap (rectangular triangles); and so on down to Bibi – a family group, with his flock of children. View: a dirty wall no more than six feet away, a series of open, stinking little windows (belonging to the other building's toilets), the wall wildly splotched white, yellow, and green, transfigured by light from above only now and then, in midsummer, towards noon. Perpetual noise of toilets being flushed. As for his place of work: one of fifty other Bookkeepers in a mammoth room divided by glass partitions, labyrinthine, traversable only on the zigzag; on the seventh floor, Obstetrical Forceps Division, pencil behind his ear, grey work smock, its elbows reinforced with patches of leather; lunch in the canteen, where he pined for a picture of the President and the Bishop, but only Petit-Paysan hung there (Number Three). Archilochos was not a real Bookkeeper, only an Assistant Bookkeeper. Or, to be more precise: the Assistant Bookkeeper of an Assistant Bookkeeper. In short, one of the lowest of the Assistant Bookkeepers, insofar as it is possible to speak of a lowest, for the number of Bookkeepers and Assistant Bookkeepers in Petit-Paysan, Inc., was practically infinite. But even in this modest, this almost lowest job, he was still far better paid than the garret would have indicated. What had banished him to this dark den, flanked by toilets, was Bibi.

Madame Bieler also made the acquaintance of Number Eight (the brother).

It was on a Sunday. Arnolph had invited Bibi Archilochos to dinner. Chez Auguste.

Bibi came with his wife, two mistresses, and seven little ones, the oldest of whom, Théophile and Gottlieb, were almost grown up. Magda-Maria, thirteen years old, brought along a lover. Bibi proved to be a hardened drinker; his wife was accompanied by 'Uncle', as he was called: a retired sea captain who could not be got rid of. It was a rich spectacle, too rich even for the cycling fans. Théophile boasted of his session in the reformatory, Gottlieb of a bank robbery; Matthew and Sebastian, respectively twelve and nine years old, went around playfully threatening people with their knives; and the two youngest, the six-year-old twins, Jean-Christophe and Jean-Daniel, had a fight over a bottle of absinthe.

'What a bunch!' Georgette cried in horror after the devil's brood had finally cleared out of the establishment.

'Just youthful high spirits,' Archilochos said to placate her. He paid the bill – half a month's salary.

'Look here,' Madame Bieler remonstrated, 'that brother of yours seems to be raising a gang of criminals. You mean to say you give him money? Almost everything you earn?'

Archilochos' faith was unshakable. 'One must always try to see the heart, Madame Bieler,' he said. 'And the heart is good. In every human being. Appearances are deceitful. My brother, his wife, and his dear little ones have an inner nobility, only life is a bit too much for them; they need help.'

But now – it was a Sunday once again, half past nine in the morning – he entered the restaurant for different purposes. He had a red rose in his lapel. Georgette was impatiently awaiting him. It was really all the doing of the unceasing rain, the fogs, the cold, the constantly damp socks, and the epidemic of grippe, which in the course of time had changed into intestinal grippe – the result being that Archilochos (we know the location of his room) could not sleep for the constant gurgling roar. All this had gradually changed Arnolph's mind, as the water deepened in the gutters of the streets, and he had finally yielded to Madame Bieler's insistent urgings.

'You ought to get married, Monsieur Arnolph,' she kept telling him. 'This isn't any life for you, holed up in that garret of yours, or sitting around with cycling fans. A man with higher interests shouldn't live that way. You need a wife to take care of you.'

'You take care of me, Madame Bieler.'

'Oh come now, a wife is something completely different. A woman keeps a man snug and warm. You'll see.'

At last she brought him round. He agreed to place a want ad in *Le Soir*. Georgette at once brought paper, pen, and ink to his table.

'Bachelor, Bookkeeper, forty-five, Old New Presbyterian, refined, seeks Old New Presbyterian wife . . .' she suggested.

'That wouldn't be necessary,' Archilochos said. 'I would convert my wife to the right faith.'

Georgette granted that this was reasonable. 'Seeks a loving wife, good disposition, own age, widow not excluded. . . .'

She would have to be an innocent girl, Archilochos demurred.

Georgette would have none of that. 'Put the idea of a girl out of your head,' she told him. 'You've never even been with a woman; one of you has to know how to do it.'

The ad he had in mind was somewhat different, Monsieur Arnolph faltered.

'How would you write it?'

'Greek seeks Greek wife.'

'*Mon Dieu*,' Madame Bieler exclaimed. 'Don't tell me you're a Greek?' She stared at the plumpish, graceless, rather northern-looking frame of Monsieur Archilochos.

'You see, Madame Bieler,' he replied shyly. 'I know I hardly conform to the picture most people have of Greeks. It's a long time since my ancestor came to this country and died at the side of Charles the Bold in the Battle of Nancy. That's the reason I don't look much like a Greek. I admit it. But now, Madame Bieler, with this fog and cold and rain, I feel such a longing to return to my homeland, though I've never seen it. It usually comes over me in the wintertime – I long for the Peloponnesus, for the red cliffs and the blue sky – I've read all about it in *Match*. So if I were to get married, I'd want my bride to be a Greek, because she'd feel the same loneliness I feel in this country.'

'You're a poet and no mistake,' Georgette had replied, drying her eyes.

And sure enough, in two days Archilochos received an answer to his ad. A small, perfumed envelope; a card inside as blue as the sky of the Peloponnesus. Chloé Saloniki was writing to say that she was lonely and wished that she and he could meet.

With Georgette's coaching he wrote to Chloé: Chez Auguste, Sunday, January so and so. Identification: a red rose.

Archilochos had on the dark-blue suit he had worn to his confirmation, but had forgotten his overcoat. He was nervous. He wondered whether he should not turn back and hide in his garret. For the first time in his life he was irked when he found Bibi waiting for him in front of Chez Auguste, almost unrecognizable in the fog.

'Let me have a couple of centuries,' Bibi said, extending his fraternal hand, palm upward, 'Magda-Maria needs English lessons.'

Archilochos expressed surprise.

'She's found herself a new steady,' Bibi explained. 'A hell of a nice guy, but he only speaks English.'

Archilochos, red rose in his lapel, handed over the money.

Georgette, too, was in a state of suspense. Only Auguste seemed unperturbed; as was his custom when there were no guests in the restaurant, he sat by the stove in his cyclist's costume, rubbing his bare legs.

Madame Bieler wiped off the counter. 'I wonder what she'll be like,' she said. 'Plump and pleasant is my guess. Not too old, I hope, though she doesn't mention her age on the card. But what woman likes to?'

Archilochos, shivering, ordered a cup of hot milk.

While he was cleaning his glasses, which had misted over from the steam of the milk, Chloé Saloniki entered the restaurant.

Nearsighted Archilochos at first saw Chloé only in outline, with a blotch of red somewhere to the right below the oval of the face – the rose, he surmised. But the silence that suddenly reigned over the place, this ghostly silence in which not the tinkle of a glass could be heard, nor the sound of anyone so much as drawing a breath, was so consternating that he did not instantly put on his glasses. In fact, as soon as he had, he snatched them off again and began to polish them in extreme excitement. It was unbelievable. A miracle had taken place, here in this little bistro, amid fog and rain. To this plumpish bachelor and timorous idealist, this prisoner of a stinking garret, barricaded behind his milk and mineral water, to this overscrupulous and over-inhibited Assistant Bookkeeper of an Assistant Bookkeeper with his eternally damp and holey socks, his unironed shirt, ill-fitting clothes, worn shoes, and queer opinions, had come this good fairy, this vision of loveliness and grace, so perfect a little lady that Georgette did not dare stir and Auguste, abashed, hid his cyclist's legs behind the stove.

'Monsieur Archilochos?' a soft, hesitant voice inquired. Archilochos stood up, bumping his cuff into his cup, so that the milk spattered over his glasses. At last he managed to don them again, and through splashes of milk he blinked at Chloé Saloniki, frozen.

'Another cup of milk,' he said at last.

'Oh,' Chloé laughed. 'I'd like one, too.'

Archilochos sat down, unable to take his eyes off her or to invite her to take a seat, although he wanted to. He was terrified, depressed, and did not dare think of his ad. Miserably, he removed the rose from his lapel. He thought that any moment she would turn in disappointment and go away. Perhaps, too, he thought he was only dreaming. He had so quickly and so completely succumbed to the beauty of this girl, to the miracle of this moment, that he was utterly defenceless. It was incomprehensible, this wonder of wonders, and he dared not hope that it would last for more than a moment. He felt ridiculous and ugly; suddenly the condition of his garret loomed in all its enormity before him, the dreariness of the working-class district in which he lived, the monotony of his work as a Bookkeeper. But she simply sat down at the table opposite him and looked at him with enormous black eyes.

'Oh,' she said happily, 'I never imagined you would be so nice. I'm so pleased we Greeks have found each other. Come, let me have your glasses. There's milk all over them.'

She took the glasses from his nose and wiped them with her scarf, or so it seemed to Archilochos, who could not see very well. She breathed on the glasses.

'Mademoiselle Saloniki,' he at last choked out, as if pronouncing his own death sentence, 'it may be I'm not quite a real Greek. My family emigrated in the days of Charles the Bold.'

Chloé laughed. 'Once a Greek, always a Greek.'

Then she put the glasses on for him, and Auguste served them their milk.

'Mademoiselle Saloniki ...'

'You must call me Chloé,' she said. 'Now that we're going to be married. I want to marry you because you're a Greek. My greatest desire is to make you happy.'

Archilochos flushed. 'This is the first time I've ever talked with a girl, Chloé,' he said at last. 'Up to now, my only contact with ladies has been with Madame Bieler.'

Chloé did not reply. She seemed to be considering something, and the pair drank the hot, steaming milk.

After Chloé and Archilochos had left the restaurant together, Madame Bieler found her tongue again.

'What a looker,' she said. 'You wouldn't believe it. And that bracelet she was wearing, and her necklace – hundreds of thousands of francs. That girl must have worked! And did you see her coat. Some fur! A man couldn't want a finer wife.'

'And so young,' Auguste said, still staggered.

'Come on,' Georgette replied, mixing herself a glass of Campari and soda, 'she's seen thirty. But dolled up. I bet you she has herself massaged seven times a week.'

'So did I,' Auguste commented, 'when I won the Tour de Suisse.' He looked mournfully at his skinny legs.

'And some perfume!'

Chloé and Archilochos stood in the street. It was still raining. The fog, too, still lurked in the air, and the cold that pierced through clothing.

'There's a temperance restaurant opposite the World Health Office,' he said at last. 'Very reasonable.'

He shivered in his damp and threadbare confirmation suit.

'Won't you give me your arm?' Chloé asked him.

The Assistant Bookkeeper was embarrassed. He did not quite know how it was done. He scarcely dared to look at the vision tripping along beside him through the fog, with a silvery blue scarf thrown over her black hair. He felt rather uneasy. This was the first time he had ever walked through the city with a girl, and so he was actually grateful for the fog. A church bell struck half past ten. They walked through deserted suburban streets, whose buildings were mirrored in the wet asphalt. Their footsteps echoed from the walls of houses. It was as if they were passing through an underground vault. Not a person was in sight. A half-starved dog trotted towards them out of the gloom, a dirty black-and-white spaniel, dripping with wetness, with drooping ears and dropping tongue. The red lights at intersections shimmered through the mist. Then a bus rolled past, pointlessly sounding its horn, evidently headed for North Station. Archilochos pressed his head into the soft fur of her coat, to find room under her dainty red umbrella. He was overwhelmed by the deserted street, the Sunday, the weather. They walked along in step, almost like a regular pair of lovers. Somewhere the Salvation Army was singing nasally in the fog, and now and then the Télédiffusion's Sunday-morning concert could be heard coming from a house – some symphony or other, Beethoven or Schubert, mingled with the tooting of automobiles lost in the fog. The two of them were drifting toward the river, they guessed, through uniform streets, only snatches of which were disclosed as it grew somewhat brighter, though everything was still swathed in greyness. Then they walked along an endless boulevard past monotonously similar façades, which now showed clearly through the mist, past the villas of long-since ruined bankers and faded cocottes, with Doric and Corinthian columns at the doors, with stiff balconies and tall windows on the second floor, most of them illuminated, most of them battered, phantomlike, dripping.

Chloé began to tell the story of her life, which was as wondrous as she herself. She spoke shyly, haltingly. But to the Assistant Book-keeper, everything fantastic seemed perfectly natural. After all, he was living a fairy tale.

She was an orphan, she said, her parents poor wanderers from Crete who had frozen to death in the terrible winters. In barracks. That was the beginning of the great loneliness. She grew up in the slums, unkempt, ragged, just like that black-and-white spaniel, had stolen fruit and robbed poor boxes. The police hounded her. Procurers pursued her. She slept under bridges, among tramps and in empty barrels, shy and suspicious as a wild animal. Then she was picked up, literally that is, by an archaeological couple out for an evening walk, and placed in a convent school. At present she was living as a maid in the home of her benefactors, was decently dressed, decently fed – a touching story, all in all.

'An archaeological couple?' Arnolph asked wonderingly. He had never heard of anything of the sort.

'A couple who studied archaeology,' Chloé Saloniki explained, 'and who had made excavations in Greece. They discovered a temple there, with precious statues, buried in a bog, and golden columns.'

What was their name?

Chloé hesitated. She seemed to be seeking a name.

'Gilbert and Elizabeth Weeman.'

'The famous Weemans?'

(An article on them with coloured photos had just appeared in *Match*.)

'Yes.'

He would incorporate them into his ethical cosmos, Arnolph said. As Numbers Nine and Ten. Or perhaps as Numbers Six and Seven, with Maître Dutour and the Rector magnificus shifted to Numbers Nine and Ten – still positions of considerable honour.

'You have an ethical cosmos?' Chloé asked in astonishment. 'What in the world is that?'

A man must have something to lean on in life, ethical models, Archilochos said. He, too, had not had an easy life, although he had not grown up among murderers and tramps, as she had done, but only with his brother Bibi in an orphanage. And he began describing to her the structure of his moral universe.

The weather had changed although at first they scarcely noticed. The rain had stopped and the fog was lifting. It turned into ghostly figures, long, sinuous dragons, clumsy bears, and giant men that slid over houses, banks, and government buildings, intertwining, rising, and dissolving. Blue sky shimmered between masses of fog, delicate and elusive at first, a mere hint of spring, which was still months away, faintly tinged by sunlight, then clearer, brighter, stronger. Suddenly the wet asphalt was printed with the reflections of buildings, street lamps, monuments, people, and the city burst forth with superclarity, bathed in the flood of new light.

They were on the Quai in front of the President's Palace. The river had swollen to a brown torrent. Spanning it were bridges with rusty iron railings; empty barges, hung with diapers, moved downstream while shivering skippers, smoking pipes, paced up and down their decks. The streets now swarmed with strollers, dignified grandfathers accompanied by grandchildren in their Sunday best, families marching in solid rows down the sidewalks. There were many policemen about, and reporters obviously waiting for the President, who now came charging out of the palace in his historic chariot, drawn by six white horses, accompanied by his mounted bodyguard with their golden helmets and white plumes. He was off to perform some political act somewhere, to dedicate a monument, pin a medal on someone's chest, or open an orphanage. The tramp of hooves, blare of trumpets and drums, cheers, and hats filled the rain-washed air.

Then the incomprehensible happened.

The President rode past Chloé and Archilochos. Arnolph, overjoyed at this unexpected meeting with Number One in his cosmos, which he was just explaining, peered at the goateed, grey-haired dignitary who sat, resplendent in gold braid, framed by the window of his carriage, just like the picture that hung above Madame Bieler's bottles of Pernod and Campari. And just at this moment the President suddenly greeted the Assistant Bookkeeper. His Excellency waved his right hand just as if Archilochos were an old acquaintance. So conspicuous was this fluttering motion of a white glove, and so plainly was it intended for him, that two policemen with impressive moustaches snapped to attention in front of Archilochos.

'The President greeted me,' Archilochos stammered incredulously.

'Why shouldn't he greet you?' Chloé Saloniki asked.

'But I'm only an insignificant ordinary citizen.'

'But isn't the President the father of us all?' Chloé suggested.

Almost immediately there took place another episode which Archilochos could not understand, but which filled him with fresh pride.

He was just about to speak of Number Two in his cosmos, Bishop Moser, and of the vital difference between the Old New and the Old Presbyterians of the Penultimate Christians, with a brief mention of the New Presbyterians (that scandal within the Presbyterian Church) – he was just about to speak of all this when, out of turn, Number Three of the cosmos met them: Petit-Paysan. He must have come either from the World Bank, five hundred yards away from the President's Palace, or from St Luke's Cathedral, which adjoined the World Bank. He was dressed in an immaculate coat, top hat, and white scarf, fairly crackling with elegance. His chauffeur had already opened the door of the Rolls-Royce when Arnolph caught sight of him. Arnolph did not know quite what to do. This event was unique, and would serve to illustrate the explanations he was at this moment giving Chloé about his cosmos. The great industrialist did not know Archilochos, could not possibly know him who was only an Assistant Bookkeeper in the Obstetrical Forceps Division. But that very fact gave Archilochos the courage to point out this superior being, though not to greet him (one does not greet a god). And so, though frightened, Archilochos felt safe in the consciousness that he could pass by this man of might unrecognized. But for the second time the incomprehensible thing happened: Petit-Paysan smiled, doffed his top hat, waved it, bowed graciously to a pale Archilochos, then dropped into the upholstery of his limousine, waved once more, and roared off.

'But that was Petit-Paysan!' Archilochos panted.

'So what?'

'Number Three in my cosmos.'

'What about him?'

'He greeted me!'

'I should hope so.'

'But I'm only an Assistant Bookkeeper and work with fifty other Assistant Bookkeepers in the lowest department of the Obstetrical Forceps Division,' Archilochos exclaimed.

'Then he must be a man with a social conscience,' Chloé declared, 'worthy of holding third place in your moral universe.'

Evidently she did not really grasp the truly amazing nature of this meeting.

But the wonders of this Sunday had not yet ceased. The weather, in the middle of winter, grew steadily warmer and more brilliant, the sky steadily bluer and more unreal, and the whole metropolis seemed suddenly determined to greet Archilochos as he strolled, his Greek girl at his side, over the bridges with their wrought-iron railings and through the gardens and parks outside the decaying castles. Arnolph became prouder, more self-assured, his gait freer, his face radiant. He was more than an Assistant Bookkeeper now. He was a happy man. Fashionable young fellows hailed him, waved from cafés, buses, and Vespas. So did *soigné* gentlemen with greying temples, and even a Belgian general with many decorations, evidently attached to NATO headquarters, who was getting out of a jeep. In front of the American Embassy, Ambassador Bob Forster-Monroe, accompanied by two Scotch sheep dogs, called out a hearty 'hello'; while Number Two (Bishop Moser, who looked even more well-fed in the flesh than he did in the picture hanging in Madame Bieler's bistro) encountered them between the National Museum and the crematorium, as they were about to enter the temperance restaurant opposite the World Health Office. Bishop Moser also greeted him. By now this somehow seemed only right and proper, although Archilochos did not know him personally at all, had only sat in a crowd of hymn-singing females listening to him preach the Easter sermon. However, Archilochos had read his biography at least a hundred times, in the pamphlet on this exemplary personage which was distributed among the congregation. The Bishop seemed even more startled than the lowly member of his

Old New Presbyterian Church, for he scurried down an absurd side street with remarkable haste.

Then they dined together in the temperance restaurant. They sat at a window table and looked out across the river at the World Health Office with the monument to a famous World Health official in front of it, on which the gulls rested, rose, swooped around, and rested again. They were both tired from the long walk, and they continued merely to sit and hold hands even after the soup had been placed before them. The restaurant was mainly patronized by Old New Presbyterians (and a scattering of Old Presbyterians), mostly spinsters and eccentric bachelors who came to dine here on Sundays for the cause of temperance, although the proprietor, an obstinate Catholic, stubbornly refused to hang Bishop Moser's portrait. On the contrary, the Archbishop hung beside the President.

Later, they sat, two Greeks beneath two Greeks, moving closer and closer to each other, on a bench in the old municipal park under a mildewed statue which was described, by guides and city maps, as representing Daphnis and Chloé. They watched the sun drop behind the trees, a red child's balloon. Here, too, everyone greeted Archilochos. Usually only cycling fans and Assistant Bookkeepers noticed him; but now this pallid, bespectacled, plumpish, and altogether inconspicuous man seemed to interest the entire city, to be the centre of society. The fairy tale went on. Number Four (Passap) passed by, followed by a band of bewildered or enthusiastic art critics, for the master had just abandoned his rectangular period with its circles and hyperbolas and was now painting only angles of sixty degrees with ellipses and parabolas, and from red and green had turned to cobalt blue and ochre. The master of modern painting came to a stop, growled, looked keenly at Archilochos, nodded, and strolled on, continuing his lecture to the critics. On the other hand, the former Numbers Six and Seven (now Nine and Ten), Maître Dutour and the Rector magnificus, greeted Archilochos with a barely perceptible wink, for they were walking at the side of imposing wives.

Archilochos told Chloé about his life. 'I don't earn very much,' he said. 'The work is monotonous; it involves checking over the reports on our obstetrical forceps, and calls for the utmost care and precision. My superior, a Vice Bookkeeper, is strict, and I also have to support my brother Bibi and his dear little ones, lovable people, perhaps a little rough and wild, but good at heart. We will save, and in twenty years we'll be able to visit Greece together. The Peloponnesus. The islands. I've dreamed of that for ever so long, and now that I know I'll go there with you, the dream has become even more beautiful.'

She said she was thrilled. 'It will be a lovely trip,' she said.

'On an ocean liner.'

'On the *Julia*.'

He looked inquiringly at her.

'That's a luxury ship. Mrs and Mr Weeman sail on it.'

'Of course,' he recalled, 'I read about that in *Match*. But the *Julia* will be too expensive for us, and in twenty years they'll have scrapped it. We'll go on a freighter. They're cheaper.'

He often thought about Greece, he went on, looking out at the fog, which was beginning to settle in again, drifting down toward the ground like thin white smoke. He could see the broken pillars of the ancient temples, and the red cliffs shimmering through the olive groves. 'Sometimes I feel I am in exile in this city, like the Jews in Babylon, and that the whole meaning of my life is to return someday to the old homeland my ancestors abandoned so long ago.'

Now the fog lay like great heaps of cotton batting behind the trees by the banks of the river, swaddling the slow-moving barges, which howled ruttishly. The masses of fog rose, flared violet, and began to spread as soon as the big red sun had dropped below the horizon. Archilochos escorted Chloé to the boulevard where the Weemans lived – a fine expensive neighbourhood, he noted. They passed wrought-iron fences, big gardens with noble old trees which screened the houses from the public view. Poplars, elms, beeches, and black fir trees towered into the silvery evening sky, their tops vanishing in the thickening billows of fog. Chloé stopped in front of an iron gate decorated with putti and dolphins, exotic foliage and arabesques, flanked by two huge stone pillars and surmounted by a red lamp.

'Tomorrow night?'

'Chloé!'

'Will you ring?' she asked, pointing to an old-fashioned bellpull. 'At eight?'

Then she kissed the Assistant Bookkeeper. She put her arms around his neck, kissed him once more, then a third time.

'We'll go to Greece,' she whispered. 'To our old homeland. Soon. And on the *Julia*.'

She opened the iron gate and vanished into the mist among the trees, waving to him once more and calling out something, some tender phrase, like a mysterious bird as she walked towards some invisible building deep in the spacious garden.

Archilochos, for his part, trudged back to his working-class neighbourhood. It was a long walk; he retraced the whole route he had taken with Chloé. And he thought over the phases of this fabulous Sunday, stood still on the deserted pavement in front of the closed-up World Bank, beneath Daphnis and Chloé, then in front of the temperance restaurant, which the last of the Old New Presbyterian spinsters were just leaving. One of them greeted him, and perhaps waited for him on the next street corner. Then he walked past the crematorium, the National Museum, and the Quai. The fog was thick again, but not dirty as it had been on previous days; it was soft and milky, a miraculous fog, it seemed to him, shot through with long golden rays of light, with delicate, needlelike stars. He reached the Ritz, and as he passed the pompous portal with its six-foot doorman in green coat and red trousers and carrying a long silver staff, Gilbert and Elizabeth Weeman emerged from the hotel. He recognized the world-famous archaeologists from their pictures in the newspapers. They were both exceedingly English; she looked more like a man than a woman, with her hair cut short just like her husband's, and both had pince-nez. The only salient difference was that Gilbert had a red moustache and stubby pipe.

Archilochos plucked up his courage. 'Madame, monsieur,' he said. 'My respects.'

'Well,' the scientist said, staring at the Assistant Bookkeeper, who stood before him in his threadbare confirmation suit and down-at-heel shoes. Mrs Weeman likewise examined him through her pince-nez.

'Well,' Mr Weeman said again. And then he added: 'Yes?'

'I have appointed you Numbers Six and Seven in my ethical cosmos.'

'Yes?'

'You have given a home to a Greek girl,' Archilochos continued.

'Well,' Mr Weeman said.

'I, too, am a Greek.'

'Oh,' Mr Weeman said, taking out his wallet.

Archilochos made a gesture of refusal. 'No, monsieur, no, madame,' he said. 'I know I do not look very trustworthy, and perhaps not even Greek, but my salary at the Petit-Paysan Engineering Works will suffice for me to set up a modest household with her. Yes, we will even be able to think of starting a family, though only of three or four, because the Petit-Paysan Engineering Works maintains an excellent maternity clinic for its employees.'

'Well,' Mr Weeman said, pocketing his wallet.

'Good-bye,' Archilochos said. 'God bless you. I will pray for you in the Old New Presbyterian Church.'

But at the door of his house he met Bibi, whose brotherly hand was extended, palm upwards.

'Théophile was trying a snatch in the National Bank,' he said in his argot. 'The bulls caught wise.'

'So?'

'He has to beat it to the south till things quiet down. I need five centuries. You'll have 'em back at Christmas.'

Archilochos gave him money.

'What's this, Brother,' Bibi protested in disappointment. 'No more than a tenner?'

'I can't give you any more, Bibi,' Archilochos apologized, embarrassed and, to his surprise, a little annoyed. 'Really not. I had dinner with a girl in the temperance restaurant opposite the World Health Office. The regular Sunday dinner and a bottle of grape juice besides. I'm thinking about starting a family of my own.'

Brother Bibi looked alarmed.

'What do you want with a family?' he cried out indignantly. 'I've got one already. Does the chick have any money at least?'

'No.'

'What line she in?'

'She works for some rich people as housemaid.'

'Where?'

'Number 12 Boulevard Saint-Père.'

Bibi whistled through his teeth.

'Go hit the hay, Arnolph, but lemme have another tenner.'

After climbing the six flights of stairs to his garret, Archilochos undressed. He went to bed. He wished he could open the window. The air was stale. But the toilets were more odoriferous than usual. He lay in semi-darkness. Lights went on and off, first in one narrow little window, then in another, across the areaway. The roar of flushing never stopped. Alternately lights flashed against the wall of his room, illuminating one of the pictures in his ethical cosmos, now the Bishop, now the President, now Bibi with his little brood, now the triangular rectangles in Passap's painting, now one of the other figures.

'Tomorrow I must obtain a photograph of the Weemans and have it framed,' he mused.

The air was so stuffy that he could hardly breathe. Sleep was out of the question. He had gone to bed happy, but now worries descended. It would be impossible to live in this garret with Chloé, to found a household, to accommodate the three or four dear little children he had planned for on the way home. He must find new lodgings. But he had no money for a better place, no savings. He had given all he earned to Brother Bibi. He owned nothing. Not even this wretched bed, the miserable table, and the rickety stool. It all belonged to the landlord of this furnished room. Only the pictures which comprised his moral cosmos were his own property. His poverty weighed on him. Chloé's delicacy and beauty called for beautiful and delicate surroundings, he sensed. She must never again return to the bridges by the river and the empty barrels at garbage dumps. The roar of the flushing toilets began to strike him as more and more malignant, more and more repulsive. He vowed to leave this garret. Tomorrow, he decided, he would look for another apartment. But as he considered how he would go about moving, a feeling of helplessness overcame him. He saw no way. He realized that he was caught in a merciless machine, without any way to make anything of the miracle that had been offered to him this glorious Sunday. Drearily, in complete despair, he lay awake waiting for morning, which at last announced its coming with an intensified thunder of water closets.

*

Towards eight o'clock, as on every Monday morning – and at this time of year it was still dark – Archilochos hustled into the administrative offices of the Petit-Paysan Engineering Works. He was one more in an army of Bookkeepers, stenographers, and Assistant Bookkeepers, an insignificant particle in the grey stream of humanity which poured out of the subway, the buses, the streetcars, and the suburban railroad cars, and flowed sadly towards the gigantic steel-and-glass cube which swallowed, divided, and sorted them out, pushed them up and down elevators and escalators, crowded them along corridors. First floor: Tank Division. Second floor: Atomic Cannon. Third floor: Machine Gun Division. And so on. Archilochos, wedged among the crowds, pushed around and shoved about, worked on the seventh floor, Obstetrical Forceps Division. Office 122-OF, in one of the many featureless spaces partitioned off with glass walls. Before he entered, however, he had to step into the Hygiene Room, gargle, and take a pill (against intestinal grippe); these measures were required by Social Welfare. Then he put on his grey working smock, still shivering; for the first intense, cutting frost of winter had descended overnight, laying a light, smooth polish over all surfaces. He had to hurry, for it was already a minute before eight and lateness was not tolerated (time is money). He sat down at a desk, likewise of steel and glass, which he shared with three other Assistant Bookkeepers, who bore numbers, AB122-OF28, AB122-OF29, AB122-OF30, and uncovered his typewriter. The number on his smock was AB122-OF31. Fingers still stiff, he began to type; the hand of the big clock had moved to eight. This morning he had to complete a summary of the upsurge in obstetrical forceps sales in the Canton of Appenzell Inner Rhoden.

Like himself, the three other Assistant Bookkeepers at his desk clattered away at their typewriters, and the forty-six others in the room, the hundreds, thousands in the building, from eight to twelve and from two to five, with meals in the Works Canteen in between. It was all part of the exemplary Petit-Paysan organization, which was so often visited by cabinet ministers, foreign delegations, bespectacled Chinese, and sensuous Hindus, who, having an interest in social conditions, floated through the big rooms, silken wives at their sides.

But sometimes, though seldom, the miracles of Sunday continue on Monday.

An announcement came over the loudspeaker, telling Archilochos to report to his office head, Bookkeeper B121-OF. For a moment there was deathly silence in Room 122-OF. Not a breath could be heard. Not the timid click of a single typewriter key. The Greek stood up. Pale, reeling. He had a foreboding of bad news. Dismissals were impending.

But Bookkeeper B121-OF received him in his office, which adjoined 122-OF, with real cordiality, as Archilochos discovered to his amazement; he had halted on the threshold, hardly daring to enter, for awful stories went the rounds of B121-OF's outbursts of temper.

'Monsieur Archilochos,' B121-OF called out, striding forward to meet the Assistant Bookkeeper and actually shaking his hand, 'I have been keeping my eye on your remarkable talents for a long time, I must say.'

'Oh, thank you,' Archilochos said, surprised at the praise and still on guard.

B121-OF rubbed his hands. He was a small, nimble chap of fifty, bald, with nearsighted eyes, dressed in a white Bookkeeper's smock with grey elbow pads. 'Your follow-up on the distribution and maintenance standards of obstetrical forceps in the canton of Appenzell Inner Rhoden is exemplary.'

He was glad to hear that, Archilochos said, still certain that he was the candidate for some cruel whim on the Bookkeeper's part, and that this friendliness was only a trick.

The Bookkeeper offered his suspicious assistant a chair, and began nervously pacing his office.

'In view of your excellent work, my dear Monsieur Archilochos, I have been planning to take certain steps.'

'I am greatly honoured,' Archilochos stammered.

He had been thinking of promotion to the post of Vice Bookkeeper, B121-OF murmured. 'I have just sent the proposal to the Chief of Personnel responsible for our office.'

Archilochos stood up, with an appropriate look of gratitude; but the Bookkeeper had still another matter on his mind. He looked anxious and unhappy as he came out with it, just as if he were an Assistant Bookkeeper.

'I'd almost forgotten,' B121-OF said softly, trying not to show his emotion, 'Chief Bookkeeper CB9-OF wishes to see Monsieur Archilochos. This very morning.'

The Bookkeeper wiped the sweat from his brow with a red checked handkerchief.

'The Chief Bookkeeper,' he continued, 'wishes to see you right away. Sit down again, my dear friend; we have another minute. Above all, collect yourself, don't lose your nerve, take courage, meet the situation like a man.'

'Certainly,' Archilochos said. 'I'll try.'

'Good Lord,' his superior said, seating himself behind his desk. 'Good Lord, Monsieur Archilochos, I'm sure I may call you my good friend, in confidence and just between the two of us – my name is Rummel, Emil Rummel. This is an event. It has never happened to me before, and I have been working in the Petit-Paysan Engineering Works for thirty-three years. A Chief Bookkeeper wishes to see an Assistant Bookkeeper, just like that. Never in my life have I seen such a dramatic jump outside of the regular channels. I feel faint, my dear friend. Of course, I believed in your brilliance all along, but still. Why, never in my whole life have I stood in the presence of a Chief Bookkeeper; I'd tremble like an aspen leaf if I did. A Bookkeeper deals only with Vice Chief Bookkeepers, of course! And now this happening to you! Being interviewed by a Chief Bookkeeper! No doubt there are reasons for it, a secret intent. I foresee a promotion; you will receive my post, that's it' (at this point B121-OF dried his eyes). 'Perhaps you'll even be made Vice Chief Bookkeeper, as happened recently in the Atomic Cannon Division to a Bookkeeper who had the honour to become somewhat intimate with the wife of a Chief of Personnel – I'm not referring to you, my friend, not you – in your case it's only your ability, that marvellous report on Appenzell Inner Rhoden, I know. But just between you and me, my dear friend: it was only by sheer chance that my proposal to promote you to Vice Bookkeeper and the summons from the Chief Bookkeeper came at virtually the same moment. I give you my word of honour, that's the case. My petition for your promotion was already written when out of a clear sky the telephone call from our respected Chief Bookkeeper's secretary reached me. But it's time, it's time, my good friend – incidentally my wife would be delighted to have you to dinner – my daughter likewise, very charming, very pretty, takes singing lessons – if you'd care to – if you'd do us the honour – fifth corridor southeast, sixth office – good Lord, and my heart isn't what it should be – trouble with my kidneys, too.'

CB9-OF, fifth corridor southeast, sixth office, a substantial man with neatly trimmed black beard, flashing gold teeth, paunch, and odour of cologne water, the photograph of a scantily clad dancer in a platinum frame on his desk, received the Assistant Bookkeeper with respect, shooed flocks of stenographers out of his office, and with an expansive wave of his hand offered his caller a comfortable easy chair.

'My dear Monsieur Archilochos,' he began, 'your excellent reports have attracted notice among our staff of Chief Bookkeepers for some time, especially your study of the new market for obstetrical forceps in the Far North, with special attention to Alaska. Your charts have created a sensation, have, I may say, evoked a storm of admiration. There has been much discussion of the matter within our circles, and word has gone around that the Directors have also been enormously impressed.'

'There must be some mistake, sir,' Arnolph demurred. 'I deal only with the canton of Appenzell Inner Rhoden and the Tyrol.'

'Just call me Petit-Pierre,' CB9-OF said. 'After all, we're among ourselves here, not in a crowd of philistines. Whether or not the Alaska report was written by you, it was inspired by you, breathes your spirit, reflects the incomparable style of your classical reports on the canton of Appenzell Inner Rhoden and the Tyrol. One more happy sign that your work is setting the tone. I always used to exclaim to my colleague Chief Bookkeeper Schränzle: Archilochos is a writer, a great prose stylist. Incidentally, Schränzle sends his regards. As does Chief Bookkeeper Häberlin. I have long been disturbed over the subordinate post you occupy in our esteemed organization, a post entirely out of keeping with your remarkable abilities. By the way, may I offer you a glass of vermouth . . . ?'

'Thank you, Monsieur Petit-Pierre,' Archilochos said. 'I am a teetotaller.'

'It seems to me a particular scandal that you should be working under Bookkeeper B121-OF, Monsieur Rummler, or whatever his name is. There's a true mediocrity for you.'

'He has just proposed my promotion to Vice Bookkeeper.'

'I wouldn't put it past him,' CB9-OF said irately. 'Vice Bookkeeper indeed! He'd like that! A man of your talent! Why, the Petit-Paysan Engineering Works owes the surge in obstetrical forceps production during the last quarter entirely to you.'

'But Monsieur Petit-Pierre. . . .'

'Don't be too modest, my dear sir, don't be too modest. Everything has its limits. Here I've been waiting patiently for years, hoping that you would turn to me in confidence as your most faithful friend and admirer, and you simply go on sticking it out under that unbearable, low-minded Bookkeeper, staying on as an Assistant Bookkeeper among Assistant Bookkeepers, in an environment that really doesn't suit you at all. Instead of pounding your fist on the table! It must have been sheer hell to be with that beastly crew. So I've had to intervene directly. Of course I'm only a helpless little Chief Bookkeeper in the labyrinth of our administration, a cipher, a zero. But I've screwed up my courage. After all, someone had to speak up for you, no matter if the world comes to an end, no matter if it costs him his own head. Pluck, my dear fellow! If we don't have that, the moral fibre of the Petit-Paysan Engineering Works is gone and what have we left but down-and-out tyranny of bureaucracy, as I've been yelling all my life. I telephoned personally to the Chief of Personnel of our division, who incidentally sends his regards to you. I wanted to propose you as Vice Director; fact is, I couldn't think of anything finer than continuing to work under you, my dear Monsieur Archilochos, serving our common cause, the constant improvement and widening market for obstetrical forceps. But Petit-Paysan himself, Our Father in Heaven, as it were, or destiny, if you will, has alas, alas, anticipated me – a bit of personal ill luck which, of course, as far as you're concerned, represents a great though not undeserved good fortune.'

'Petit-Paysan?' Archilochos thought he was dreaming. 'But that's simply impossible!'

'He wants to see you today, this very morning, this very hour, Monsieur Archilochos,' CB9-OF said.

'But . . .'

'No buts.'

'I mean . . .'

'Monsieur Archilochos,' the Chief Bookkeeper said earnestly, running his hand down his well-tended beard, 'let us speak frankly with one another. As man to man, as friend to friend. I tell you in all honesty: This is a historic day, a day of candour, of clarification. My whole soul demands that I assure you, on my word of honour, that the fact that I have proposed you for Vice Director and the fact that our revered Petit-Paysan, hats off to him, wishes to see you, have nothing whatsoever to do with one another. On the contrary. I had just dictated the formal proposal for your promotion when Director Zeus sent for me.'

'Director Zeus?'

'Head of the Obstetrical Forceps Division.'

Archilochos apologized for his ignorance. He had never heard the name.

'I know,' the Chief Bookkeeper replied, 'the names of Directors have not reached down to the circles of Bookkeepers and Assistant Bookkeepers. What would be the point? Such coolies are supposed to keep scribbling, composing drivel on the canton of Appenzell Inner Rhoden or God knows what out-of-the-way corners of the world that between you and me, my dear Monsieur Archilochos, nobody gives a damn about – your papers excepted, of course – we rely on them, we Chief Bookkeepers can't wait to read them. But then your reports on the canton of Basel or Costa Rica are magnificent, classics, as I've already said. As for the rest – overpaid, useless buffoons, all those Bookkeepers and Assistant Bookkeepers. I've been trying to get that across to my superiors in the administration for ages. I'd do the work of that whole crew with my stenographers alone. The Petit-Paysan Engineering Works isn't a sanatorium for morons. Incidentally, Director Zeus wishes me to give you his regards.'

'Thank you.'

'Unfortunately he's in the hospital now.'

'Oh.'

'Nervous breakdown.'

'I'm sorry to hear that.'

'You see, my dear friend, you've introduced sheer disaster into the upper echelons of the Obstetrical Forceps Division. Sodom and

Gomorrah were a harmless little bonfire by comparison. Petit-Paysan wants to see you! Very well, that's his right, the Lord can turn the moon into green cheese if He likes, but all the same we'd be taken aback if He did. Petit-Paysan and an Assistant Bookkeeper! It's about the same kind of miracle. No wonder the poor Director heard the bell tolling. And the Vice Director? He went to pieces too.'

'But why?'

'My dear sir, because you are going to be appointed Director of the Obstetrical Forceps Division. Any child can see that. Otherwise there'd be no point to all this. When Petit-Paysan sends for a man, he is slated for the directorship. We know what we know. Firing is done by the Chief of Personnel.'

'Director? Me?'

'Certainly. The promotion has already been communicated to Personnel Chief Feuz, who incidentally also asks me to give you his regards.'

'Of the Obstetrical Forceps Division?'

'Possibly of the Atomic Cannon Division also. Who knows? Personnel Chief Feuz thinks anything is possible.'

'But why in the world?' Archilochos cried out. Nothing made sense.

'My dear, dear fellow! You forget your distinguished reports on Upper Italy....'

His territory was eastern Switzerland and the Tyrol, the Assistant Bookkeeper obstinately repeated.

'Eastern Switzerland and the Tyrol – I mix places up – I'm not a geographer, you know.'

'But that can't be a reason for appointing me Director of Obstetrical Forceps.'

'Come now!'

'I don't have the qualities for a Director,' Archilochos protested.

CB9-OF shook his head and threw a mysterious look at Archilochos. He smiled, flashing his gold teeth, and folded his hands over his impressive paunch. 'The reason,' he said, 'my dearest, my most honoured friend, the reason you are being promoted to the directorship is something you must know, not I. And if you do not know it, don't try to find out. It's better that way. Take my advice. This is probably the last time we will sit face to face. Directors and Chief Bookkeepers do not ordinarily associate; that would be a breach of the unwritten rules of our great firm. Why, I myself met Director

Zeus for the first time today, in the hour of his downfall, to be sure. And that was only because poor Vice Director Stüssi, who is my proper superior and who alone associates with Chief Bookkeepers, was being carried out on a stretcher. Truly, a twilight of the gods. But let us pass over this memorable scene in silence. As for your scruples, your fears that you cannot manage the métier of a Director – my dearest friend, between you and me, anybody can master the métier of a Director. Any idiot can do it. All you need do is simply be the Director, exist as Director, assume the dignity, represent the company, lead Indians, Chinese, and Zulus through the building, show around members of UNESCO and medical associations and anybody else in God's great world who is interested in that noble instrument the obstetrical forceps. The practical affairs, the plant, the technology, the computations, the market research – all that is handled by the Chief Bookkeepers, if I may express myself rather candidly to an honoured friend. No need for you to grow any grey hairs over that. What will be important, of course, is whom you pick from the ranks of the Chief Bookkeepers to be Vice Director. Stüssi's finished now, you see, and high time too; the man was too closely linked with Director Zeus, nothing but His Lordship's tool – but, well, I don't want to express an opinion on Zeus's professional qualifications. Wouldn't be right at this point. He has his nervous breakdown. Far be it from me to criticize. Though it was a cross working under him, just between you and me. Why, the man was totally incapable of comprehending the reports on Dalmatia which you composed, my dearest friend and respected patron. And in general, the man hadn't a glimmer – I know, I know, it wasn't Dalmatia, it was Toggenburg or Turkey. Let's forget that. You were born for higher things. Like an eagle, you soar above the heads of us wonder-struck Chief Book-keepers, into the empyrean. At any rate, just this one more confidential remark: We Chief Bookkeepers are delighted to have you as our Director! I don't even want to stress that as your best friend I particularly will sing hallelujah and hosannah' (at this point CB9-OF's eyes grew moist); 'it really wouldn't do, would seem as if I were angling for the post of Vice Director, although of course I do have seniority. Whatever your choice among us Chief Bookkeepers, whomever you appoint to be your deputy, I shall accept the decision with humility and remain your greatest admirer. . . . Colleague Spätzle would like a chance to see you, and then colleague Schränzle, but I'm afraid,

I'm afraid, I must now take you to Petit-Paysan without more ado, deliver you undamaged to his waiting room, it's growing late. So come now, head up, enjoy your good fortune; after all, you are the worthiest, the most talented of all of us, a golden boy, so to speak, born under a bright star. The Obstetrical Forceps Division will outstrip the Machine Gun Division with colours flying, I predict. My dear sir, dear Director Archilochos, as I may as well address you from now on, would you do me the honour of coming with me, it's a great pleasure, we may as well take the Directors' elevator right away.'

With CB9-OF, Archilochos entered rooms whose existence he had never suspected, realms of glass and unknown materials, sparkling with cleanliness; superb elevators which bore him to the upper, mysterious storeys of the administration building. Pretty stenographers swept fragrantly past, smiling, blonde, brunette, and raven, and one with glorious vermilion hair. Male secretaries made way for him, Directors bowed, General Directors nodded; velvety corridors received him, the red or green lights blinking over their doors the only signs of discreet administrative activity. They walked soundlessly on soft carpets; all noise, even the slightest clearing of throats or suppressed coughs, seemed banned from these regions. French Impressionists glowed on the walls (Petit-Paysan's collection of paintings was famous); a dancer by Degas, a bather by Renoir. Flowers in tall vases exuded their scents. The higher they mounted, the fewer people they encountered in the corridors and rooms, which ceased to be functional, supermodern, and cold, though their proportions remained the same. The ambience here was more imaginative, warmer, more human; the walls were tapestried, hung with gilded rococo and Louis Quatorze mirrors, a few Poussins, a sprinkling of Watteaus, a Claude Lorrain. And when they reached the topmost floor (CB9-OF, by now as overawed as Archilochos, for he had never penetrated so far, bid good-bye at this point), the Assistant Bookkeeper was received by a stately grey-haired gentleman in faultless dinner jacket, probably a secretary, who led him down peaceful corridors and through big, bright rooms filled with antique vases and

Gothic madonnas, Asiatic idols and Indian hangings. Here was no reminder at all of the manufacture of atomic cannon and machine guns, though possibly the sight of a few cherubic babes and dwarfs, which smiled at Archilochos out of a Rubens painting, might remotely call to mind obstetrical forceps. Everything was bright and serene in these altitudes. The sun was a magnanimous disc shining warmly through the windows, although in reality it stood in an icy sky. Comfortable easy chairs and sofas stood about. Somewhere hearty laughter could be heard; it reminded Archilochos, in his grey working smock, of Chloé's laughter on the bright Sunday which was now having so fabulous a continuation. Somewhere music trembled in the air, Haydn or Mozart; there was no clattering of typewriters, no rushing back and forth of frenzied Bookkeepers, nothing that reminded him of the world he had just risen out of, which now lay so far below him, like a bad dream. Then they were standing in a bright room whose walls were covered with red silk, with a large painting representing a nude woman, probably the famous Titian people were talking about, whose price was everywhere repeated in excited whispers. Delicate little pieces of furniture, a dainty desk, a small wall clock with silver pendulum, a gaming table surrounded by petite chairs, and flowers, roses, camellias, tulips, orchids, gladioli in spendthrift profusion, as though there were no seasons, no cold, no fog, and no winter. Almost as soon as they entered, a small side door opened and Petit-Paysan came in, dressed in a dinner jacket like the secretary, an India-paper edition of Hölderlin's poems in his left hand, index finger between the pages. The secretary withdrew. Archilochos and Petit-Paysan confronted one another.

'Well,' Petit-Paysan said, 'my dear Monsieur Anaximander....'

His name was Arnolph Archilochos, the Assistant Bookkeeper corrected him, bowing.

'Archilochos. Very good. I knew your name was something Greekish, Balkan, my dear Chief Bookkeeper.'

Assistant Bookkeeper.' Archilochos set straight his social status.

'Assistant Bookkeeper, Chief Bookkeeper, it comes pretty much to the same thing, doesn't it?' the captain of industry said, smiling. 'At least I don't make any distinction. How do you like my quarters up here? A lovely view, if I do say so myself. You can see the whole city, the river and even the Palace of the President, not to speak of the cathedral, and in the distance North Station.'

'Very lovely, Monsieur Petit-Paysan.'

'You are, incidentally, the first person from the Atomic Cannon Division to enter this floor,' the industrialist said, as though congratulating Archilochos for performing an athletic feat.

'I am from the Obstetrical Forceps Division,' Archilochos replied. 'My territory is eastern Switzerland and the Tyrol, at present the canton of Appenzell Inner Rhoden.'

'Well, well,' Petit-Paysan exclaimed in surprise, 'you come from the Obstetrical Forceps Division. I didn't know we made such things. What exactly are they?'

An obstetrical forceps, Archilochos explained, was an instrument used in childbirth. With it, the doctor grasped the baby's head, during parturition, to speed delivery. The Petit-Paysan Engineering Works, Inc., manufactured forceps of various types; the differences lay in the shapes of the two fenestrated blades, which were curved to hold the head and also had a second curve known as the pelvic crook, to facilitate introduction of the instrument. The handles also varied; they might be short or long, of wood or metal, with or without special knobs, and cross-grips; and furthermore there were distinctions in the type of hinge, that is, the arrangement which allowed the blades to open crosswise when in use. The prices . . .

'Why, you certainly know your subject,' Petit-Paysan said smilingly. 'But let's leave aside the question of price. Now, my dear Monsieur . . .'

'Archilochos.'

'Archilochos, to make a long story short and not keep you in suspense any longer, I have appointed you Director of the Atomic Cannon. To be sure, you have just confessed that you belong to the Obstetrical Forceps Division, of whose existence I really had no inkling. That surprises me a little; something must have got mixed up somewhere; there are always mix-ups in a vast enterprise like this. Very well, it doesn't matter; let us simply combine the two divisions. Consider yourself hereafter Director of the Atomic Cannon and Obstetrical Forceps Division. I shall order the present Directors to be pensioned. I am happy to have the opportunity to inform you personally of your promotion, and to congratulate you.'

'Director Zeus of the Obstetrical Forceps Division is already in the hospital.'

'Why, what is his trouble?'

'Nervous breakdown.'

'Goodness, then my intention must already have reached him.' Petit-Paysan shook his head in wonder. 'And yet I only meant to dismiss Director Jehudi of the Atomic Cannon Division. Somehow there are always these leaks – too many loose tongues around. Well, good, Director Zeus has anticipated me with his nervous breakdown. I would have had to discharge him anyhow. Let us hope that Director Jehudi will receive the news with greater composure.'

Archilochos pulled himself together, and for the first time ventured to look straight at Petit-Paysan, who still held the India-paper volume in his hand. 'May I ask,' he said, 'what all this means? You send for me, promote me to the directorship of the Atomic Cannon and Obstetrical Forceps Division. I am disturbed because I must confess I do not understand any of this.'

Petit-Paysan regarded the Assistant Bookkeeper calmly. He put the volume of Hölderlin down on the green gaming table, and with a gesture invited Archilochos to take a seat. They sat facing one another in the sunlight, on soft cushions. Archilochos scarcely dared breathe, so solemn was this moment. At last he would learn the reason for these mysterious events, he thought.

'Monsieur Petit-Paysan,' he began anew, in a shy, halting voice, 'I have always revered you. You are Number Three in my ethical cosmos, the framework I have put together as best I could, in order to have a moral footing. You come immediately after our honoured President and Bishop Moser of the Old New Presbyterian Church. I feel I should tell you all this. Hence I beg you all the more earnestly to explain the reason for your action to me. Bookkeeper Rummel and Chief Bookkeeper Petit-Pierre have tried to tell me that it is because of my reports on eastern Switzerland and the Tyrol, but I know nobody reads them.'

'Dear Monsieur Agesilaus . . .' Petit-Paysan began solemnly.

'Archilochos.'

"Dear Monsieur Archilochos, you were a Bookkeeper or Chief Bookkeeper – as I've said, I can't fathom the difference – and are now a Director. This seems to perplex you. Look here, my friend, you must see all these remarkable events in their worldwide connections, as a part of the highly diversified activities of my beloved Engineering Works. Why, the firm even – as I have just heard to my delight for the first time – manufactures obstetrical forceps. I hope this branch also turns a profit.' Archilochos beamed. During the past three years, sixty-two obstetrical forceps had been sold in the canton of Appenzell Inner Rhoden alone, he reported.

'Hmm, not much of a turnover. But let that be. I suppose it is more or less a humanitarian division. Good to think that in addition to things that remove human beings from the world we also manufacture things that bring them into it. There must be a certain equilibrium, even if some products do not show a profit. So let us be grateful.

Petit-Paysan paused and looked grateful.

'In his poem "Archipelagos",' he continued at last with a bit of a sigh, 'Hölderlin refers to the businessman, the industrialist, as "far-thinking". The phrase has moved me deeply. A company like this is monstrous, my dear Monsieur Aristippus; the number of workmen and white-collar people, of Bookkeepers and stenographers, is vast, too vast to grasp. Why, I scarcely even know the Directors and have only a nodding acquaintance with the General Directors. The near-sighted go astray in this jungle. Only the man so farsighted that he does not keep his eye on details and individual destinies, but sees only the whole, will not lose sight of the distant goal, is far-thinking, as the poet puts it – you know his works, of course – only the man who knows how to dream, how to launch ever new enterprises, in India, in Turkey, in the Andes, in Canada – only such a man is not mired in the swamps of competition and cartels. Far-thinking. . . . I am on the point of making a merger with the Rubber and Lubricating Oil Cartel. That will be the coup of the century.'

Petit-Paysan paused and looked far-thinking.

'So I plan, I work,' he went on. 'I add my few threads to the fabric being woven at the roaring loom of time. In my modest way, to be sure. What is the Petit-Paysan Engineering Works beside the Steel Trust or the Forever-Joyous Mines, the Pestalozzi Corporation or the Hösler-LaBiche! Nothing! But now, how does it stand with my employees? With all the individuals whose destinies I must overlook in order to keep my eye on the whole? This question frequently troubles me. Are they happy? World freedom is at stake; are my workers free? I have provided them with social benefits, with gymnasiums, swimming pools, canteens, vitamin pills, theatrical performances, concerts. But are the people to whom I give work still caught in material things, in filthy lucre? That is a question that haunts me. A Director goes to pieces merely because he is about to lose his job. Why, that's disgusting. How can anyone take money so seriously? Only the spirit counts, my dear Monsieur Artaxerxes; there is nothing more contemptible, more paltry than money.'

Petit-Paysan paused once again and looked grave.

Archilochos scarcely dared stir.

But now the industrialist straightened up, stiffened; his voice rang out forcefully and coldly.

'You ask why I am appointing you Director. Very well, I shall give you the answer: In order not only to preach but to practise freedom. I do not know my employees, do not understand them; but evidently they have not yet fought through to a purely spiritual comprehension of the phenomenal world. Diogenes, Albert Schweitzer, St Francis, do not seem to be their ideals, as they are mine. Apparently the members of the masses would forgo meditation, helpful service to others, the joys of poverty for the tinselly illusions of social status. Very well, let us give the world what it desires. I have always followed this rule of Lao-tse. For that very reason I have appointed you Director. So that justice may prevail in this regard also. The man who has risen from the ranks, who knows the cares and tribulations of employees from the very bottom, ought to be a Director. I plan the enterprise as a whole, but the man who deals with Bookkeepers and Chief Bookkeepers, with stenographers and secretaries, with errand boys and cleaning women, should be someone from their ranks. Director Zeus and Director Jehudi did not come from the ranks; I bought them as ready-made Directors from ruined rivals. Let us make an end to that. It is time for radical revision in our Western world. The politicians have failed. If industry should also fail, everything will go to the dogs, dear Monsieur Agamemnon. Man is wholly man only when he is creative. Your appointment represents a creative act, an act of creative socialism, which we *must* oppose to uncreative communism. That is all I have to say to you. From now on you are a Director – a General Director. But first take a vacation,' he continued with a smile. 'The cashier already has a cheque for you. Set yourself up. I saw you recently with a charming girl. . . .'

'My fiancée, Monsieur Petit-Paysan.'

'So you are about to marry. I congratulate you. Do so. Unfortunately, this happiness does not lie in my destiny. I have had a cheque for a General Director's annual salary made out to you. It will now be doubled, since you are also taking over the Obstetrical Forceps

Division in addition to the Atomic Cannon Division— I have an important call to Santiago coming up – good luck, my dear Monsieur Anaxagoras. . . .'

As soon as General Director Archilochos, once AB122-OF31, escorted to the elevator by the secretary, left the most holy precincts of the administrative building, he was received like a prince, was warmly embraced by General Directors, greeted with low bows by Directors. Stenographers cooed flatteringly around him, Chief Book-keepers crept around the outskirts of the crowd, CB9-OF lurked in the background, dripping with servility, and from the Atomic Cannon Division, Director Jehudi was carried out on a stretcher, evidently in a straitjacket, exhausted and now unconscious. It was said that he had smashed all the furniture in his office. But it was the cheque that allured Archilochos, and he at once took possession of it. At least this is certain, he thought, still distrustful. He promoted CB9-OF to Vice Director of the Obstetrical Forceps Division, Numbers AB122-OF28, AB122-OF29, and AB122-OF30 to Bookkeepers, issued a few memos concerning the sales campaign for obstetrical forceps in the canton of Appenzell Inner Rhoden, and left the administrative building.

Now he sat in a taxi for the first time in his life. Tired, hungry, bewildered by his precipitate rise in life, he had himself driven to Madame Bieler's.

The city lay in the grip of icy cold, under a clear sky. Everything looked abnormally distinct: palaces, churches, bridges; the big flag above the President's Palace seemed frozen stiff; the river was like a mirror; colours were stratified without blending; the shadows on streets and avenues had sharp outlines drawn around them.

Archilochos entered the bistro. The door tinkled as always, and he took off his shabby winter coat.

'Heavens above,' Georgette said. She stood behind her counter, pouring herself a Campari, surrounded by bottles and glasses that sparkled in the cold sunlight. 'Heavens above, Monsieur Arnolph!

What's happened to you? You look pale and haggard, as though you've had no sleep, and turn up at a time when you should have been at the office long ago! Is anything wrong? Have you been to bed with a woman for the first time, or drunk wine? Have they gone and fired you?' 'On the contrary,' Archilochos said, taking his corner seat.

Auguste brought him his milk.

'What does "on the contrary" mean?' Georgette asked, perplexed. She lit a cigarette and puffed smoke into the slanting rays of sunlight.

'This morning I was appointed General Director of the Atomic Cannon and Obstetrical Forceps Division. By Petit-Paysan personally.' Archilochos still spoke breathlessly.

Thereupon Auguste brought a bowl of applesauce, noodles, and salad to the table.

'Hmm,' Georgette murmured. She did not seem overcome by the news. 'Why?'

'As an act of creative socialism.'

'Could be. And how did it go with the Greek girl yesterday?'

'We are engaged,' Archilochos said shyly, blushing.

'That makes sense,' Madame Bieler declared approvingly. 'What sort of work does she do?'

'Housemaid.'

'Funny sort of household she must work in,' Auguste commented. 'To afford a coat like that.'

'Quiet!' said Georgette.

They had gone for a walk, Arnolph told them, and everything had been so strange, so odd, almost like a dream. All of a sudden everyone was greeting him, waving from cars and buses – the President, Bishop Moser, the painter Passap, and even the American Ambassador had called out 'hello' to him.

'Aha,' Georgette said.

'Maître Dutour also greeted me,' Arnolph continued, 'and Hercule Wagner, though he only winked.'

'Only winked,' Georgette repeated.

'Well, that kind,' Auguste growled.

'Shut up!' Madame Bieler snapped at him, so violently that he skulked off behind the stove with his livid legs. 'You don't have to put your oar in; this isn't anything a man could understand! So now you'll be able to marry your Chloé right away, I guess,' she said, turning back to Archilochos and finishing her glass of Campari.

'I was thinking, as soon as possible.'

'A good idea. It always pays to be decisive with women, especially when they're named Chloé. And where are you planning to live with your Greek wife?'

'I don't know,' Archilochos sighed, as he buckled down to his applesauce and noodles. 'My garret wouldn't do, of course, on account of the water closets and the bad air. In a boarding house, for the time being.'

'Go on, Monsieur Archilochos,' Georgette laughed. 'With the dough you're going to be making! Stay at the Ritz; that's where you belong. And from now on we're doubling your rates here. General Directors have to be exploited or they're no use to anyone.'

She poured herself another Campari.

After Archilochos left, there was silence for a while in Chez Auguste. Madame Bieler washed glasses and her husband sat motionless behind the stove.

'That kind,' Auguste said at last, rubbing his lean legs. 'When I came in second in the Tour de France, I could have had one of that kind too, with a fur coat, fancy perfume, and an industrialist in tow – fellow who owned coal mines in Belgium. By now I'd probably be a General Director myself.'

'Rot,' Georgette said, drying her hands. 'You weren't born for higher things. That kind of woman wouldn't marry you. There's nothing to wake up in you. Archilochos is a Sunday child – I've always felt that – and a Greek besides. You wait and see how he develops. He'll thaw out, and how! The woman is first class. Only natural that she wants to get out of her trade. After all, it isn't always pleasant and it takes a lot out of you, in the long run. All of them want to get married; so did I. Of course the majority don't make it; they do end up in the gutter, as it always says in the sermons; some just about manage to land an Auguste with bare legs and a yellow bicycle rider's outfit – *eh bien*, I'm not complaining, if we're going to talk about bygone days, and I never had me an industrialist. I wasn't ever that classy. The only kind that came to me were petty bourgeois, a few boys from the Treasury, and once an aristocrat for two weeks, Count Dodo of Malchern, the last of his family. He's been dead and buried these many years. But that girl Chloé will pull it off. She has her Archilochos, and it's going to turn out pretty nice.'

Meanwhile, Archilochos took a cab to the World Bank and then to a travel bureau on the Quai de l'État. He entered a big office with maps and bright posters on the walls. Visit Switzerland. The Sunny South Is for You. Air France to Rio. The Emerald Isle. Clerks with courteous, smooth faces. Rattle of typewriters. Neon lights. Foreigners speaking strange languages.

He wanted to go to Greece, Archilochos explained. To Corfu, the Peloponnesus, Athens.

'Sorry, our agency doesn't handle freighter travel,' the clerk said.

But he wanted to go on the *Julia*, Archilochos explained. He would like to have a first-class stateroom for himself and his wife.

The clerk leafed through a timetable and gave a Spanish pimp (Don Ruiz) information on a train. 'The *Julia* is booked up,' he said at last, and turned to a businessman from Cairo.

Archilochos left the travel bureau and went back to his waiting taxi. He considered. Then he asked the driver who was the best tailor in the city.

The cab driver was surprised. 'There's O'Neill-Papperer on the Avenue Bikini and Vatti on the rue St Honoré,' he replied.

'The best barber?'

'José on the Quai Offenbach.'

'The best haberdasher?'

'Goschenbauer.'

'Where does one buy the best gloves?'

'At De Stutz-Kalbermatten.'

'Good,' Archilochos said. 'Take me to each of them in turn.'

And so they drove to O'Neill-Papperer on the Avenue Bikini and to Vatti on the rue St Honoré, to José on the Quai Offenbach, to De Stutz-Kalbermatten for gloves, and to Goschenbauer for hats. Archilochos passed through a thousand hands which smoothed, measured, cleaned, cut, massaged him; each time he entered the cab he was visibly changed, looking more suave and smelling more fragrant. After Goschenbauer's he wore a silver-grey Anthony Eden hat, and late in the afternoon he again drove up to the travel bureau on the Quai de l'État.

He wanted a first-class stateroom with twin beds on the *Julia*, he said in an unchanged voice to the clerk who had turned him away. He laid his silver-grey Anthony Eden hat on the glass counter.

The clerk began filling out a form. 'The *Julia* sails next Friday,' he said. 'Corfu, the Peloponnesus, Athens, Rhodes, and Samos. May I have your name please?'

But after Arnolph had paid for the two bookings and left, the clerk turned to the Spanish pimp, who was still hanging around, leafing through travel folders and now and then conferring with various ladies who (likewise studying travel folders) slipped money into his thin, aristocratic hands.

'Scandalous, señor,' the clerk said, practising his night-school Spanish. 'Some street cleaner or chimney sweep comes along and asks for two tickets on the *Julia*, which is really reserved only for the aristocracy and the best society' (he bowed to Don Ruiz). 'Why, the passenger list for the next voyage includes the Prince of Hesse, and Mr and Mrs Weeman, and Sophia Loren. And when I head him off, out of pure kindness, because he'd find himself completely out of his element, the fellow comes back, sheer gall, dressed like a lord, rich as a tycoon, and I have no choice but to book a cabin for him – what can I do against capitalism? One of your cool customers who can make a fortune in three hours. Probably bank robbery, rape, murder, or politics.'

'Simply outrageous,' Don Ruiz replied in his night-school Spanish.

Darkness was beginning to fall and lights were going on in streets and houses when Archilochos drove across New Bridge to the Boulevard Künnecke and the residence of the Bishop of the Old New Presbyterians of the Penultimate Christians. But in front of the small Victorian house he found Bibi, ragged and dirty, with crushed hat, sitting on the curb, reeking of alcohol, his back propped against a lamp post, reading a newspaper he had found in the gutter.

'How come you're dressed up like that, Brother Arnolph?' he asked, whistling through his teeth, clucking his tongue, blowing his nose with his fingers, and carefully folding the filthy newspaper. 'That's a pretty sharp outfit you've got on. Real high-class.'

'I've become a General Director,' Arnolph said.

'Well, I'll be damned.'

'I'll give you a job as Bookkeeper in the Obstetrical Forceps Division if you promise to pull yourself together. Things have to be done right.'

'No, Arnolph, I've got too much temperament for office work. Can you spare twenty centuries?'

'What's wrong now?'

'Gottlieb slipped down a building front and broke his arm.'

'What building?'

'Petit-Paysan.'

Archilochos became angry, for the first time in his life.

'Gottlieb has no business burgling Petit-Paysan's,' he exclaimed. 'He shouldn't be burgling at all. Petit-Paysan is my benefactor. As an act of creative socialism he has appointed me General Director, and now you ask me for money, money that comes to me from Petit-Paysan, after all.'

'Won't happen again, Brother Arnolph,' Bibi replied with dignity. 'It was just practice. Gottlieb was a bit muddled. He'd heard there was a nice cache of Spanish gold at the Chilean Embassy; besides, the Embassy building is easier to climb. He just mixed up the house numbers; after all, he's only a kid.' He held out his fraternal palm. 'Well, what about those centuries?'

'No,' Archilochos said, 'I cannot finance such dishonesty. I must see the Bishop now.'

'I'll wait for you, Brother Arnolph,' Bibi said, unabashed. He unfolded the newspaper again. 'I have to study up on current events.'

Bishop Moser, stout and pink, in ministerial black and stiff white collar, received Archilochos in his study, a small, high-ceilinged, smoke-stained room lit only by a single lamp, with spiritual and secular books lining all the walls, a high window behind heavy drapes, through which fell the light of the lamp post under which Brother Bibi was ensconced.

The visitor introduced himself. He was actually an Assistant Book-keeper, he said, but had just become General Director of the Atomic Cannon and Obstetrical Forceps Division in the Petit-Paysan Engineering Works.

Bishop Moser regarded him benevolently.

'I know, my good friend,' he murmured. 'You attend Preacher Thürcker's services at the Héloïse Chapel, don't you? I keep my eye on our dear Old New Presbyterian congregation. Welcome, welcome.'

The Bishop vigorously shook the General Director's hand.

'Do sit down,' he said, gesturing to a comfortable armchair and himself taking a seat behind his desk.

'Thank you,' Archilochos said.

'Before you pour out your heart to me, I'd like to pour mine out to you,' the Bishop murmured. 'Will you have a cigar?'

'I am a non-smoker.'

'A glass of wine? Brandy?'

'I am a teetotaller.'

'Do you mind if I permit myself a cigar? A good Dannemann sets the mood for cosy talk and man-to-man confession. Sin bravely, Luther said. And I might say: Smoke bravely. And add: Drink bravely. Permit me?'

He filled a small glass with brandy which he kept in an old bottle behind some books.

'Oh, certainly,' Archilochos said, somewhat perturbed. He was sorry that his Bishop was not quite the paragon he had always pictured.

Bishop Moser lit a Dannemann.

'You see, dear brother, as I hope I may call you, it has long been my heart's desire to have you in for a chat.' (He puffed a first cloud of Dannemann smoke.) 'But, dear God, you can't imagine how busy a bishop is. There are Old Age homes to visit, Youth Camps to organize, straying girls to find Christian homes for, the Sunday schools and confirmation instruction to be inspected, candidates to be examined, negotiations with the New Presbyterians to be conducted, our preachers to be given dressings down. There are a thousand things and trivia to take care of, and one never gets anything done. Our dear friend Thürcker has talked about you frequently; why, you never miss a single service and display a truly rare zeal for the work of our congregation.'

His whole soul demanded that he attend services, Archilochos said simply.

Bishop Moser poured himself another pony of brandy.

'Exactly. We have all been most favourably impressed by you. Two months ago our Old New Presbyterian World Church Council lost

one of its most venerable members and I have been considering
whether you would not be the best candidate for this honorific post.
It could certainly be combined with your duties as General Director
– one would only have to play down the Atomic Cannon Division
somewhat. But we need people who stand with both feet in the midst
of the hard and often cruel struggle of life, Monsieur Archilochos.'

'But Bishop Moser ...'

'Well, are you willing?'

'It's an honour I'd never hoped ...'

'Then may I propose you to the World Church Council?'

'If you think ...'

'I would not want to conceal from you the fact that the World
Church Council is receptive to my suggestions, often only too receptive. Only too often I live in the odour of tyranny; I have the reputation
of being an overbearing Bishop of Bishops. They're all good-natured
gentlemen and good Christians, to be sure – I'll say that for the World
Church Council. They're grateful if I relieve them of organizational
burdens and occasionally think for them – unfortunately not everyone
has a bent for thinking, and that includes the World Church Council.
The next World Council meeting is taking place in Sydney, Australia.
After all, it's one of God's gifts to take a little trip like that, to get to
know other countries and other peoples, foreign morals and foreign
customs, the needs and problems of the common man the world over.
Naturally the Old New Presbyterian Church pays the expenses.'

'I am overcome.'

'Well, that was my problem,' the Bishop murmured. 'Now let us
come to yours. Speaking as man to man, sir. I can already guess it.
You are considering marriage, contemplating linking your fortunes
with a dear little woman. I saw you yesterday between the crematorium
and the National Museum, and even greeted you, but I had to scurry
down a depressing side street, there was a dying old woman I had to
see, poor dear – another of God's hidden saints.'

'Of course, Your Reverence.'

'Well, have I guessed it?'

'Yes.'

Bishop Moser closed the Greek Bible which lay on the desk before
him.

'She was a pretty little thing,' he said. 'I congratulate you. When is
the wedding to be?'

'Tomorrow. In the Héloïse Chapel, if possible – and I would be very happy if you could perform the ceremony.'

The Bishop was somewhat embarrassed.

'That really is the job of your regular minister,' he said. 'Thürcker performs weddings splendidly; he has a remarkable sonorous voice.'

'Won't you please make an exception?' Archilochos pleaded. 'Since I'm going to be a World Church Councillor.'

'Hmm. Do you think you can take care of the legal formalities so quickly?' the Bishop asked. Plainly, he was quite embarrassed about something.

'I shall ask Maître Dutour to take care of them.'

The Bishop at last yielded. 'Very well then. Shall we say tomorrow afternoon at three, in the Héloïse Chapel? May I have the name of your fiancée, address and so on?'

The Bishop noted down the necessary data.

'Your Reverence,' Archilochos said, 'my imminent marriage may be a sufficient reason for my taking up so much of your time, but it is not the prime reason, if I may say so, if it is not sinful to put it that way, since it would be difficult to find anything more important than entering on the obligation to live with a woman for a whole lifetime. Nevertheless, at this moment there is something far more important to me, something that lies heavily indeed upon my heart.'

'My dear General Director, say all you wish to say,' the Bishop replied genially. 'Courage. Cast the cares from your soul, whether your burden is a human or an all-too-human one.'

'Your Reverence,' Archilochos said timidly, straightening up in his easy chair and crossing his legs, 'please forgive me if I seem to be talking confused nonsense. Only this morning I was dressed quite differently; I was frankly shabby, and the suit I wore was the one I'd worn at my confirmation. And now I suddenly find myself in expensive clothing made by O'Neill-Papperer and Vatti. I am distressed, Your Reverence; you must think I have succumbed completely to the world and its tinselly illusions, as Preacher Thürcker always says.'

'On the contrary,' the Bishop said, smiling. 'An agreeable exterior, pleasing clothing, are entirely commendable, especially nowadays when it has become the mode in certain circles devoted to a Godless philosophy to dress with ostentatious carelessness, to look almost beggarly, with gaudy shirts hanging outside the trousers and similar outlandish attire. Decent nattiness and Christianity are by no means mutually exclusive.'

'Your Reverence,' Archilochos went on, encouraged, 'it is a shock to a Christian, I think, when misfortune after misfortune suddenly descends upon him. He may look upon himself as a Job who lost his goods and his health, his sons and his daughters; but for all that, he will be able to come to terms with the matter and regard his calamities as a consequence of his sins. But when the opposite happens, when one piece of good luck follows upon another, it seems to me the time has come for a man to be really disturbed. For where is there a human being who has deserved so much good fortune?'

'My dear Monsieur Archilochos,' Bishop Moser said, smiling, 'the nature of creation is such that this sort of case is extremely rare. The whole creation groaneth, as Paul says, and so we all groan under a greater or smaller accumulation of misfortunes, which, however, we should not take too tragically but understand more in the sense of Job, as you have so finely and correctly said, almost as eloquently as Preacher Thürcker. A case such as you have cited, such an accumulation of good fortune, is hardly likely to be found and produced anywhere.'

'I am such a case,' Archilochos said.

It was very quiet in the sombre study. The last light of day was gone by now, blackest night reigned, and from the street scarcely a sound penetrated into the room, only the occasional hum of a passing automobile or the fading footsteps of a pedestrian.

'I have been struck by one piece of good fortune after the other,' the former Assistant Bookkeeper continued softly. He sat there in his flawless suit, a chrysanthemum in his lapel (the silver-grey Eden hat, the immaculate white gloves, and the elegant fur coat were in the coat closet). 'I inserted a notice among the matrimonials in *Le Soir*. The most charming girl imaginable answers my ad, loves me at first sight, and I love her at first sight; everything happens as in a cheap movie, so that I'm almost ashamed to talk about it. The whole city begins to greet me as I walk through the streets with this girl: the President, you, all sorts of important people; and today I've been accorded the most improbable sort of advancement both in the secular and in the ecclesiastical realm. I've been raised up out of nothing, from the miserable existence of an Assistant Bookkeeper to General Director and World Church Councillor. It's all inexplicable and deeply disturbs me.'

For a long time the Bishop did not say a word. He suddenly looked old and grey. He stared into space, and had even laid the Dannemann in the ashtray, where it remained, abandoned and cold.

'Monsieur Archilochos,' the Bishop said at last, abruptly ceasing to murmur and speaking in a different, firm voice, 'all these events of which you tell me in private on this quiet evening are indeed strange and extraordinary. Whatever their underlying causes may be, I believe that these unknown causes' (here his voice trembled and for a moment dropped to a murmur again) 'are not important to us, certainly not crucial, for they lie in the human realm, and in that realm we are all sinners. What is important, what all this means, is that you are a blessed person upon whom all the proofs of blessing are being heaped in their most visible manner. The man who must stand up before the world now is not Archilochos the Assistant Bookkeeper, but Archilochos the General Director and World Church Councillor. It must mean that you are now obligated to prove whether you deserve all these blessings. Take these events as humbly as you would if they were misfortunes; that is all I can think to tell you. Perhaps you are destined to tread an unusually difficult road, the road of good fortune, which is not imposed upon most people because they would understand even less how to tread it than the road of misfortune, which as a rule we have to traverse upon this earth. Good-bye now.' (He rose.) 'We will see each other again tomorrow in the Héloïse Chapel. By then, perhaps, many mysteries will have been clarified for you, and I can only pray that you will not forget my words, no matter what befalls you henceforth.'

After the conversation with Bishop Moser in the smoke-stained, book-lined room with its sets of classics and rows of Bibles, its massive desk and heavy drapes, and after Bibi, still reading the newspaper (*Le Soir*) under the Bishop's window, had been paid off, the World Church Councillor would have liked to go straight to the Boulevard Saint-Père. But the clock on the Jesuit church at the Place Guillaume had only just struck six, and so he decided to wait until eight, as had been arranged, although he was painfully aware that this meant prolonging

Chloé's life as a housemaid for two unnecessary hours. He resolved to move into the Ritz with her this very evening, and made the necessary arrangements, reserving two rooms, one on the second and one on the sixth floor, so that the girl should not feel awkward, and he himself, as a World Church Councillor, not be placed in a false position. Then he tried to locate Maître Dutour, but his efforts were unfortunately in vain. He was told that the lawyer and notary was out completing the transfer of title of a house. Even with all this, he still had more than an hour and a half to kill. He prepared himself, buying flowers and inquiring about a good restaurant. For he did not want to go back to his old temperance restaurant opposite the World Health Office; and Chez Auguste was not the right place either, for he felt with secret sorrow that his fine clothing excluded him from the bistro. An O'Neill-Papperer suit would not do alongside Monsieur Bieler's yellow jersey! He therefore decided, though with some twinges of conscience, to dine at the Ritz itself – a temperance meal, of course – and reserved a table. Then, a-tingle with happy anticipation, he went to the Passap show which he happened to notice at the Nadelör Gallery, just across the street from the Ritz; the attendance had been so large that the gallery was being kept open in the evening. Passap's latest paintings were on view (sixty-degree angles, ellipses, and parabolas). Archilochos, holding his flowers – white roses – moved slowly through the brightly lit rooms amid a throng of American women, journalists, and artists, enthusiastically and reverently studying the paintings. Suddenly he started at a canvas in cobalt blue and ochre which actually showed nothing but two ellipses and a parabola. Convulsively clutching his flowers, he stared in consternation at the painting. Then he suddenly whirled around, seized by deep dread, bathed in sweat and simultaneously shivering. He stopped for a moment at the cash register, where Nadelör, the gallery owner, stood in a black dinner jacket, smiling and rubbing his hands, and asked the painter's address. Then he dashed into a cab. The dealer, without bothering to take his coat, flew out the door after him and likewise jumped into a cab; he scented a secret purchase and was determined to make sure of his percentage. Passap lived on the Rue Funèbre in the Old Town. The cab (with Nadelör's close behind) finally reached the street by way of Marshal Vögeli Boulevard, but with considerable difficulty, for Fahrcks's followers were at the moment holding a demonstration, with pictures of the anarchist on long poles, red flags, and gigantic placards bearing such slogans as 'Down with the President!' 'Away with the Treaty of Lugano!' and so on. Somewhere in the mob Fahrcks himself was making a speech. Gales of shouting and screeching filled the air, whistles shrilled, horses' hooves thudded, and as the police began wielding nightsticks and fire hoses, the cabs containing the General Director and the art dealer were drenched. The latter had unfortunately opened a window, probably from curiosity. But then both vehicles with their swearing drivers turned into the Old Town. The roughly paved streets rose steeply, lined with ramshackle houses and low dives. The whores stood around in swarms, like black birds, waving and uttering sharp, hissing sounds. It was so cold that the wet cabs became coated with ice.

At No. 43 on the ill-lighted rue Funèbre (where Passap lived), Archilochos got out, still holding the white roses. It was like stepping out of a fairy vehicle encrusted with sparkling, tinkling icicles. He told the cab driver to wait, and besieged by street urchins who clung to his trouser legs, he pressed on past a malignant, drunken concierge into the interior of the tall, ancient building. He began climbing endless flights of stairs which were so rotten that his foot broke through the steps several times and he hung for a moment in space, clinging to the banister. Wearily, he climbed from storey to storey, splinters in his aching hands, almost in darkness, peering at all the doors in search of Passap's name, hearing close behind him the panting of Nadelör, to whom he paid no attention. It was bitterly cold in the stairwell. Somewhere a piano tinkled and somewhere a window banged open and shut. Behind one door a woman was screeching and a man whooping; this landing smelled of wild orgies. Archilochos climbed higher and higher, once sinking through a step to his knee. He barged into a spider web; a fat, half-frozen spider ran across his forehead. Irritably, he brushed it aside. At last, Vatti's fur coat and O'Neill-Papperer's handsome suit covered with dust and his trousers already ripped, but with the flowers safe, he came to the end of a narrow, steep attic staircase and found a rickety door with Passap's name scrawled diagonally across it in gigantic chalked letters. He knocked. Two flights lower down, Nadelör waited in the icy cold. He knocked again, then a second, third, and fourth time. No one. World Church Councillor Archilochos pressed the latch. The door was unlocked, and he went in.

He found himself inside a vast attic, big as a barn. It was a tangle of beams, with various levels of flooring. Everywhere African idols stood around, piles of paintings, empty frames, sculptures, strangely twisted wire constructions, a glowing iron stove with a fantastically long, grotesquely winding stovepipe. Wine and whisky bottles lay about, squeezed-out tubes of pigment, cans of paint, brushes; cats were everywhere, and books lay piled on chairs and scattered on the floor. In the centre of the room stood Passap in a once-white painter's smock, now splotched with colour, dabbing away with his spatula at a canvas on the easel: parabolas and ellipses. Before him, close to the stove, a fat girl sat on a rickety chair, stark naked, with long blonde hair, hands clasped at the nape of her neck. The World Church Councillor stood petrified, scarcely daring to breathe; this was the first time he had ever seen a naked woman.

'Who the devil are you?' Passap asked.

Archilochos introduced himself, though he was rather surprised at the question, for the painter had greeted him on Sunday.

'What do you want?'

'You painted my fiancée, Chloé, naked,' the Greek choked out.

'You mean the painting *Venus, July 11*, which is now hanging in the Nadelör Gallery.'

'Exactly.'

'Get dressed,' Passap snarled at the model, who vanished behind a screen. Pipe in mouth, its smoke curling up among the tangle of beams, Passap stood looking long and attentively at Archilochos.

'So what?'

'Sir,' Archilochos replied with the utmost dignity, 'I am an admirer of your genius. I have followed your career with rapt interest, have even elevated you to the rank of Number Four in my cosmos.'

'Your cosmos? What nonsense is this?' Passap asked, heaping fresh mounds of paint (cobalt blue and ochre) on his palette.

'I have drawn up a list of the worthiest representatives of our age, a list of my moral exemplars.'

'Well?'

'Sir, in spite of the enthusiasm I feel for your work, in spite of my deep respect, I must ask you for an explanation. It is certainly not an everyday occurrence for a bridegroom to see his bride depicted naked as Venus. And even though the painting is an abstraction, a sensitive observer cannot fail to recognize the subject.'

'Pretty damn good,' Passap said. 'More than the critics can do.'

He studied Archilochos once more, stepped up to him, felt him over like a horse, took several steps back again and squinted at him.

'Undress,' he said then. He poured himself a glass of whisky and filled a fresh pipe.

'But . . .' Arnolph attempted to protest.

'No buts,' Passap snarled at him, his small black eyes so fierce and piercing that Archilochos fell silent. 'I want to paint you as Ares.'

'Ares?'

'The war god of the Greeks,' Passap explained. 'I have been searching for years for a suitable model, for the pendant to my Venus. You are it. The typical raging lion, lover of the heat of battle, organizer of bloodbaths. You are Greek?'

'Certainly, but . . .'

'There you are.'

'Monsieur Passap,' Archilochos said at last, 'you are mistaken. I am no raging lion, neither an organizer of bloodbaths nor a lover of the heat of battle. I am a peace-loving man, World Church Councillor of the Old New Presbyterian Church, a strict teetotaller, and I also refrain from smoking. Moreover, I am a vegetarian.'

'Nonsense,' Passap said. 'What is your occupation?'

'General Director of the Atomic Cannon Division and the . . .'

'There we have it,' Passap interrupted. 'A war god after all. And a raging lion. You are simply repressed and have not yet arrived at the mode of life which is appropriate for you. You are also a born swiller and lecher, the most magnificent Ares that has ever come my way. So get undressed and be quick about it. My business is painting, not gabbing.'

'Not while this woman you were painting is still in the room,' Archilochos protested.

'Scram, Catherine, he's bashful,' the painter shouted. 'I won't need you again till tomorrow, fatty.'

'The fat, blonde-haired girl, now with her clothes on, departed. As she opened the door, she confronted Nadelör, covered with ice, shaking in every limb from cold.

'I must protest,' the art dealer called out hoarsely. 'I must protest, Monsieur Passap. We agreed . . .'

'Go to the devil!'

'I'm trembling in every limb from cold,' the art dealer cried desperately. 'We agreed . . .'

'Freeze to death.'

The girl shut the door. She could be heard clumping down the stairs.

'Well,' the painter impatiently asked Archilochos, 'aren't you out of your pants yet?'

'All right,' the General Director replied, undressing. 'My shirt, too?'

'Everything.'

'The flowers? They're for my fiancée, you see.'

'Put them on the floor.'

The World Church Councillor laid his clothes neatly over a chair, brushed them out with his hand (for they were covered with dust from the laborious climb up the stairs), and at last stood naked.

He shivered with cold.

'Move the chair over to the stove.'

'But.'

'Stand on the chair and take a boxer's pose, arms at angles of sixty degrees,' Passap ordered. 'That is how I have always imagined a war god.'

The chair teetered on its rickety legs, but Archilochos obeyed.

'You're too fat,' the painter growled irritably, pouring himself another glass of whisky. 'I only go for that in certain women. But I can get around it. The main thing is the face and chest. All that hair on your chest is good, has a martial look. And the thighs are all right. But take those glasses off; they spoil the whole illusion for me.'

Then he began to paint, angles of sixty degrees, ellipses, and parabolas.

'Sir,' the World Church Councillor began anew (in his boxer's pose), 'you owe me an explanation. . . .'

'Shut up!' Passap thundered. 'If there's to be any talking here, I'll do it. It's the most natural thing in the world that I painted your fiancée. A magnificent woman. You'll find that out when you get to know her breasts.'

'Sir. . . .'

'And her thighs, her navel.'

'But I must . . .'

'Get back into a decent boxer's pose, damnitall,' the painter snarled, smearing wads of ochre on the canvas, followed by cobalt blue. 'Why, you don't even know your girl nude and yet you risk an engagement.'

'You're stepping on my flowers. White roses.'

'So what. A revelation, that nude. I had to force myself not to become a banal naturalist or a bright-buoyant-bouncy-beatific impressionist when I saw that glorious flesh, that breathing skin. Pull your belly in, damnitall! I never had a more divine model than Chloé with her divine back, those perfect shoulders, and those two rounded buttocks, like the twin halves of the universe. A sight like that puts cosmic ideas into your mind. Painting became a pleasure such as it hadn't been for ages. Ordinarily I don't much care for women as subjects – only now and then, like that fat one I had here. Artistically they don't yield anything special. A man is different; there the deviations from the classic ideal are precisely the interesting feature. But with Chloé now – that was different! In her you still see the unity of Paradise – her legs, her arms, her neck, grow out of her body with perfect naturalness, and her head is still a woman's head. I've also done a sculpture of her. Here!'

He pointed to a structure of tangled wires.

'But . . .'

'Boxer's pose,' Passap admonished; he stepped back several times, examined his painting, changed an ellipse, removed the canvas from the easel, and screwed a fresh one into place.

'There,' he commanded. 'Now kneel. Ares after the heat of battle. Lean forward more; after all, I don't have you available every day.'

Archilochos, confused and half roasted by the stove, put up only a feeble resistance.

'I would really like to ask you . . .' he said, but was interrupted by Nadelör, who came tottering, shaking in every limb, into the attic, a moving, tinkling lump of ice, convinced that a sale was being negotiated.

Passap flew into a rage.

'Clear out!' he cried, and the art dealer crept back into the arctic cold of the stairwell.

'Art is my explanation,' the painter said at last, drinking whisky, painting, and simultaneously caressing the tomcat which had climbed on his shoulders. 'I don't give a damn whether or not this explanation satisfies you. I have made something out of your nude fiancée, a masterpiece in proportions, in distribution of planes and rhythms, in colours, in painterly poetry – a world of cobalt blue and ochre. You, on the other hand, want to make something entirely different out of Chloé, once you have her at your disposal in the nude. A mama with a flock of kids, I guess. You will destroy a masterpiece of Creation, sir, not I, who glorify this masterpiece, raise it to the realm of the Absolute, the Ultimate, the dream.'

'It's a quarter after eight,' Archilochos exclaimed in alarm, although at the same time he felt relieved by the painter's explanation.

'So what?'

'I'm supposed to meet Chloé at eight,' Arnolph explained anxiously. Cats purring around his legs, he started to step down from his chair. 'She's waiting for me at the boulevard Saint-Père.'

'Let her wait. Keep your pose!' Passap roared. 'Art is more important than your love affair.' He went on painting.

Archilochos groaned. The cat, a grey one with white paws, had now climbed to his shoulders, and its claws dug painfully into his flesh.

'Quiet,' Passap ordered. 'Don't move.'

'The cat.'

'There's nothing wrong with the cat, but there is with you,' the painter said angrily. 'How can anyone develop such an enormous belly, and without drinking, too?'

Nadelör once more appeared at the door (numb, coated with ice). He was frozen through, he snivelled, his voice so hoarse as to be almost inaudible.

'Nobody's asked you to wait outside my door, and I don't want you in my studio,' Passap retorted roughly.

'You do business with me,' the art dealer croaked; he had to sneeze but could not get his hand out of his pocket because his sleeve was frozen to his trousers.

'On the contrary, you do business with me,' the painter thundered. 'Get out!'

The art dealer withdrew for a third time.

Archilochos did not dare say another word. Passap drank whisky, painted angles of sixty degrees, parabolas and ellipses, heaped cobalt on ochre and ochre on cobalt, and after half an hour allowed the General Director to dress.

'Here,' Passap said, putting the wire construction in his arms, 'put this beside your marital bed. My wedding present. So that you will remember your wife's beauty when it fades. And I'll send you one of your portraits after it dries. And now get out. I dislike World Church Councillors and General Directors almost as much as I do art dealers.

Your luck that you look like the Greek god of war. Otherwise I would have thrown you out long ago, naked, believe me!'

Archilochos departed, the white roses in one arm, while the other clasped the wire construction which allegedly represented his naked fiancée. On the steep, narrow stairway, which was really rather a ladder, he encountered Nadelör. Icicles had now formed under the art dealer's nose. He stood huddled next to the wall, utterly miserable and frozen through from the icy draught.

'There you are,' the man lamented, his voice as faint as if it were coming from a crevice in a glacier. 'I thought so. You've bought something. I protest.'

'It's a wedding gift,' Arnolph explained. He began cautiously descending the stairs, hampered by the flowers and his wire sculpture, vexed with himself at his senseless adventure, for it was going on nine o'clock. But the condition of the stairs did not allow any more rapid descent.

The art dealer followed him.

'You ought to be ashamed,' Nadelör grumbled, to the extent that his words were at all comprehensible. 'I heard you telling Passap that you're a World Church Councillor. Scandalous. A high churchman acting as a model! Stark naked!'

'Would you please hold the sculpture for me?' Archilochos was forced to ask him after a time (between the fourth and third floors, near the still screeching woman and whooping man). 'Just for a moment; my foot has gone through the step.'

'Impossible,' Nadelör whispered. 'I never touch a sculpture unless I get my percentage.'

'Then hold the flowers.'

'I can't. My sleeves are frozen hard.'

At last they reached the street. The icicled cab gleamed like silver. Only the radiator was free of ice, and the motor was still running. Inside, it was frigid. The heater was out of order, the shivering driver explained.

'Twelve boulevard Saint-Père,' Archilochos said, his spirits reviving at the prospect of seeing his fiancée shortly.

The cab was just about to start when the art dealer tapped on the windowpane.

'I must ask you to give me a lift,' came indistinctly from the mass of ice as Arnolph lowered the window and leaned towards the glittering blob. He managed to make out the art dealer's plaint that he could not go a step further and that taxis were few and far between in the Old Town.

'Impossible,' Archilochos said. 'I must get to the boulevard Saint-Père. I'm already terribly late.'

'You're a Christian and a World Church Councillor,' Nadelör replied accusingly. 'You can't leave me in this condition. I'm already beginning to freeze to the pavement.'

'Get in,' Archilochos said, flinging open the cab door.

'A bit warmer in here anyhow, it seems to me,' the art dealer said when he at last managed to bend himself and sit beside Archilochos. 'I hope I thaw out.'

But by the time they turned into the boulevard Saint-Père, Nadelör had not yet thawed. Nevertheless, he also had to leave the cab. The driver refused to go back to the Quai. He'd had enough of the cold, he said, and off he drove. So the two stood before the wrought-iron gate with its putti and dolphins, with the red lamp, which was now dark, and two stone pillars. Archilochos pulled at the old-fashioned bellpull. No one answered. The boulevard was deserted. In the distance the noise and shouts of the demonstrating followers of Fahrcks could be heard.

'Sir,' Archilochos said, upset by his lateness, the flowers and wire sculpture in his arms, 'I must leave you now.'

Resolutely he opened the gate; but Nadelör followed him into the depths of the garden.

'What do you want now?' Arnolph asked, vexed that he could not get rid of the ice-coated art dealer.

'I must telephone a cab.'

'I hardly know the people here. . . .'

'You as a World Church Councillor . . .'

'All right, all right,' Archilochos said. 'Come along.'

The cold was merciless. The art dealer rang like a glockenspiel as he walked. The fir and elm trees stood motionless; huge stars twinkled in the sky, reddish and yellowish amid the silvery ribbon of the Milky Way. Among the tree trunks the windows of a villa glowed in muted gold. As they came closer they saw that the building was really a small rococo palace, daintily ornate, with slender columns, the whole bedecked with vines of wild grape, which showed up plainly on this clear night. A gently curving staircase led up to the front door, which was brightly lit and without a nameplate. Beside it hung a heavy bellpull, but once again no one answered the ring.

Another minute in this cold and he would be frozen to death, the art dealer wailed.

Archilochos pressed the latch. The door was unlocked. He would go and see, he said.

Nadelör entered with him.

'Are you crazy?' demanded Archilochos.

'I can't stand outside in this cold. . . .'

'I'm not at home here.'

'You as a Christian. . . .'

'Then wait here,' Arnolph ordered him.

They had entered a large salon. Furniture which reminded Archilochos of Petit-Paysan's quarters, flowers and little mirrors, beneficent warmth everywhere. The art dealer began thawing immediately. Little streams of water ran down him.

'Don't stand on the rug,' the World Church Councillor snapped, but he felt somewhat alarmed for the gallery owner at the sight of all the drip.

'Certainly,' Nadelör said, posting himself beside the umbrella stand. 'If only I may use the phone.'

'I'll ask the master of the house.'

'As soon as possible.'

'At least hold the wire sculpture,' Archilochos suggested.

'Only for a percentage.'

Arnolph placed the work of art beside Nadelör and opened a door. He looked into a small salon with a settee, a small tea table, a spinet, and delicate little armchairs. He cleared his throat. The room was empty, but he heard footsteps behind a double door. Evidently Mr Weeman. He crossed the room, knocked.

'Come in!'

To his astonishment Arnolph found himself confronting Maître Dutour.

Maître Dutour, a small, spry man with a black moustache and an artistic mop of white hair, stood at a large, handsome table in a room walled with golden mirrors. A chandelier full of real candles hung from the ceiling, brilliant as a Christmas tree.

'I have been expecting you, Monsieur Archilochos,' Maître Dutour said, bowing. 'May I ask you to take a seat.'

He indicated a chair, and sat down facing the World Church Councillor. A document was spread out on the table.

'I don't understand,' Archilochos said.

'My dear General Director,' the lawyer said, smiling, 'I have the pleasure of transferring this house to you as a gift. It is free of mortgage and in excellent condition, except for the west side of the roof, which ought to be repaired one of these days.'

'I still don't understand,' Archilochos said. Though surprised, he was already somewhat inured to so much good fortune. He was in the way of it, after all. 'Would you mind explaining. . . .'

'The former owner of the house does not wish his name mentioned.'

Oh, he knew who that was, Arnolph declared. The owner was Mr Weeman, the famous archaeologist and excavator of Greek antiquities, who'd dug up some ancient temple with precious statues buried in a bog, and golden columns.

Maître Dutour started, stared wonderingly at Archilochos, and shook his head. He was not permitted to dispense any information, he said; the previous owner wished to have his house in Greek hands, and was happy to have found in Archilochos a man who met these conditions. In an age of corruption and immorality, he continued, an age in which the most unnatural crimes seemed to be the most natural, in which all right-thinking was on its way out and people were turning individually and collectively to the fist-and-club morality of primitive eras, a man of law would lose all hope of ever seeing any meaning in his efforts for order and justice if he were not privileged now and then to prepare and execute an act of pure *caritas* such as the transfer of this mansion. The documents were all ready; the General Director had only to glance through them and sign his name. The tax required by the government – Moloch demanded his victims – had already been paid.

'Thank you very much,' Archilochos said.

Maître Dutour read the documents aloud, and the World Church Councillor signed his name in the proper places.

'This little palace now belongs to you,' the lawyer said, rising.

Archilochos likewise rose. 'Sir,' he said solemnly, 'let me express my pleasure at meeting a man whom I have always revered. You were the defence attorney for that poor curate. It was a case of the flesh overpowering the spirit, you cried out at the time; the soul remained untainted. Those words made a deep impression upon me.'

'Now, now,' Dutour said, 'I was only doing my duty. Unfortunately the curate was beheaded; I still feel bad about it. I plumped for twelve years in the penitentiary, you know. Though at least I was able to avert the worst: the poor fellow was not hanged.'

'May I trouble you for a moment longer?' Archilochos said.

Dutour bowed.

'I wish to ask you, *cher Maître*, to prepare the papers for my marriage.'

'They are prepared,' the lawyer replied. 'Your dear fiancée has already asked me to.'

'Oh,' Arnolph exclaimed joyfully, 'you know my dear fiancée?'

'I have had the pleasure.'

'Isn't she a wonderful girl?'

'Very.'

'I am the happiest man in the world.'

'Whom do you suggest as witnesses?'

He had not yet thought about it, Archilochos admitted.

'I would recommend the American Ambassador and the Rector of the University,' Dutour proposed.

Arnolph hesitated.

'I have already won their consent,' Maître Dutour said. 'It will not be necessary for you to do anything further. The marriage is already creating a sensation in society – word of your amazing career has got around, my dear Monsieur Archilochos.'

'But these gentlemen do not know my bride.'

The little lawyer threw back his mop of hair, stroked his moustache, and contemplated Arnolph with an almost spiteful stare.

'Oh, I fancy they do,' he said.

'I understand.' It suddenly dawned on Archilochos. 'The gentlemen have been guests of Gilbert and Elizabeth Weeman.'

Again Maître Dutour started and seemed surprised. 'So to speak,' he said finally.

Arnolph was not altogether enthusiastic. 'Of course I have great esteem for the Rector of the University. . . .'

'There you are.'

'But the American Ambassador . . .'

'Do you have political objections?'

'Not that,' Archilochos replied falteringly. 'Mr Forster-Monroe does after all take fifth place in my moral cosmos; but he belongs to the Old Presbyterian Church, whose dogma of Universal Reconciliation I cannot share, for I believe unshakeably in the eternity of hellfire.'

Maître Dutour shook his head. 'I don't want to say anything against your religion,' he said. 'But surely all that's beside the point. There should not be much in common between the eternity of hellfire and your marriage.'

Archilochos sighed with relief. 'I quite agree with that,' he said.

Maître Dutour closed his briefcase. 'I will bid you good-bye now,' he said. 'The civil ceremony will take place at two o'clock at City Hall.'

Arnolph wanted to see him to the door.

He would rather go across the garden, the lawyer said. He pushed aside a red drape and opened a tall casement. 'This is the shortest way.'

Icy air streamed into the room.

He must have been a frequent guest here, Archilochos thought as the lawyer's swift footsteps faded into the night. For a few moments Arnolph stood on the terrace outside the glass door. He gazed at the twinkling stars above the trees. Then, shivering, he stepped back into the room and closed the casement. 'The Weemans must have entertained a great deal,' he murmured.

Archilochos began wandering through the little rococo palace which now belonged to him. It had seemed to him that he heard faint footsteps in an adjoining room, but he found no one. The whole house was illuminated, either by big white candles or by small lamps. He passed through parlours and small sitting rooms, filled with graceful, delicate furniture, the floors covered with soft rugs. On the walls hung precious antique wallpapers, sometimes rather frayed, with pale-gold lilies against a silver-grey background and fine oil paintings which, however, he did not dare to look straight at; rather, Archilochos blushed several times, for most of them showed nude women, occasionally joined by men equally in a state of nature. He found Chloé nowhere.

At first he had wandered about planlessly, but after a while he began following a coloured trail, paper cutouts of blue, red, and golden stars which lay on the soft rugs and seemed obviously meant to guide him. He came at last to an unexpected narrow, winding staircase which he reached through a secret door in the wallpaper, and so climbed to the upper floor (he had stood baffled for a long time in front of the wall where the stars ended, until at last he discovered the door). On every step lay either a paper star or a paper comet, and once the planet Saturn with its ring, then the moon, then the sun. From step to step Archilochos grew more and more irresolute; his courage had fled and his old timidity had overcome him. He breathed heavily, clutching the white roses which he had never let out of his hand, even during the conversation with Maître Dutour. The winding staircase ended in a round room with a large desk and three high windows, a globe of the world, a high-backed chair, a big standing lamp, and a chest – all the furniture had a medieval cast, as in Faust's study in the theatre. A sheet of yellowed parchment lay on the chair. On it was written in lipstick: *Arnolph's study*. At the sight of the telephone on the desk, Archilochos thought for a moment of the waiting gallery owner standing dripping beside the umbrella stand in the hall down below – perhaps he had thawed out completely by now. But he forgot Nadelör by the time he opened the other study door, to which the stars and comets led; for now he saw before him a bedroom with a tremendous, antique canopied bed. *Arnolph's bedroom* was inscribed on the sheet of parchment which lay on a small Renaissance table. The next room – he continued following the track of stars – switched back to rococo; it was a charming boudoir lit by little red lamps, with all the fragile objects and furniture appropriate to such a room. *Chloé's boudoir* was written here, and the lipsticked parchment lay on a chair over which some articles of clothing had been tossed in hasty disorder – clothing that befuddled Archilochos: a brassière, a girdle, a slip, panties, all gleaming white. On the floor lay stockings and shoes, and through a half-opened door he looked into a black-tiled bathroom. The tub, set into the floor, was filled with green scented water, slightly steaming; but the comets on the floor pointed not only to the bathroom but through it to another door, which he thereupon opened, holding the flowers before him like a shield. He entered a bedchamber with a delicately carved but extremely wide canopied bed in the centre. Here the stars and moons ended, except for a few pasted to the footboard; but there was no one to be seen, for the curtains of the bed were drawn. A few logs burned in a fireplace, casting Arnolph's shadow, huge and flickering, upon the red bed curtains, which were embroidered with strange golden devices. Timidly, he approached the bed. Peering through the crack between the curtains, he saw in the darkness nothing but the white cloud of bed linen. But it seemed to him that he could hear breathing and so he whispered softly, gripped by a thousand anxieties: 'Chloé.' No one answered. He had to act, much though he would have preferred to retreat, from the room, from the palace, back to his garret where he was safe and not befuddled by stars. And so at last with heavy heart he drew the curtain aside and found her lying there, her head ringed by the black tendrils of her loosened hair, sleeping.

Archilochos was so dazed that he sagged down on the edge of the bed and looked shyly at Chloé. But he only dared to look now and again. He was tired, too; the unceasing good fortune had never given him a chance to rest and reflect; so that his shadow on the filmy vermilion curtain of the canopied bed drooped closer and closer to the sleeping Chloé. But suddenly he observed that Chloé had opened her eyes slightly and was studying him, had probably been doing so for some time, from under her long lashes.

'Oh,' she said, as if awakening, 'Arnolph. Did you find the way all right, through all those rooms?'

'Chloé,' he exclaimed, startled, 'you're lying in Mrs Weeman's bed.'

'The bed belongs to you now, you know,' she laughed, stretching.

'You told Mr and Mrs Weeman about our engagement, didn't you?' She hesitated. 'Of course,' she said after a moment.

'Whereupon they gave us this little palace.'

'They have several more in England.'

'I don't know,' he said, 'I can't really take it all in yet. I had no idea Englishmen were so socially enlightened and would simply make their maid a present of a palace.'

'It seems to be the custom there in certain families,' Chloé explained.

Archilochos shook his head. 'And I have become General Director of the Atomic Cannon and Obstetrical Forceps Division.'

'I know.'

'At a huge salary.'

'So much the better.'

'And also World Church Councillor. In May I must make a trip to Sydney.'

'That can be our wedding trip.'

'No,' he said, 'this!' He took the two tickets from his pocket. 'We're sailing to Greece on Friday. On the *Julia*.'

But then he gave a start.

'How is it you know all about my career?' he asked.

She sat up, and was so beautiful that Archilochos lowered his eyes. She seemed about to say something, but then abandoned it, with a sigh, looked long and pensively at Arnolph, and sank back into the pillows. 'The whole city is talking about it,' she said at last, in an odd voice.

'And tomorrow you want to marry me,' he stammered.

'Don't you want to marry me?'

Archilochos still did not dare to look, for she had thrown aside her blanket. Altogether, it was difficult to look anywhere in this room; everywhere were pictures of naked goddesses and gods, something he would not have expected of flat-chested Mrs Weeman.

'These Englishwomen,' he thought. 'Fortunately they are good to their maids, so one can forgive them their lewd minds.' What he really wanted to do was lie down, take Chloé into his arms, and simply sleep, for hours, dreamlessly and soundly in the warm glow of the fireplace.

'Chloé,' he said softly, 'everything that has happened is so confusing to me, and probably to you also, that sometimes I scarcely feel like myself any more and I think I've turned into someone else and must really still be in my garret with its mildewed walls, and that you have never existed. It's much harder to endure happiness than unhappiness, Bishop Moser said today, and at times I think he is right. Unhappiness is not surprising; it happens because it's in the nature of things; but happiness occurs by accident, and so I'm full of fear that our happiness will end as quickly as it began, and that everything is a game people are playing with you and me, with a housemaid and an Assistant Bookkeeper.'

'You mustn't brood about all this now, darling,' Chloé said. 'I've waited for you all day, and now you're here. And how handsome you are. Won't you take off your coat? It's certainly made by O'Neill-Papperer.'

But as he started to take it off, he realized that he still held the flowers in his hands.

'Here,' he said, 'white roses.'

He wanted to give her the flowers, and had to lean across the bed, but was embraced by two soft white arms and drawn down on to it.

'Chloé,' he gasped, 'I haven't yet explained to you the fundamental dogmas of the Old New Presbyterian Church.' But at this moment someone cleared his throat behind him.

The World Church Councillor started up, and Chloé hid under the blanket with a cry. It was the gallery owner who stood beside the canopied bed, shivering, teeth rattling, wet as a drowned man just pulled out of the water, hair pasted to his forehead in thin strands, moustache dripping, clothes plastered to his body, Passap's wire sculpture in his hands. From his feet all the way to the door stretched a puddle, glistening in the candlelight, a few paper stars floating in it.

'I've thawed out,' the art dealer said.

Archilochos stared at him.

'I've brought the sculpture.'

'What do you want?' Arnolph asked at last, blushing.

'I didn't mean to intrude,' Nadelör replied, shaking his sleeves, from which water was running to the floor as if they were hoses. 'But I must ask you as a Christian and a World Church Councillor to please telephone a doctor at once. I've a terrible fever, stabbing pains in my chest, and a ghastly backache.'

'All right,' Arnolph said, rearranging his clothing and standing up. 'Perhaps you'd better put the sculpture right here.'

'As you wish,' Nadelör replied. Groaning, he placed the sculpture beside the bed. 'I also have inflammation of the bladder.'

'My fiancée,' Archilochos made the introduction, gesturing to the mound formed by the blanket.

'You ought to be ashamed,' the art dealer said, fresh fountains spurting from him. 'You as a Christian . . .'

'She really is my fiancée.'

'You may count on my discretion.'

'Will you please go now,' Archilochos said, propelling Nadelör out of the room; but in the boudoir the gallery owner stopped again beside the chair bearing the brassière, the girdle, and the panties.

A bath would do him good, he said, gesturing with trembling arm towards the open bathroom door and the steaming green water in the sunken tub.

'Impossible.'

'You as a World Church Councillor . . .'

'As you like,' Archilochos replied.

Nadelör undressed and stepped into the bath.

'Don't go away,' he begged, naked in the bathtub, soft-fleshed, drenched in sweat, his eyes large, pleading, and feverish. 'I might faint.'

Then Archilochos had to massage him.

The gallery owner showed signs of anxiety.

'What if the master of the house should turn up?' he quavered.

'I am the master of the house.'

'But you said. . . .'

'The house has just been turned over to me.'

The man had a high fever and his teeth were chattering. 'Owner or not,' he said, 'no one is going to turn me out of this place in my condition.'

'It is true, I assure you,' Archilochos said. 'Trust me.'

He still had a little common sense left, Nadelör gasped, heaving himself out of the tub. 'You as a Christian. I'm terribly disillusioned. You're no better than all the others.'

Archilochos wrapped him in a blue-striped bathrobe that hung in the bathroom.

'Take me to a bed now,' the art dealer groaned.

'But. . . .'

'You as a World Church Councillor . . .'

'All right.'

Archilochos led him to the canopied bed in the Renaissance room. He tucked him in. 'I'll telephone the doctor now,' Arnolph said.

'First a bottle of cognac,' the gallery owner demanded, shivering, his throat rattling. 'I always take it for colds. You as a Christian . . .'

'I'll look in the cellar,' Archilochos promised, and wearily started to descend the stairs.

But as soon as he reached the cellar stairs, after some wandering about, he heard a distant whooping from below. Everything was lit up, moreover, and when he reached the vaulted wine cellar he found his presentiment confirmed: Brother Bibi was sprawling on the floor, with the twins Jean-Christophe and Jean-Daniel, in the midst of emptied bottles, singing folksongs.

'Behold what cometh from on high!' Bibi cried cordially when he caught sight of his brother. 'Uncle Arnolph!'

What was he doing here? Arnolph asked anxiously.

'Digging out the brandy and practising harmony. Who'll go a-hunting? said Robin to Bob . . .'

'Bibi,' Arnolph said with dignity, 'I should like to ask you not to sing. This is the cellar of my house.'

'Well, well,' said Bibi, 'you have come up in the world. Congratulations. Plank yourself down here, Brother Arnolph, square on the sofa.' He offered his brother an empty keg that stood in a puddle of red wine.

'Come on, kids,' he urged the twins, who were doing gymnastics, like monkeys, on Arnolph's knee and shoulders, 'rap out a hymn for your uncle.'

'Be faithful, honest, true, and good. . . .' Jean-Christophe and Jean-Daniel sang screechingly.

Archilochos attempted to overcome his weariness. 'Brother Bibi,' he said, 'I have to talk to you once and for all.'

'Enough with the music, twins!' Bibi bumbled thickly. 'Listen sharp. Uncle Arnolph wants to make a speech.'

'Not that I am ashamed of you,' Arnolph said. 'You are my brother and I know that at the bottom of your heart you're a good soul, who bears no man ill-will, with inner nobility. But because of your weakness I must now be stern as a father with you. I have supported you, and the more I gave you, the worse things have gone with you and your family. And now here you are lying drunk in my cellar.'

'Sheer oversight, Brother Arnolph; I thought it was the War Minister's cellar. Just an oversight.'

'So much the worse,' Arnolph replied sadly. 'One does not break into strangers' cellars. You'll end up in prison. Now go home with your twins, and tomorrow you'll start work at Petit-Paysan in the Obstetrical Forceps Division.'

'Home? In this cold?' Bibi demanded, horrified.

'I'll call a cab for you.'

'You want my delicate twins to freeze to death?' Bibi protested indignantly. 'In our draughty barracks they'd die in this temperature. It's four below zero.'

From an adjoining section of the cellar came rumbling sounds. Matthew and Sebastian, twelve and nine years old, rushed in, dashed at their uncle, and joined the twins in clambering on his knees and shoulders.

'Put away your daggers when you play with your uncle, Matthew and Sebastian,' Brother Bibi commanded.

'Good Lord,' Arnolph asked from underneath his four nephews, 'who else have you got here?'

'Only Mama and Uncle Captain,' Bibi said, opening a bottle of vodka. 'And then just Magda-Maria with her new sport.'

'The Englishman?'

'What's this about an Englishman?' Bibi said in a tone of wonderment. 'That was all over with long ago. A Chinese now.'

When he finally returned to Nadelör, the man was asleep, though tossing with delirious dreams, and it was too late to telephone a doctor. Archilochos was exhausted. Cacophonous sounds of singing still came from the cellar. He did not dare follow the trail of stars and comets a second time to Chloé's bedroom. Instead, he lay down on the settee, near the chair with the brassière and girdle, and after removing his O'Neill-Papperer coat at last and covering himself with it, fell asleep at once.

In the morning he was awakened towards eight o'clock by a maid in a white apron.

'Hurry, sir,' this maid said, 'take your coat and leave, before the master of the house wakes up.' She opened a door which he had not noticed previously and which led out to a wide hallway.

'Nonsense,' Archilochos said, 'I am the master of the house. The man in bed is the gallery owner Nadelör.'

'Oh,' the girl said, dropping a curtsey.

'What is your name?' he asked.

'Sophie.'

'How old are you?'

'Sixteen, sir.'

'Have you been here long?'

'Six months.'

'Mrs Weeman hired you?'

'Mademoiselle Chloé, monsieur.'

Archilochos thought there must be some confusion somewhere, but he felt uneasy and forbore to ask any further questions.

'Would you like your coffee, sir?' the girl asked.

'Is Mademoiselle Choé up yet?'

'She sleeps till nine.'

'Then I wish to see her at nine,' Archilochos said.

'*Mon Dieu*, monsieur!' Sophie shook her head. 'Then Mademoiselle takes her bath.'

'And at half past nine?'

'She is massaged.'

'Ten?'

'Monsieur Spahtz comes.'

'Who is that?' Archilochos asked.

'The dressmaker.'

'But when can I see my bride?' Archilochos cried out in despair.

'*Ah non*,' Sophie declared firmly. 'There are all the wedding preparations. Mademoiselle has far too much to do.'

Archilochos submitted and told the girl to show him to the breakfast room; at least he would have something to eat.

He breakfasted in the room in which Maître Dutour had transferred the house to him, served by a stately, grey-haired butler (the whole place seemed suddenly to be swarming with servants). Eggs, ham (which he let stand), mocha, orange juice, grapes, and sweet rolls with butter and jam. Outside the tall windows, meanwhile, it grew lighter beyond the trees of the garden, and the wedding presents began pouring into the palace. Flowers, letters, telegrams, mountains of packages. Blowing their horns, the mail trucks drove up, became jammed one behind the other; the presents were heaped higher and higher in the hall, in the salon, even in front of the bed and on the blanket of the forgotten art dealer, who with mute dignity went on with his delirium.

Archilochos wiped his mouth with the damask napkin. He had eaten for almost an hour, conscientiously, silently, for since his noodles and applesauce at Georgette's he had not had so much as a morsel. On the sideboard stood bottles of apéritifs and liqueurs, boxes of cigars, brittle, fragrant Partagas, Dannemann, Costa Penna, a fine array of cigarettes. The first temptation to try something of the sort arose in him; alarmed, he fought down the feeling. He was enjoying this first hour as master of the house. To be sure, the singing and bawling of Bibi's clan, which at times sounded only too clearly from the cellar, bothered him somewhat. The fat cook, who had gone down there, came back badly dishevelled; she had almost been raped by Uncle Captain.

A band of robbers had broken in, the alarmed butler reported, and wanted to telephone the police. Archilochos waved that aside.

'Just my family.'

The butler bowed.

Arnolph asked his name.

'Tom.'

'Age?'

'Seventy-five, sir.'

'How long have you been here?'

'Ten years.'

'Mr Weeman hired you?'

'Mademoiselle Chloé.'

Again Archilochos thought there must be some confusion, but for the second time forbore to pursue his questioning. He felt slightly uneasy before this seventy-five-year-old butler.

O'Neill-Papperer would be coming at nine o'clock, the butler informed him. To prepare the wedding suit. Goschenbauer had already sent the top hat.

'Very good.'

'At ten the registrar. There are still a few formalities to settle.'

'Very well.'

'At half past ten Monsieur Wagner will call to bring the honorary doctorate of the Medical Faculty of the University, for Monsieur's services in connection with obstetrical forceps.'

'I shall be expecting him.'

'At eleven the American Ambassador is coming with a letter of congratulations from the President of the United States.'

'Delighted.'

'At one there will be a small lunch with the witnesses and at twenty minutes to two departure for the Registry Office. After the ceremony in the Héloïse Chapel, dinner at the Ritz.'

Who had organized all this? Archilochos wanted to know.

'Mademoiselle Chloé.'

'How many guests?'

Mademoiselle desired an intimate celebration. Only close friends.

'I entirely agree.'

'Therefore we have invited only two hundred persons.'

Archilochos was somewhat perplexed. 'Very well,' he said at last. I don't understand these matters. Have a cab here for me at half past eleven.'

'Wouldn't you prefer Robert to drive you?'

'Who is that?' Archilochos asked.

'The chauffeur. Your red Studebaker is the smartest in the city, sir.'

'Odd,' Archilochos thought; but at this moment O'Neill-Papperer arrived.

And so, shortly before half past eleven, he drove to the Ritz to call on Mr and Mrs Weeman. He found the two in the hotel lobby, a feudal room with plush sofas and all sorts of armchairs, with such dark paintings on the walls that the objects represented, various fruits in some and assorted game in others, were all but invisible. The couple were sitting on a sofa, reading magazines: he the *New Archaeological Survey* and she the *Journal of Antiquities*.

'Mr and Mrs Weeman,' Arnolph addressed them, stirred to his depths, handing them two orchids as they looked up in surprise, 'you are the finest persons I have ever known.'

'Well,' Mr Weeman said, pulling on his pipe and laying aside the *New Archaeological Survey*.

'I am raising you to Numbers One and Two in my ethical cosmos!'

'Yes,' Mr Weeman said.

'I revere you even more than the President and the Bishop of the Old New Presbyterians.'

'Well,' said Mr Weeman.

'Who gives from the heart deserves thanks from the heart.'

'Yes,' said Mr Weeman, staring popeyed at his wife.

'Thank you very much!'

'Well,' said Mr Weeman, and then again, 'Yes.' He took out his wallet, but Archilochos had already vanished.

'Dear good people, but rather reserved, these Englishmen,' he thought as he rode away in his red Studebaker (the smartest in the city).

It was not just a few meek little old ladies of the Old New Presbyterian congregation that awaited the wedding procession in front of the Héloïse Chapel. Huge crowds of people stood half-frozen on Emil Kappeler Street and formed long rows along the sidewalks. Every window of the dirty, battered quarter was filled with heads and shoulders. Ragged urchins hung like lime-sprayed grapes from the lamp-posts and perched in the neighbourhood's few wretched trees. The procession of automobiles turned from the Boulevard Merkling, on its way from City Hall to the Chapel, the red Studebaker in the van. Chloé and Archilochos emerged from the Studebaker. The crowd screamed and roared with enthusiasm. 'Hurrah for Archilochos!' '*Evviva Chloé!*' The bicycle-racing fans shouted themselves hoarse, and Madame Bieler and her Auguste (for once not in his cyclist's outfit) both wept. Somewhat later the President's ornate carriage came driving up, drawn by the six white horses, the bodyguard with golden helmets and white plumes on prancing black chargers. The Héloïse Chapel filled. It was not exactly a beautiful building, since it rather resembled a small factory, had no tower, and its once-white walls were badly marred. It was, in fact, in every respect an unsuccessful product of modern ecclesiastical architecture, surrounded by a few dreary cypresses. And since it had once taken over for a song the furnishings of an extremely old church which had had to be demolished to make room for a movie palace, the interior of the Héloïse Chapel corresponded to its exterior. It had a barren, poverty-stricken air, with crude wooden benches and a rude pulpit which projected, awkward and solitary, into the room. Opposite the entrance was a large, half-rotted cross. The wall behind the cross, with its yellow and greenish stains, reminded Archilochos of his former garret, as did the high windows, like loopholes; through them fell slanting rays of light in which danced particles of dust. But as the wedding guests began to occupy this poor, devout, cramped world, which smelled of old women, of cheap perfume, and perhaps also of garlic, brilliance entered; the chapel became friendly and warm; the sparkle of jewellery and pearl necklaces filled the room; shoulders and breasts glowed, and fumes of the finest perfume rose upwards into the half-charred rafters (the church had once nearly burned down). Bishop Moser mounted the pulpit, dignified in his black Old New Presbyterian robe. He laid the Bible with its bright gilt edging on the cracked wood of the lectern, clasped his hands, and looked down, somewhat embarrassed, it seemed, his pink face drenched with sweat. Directly below him sat the bridal couple, Chloé with big, black, fervent eyes, radiant with joy, in a filmy veil in which played a ray of sunlight, and Archilochos stiffly at her side, now also embarrassed, in his formal dress (O'Neill-Papperer), hardly recognizable any more, for only his rimless, dusty glasses, which were now somewhat askew, remained of his old self. The top hat (Goschenbauer) and the white gloves (De Stutz-Kalbermatten) rested on his knees. Behind the pair, but somewhat apart from the others, sat the President, goateed, his face chiselled by innumerable lines, hair white, his uniform of a cavalry general bedizened with gold, long sword along his thin legs, on which he wore highly polished boots; and behind the President sat the witnesses: the American Ambassador, with decorations on the breast of his white formal jacket, and the Rector magnificus in all his gravity; then came the guests, rather uncomfortably seated on the wooden benches: Petit-Paysan; Maître Dutour at the side of his enormous wife, who towered into the room like a mountain covered with pearls instead of snow;

Passap, he too in tails, his hands still stained with cobalt blue; in addition, men, chiefly men, of the upper one thousand, the cream of the cream of the city, all solemn-faced; and just as the Bishop was about to begin his oration even Fahrcks came in, though late: Fahrcks the revolutionary, the last and lowermost in Arnolph's ethical cosmos, huge, massive head with bristly moustache and fiery red, curly hair between mighty shoulders, double chin touching the breast of his tailcoat, from which dangled a gold decoration studded with rubies: the Order of the Kremlin.

Bishop Moser began his address in a low, faintly lisping voice, shifting back and forth in his pulpit with visible discomfort. The words of which he wished to remind the congregation assembled here to celebrate this happy occasion, he said, were to be found in the Seventy-second Psalm, a Psalm of Solomon: Blessed be the Lord, the God of Israel, who alone does wondrous things. His task today, the Bishop continued, was to bind together for life two children who undoubtedly had been dear and precious to all those gathered here in the Héloïse Chapel. There was first of all the bride (here Bishop Moser stammered a little), whom all those present had no doubt locked in their hearts with great tenderness, a bride who (here Bishop Moser became poetic) had so graciously vouchsafed to all those assembled here so much love, so much of beauty and sublimity, in brief so many glorious hours, that no one could thank her sufficiently (the Bishop wiped the sweat from his brow); and here was a bride-groom, the Bishop continued with manifest relief, also a dear, noble soul who would now partake of all the love which his bride was capable of giving so lavishly – a citizen of our town who in a few days had attracted the attention of the whole world, rising from humble estate to the eminence of General Director, World Church Councillor, Honorary Doctor of the Medical Faculty, and Honorary Consul of the United States. True though it might be that everything man undertakes, and all that he achieves, all his titles and deserts, are transitory, chaff in the wind, a nothingness in the face of the Eternal, nevertheless this precipitate rise showed that grace had intervened (here Fahrcks audibly cleared his throat). For all this was simply not a grace bestowed by men alone (now Petit-Paysan cleared his throat), but by God, as the Scriptural passage just quoted indicated; not the favour of men had elevated Archilochos, but the Lord alone, who to be sure had employed for His purposes human hearts which He guided, had indeed utilized human weakness, human fallibility, for His ends, and therefore to Him alone belonged the glory.

So Bishop Moser preached, and his voice grew more powerful, more stirring, his words more elaborate, more unctuous, the further he moved from the starting point of his oratory, the bride and bridegroom, to the realms of the infinite and the divine, painting a canvas of the wisely and majestically ordered cosmos in which the decrees of God ultimately turned all things to a good end. But after the Bishop had finished, and had descended from the pulpit and completed the ceremony, the two whispering their 'I do's', and Archilochos now stood there, his lovely wife, with her big, black, happy eyes, holding his arm, and as if awakening, he looked at the fine company through which he was now to pass, the dignified President, the ladies and gentlemen weighed down with jewellery and decorations, all these powerful, influential, and famous persons in the land, and as he noticed Fahrcks with his tousle of red hair scrutinizing him mockingly, face twisted in a malignant grimace, and as the little organ above the choir began wheezing out Mendelssohn's Wedding March – at this point, at the climax of his joy, envied by the waiting crowd outside, the Greek suddenly understood. He paled, reeled. Sweat poured down his face.

'I HAVE MARRIED A COURTESAN!' he cried out desperately, like a fatally wounded animal. He wrenched away from his wife, who anxiously pursued him in her waving veil to the portal, and ran out of the Héloïse Chapel, where the crowd received him with whoops and gales of laughter, for as they saw the bridegroom appear alone they instantly realized what had happened. Archilochos faltered for a moment among the miserable cypresses, alarmed, for only now did ne realize the vast numbers of the spectators. Then he ran past the President's carriage and the waiting line of Rolls-Royces and Buicks and dashed down Emil Kappeler Street, zigzagging because here and there people stepped in his way. He ran frantically like a hunted animal pursued by a pack of dogs.

'Hurrah for the town cuckold!'

'Down with him!'
'Tear his clothes off!'
Whistles shrilled in his ear, insulting shouts and stones were hurled after him, urchins tripped him up. Several times he fell, until finally, covered with blood, he was able to hide under the stairs in the entrance to a tenement house. He cowered there in the darkness, the thundering footsteps of the pack above his head, his face buried in his arms. After a while the pursuit stopped, since the mob had lost its quarry.

For hours he continued to crouch under the stairs, freezing, sobbing softly, while it grew darker and darker in the unheated hallway of the tenement. She had slept with all of them, all, with the President, with Passap and Maître Dutour, with all of them, he whimpered. The whole enormous weight of his moral cosmos had collapsed, crushing him in the ruins.

Finally he pulled himself to his feet. He staggered down the unknown hallway, fell over a bicycle, and stepped out on the street. Night had already fallen. He stole down to the river, through ill-lighted, dirty streets, stirring up hordes of yammering beggars who lay under the bridges wrapped in newspapers. A dog snapped at him, shadowy in the darkness. Squeaking rats scurried past and gurgling water lapped at his feet. Somewhere, a ship's whistle howled.

'That's the third one this week,' a beggar's voice squawked. 'Go on, jump in!'

'Nonsense,' another croaked. 'It's too cold.'

Laughter.

'Hang yourself, hang yourself,' the beggars bawled in chorus. 'That's the easiest, that's the easiest.'

He left the river, wandering at random through the Old Town. Somewhere the Salvation Army was playing a hymn. He drifted into the Rue Funèbre, where Passap lived, began to run, trudged for hours through quarters he had never entered before, through high-toned residential streets, working-class neighbourhoods filled with the noise of radios, past ugly taverns from which boomed the cynical songs of Fahrcks's adherents, through factory districts with ghostly foundries, and toward midnight reached his old garret. He did not turn on the light; he stood leaning against the door which he had closed behind him, trembling, filthy, O'Neill-Papperer's dress suit torn; he had long ago lost Goschenbauer's top hat. The flushing toilets still roared, and the lights from the little windows in the building across the areaway fell through the dusty windowpanes, illuminating now the curtain (behind which hung his old Sunday suit), now the iron cot, now the chair and the rickety table with the Bible, now the pictures of his former cosmos against the vague wallpaper. He opened the window. Stench welled up towards him, and a louder roaring. One after the other he ripped the pictures from the wall, hurled the President, the Bishop, the American Ambassador, even the Bible, into the dark depths of the shaftlike areaway. He left hanging only Brother Bibi with his little brood. Then he crept into the other part of the attic, where long rows of laundry hung indistinctly, untied a clothesline, left the wash of some family or other lying on the floor, and groped his way back to his room. He placed the table under the lamp, climbed up on it, fastened the clothesline to the hook from which the lamp hung. Then he knotted the noose. The window blew open and shut, and icy drafts washed across his forehead. He stood, head in the noose, and was about to throw himself from the table when the door to his room opened and the light was turned on.

It was Fahrcks, still in formal dress as at the wedding, a fur-lined coat over it, his ponderous face immobile, gigantic above the Order of the Kremlin, his tousle of hair a furious flame. Two men accompanied him. One of them was Petit-Paysan's secretary, who now bolted the door, while the other, a towering hulk of a man in the uniform of a taxicab driver, closed the window. Then, chewing gum, he placed the chair in front of the door. Archilochos stood on the swaying table, head in the noose, in the spectral light of the lamp. Fahrcks sat down on the chair and folded his arms. The secretary sat down on the bed. The three remained silent. With the window closed, the roar of flushing toilets was somewhat muted, and the anarchist sat studying the Greek closely.

'Well, Monsieur Archilochos,' he said at last, 'you really should have expected me to call.'

'You too have slept with Chloé,' Archilochos snarled at him from his stance on the table.

'Of course,' Fahrcks said. 'After all, that is the lovely lady's occupation.'

'Get out!'

The revolutionary did not stir. 'Each of her lovers gave you a wedding present,' he said. 'Now it's my turn. Luginbühl, hand him my present.'

The giant in cab driver's uniform stepped to the table, chewing, and laid a metallic, egg-shaped object between Arnolph's feet.

'What is that?'

'Justice.'

'A hand grenade?'

Fahrcks laughed. 'Exactly.'

Archilochos took his head out of the noose, climbed carefully down from the rickety table, and hesitantly picked up the grenade. It was cold and sparkled in the light.

'What am I supposed to do with it?'

The revolutionary did not answer at once. Immobile, cunning, he leaned forward on the chair, huge hands spread out over his knees.

'You wanted to commit suicide,' he said. 'Why?'

Archilochos did not answer.

'There are two ways to deal with this world,' Fahrcks said slowly and dryly. 'Either one is destroyed by it or one changes it.'

'Be still,' Archilochos screamed.

'Very well. Then hang yourself.'

'Say your say.'

Fahrcks laughed. 'Give me a cigarette, Schubert,' he said, turning to Petit-Paysan's secretary. Luginbühl gave him a light from a clumsy lighter, and he sat smoking deliberately, puffing out big, bluish clouds of smoke.

'What am I to do?' Archilochos cried.

'Accept what I am offering you.'

'What for?'

'The social order that has made a fool of you must be overthrown.'

'That's impossible.'

'Nothing is easier,' Fahrcks replied. 'You are to assassinate the President. I'll take care of the rest myself.' He tapped the Order of the Kremlin.

Archilochos reeled.

'Don't drop the bomb,' the old incendiary warned him. 'It will explode if you do.'

'You want me to become a murderer?'

'What's so awful about that? Schubert, show him the plan.'

Petit-Paysan's secretary stepped to the table and unfolded a sheet of paper.

'You're in league with Petit-Paysan!' Archilochos cried out, horrified.

'Nonsense,' Fahrcks said. 'I've just bribed the secretary. Such fellows can be had for small change.'

Here was the plan of the President's palace, the secretary began explaining matter-of-factly, running his finger over the drawing. Here the wall surrounded the palace on three sides. The front side was closed off by an iron fence thirteen feet high. The wall itself was seven feet nine inches high. To the left was the building of the Economics Ministry, to the right the Nuncio's residence. Where the wall enclosed the courtyard of the Economics Ministry, a ladder was standing.

Archilochos wanted to know whether the ladder was always there.

'It is there tonight; that ought to be enough for you,' the secretary replied. 'We will drive you as far as the Quai. You climb up the wall, draw the ladder after you, and use it to climb down. On the other side you will be in the shade of a fir tree. Step behind the trunk of it and wait until the guard has passed. Then proceed along the back of the palace. You will find a small door, with several steps leading up to it. The door is locked; here is the key.'

'And then?'

'The President's bedroom is on the second floor; from the little door you reach it by way of the main staircase. It is towards the rear. Throw the hand grenade at his bed.'

The secretary fell silent.

'And after I have thrown the grenade?'

'Go back the way you came,' the secretary said. 'The guards will all be rushing through the main entrance and you will have time to escape across the courtyard of the Economics Ministry, in front of which our car will be waiting for you.'

It was silent in the garret, and cold. Even the roar of water closets had ceased. Against the stained wallpaper Brother Bibi and his little brood hung in solitude.

'Well?' Fahrcks interrupted the silence. 'What do you say to this project?'

'No,' Archilochos cried, pale, shaking with horror. 'No!'

The old revolutionary dropped his cigarette to the rough floor (splintery wood with big knotholes), where it went on smouldering.

'They all take on like that at first,' he said. 'As though the world could be changed without killing.'

Next door, awakened by Arnolph's cry, a servant girl thumped on the wall. Archilochos saw himself, Chloé on his arm, walking through the wintry city. Fog hung over the river with its big, shadowy ships and its lights. He saw people waving from streetcars, from automobiles, handsome, elegant young men. Then he saw the wedding guests, spangled with gold and studded with diamonds, black tailcoats and evening dresses, scarlet decorations, white faces in the golden sunlight, with the dancing dust particles, and everyone wearing a benevolent smile that was in truth so false, so malicious. He felt once again the sudden, cruel moment of insight, of shame; saw himself rushing out of the Héloïse Chapel, emerging from among the cypresses; saw himself faltering, and at last beginning his wild dash down Emil Kappeler Street, right through the howling, jeering, jubilant crowd. He saw the shadows of his pursuers grow to gigantic size on the asphalt of the street, felt once again his body pitching forward, felt the impact of his fall on the hard ground, which reddened with blood, and the stones, the fists that struck him like hammers, and how he quivered as he crouched under the stairs of the hallway, with footsteps pounding above him.

'I'll do it,' he said.

Archilochos, resolved to avenge himself upon the world, was driven by Fahrcks and his companions in their American-made car to the Quai Tassigni. From here he had only two minutes' walk to the President's palace on the Quai de l'État. It was fifteen after two. The Quai was deserted. A quarter moon had risen behind St Luke's Cathedral. The ice floes in the river, and the bizarre crenellations and beards on the frozen St Cecilia's Fountain, glistened in its light. Archilochos kept in the shadow of the palace and the hotel. He passed by the Ritz with its shivering doorman who paced up and down in front of the entrance; but otherwise he met no one. Only Fahrcks's car drove by several times, as if by chance; the revolutionary was checking to see that Archilochos carried out his mission. Fahrcks also stopped to ask the policeman in front of the Economics Ministry some feigned question, so that Archilochos could slip unnoticed into the courtyard. There he found the ladder against the wall. He patted the grenade in the pocket of his patched old coat, which he had taken with him from the garret, climbed the ladder, sat down on the narrow top of the wall and drew it after him, dropped it to the other side and descended. When he reached the hard-frozen lawn, he found himself in the shadow of a fir tree, just as the secretary had said. Arc lights were playing on the side of the building toward the Quai, and an automobile blew its horn somewhere; perhaps that was Fahrcks again. The quarter moon emerged from behind the Presidential Palace, a clumsy, over-ornamented baroque structure (reproduced in all art books and extolled by all art commentators). Close to the moon a big star twinkled, and the lights of an airplane moved high up in the sky. Then footsteps resounded on the paved path that wound along outside the palace. Archilochos pressed close to the trunk of the fir, hidden in its branches, which hung down to the ground and surrounded him with their resinous scent, while the needles tickled his face. There were two guards; they approached marching in step, visible at first only as dark silhouettes with shouldered rifles and fixed bayonets, their white plumes swaying in the moonlight. In front of the fir tree, they came to a halt. One of them pushed the branches aside with his rifle. The Greek held his breath, thought himself discovered, and was already preparing to throw the grenade. But then they moved on; they had not seen him. As they advanced into the full moonlight, their golden helmets and the cuirasses of their historical uniforms flashed brightly. They turned the corner of the palace. Archilochos disentangled himself from the branches of the tree and sprinted towards the rear of the building. There everything lay in the full glare of the moonlight: tall spruces and bare weeping willows, an ice-coated pond and the Nuncio's residence. He found the door at once. The key fitted. He turned the key, but the door did not open. It must be bolted from inside. Archilochos hesitated; the guards might be back at any moment. He stepped back and looked up the rear wall of the building. The door was embedded between two nude marble giants, evidently Castor and Pollux, who carried a curving balcony on their shoulders. The balcony, he deduced, must be outside the President's bedroom.

A mad fury of determination seized him: he must carry out the assassination, come what may. He began scaling one of the statues, clambering up a thigh, a belly, a chest, digging his fingers into a marble beard, holding on to a marble ear, hoisting himself up over a gigantic head. He reached the balcony. In vain. The door would not open, and he did not dare smash the glass panes, for he could already hear the guards' footsteps. He flattened himself out on the cold floor of the balcony. The guards came along, marching in step as before, and passed by beneath him. The balcony door was surrounded by a variety of nude males and females, larger than life, with horses' heads among them, all brightly illuminated by the moon, fighting and rending one another in gruesomely complex postures. He was able to study all this while still lying on the floor of the balcony. Evidently it represented a battle with Amazons, and in the midst of the writhing bodies he detected the open hole of a round window. He ventured up into the world of marble gods, made his way between enormous breasts and thighs, fearing all the while that the bomb in his coat pocket might explode. He crawled past the bellies of heroes, along arched and twisted backs, at one point had only the drawn sword of a warrior to hang on to, snatching at it just as he thought he had already fallen. Terrified, he thrust himself into the arms of a dying Amazon whose sophisticated face beamed tenderness upon him, while far below the guards completed their tour for the third time, and stood still.

Archilochos saw them step back into the moonlit gardens and study the wall of the palace.

'There's someone up there,' one of the two said, after prolonged peering.

'Where?' the other asked.

'There.'

'Nonsense, that's only a shadow between the gods.'

'They aren't gods, they're Amazons.'

'What's that?'

'Women with only one breast.'

'But they've got two.'

'The sculptor made a mistake,' the first guard concluded. 'But someone's hanging on up there. I'll bring him down fast enough.'

He raised his rifle and took aim. Archilochos did not move.

The other man protested: 'Do you want to wake the whole neighbourhood with your target practice?'

'But there's someone there.'

'There isn't. No one could ever get up there.'

'Guess you're right.'

'You see? Let's go!'

The two marched off, in step, their rifles shouldered again. Arnolph clambered on, at last reached the window, and crawled through it. He found himself on the third floor, in a high-ceilinged bare toilet, filled with moonlight that streamed through the open window. He was exhausted, covered with dust and bird droppings from his climb, and sobered by the abrupt change between the world of marble gods and his present place. Breathing heavily, he opened the door and found himself in a spacious hall which opened up on both sides into large rooms of state, they too moonlit, with statues among the columns. Vaguely, he made out a wide, curving staircase. He descended cautiously to the second floor, reached the corridor the secretary had described, peered through the tall windows on the side toward the Quai, and started back in alarm, momentarily blinded by the lights of the city. In the yard below the guard was being relieved: a solemn ceremony with salutes, clicking heels, standing at attention, and goose-stepping. He glided back into the darkness, crept towards the bedroom door at the farther end of the corridor, and opened it softly, hand grenade in his right hand. Through the tall balcony door fell quivering moonlight; that was the door he had stood in front of when he was outside. He entered the room, looking for the bed, prepared to throw the hand grenade; but there was no bed in the room, no sleeping President, only a basket with dishware. Otherwise the room was empty. He had been wrongly informed. Anarchists, too, must go astray sometimes. Confused, he withdrew, and began stubbornly searching for his victim. He went up to the third floor again, the bomb held ready, then to the fourth, wandering through sumptuous reception rooms, conference rooms, corridors, small parlours, entering offices with covered typewriters, picture galleries, a weapons room with ancient armour, cannon, and banners, where a halberd ripped his sleeve. At last, when he climbed to the fifth floor and was stealing cautiously along the marble wall, he saw a crack of light ahead. Someone must have turned on a light. He summoned up his courage and walked on. The hand grenade gave him a sense of power. He entered the corridor. His weariness had vanished. He looked down the corridor, which ended at a door. It was ajar. In the room, a light was burning. He hurried over the soft rug; but when he wrenched open the door, hand with the grenade raised, the President stood before him in his bathrobe. The sight was so sudden and surprising that Archilochos barely had time to conceal the grenade in his coat pocket.

'I beg your pardon,' the assassin stammered.

'Ah, there you are, my dear Monsieur Archilochos,' the President exclaimed joyfully, grasping the confused Greek's hand and shaking it vigorously. 'I've been expecting you all evening, and a while ago I happened to see you from my window, climbing over the wall. A good idea. My bodyguard is far too pedantic. The fellows would never have admitted you. But now you're here, and I'm so delighted. How ever did you get into the building? I was just about to send my valet down. I've been living on the fifth floor only for the past week; it's much more comfortable here than on the second, although there is the difficulty that the elevator doesn't always work.'

The back door had been unlocked, Archilochos stammered; he felt that he had missed the right moment, and besides he was standing too close to his victim.

'How fortunate,' the President said warmly. 'My valet, old Ludwig – he really looks much more like a President than I do – has rustled up a little supper.'

'I beg your pardon,' Archilochos said, flushing. 'I didn't mean to intrude.'

'Not at all, not at all,' the goateed old man assured him. 'At my age one doesn't sleep much – cold feet, rheumatism, worries, personal and public, what with the present tendency of nations to collapse, and so I often have a bite to eat during the long nights in my lonely palace. Luckily we had central heating installed last year.'

'It really is pleasantly warm,' Archilochos observed.

'Why, what a sight you are!' the President said. 'Covered with dust. Ludwig, brush him off a little.'

'Permit me,' the valet said, and began cleaning the dust and bird droppings off the assassin's clothing. Archilochos did not dare to fend him off, though he was afraid the bomb in his coat pocket might explode as a result of the brushing. He was relieved when the valet helped him out of his coat.

'You resemble my butler at the Boulevard Saint-Père,' he said.

'As a matter of fact he is my half-brother,' the valet replied. 'Twenty years my junior.'

'We have a great deal to chat about, I imagine,' the President said, leading his would-be murderer down the now brightly illuminated corridor.

They entered a small room on the Quai side of the building, lit by candles. In a window embrasure stood a small table set with precious china and sparkling crystal on a white linen cloth.

'I'll strangle him,' Archilochos thought surlily. 'That's the simplest way.'

'Let us sit down, my dear good friend,' the courteous old President said, lightly touching Arnolph's arm. 'From here we can gaze down into the yard if we like, at those upstanding young men with their white plumes, who would be surprised to learn that someone has made his way in to me. The idea of the ladder is excellent, and delights me all the more because I too sometimes climb over the wall by means of a ladder, in the dead of night, as you have just done – but that is between the two of us. An old President must sometimes employ such means, for there are aspects of life that concern a man of honour but not the gentlemen of the press. Ludwig, pour us the champagne.'

'Thank you,' Archilochos said. 'But I'll kill him nevertheless,' he thought.

'And a bit of chicken,' the old man said with unconcealed pleasure. 'Ludwig and I always have that in the kitchen, champagne and chicken at three o'clock in the morning. Good, simple fare. I assume your climb over the wall has made you good and hungry.'

'Rather,' Archilochos said honestly, thinking of his climb up the face of the building. The valet served them with perfect dignity, although his hands trembled in an alarming manner.

'Don't be upset by Ludwig's shaking,' the President said. 'He has already served six of my predecessors.'

Arnolph cleaned his glasses with the napkin. The grenade would have been more convenient, he thought. He did not yet know how he would go about it. He could not very well say, 'Excuse me,' and begin strangling the President. Besides, the valet would have to be done away with, lest he call the guards. And so Archilochos ate and drank, in the first place in order to gain time and adjust to the novel circumstances, and then because he was enjoying it. The dignified old man had a benign effect upon him. It was as though he were sitting with a father to whom he could confess everything.

'The chicken is first-rate,' the President opined.

'It really is,' Archilochos conceded.

'And the champagne is also excellent.'

'I never thought anything so good existed,' Archilochos confessed.

'Let us chat as we eat; let's not shirk it. Let us talk about your lovely Chloé, who is your problem, who perplexes you,' the old man proposed.

'I was terribly shocked today in the Héloïse Chapel,' Archilochos said, 'when I realized the truth for the first time.'

'I rather had that impression,' the President said.

'As I saw you sitting there,' Arnolph confessed, 'in the church, with all your decorations, it suddenly entered my mind that you had come to the wedding only because you and Chloé . . .'

'Had you had such a high opinion of me?' the old gentleman asked.

'You were my model. I thought you were a strict opponent of alcohol,' Archilochos told him shyly.

'The newspapers cooked that up for me,' the President growled. 'The government is waging a campaign against alcoholism, so they always photograph me holding a glass of milk.'

'It was also said that you are extremely austere in regard to morals.'

'That's for the consumption of the Federation of Women's Clubs. Are you a teetotaller?'

'A vegetarian also.'

'But now you're drinking champagne and eating chicken.'

'I no longer have any ideals.'

'I'm sorry to hear it.'

'Everyone is a hypocrite.'

'Including Chloé?'

'You know very well what Chloé is.'

'The truth,' the President remarked, laying aside a gnawed chicken bone and moving the candelabrum so that it no longer stood between them, 'the truth is always rather embarrassing when it comes to light, not only in the case of women, but in the case of all human beings, and especially in the case of the government. Sometimes I too would like to rush out of my palace, which I consider monstrous from a purely architectural point of view, just as you rushed out of the Héloïse Chapel; but the way things are, I don't quite have the courage, and so I climb surreptitiously over the wall. I don't want to defend any of the persons involved, least of all myself. This is, in general, an area which is hard to discuss in a decent way, and if it can be done at all, then only at night between two people. Because views and moralities which don't belong are too apt to get mixed up in the matter, and because the virtues, passions, and defects of men lie so close together and contempt and hatred can easily arise where respect and love would be the only proper sentiments. I want to say only one thing to you, my dear good fellow: If there is one person in the world whom I envy, it is you, and if there is one person for whose future I am gravely alarmed, it is also you. . . . I had to share Chloé with many others,' he said after a while, hunched in the Biedermeier chair, educating Archilochos with an almost tender note in his voice. 'She was a queen in a dark, elemental kingdom. She was a courtesan. The most famous in the city. I do not want to make this out any better than it is; I am too old to do that. But I am grateful that she gave me her love, and I think back on no one in this world with greater gratitude. Now she has turned away from all of us and come to you. Therefore her day of rejoicing was for us a farewell and a thanksgiving.'

The aged President fell silent. Dreamily, he ran his hand over his carefully groomed goatee. The valet poured champagne, and from outside they heard the staccato commands and goose-stepping of the bodyguard. Archilochos, too, leaned back in his chair, musing with wonderment at the now utterly useless grenade in his coat pocket. Through the window curtain he spied Fahrcks's car waiting in front of the Economics Ministry.

'Now as for you, my dear, good fellow,' the President continued softly after a while, lighting a small cigar which the valet had handed him (Archilochos, too, was smoking), 'I understand your tempestuous feelings. What man in your situation would not be offended? But these altogether natural emotions are precisely those we should combat, for they can do the greatest harm. I cannot help you – who could do that? I can only hope that you will learn to ignore a fact which no one can deny, but which will become inconsequential if you have the strength to believe in the love that Chloé is offering you. The miracle which has happened between you two is only possible and only credible through the workings of love. Outside that love, it becomes a farce. Thus you must walk across a narrow bridge over dangerous abysses, as Mohammedans must tread the edge of a sword when they enter their paradise – I read something of the sort once upon a time. But do take a little more chicken,' he urged the thwarted murderer. 'It really is excellent, and there's always comfort to be found in good food.'

Archilochos sat there, surrounded by the glow of candles, absorbing the delicious warmth of the room. On the walls, in heavy gold frames, hung earnest, long-since-deceased statesmen and heroes who had entered into eternity and regarded him thoughtfully, strangely, sublimely. A hitherto unknown peace had entered his soul, an incomprehensible serenity, evoked not only by the President's words – what did words amount to, after all? – but by his kindly, paternal, courteous manner.

'A grace has been conferred upon you,' the old statesman added. 'There are two possible reasons for this grace, and it depends upon you which of them is the valid one: love, if you believe in that love, or evil, if you do not believe in that love. Love is a miracle that is eternally possible; evil is a fact that is eternally present. Justice condemns evil, hope longs to reform it, and love overlooks it. Only love is capable of accepting grace as it is. There is nothing more difficult, I know. The world is terrible and meaningless. The hope of finding a meaning behind all the meaninglessness, behind all the terror, can be preserved only by those who nevertheless can love.'

He fell silent, and for the first time Archilochos was again able to think of Chloé without a shudder, without horror.

Then, when the candles had burned down, the President helped Archilochos into the coat with the now useless grenade in its pocket and accompanied him, since the elevator happened to be out of order, down to the main entrance. Because, as he said, he did not want to bother Ludwig, who, stiff and impeccable, had fallen asleep standing beside his master's chair – a feat which, the old man declared, should certainly be respected. And so the two walked down through the deserted palace, down the broad, curving staircase, Archilochos consoled, content with the world, longing for Chloé, the President behaving rather like a museum curator, turning on the lights in this or that hall and making the necessary explanations. Here he received state visitors, he would remark, pointing into a lofty reception room; or here he accepted the resignation of the Premier, twice a month; and here in this intimate salon with its nearly genuine Raphael he had had tea with the Queen of England and her prince consort, and had nearly fallen asleep when the prince consort began talking about the navy; nothing bored him so much as naval stories, and only the quick-wittedness of the Chief of Protocol had averted a national disaster; the Chief of Protocol had awakened him at the crucial moment and whispered to him a properly naval reply. Otherwise, he must say, the two English visitors had been very nice.

Then they bade each other good-bye, two friends who had had a full talk, who had made peace with one another. From the main entrance the old man once more waved, smiling, serene. Archilochos looked back. The palace loomed into the cold night, dark now, like a gigantic, over-ornamented chest of drawers. The quarter moon was no longer visible. He walked between the saluting bodyguards and reached the Quai de l'État, but then turned into Etter Lane between the Nuncio's residence and the Swiss Embassy, for he saw Fahrcks's car roaring towards him from the direction of the Economics Ministry. In front of Pfyffer's Bar on the rue Stäbi he took a cab; he had no desire to meet Fahrcks again. Back home, he raced across the garden, obsessed by the single thought of taking Chloé into his arms. The rococo palace was brightly lit. Uproarious singing surged towards him. The front door was open. Dense yellow swathes of pipe and cigar smoke filled the air. Brother Bibi with his brood had now taken possession of the entire house. Everywhere, members of the gang were sitting and lying around, drunk, jabbering, on the sofas, under the tables, tangled in curtains that had been dragged from the windows. All the tramps, pimps, and fancy-boys of the city seemed to be assembled. In the beds women screeched, bare breasts gleamed; gallow birds sat in the kitchen, stuffing their bellies, smacking their lips, drinking up the liquor closets and the cellar. Matthew and Sebastian were playing hockey in the dining room with two wooden legs for sticks. In the hall Uncle Captain was practising knife throwing with Mama dear, while Jean-Christophe and Jean-Daniel were playing marbles with his glass eye and Théophile and Gottlieb, sluts on their laps, were sliding down the banisters. Filled with an evil presentiment, Arnolph ran upstairs, past the art dealer Nadelör, who still lay delirious in his bed, through the boudoir, where a male chorus and the splash of water could be heard from the bathroom, along with Magda-Maria's shrill voice; when he rushed into the bedroom, Brother Bibi lay in bed with a mistress (undressed). Nowhere in the house had there been any sign of Chloé.

'Where is Chloé?'

'What's this, Brother,' Bibi said reproachfully, puffing at a cigar. 'Never enter a bedroom without knocking.'

That was as far as Bibi got. His brother had undergone a metamorphosis. He had rushed into his palace filled with the tenderest emotions, full of love, full of longing for Chloé. Now all these emotions turned to wrath. The folly of having supported this family for years, the impudence with which they had taken over his house, the fear that he had lost Chloé through his own fault, transformed him into a raging lion. He became an Ares, a Greek god of war, as Passap had predicted. Picking up Passap's wire sculpture, he smashed it down upon his cigar-smoking brother sprawled out in the marital bed with his trull. With a cry, Brother Bibi leaped out of bed, received a right hook to the jaw, and staggered to the door, where Arnolph pounded him again, then turned to the trull, whom he dragged by the hair into the hall and hurled at the Captain, who, alarmed by Bibi's roars, had come racing forward, whereupon the two went bouncing down the stairs. From all the doors sharpers, pimps, and other scum came rushing at him, some members of his own family, like Théophile and Gottlieb, whom he sent flying down the winding staircase, together with Nadelör, Renaissance bed and all, then Sebastian and Matthew, whom he pounded to a pulp, then Magda-Maria with her lover (Chinese), whom he threw naked through the splintering panes of the window into the garden outside, then unknown creatures. Wooden legs whistled through the air, chair legs, blood spurted, whores fled, Mama dear fainted dead away, fancy boys and counterfeiters, shoulders hunched, whistling like rats in their terror, beat a quick retreat. Arnolph swung, choked, scratched, struck, smashed, pounded heads together, raped a mistress while wooden legs, brass knuckles, rubber truncheons, and bottles hailed down on him, rose again, freed himself, foaming at the mouth, used a round table as a shield, vases, chairs, oil paintings, Jean-Christophe, and Jean-Daniel as missiles, and steadily advancing, crushing all resistance, his clothes in tatters, cursing steadily, drove the whole scurvy band out of his house, in which the wallpaper now hung in shreds, waving banners in the icy draughts that swept out the billows of tobacco smoke. Finally, when they were all outside, he threw the hand grenade after the howling crew, and the explosion illuminated the garden along with the first light of morning.

Then he stood for a long time at the entrance of his demolished mansion, staring into the quickening dawn which rose silvery behind the elms and the firs of the garden. Warm gusts of wind lashed the trees, shook them. A thaw was beginning. The ice of the roof melted; water gurgled in the gutter. Everything dripped; huge banks of cloud swept over the roofs and gardens, heavy and fecund; rain sifted down in thin sheets. Bruised, half dressed, shivering, Nadelör limped past him into the damp morning.

'You as a Christian!'

Archilochos paid no attention to him. He stared into space out of swollen eyes, bloodstained, his wedding suit tattered, the lining of the jacket hanging out, his glasses lost.

He began searching for Chloé.

'Good Lord, Monsieur Arnolph!' Georgette cried when he appeared at the counter and demanded a Pernod. 'Good Lord, what is the matter with you?'

'I can't find Chloé.'

The restaurant was full of customers. Auguste was waiting on tables. Archilochos finished his Pernod and asked for another.

'Have you looked everywhere?' Madame Bieler asked.

'At Passap's, at the Bishop's, everywhere.'

'She will turn up,' Georgette encouraged him. 'Women don't get lost so easily, and they're often just where you least expect them.'

Then she poured him a third Pernod.

'At last,' Auguste said with a sigh of relief to the cycling fans. 'Now he's drinking.'

Archilochos went on with his search. He forced his way into convents, boarding houses, furnished apartments. Chloé could not be found. He wandered through his deserted palace, through the empty gardens, stood in the wet leaves. Nothing. The trees sighed, the clouds raced above the roofs. Suddenly homesickness overcame him, a longing for Greece, for red cliffs and dark groves, for the Peloponnesus.

Two hours later he embarked. As the *Julia*, siren wailing, wrapped in her own smoke, glided into the fog, a car filled with Fahrcks's activists came roaring up and fired a few bullets after the ship, meant for the deserting assassin; but they only slashed the wearily waving green and golden landing flag.

Mr and Mrs Weeman were on the *Julia*, and they regarded him anxiously when, one afternoon, he came up to them.

Mediterranean. The deck in sunlight. Deck chairs everywhere. Archilochos said: 'I have had the honour of speaking with you several times.'

'Well,' Mr Weeman rumbled.

Arnolph apologized. It had all been a misunderstanding, he said.

'Yes,' Mr Weeman agreed.

Then Archilochos asked permission to help with the excavations in his old homeland.

'Well,' Mr Weeman replied, folding the *Journal of Antiquities*. Then he said, while filling his stubby pipe: 'Yes. . . .'

And so Archilochos dug for antiquities in Greece, in a part of the Peloponnesus which did not in the least conform to the picture he had conceived of his land of origin. He shovelled under a merciless sun. Gravel, snakes, scorpions, and a few crippled olive trees against the horizon. Low, barren hills, dried-up springs, not even bushes. A vulture circled over his head, stubborn, refusing to be frightened off. He hacked for weeks with a pick at a hill, streaming sweat, slowly hollowing out the hill. At last he exposed some shabby walls filled with sand, sand that grew fiery hot in the sun, crept under his finger-nails, inflamed his eyes. Mr Weeman hoped they had uncovered a temple of Zeus, Mrs Weeman thought it a sanctuary of Aphrodite. The altercations of the pair could be heard for miles. Their Greek helpers had long since quit work. Mosquitoes buzzed, flies covered Arnolph's face, crawled over his eyes. Dusk fell. In the distance a mule brayed, shrill and wailing. The night was cold. Archilochos lay in his tent beside the excavation site, Mr and Mrs Weeman in the hotel in the capital of the district, a miserable hole some seven miles away. Nocturnal birds and bats fluttered around the tent. In the distance an unknown animal howled, perhaps a wolf; then it was quiet again. He fell asleep. Towards morning he imagined he heard soft footsteps. He slept on. As soon as the sun, red and fierce above the senselessly barren hills, touched his tent, he got up. He staggered to his solitary place of work, by the walls. It was still cold. High above, the vulture was still circling. Inside the walls it was still almost entirely dark. His limbs ached. He set to work with the shovel. Before him lay an oblong heap of sand, glistening in the semi-darkness; but after the first few cautious probes he felt resistance. Is it Zeus or the goddess of love? he wondered, curious as to which of the two archaeologists was right. He set to work with both hands, scuffed the sand away, and exposed Chloé.

Scarcely daring to breathe, he stared at his beloved.

'Chloé,' he cried, 'Chloé, what are you doing here?'

She opened her eyes, but remained lying in the sand.

'Very simple,' she said. 'I followed you. We had two tickets, you know.'

Then they sat on the wall and looked out over the Greek land, at the low, barren hills with the tremendous sun above them, at the crippled olive trees in the distance, and at the white gleam of the capital of the district on the horizon.

'This is our native land,' she said. 'Yours and mine.'

'Where were you?' he asked. 'I searched the whole city for you.'

'At Georgette's. In the apartment upstairs.'

Two dots moved in the distance, approaching. Mr and Mrs Weeman.

Then she delivered her speech on love, somewhat as Diotima long ago to Socrates – though not so profound a one, of course, for as the child of a Greek businessman (to straighten out the matter of her origins) Chloé Saloniki was of a more robust and practical temper.

'You see,' she said, while the wind played with her hair and the sun moved ponderously higher and higher in the sky and the English couple approached steadily closer on their mules, 'now you know what I was; that has been cleared up between us. I was sick of my work, which is hard work, like any honest work. But it made me sad. I had a longing for love, for someone to care for; I wanted to be available not only for a man's pleasure, but also for his sorrows. And one morning when the fog wrapped my little palace, one wintry, dark morning, as it had been for weeks, I read in *Le Soir* that a Greek wanted a Greek wife. Then I made up my mind to love *that* Greek, him alone and no one else, no matter what happened, no matter what he was like. And so I came to you, that Sunday morning at ten, with the rose. I didn't mean to hide what I was. I came in my best clothes. As I wanted to accept you as you were, I meant you to accept me as I was, and when I saw you sitting at the table, bashful, awkward, with the steaming milk and cleaning your glasses, I fell in love with you. But since you thought I was still an innocent girl, since you showed so little knowledge of the world that you did not guess my profession, as Georgette and her husband guessed it, I didn't dare to destroy your illusion. I was afraid of losing you, and so only made everything worse. Your love became a thing of ridicule, and when you realized the truth in the Héloïse Chapel, your love was shattered along with your world. It was good that that happened. You could not love me without the truth, and only love is stronger than truth, which threatened to destroy us. The love you had in your blindness had to be destroyed for the sake of clear-eyed love, which is the only kind that counts.'

But some time passed before Chloé and Archilochos were able to return home. The government crashed. Fahrcks, the Order of the Kremlin under his double chin, took the rudder. The night sky flared red. Everywhere flags, everywhere choruses chanting: 'Ami, go home.' Everywhere banners, huge portraits of Lenin and of the Russian Premier, who had just barely escaped overthrow. But the Kremlin was far away, the dollar needed, personal power tempting. Fahrcks moved into the Western camp, had the Chief of the Secret Police (Petit-Paysan's secretary) strung up, and thereafter resided in the most dignified manner in the Presidential Palace on the Quai de l'État, protected like his predecessor by the same bodyguard with golden helmets and white plumes, his red hair carefully barbered, his moustache cropped. He relaxed the stringency of his regime, his ideology faded, and one fine Easter Sunday he attended services at St Luke's Cathedral. The bourgeois order returned, and with it Chloé and Archilochos; but they could no longer feel at ease. However, they tried it for a while. They turned their little palace into a boarding-house. Passap rented a room; he was no longer in favour (in artistic matters Fahrcks stuck by socialist realism). Maître Dutour moved in, he too in reduced circumstances. So did Hercule Wagner with his enormous wife, he too deposed; likewise the overthrown President, still courteous, serenely surveying the course of affairs; finally Petit-Paysan (the merger with the Rubber and Lubricating Oil Cartel had proved his ruin), doing light housework: a bankrupt crew. Only the Bishop was missing. He had gone over to the New Presbyterians of the Penultimate Christians. The boarders drank milk, Perrier on Sundays, lived quietly, spending the summers under the trees of the garden, dreamy, at peace with their undemanding world. Archilochos was deeply troubled. He went to see his brother, who lived in a suburb with Mama, Uncle Captain, and the dear little ones, running a small plant nursery – the beating Arnolph had given him had worked wonders. (Matthew passed his teacher's examination, Magda-Maria taught kindergarten, the others worked in factories or entered the Salvation Army.) But Arnolph did not stay long at his brother's. The sturdy, upstanding atmosphere, the pipe-smoking captain, and Mama knitting bored him, as did Bibi, who now regularly attended the Héloïse Chapel in his stead. Four times a week.

'You look pale, Monsieur Arnolph,' said Georgette, as he once again stood at the counter before her (behind her, above the bottles of brandy and liqueurs, Fahrcks now hung in the carved picture frame). 'Do you have troubles?'

She handed him a glass of Pernod.

'Everyone drinks milk,' he growled. 'The cycling fans and even your husband now.'

'What can little guys like us do?' Auguste said, still in his yellow jersey, rubbing his gleaming legs. 'The government has launched another anti-alcohol campaign. Besides, I'm an athlete, after all.'

Then Archilochos observed Georgette opening a bottle of Perrier.

'She, too,' he thought regretfully. And while he lay beside Chloé in the canopied bed, behind the red curtain, logs burning in the fireplace, he said: 'It's really very pleasant in our little palace with these contented, ageing boarders. I don't want to complain, but this virtuous world we live in strikes me as uncanny. It seems to me that I have converted the world and it has converted me, so that it comes down to the same thing in the end and everything has been in vain.'

Chloé had sat up while he talked.

'All this time I've been thinking about our wall, back in our native land,' she said. 'That time I covered myself with sand to surprise you, and lay there that dark morning, looking up at the vulture circling above the field, I felt something hard underneath me, something stony, like two big round breasts.'

'The goddess of love!' Archilochos cried, leaping out of bed. Chloé, too, got up.

'We must never stop seeking the goddess of love,' she whispered. 'Otherwise she will abandon us.'

They dressed noiselessly, packed a suitcase, and when Sophie entered the bedroom at eleven o'clock next morning, after knocking in vain for a long time, she and the anxious boarders who pressed in after her found the room empty.

A Dangerous Game

First part

Are there any feasible stories still left for writers to write? Suppose a man does not want to romanticize himself and talk about his own ego – feels no urge to discuss his personal ambitions or to describe his sex life, however frankly: suppose he prefers instead to withdraw into himself and maintain a decent reserve about his private life, resting content to work at his material like a sculptor at his stone and trying to retain a classical detachment in the face of the often inane result. If this is his aim, then the task of being a writer becomes more difficult – and more lonely; it also becomes meaningless, an isolated, pointless activity. For what good are literary honours in themselves? How many writers have not already gained such distinctions – and what botches have not received their prizes?

Or suppose a writer tries the contemporary scene. He is hardly likely to find a way out of his dilemma here, for the cinema and the newspapers already provide the more mundane distractions, and at any level above that of the gutter press the cry is all for 'depth'. The reading public are prepared to pay only if they are offered what passes for 'deeper significance': moral platitudes, sententious observations, the denial or affirmation of some belief, past or present. In short, they want Literature.

But suppose the writer doggedly refuses to produce this kind of thing, being convinced that the basis of his art is essentially personal and is his own affair entirely – what then? What if he believes that creation is an end in itself and refuses to indulge in comment or criticism? Once he reaches this point he will be brought up short; he cannot avoid it. He is bound to suspect that there is nothing left for him to write about and that life offers him no scope as an artist. He had better give up.

Of course a few odd sentences may still be possible, but apart from these a writer can give the reading public only what they want: speculations on the future of mankind, or some interpretation implying order and harmony in the riddle of the universe. The rest adds up to no more than the doings of royalty, politicians, film stars, millionaires – all interchangeable, no sooner in the public eye than out of it, and thus belonging to the gossip columns and the illustrated weeklies rather than to art.

In contrast to all this is the everyday life of the individual: in my case West European – Swiss, to be precise – an average life, subject to changes in the weather and fluctuations on the stock exchange, beset with minor trials and tribulations and the emotional upheavals attendant upon personal crises, but seemingly without any universal or cosmic significance. Fate has been banished from the stage on which the scene unfolds, and now waits impatiently in the wings – outside the modern concept of life which allots the principal roles to misfortune, illness and catastrophe. Even something so momentous as war is now made dependent on whether electronic brains can forecast it correctly, and the possibility of defeat is reduced to a mathematical hazard. This in itself is a miscalculation, but it is less disturbing than the thought that a screw may work loose, a coil unwind, a control device fail, and our whole civilization be shattered by a short circuit or a faulty connection.

We no longer walk in the fear of the Lord, under the shadow of righteousness and justice, the ever-present Fate of the Fifth Symphony. Instead we have car crashes, dams that burst because of faulty construction, explosions at atomic plants caused by the carelessness of some technician who has not properly switched off a machine. Our headlong and commercialized course is haunted only by the fear of mechanical breakdown; we are reminded of Fate only by the little cairns commemorating previous victims. And in our modern world there are only one or two feasible stories left, in which the fundamental nature of man can still be glimpsed in an ordinary face: in which some trifling misfortune accidentally impinges on the universal: and in which righteousness, justice, and perhaps even grace, are still made manifest, caught for a fleeting instant in the monocle of a drunken old man.

Second part

An accident too, though a minor one: a simple breakdown. Alfredo Traps, connected with the textile industry, forty-five years of age, still far from stout, of likeable exterior and adequate manners (though these somehow betrayed mechanical training so that, beneath the veneer, the salesman – a certain underlying element of crudity – showed through) – this fellow-citizen of ours had just been sailing down one of our great national highways in his Studebaker, and had every reason to believe he would reach his home in a fairly large city within the hour, when his car gave out. Simply would not go. Useless, the shining red car sat at the foot of a small hill over which the road wound. In the north a cumulus cloud had formed, and in the west the sun still stood high, shedding an afternoonish light. Traps smoked a cigarette and then made a phone call. The garage man who finally arrived to tow the Studebaker away pronounced that he could not repair the defect before next morning; there was something wrong with the fuel line. Whether or not this was true could not be determined, nor was it advisable to try to determine it: we are as thoroughly a prey to garage men as once we were to robber knights and, in still earlier times, to local gods and demons. Too lazy to take the half-hour walk to the nearest railway station and then the short, but rather complicated, rail journey home to his wife and four children, all boys, Traps decided to spend the night where he was. It was six o'clock in the evening – hot, not far off the longest day of the year.

The garage was on the outskirts of a village. The village itself was a pleasant place that straggled away towards wooded hills, with a hillock in its centre on which stood church, parsonage, and an age-old oak with iron rings and props. Everything was solid and clean; even the manure heaps in front of the farmhouses were carefully layered and neatly squared off. There was a small factory, too, and several taverns and country inns. One of the inns, Traps had often heard praised: but the rooms were all taken – there was a poultry farmers' meeting – and Traps was directed to a large private house which sometimes took the odd guest.

Traps hesitated. It was still possible to return home by train, but on the other hand he was tempted by the hope of a possible adventure. Sometimes there were girls in the villages – as in Grosbiestringen recently – who appreciated a traveller in textiles. With renewed spirits, he set out towards the house. Bells clanged from the church. Cows were making for their various barns, mooing.

The house stood in a sizeable garden. It was a two-storeyed building, with dazzling white walls, flat roof, green shutters. It was half concealed by shrubs, clipped beech and evergreens. Towards the street there were flowers, mainly roses, and in the midst of them an aged little man wearing a leather apron – possibly the master of the house – was pruning and snipping.

Traps introduced himself and asked for lodgings.

'What is it you do?' the old man asked. He had come up to the garden gate, smoking a cigar, and was barely higher than the gate itself.

'I am in textiles.'

The old man examined Traps closely, peering over small rimless glasses in the way that longsighted people do. 'Yes, certainly, you can stay here overnight.'

Traps asked the price of the room.

He was not in the habit of charging, the old man replied. He was alone, his son having gone to the United States. He had a house-keeper, Mlle Simone, who took good care of him, and he enjoyed having a guest now and then.

The commercial traveller thanked him. He was touched by this offer of hospitality, and said how pleasant it was to find that in the country the good old customs had evidently not yet died out.

The garden gate was opened to him.

Traps looked around. Gravel paths, lawn, large shaded areas interspersed with patches of sunlight . . .

When they reached the roses the old man remarked that he was expecting several guests for the evening. With great care he snipped away at a rose-bush. Some friends from the neighbourhood were coming, he said. Two of them lived in the village, one farther off towards the hill. They were retired like himself, attracted here by the mild climate and the absence of the Föhn. All were lonely, and widowed, and eager to know about anything that was new, stimulating and lively; so he would be delighted if Herr Trapps would join them for dinner and spend the evening with them.

It was not what the commercial traveller had intended. He had been looking forward to eating in the village, at that celebrated inn. Still, he could not very well turn down the invitation. He felt under an obligation – after all, he had been offered a night's lodging for nothing. He did not want to seem the typical discourteous urbanite. So he pretended to be overjoyed.

His host showed him up to the first floor.

The room was pleasant, with running water, a wide bed, table, comfortable chair, a Hodler painting on the wall, old leather-bound volumes in the bookcase. Traps opened his valise, washed, shaved, patted himself with eau de Cologne, walked over to the window, lit a cigarette.

A great disc of sun was sliding down towards the hills, irradiating the beeches.

He ran quickly over the day's business. The order from Roacher & Co. – not bad. The difficulties with Wilholz – the fellow was asking for five per cent; by God, he would wring his neck for him. Then memories bobbed to the surface. Disordered commonplaces. A planned adultery at the Touring Hotel. The question of whether he should buy his youngest boy (his favourite child) a set of electric trains. The thought that he really ought to telephone his wife and let her know what was detaining him . . . But he couldn't be bothered; it was an old story – she was used to it, and would not believe him anyway.

He yawned, allowed himself another cigarette. Watching through the window he saw three old gentlemen come marching up the gravel path, two of them arm in arm, the third a fat, bald-headed old fellow bringing up the rear. Greetings, handshakes, embraces, chatter about roses.

Traps moved away from the window and examined the bookshelves. To judge by the titles, he was in for a dull evening. Hotzendorff, *Homicide and the Death Penalty*; Savigny, *System of Contemporary Roman Law*; Ernst David Hölle, *Interrogation Practice* . . .

The commercial traveller knew what the evening would amount to. His host was a former lawyer. The conversation would be one long succession of boring discourses. After all, what did these educated fellows know about real life? Nothing. And then there was the unpleasant possibility that the talk would turn to art or such matters, and he would make a bit of a fool of himself. Well, what of it? If he didn't always have to cope with the struggle for existence, if he weren't in business, he could know just as much as they did about the higher things.

Without much enthusiasm, he went downstairs. The old parties had settled down on the still sunlit open veranda, while the housekeeper, a woman of robust proportions, set the table in the adjoining dining-room.

When he saw the company more closely he got quite a jolt. Fortunately his host, by coming forward to greet him, gave him a chance to recover.

The master of the house was now dressed with almost dandyish care. His sparse hair was carefully brushed. His frock-coat, however, was much too big for him. He welcomed Traps with a little speech which gave the commercial traveller some cue to his further conduct.

Traps murmured that the pleasure was all on his side. He bowed coolly and aloofly, playing the part of the worldly businessman – though he was reflecting wistfully that he had only stayed in this village in the hope of picking up some girl, which was quite out of the question now.

He found himself confronting three more old codgers no less extraordinary than their ancient host. Like monstrous crows, their black-clad figures filled the summery veranda with its wicker chairs and gay awnings. Their frock-coats were of the best quality, as he immediately noted, yet the old men looked slovenly, superannuated, untidy – except for the bald-headed one (Pilet by name, seventy-seven years old, as his host informed Traps in the course of the introductions which now began), who sat stiffly and dignifiedly upon an extremely uncomfortable stool, although there were several easy chairs available. Herr Pilet was if anything decked out with excessive formality, had a white carnation in his buttonhole, and constantly stroked his black-dyed, bushy moustache – a man obviously retired on a pension, perhaps a former sexton or chimney-sweep whom luck had raised to prosperity, perhaps even a railway engineer. By contrast the other two looked all the sloppier. One of them (Herr Kummer, eighty-two) was even fatter than Pilet – simply enormous. He looked as though he were made of greasy sausages. He sat in a rocking-chair, his face blowzy, sporting the swollen nose of an alcoholic and jovial pop-eyes behind gold-rimmed pince-nez. He was wearing a nightshirt under his black suit – probably because he had forgotten to remove it – and his pockets leaked newspapers. The other (Herr Zorn, eighty-six) lank and cadaverous, had a monocle clamped into his left eye, duelling scars on his face, a hooked nose, snow-white lion's mane, sunken mouth: all in all an antediluvian phenomenon, waistcoat buttoned awry and socks of two different patterns.

'A drink?' the host asked.

'Yes, thank you,' Traps replied, dropping into an armchair. The lank, cadaverous fellow eyed him with interest through the monocle. 'I trust Herr Traps will take part in our game?' he asked.

'Why, of course. I always like games.'

The old parties smiled, rocking their heads.

'Our game is possibly a little strange,' his host confessed cautiously. 'What we do at these evenings is to play at our old professions.'

The guests smiled again, politely, discreetly.

Traps was perplexed. How was he to interpret that?

'I used to be a judge,' his host explained.' Herr Zorn was a prosecuting counsel, and Herr Kummer a lawyer for the defence. And we play at holding court.'

'Ah, I see,' Traps said. The idea struck him as not bad. Perhaps the evening wasn't altogether lost after all.

His host regarded him solemnly. In general, he explained in a gentle voice, they did revivals of famous historical trials: the Trial of Socrates, the Trial of Jesus, the Trial of Joan of Arc, the Trial of Dreyfus. Recently they had held the Reichstag Fire Trial, and once they had found Frederick the Great *non compos mentis*.

Traps was fascinated. 'Do you play this every evening?' he asked.

The judge nodded. But of course, he continued, it was most fun when they were able to play with living material, which frequently resulted in especially piquant situations. Only the day before yesterday, for example, they had had up before them a politician who had delivered an election speech in the village and missed the last train. He had been sentenced to fourteen years for extortion and bribery.

'A tough court you have here,' Traps declared with amusement.

'A matter of principle with us,' the old men beamed.

Then what part could he play in the game, Traps asked.

More smiles, almost laughter.

His host pointed out that they already had the judge, the prosecutor, and the counsel for the defence – posts which in any case required knowledge of the subject and of the rules of the game. Only the post

of defendant was unoccupied. But he wanted it to be clearly understood that Herr Traps was under no obligation to join in the game
unless he wished to.

The idea quite appealed to the commercial traveller. The evening
was saved – and far from being high-toned and boring, as he had
feared, it promised to be very good fun. For Traps was a simple
fellow, without any great mental powers or bent for thinking: a
businessman, clever enough when he had to be, out for all he could
get in his own line of work, but also fond of good food and drink,
with a liking for crude practical jokes. He would be glad to play, he
said, and would be honoured to take over the vacant post of defendant.

'Bravo!' the prosecutor cawed, clapping his hands. 'Bravo, there's
a man speaking. I call that courage.'

Traps asked curiously what crime would be attributed to him.

'An altogether minor matter,' the prosecutor replied, polishing his
monocle. 'A crime can always be found.'

All laughed.

Herr Kummer rose. 'Come, Herr Traps,' he said almost paternally.
'We want to try the port this house has to offer. It's wonderful stuff,
you must not miss it.' He led Traps into the dining-room.

The big round table had been set most festively. The chairs were
all high-backed; there were dark pictures on the walls; everything was
solid and old-fashioned. From the veranda came the chatter of the old
men's voices; the sunset shimmered through the open windows; birds
twittered outside. On a smaller table stood an array of bottles, and there
were more bottles on the hearth, the Bordeaux cradled in baskets.

The defending counsel poured carefully, with somewhat tremulous
hands, from an old bottle of port. He filled two small glasses to
the brim, then touched glasses with the commercial traveller – but
circumspectly, barely permitting contact between the two glasses with
their precious liquid.

Traps tasted the wine, and approved it. 'Excellent,' he said.

'I am your counsel for the defence, Herr Traps,' said Herr
Kummer. 'Therefore let the two of us drink to good friendship!'

'To good friendship!'

It would be best, the lawyer said, moving his red face with its
alcoholic's nose and pince-nez closer to Traps, so that his huge belly,
a soft unpleasant mass, actually touched our friend – it would be best
for the gentleman to confide his crime to him at once. If Traps would

only do that, Herr Kummer could guarantee to bring him safely through the trial. The situation was not dangerous, of course, but its difficulties should not be underestimated. The cadaverous prosecutor was still in full possession of his intellectual powers, and he was certainly someone to be handled carefully. As for the judge, their host, unfortunately he was inclined to strictness, and possibly even to pedantry – traits which had worsened with age: after all, the good man was eighty-seven. All the same, he, the counsel for the defence, had succeeded in saving most of his clients, or at least preserving them from the worst; and as a matter of fact, only in one case – that of a robbery accompanied by homicide – had he been unable to do anything to save his client. But then, he would guess that robbery with homicide was hardly in Herr Traps's line. Or was it?

Traps laughed. Unfortunately, he said, he had committed no crime. 'Your health!'

'Better confess it to me,' his defending counsel encouraged him. 'There's no need for you to be ashamed. I know life; nothing surprises me any longer. Human destinies have filed past me, Herr Traps, frightful abysses have yawned before me – I can assure you!'

'Sorry,' said Traps with a grin, 'terribly sorry. But here I stand, a defendant without a crime. Anyway, it's the prosecutor's business to find the crime – he said so himself, so let's take him at his word. A game's a game.'

He was curious to see what would come of it, Traps went on. Would there be a real interrogation?

'I should think so!'

'I'm looking forward to it.'

The defending lawyer looked grave.

'Do you feel yourself to be innocent, Herr Traps?'

The commercial traveller laughed. 'Absolutely so.' He thought the whole thing was extremely amusing.

The defending counsel cleaned his glasses.

'Mark my words, young friend,' he said, 'innocence doesn't matter one way or the other. Tactics are what count. It is sheer recklessness – to put it mildly – to feign innocence before our court. On the contrary, the most prudent thing is to accuse oneself of a crime right off. A good choice for businessmen, for example, is fraud. It may always turn out in the course of the trial that the defendant is exaggerating, that he really has not committed any actual fraud, but has only, say, suppressed a few facts, as is customary in business. The road from guilt to acquittal is difficult but not impossible. On the other hand, it is literally hopeless to try to maintain innocence, and the result is devastating. You will lose where you could win; moreover, the choice you are making forces you into a situation where you can no longer select your crime; you will have to have it imposed upon you.'

Amused, the commercial traveller shrugged his shoulders. He was sorry he couldn't oblige, he said, but he couldn't think of a single misdeed that had ever brought him into conflict with the law.

The defending counsel replaced his pince-nez. He could see he was going to have his troubles with Traps; it wasn't going to be an easy matter. He concluded their conversation by saying: 'Above all, consider every word you utter; don't start blabbing, or you will suddenly find yourself condemned to years of penal servitude and nothing to be done about it.'

The others came in. They sat down at the round table, made themselves comfortable, exchanged jests. First various hors-d'oeuvres were served, cold cuts, eggs à la russe, snails, and then turtle soup. All of the company were in fine fettle; they spooned away contentedly, slurped without restraint.

'Well, defendant, what have you to offer us?' the prosecutor croaked. 'A fine substantial murder, I hope.'

The counsel for the defence protested: 'My client is a defendant without a crime – a judicial rarity, as it were. He maintains he is innocent.'

'*Innocent*?' the prosecutor exclaimed in astonishment. His duelling scars reddened, and his monocle slipped from his eye, almost falling into his plate, and swung back and forth at the end of its black cord.

The stunted little judge, who was breaking bread into his soup, paused, cast a reproachful look at Traps, and shook his head gravely. The bald, taciturn gentleman with the white carnation likewise stared at him in astonishment.

The sudden silence was frightening. Not the clink of a fork or spoon could be heard, not a heavily drawn breath or sipping of soup: only the sound of Mlle Simone giggling softly at the back of the room.

At last the prosecutor recovered his composure. 'We'll have to look into this,' he said. 'If a thing cannot be, it does not exist.'

'Go to it,' Traps laughed. 'I am at your disposal.'

Wine was served with the fish – a light, sparkling Neuchâtel.

'Well then,' the prosecutor said as he dissected his trout, 'let us see. Married?'

'For eleven years.'

'Children?'

'Four.'

'Occupation?'

'I am in the textile industry.'

'Ah, then you are a salesman, my dear Herr Traps?'

'Sales manager.'

'Good. And your car broke down?'

'As luck would have it. First time in a year.'

'Aha. And before that?'

'Oh, in those days I still had my old car,' Traps explained. 'A 1939 Citroën. But now I've got a Studebaker – red – a special job.'

'An American car, eh? Well, well. Interesting. And acquired only recently, I take it? I suppose you were not a sales manager before?'

'No, I was just a plain ordinary traveller in textiles.'

The prosecutor nodded. 'Boom times, eh?'

The defending counsel was seated next to Traps. 'Watch your step,' he whispered.

But the commercial traveller, or rather the sales manager as we may now call him, proceeded without a care in the world to doctor up his steak tartare. He had his private recipe: a few drops of lemon, a dash of cognac, paprika, and salt. Really, he declared happily, he had never enjoyed a pleasanter meal. He had always thought the meetings of the Utopia Club must be the best fun a fellow of his sort could ever hope for, but they were nothing compared with this evening.

'Ah,' observed the prosecutor, 'you are a member of the Utopia Club, then. May I ask what nickname they give you in the club?'

'Casanova.'

'Wonderful!' the prosecutor bawled joyously, as though this information were of the greatest importance. He tucked the monocle back into its place. 'We are all delighted to hear it. Does this nickname entitle us, my dear Traps, to draw any conclusions about your private life?'

'"Careful,' the defending counsel whispered.

'Within limits, my dear sir, within limits,' Traps replied. 'If I do have any extramarital experiences, it's a matter of pure chance. I don't make a point of it.'

The judge refilled their glasses with Neuchâtel and took occasion to ask a question of his own. Would Traps have the kindness to give the assembled company a brief summary of his life? As they had decided to sit in judgment upon their dear guest and delightful miscreant, and perhaps to put him behind bars for years, it was only right that they should hear some of the more intimate details of his personal life. Affairs with women would be much to the point, of course, and let him not spare the salt and spice.

'Let's have it, let's have it!' the old gentlemen cackled in chorus. After all, they told him, they had once had a procurer at their table who had favoured them with a host of anecdotes of the most sensational kind concerning his business – despite which, they had sentenced him to only four years' hard labour.

'Now, now,' Traps joined in their laughter. 'I haven't anything so colourful to offer. I lead a very ordinary life, gentlemen – a life no different from anyone else's, I may as well admit. Bottoms up!'

'Bottoms up!'

The sales manager raised his glass. With the utmost cordiality he met the birdlike eyes of the four old men, who gazed at him as if he were a particularly juicy morsel. Then they touched glasses.

Outside, the sun had set, and the noise of the birds had subsided. But the countryside was still lapped in daylight – close by, the red roofs of the village, set among trees; farther off, the wooded hills; and in the distance the mountains, with glaciers still catching rays of sunlight: a panorama of felicity, divine blessing and cosmic harmony, in an atmosphere of sweet peace and rustic silence.

While Mlle Simone changed their plates and placed on the table a huge, steaming bowl of mushrooms stewed in cream, Traps began his story.

He had buffeted his way through a hard youth. His father had been a factory worker – a proletarian led astray by the false doctrines of Marx and Engels: an embittered, joyless man who had never paid any attention to his only child. His mother had been a washerwoman, and had come to an early end.

'I never went farther than elementary school.' There were tears in his eyes; he was torn between bitterness and deep sentimentality over his own meagre lot. 'No farther than elementary school.'

They raised their glasses and toasted one another in Réserve des Maréchaux.

'Remarkable,' the prosecutor said. 'Remarkable. No farther than elementary school. You certainly have worked your way up in the world, haven't you?'

'I should think I have,' Traps boasted, heated by the Maréchaux and inspired by the conviviality of the occasion and the serene beauty of the countryside outside the windows. 'I should think I have. Only ten years ago I was nothing but a door-to-door salesman, trudging round with a little suitcase full of odds and ends. Hard work it was, tramping the roads, spending the night in haylofts and low-class inns. I started at the bottom in my trade, at the very bottom. And now, gentlemen, you ought to see my bank account. I don't want to brag, but does any one of you own a Studebaker?'

'Be careful,' his defending counsel whispered anxiously.

And what was his position now, the prosecutor inquired.

Again the counsel for the defence warned Traps to watch his step and not talk so much.

'Now – now I'm the sole agent for Hephaeston in the whole of Europe,' Traps announced, looking around him with an air of triumph. 'Apart from Spain and the Balkans – someone else has that territory.'

The little judge heaped mushrooms on his plate. 'I am familiar with the name Hephaestos,' he said, chuckling. 'A Greek god he was, and a great and subtle smith, who trapped the goddess of love and her lover, the god of war, in a net forged so fine as to be invisible. The other gods laughed till their sides ached to see the queer fish he had caught. But what Hephaeston may be, of which our friend has the honour to be sole agent, is a mystery wrapped in seven veils to me.'

'You're on the track, my dear host and judge,' Traps guffawed. 'You said the key word yourself – veils. So there was this Greek god – I never heard of him before this moment – who wore a fine, invisible net. You gentlemen of the court have no doubt heard of nylon, perlon, myrlon, and the other synthetics. Well, there is also Hephaeston, the greatest synthetic of them all. Transparent, tough as steel, equally useful in industry and in fashion, in wartime and peacetime. The perfect material for parachutes, and at the same time the most delectable stuff for ladies' nightgowns, as I know from first-hand experience.'

'Aha!' the old men chuckled. 'First-hand experience, eh?'

Mlle Simone whisked away the plates again, and brought in a roast loin of veal.

'A regular banquet!' the sales manager exclaimed with delight.

'I am pleased to see that you appreciate such delicacies,' the prosecutor said. 'And right you are. Our food is of the finest, and we enjoy quantity as well as quality, a menu that would have done honour to the last century, when people still had the courage to eat heartily. Let us praise Mlle Simone! Let us praise our host, too – the little shrimp is a gourmet of the first water and does all the shopping himself. And as for the wines, they are provided by our friend Pilet, proprietor of the Bull and Stirrup in the next village. All praise to him too.

'But now let us see how things stand with you, our virtuoso of the business world. We know something of your life now; it was a pleasure to be let into some of its secrets; and we are now fully briefed as to the nature of your occupation. There is only one minor point that has not yet been clarified: how in your professional life did you arrive at so lucrative a position? By sheer discipline and unflagging effort?'

'Be careful,' the defending counsel whispered. 'This is the danger-point.'

It had not by any means been easy, Traps replied, watching greedily as the judge began to carve the roast. First of all, he had had to undercut Gygax, and that had been a tough proposition.

'Ah, indeed. And who may Herr Gygax be?'

'My former boss.'

'He had to be supplanted, you mean?'

'Got rid of, to give it to you without mincing words, as we do in my line,' Traps replied. He ladled gravy on to his meat. 'You gentlemen won't mind if I speak frankly. It's dog eat dog in business, you know – an eye for an eye and a tooth for a tooth. If you try to handle people with kid gloves, you get kicked in the guts for your pains. I'm raking in the cash nowadays, but I slave like ten elephants for it, do four hundred miles a day in my Studebaker. I must admit I didn't exactly play fair when it came to cutting old Gygax's throat, but I had to get on – no help for it. Business is business, after all.'

The prosecutor looked up from his veal with a gleam in his eye. ' "Ged rid of", "cut old Gygax's throat" – those are pretty strong expressions, my dear Traps.'

The sales manager laughed. 'I mean them only as figures of speech, of course.'

'And how is Herr Gygax these days?'

'He's dead – died last year.'

Traps's lawyer whispered to him: 'Are you mad? You've gone clean out of your mind!'

'Last year,' the prosecutor repeated sympathetically. 'What a pity. How old was the man?'

'Fifty-two.'

'So very young! And what did he die of?'

'Some disease or other.'

'After you had taken his job?'

'Shortly before.'

'Good. For the present that is all I need to know,' the prosecutor said. 'What luck, what luck we are having tonight! We've turned up a corpse, and that is the main thing, after all.'

They all laughed. Even bald Pilet, who was reverently, pedantically devoting himself to his eating, refusing to be distracted from his pious occupation of devouring enormous quantities of food, looked up.

'Good!' he said, stroking his black moustache.

He said no more, and returned to his plate.

The prosecutor solemnly raised his glass. 'Gentlemen,' he declared, 'in honour of this newest piece of data let us imbibe the Pichon-Longueville 1933. A good Bordeaux to go with a good game.'

They clinked glasses once more and drank to one another.

'Uhm!' Traps emptied his glass at one draught and held it out to the judge for refilling. 'My God, that went down well.'

Twilight had fallen, and the faces of the men at table could scarcely be distinguished in the dusk. In the sky outside the window the first stars could be seen. The housekeeper applied a match to the candles on the three silver candelabra on the table, and the shadows of the assembled company danced on the walls like the wondrous chalice of some fantastic flower. A cosy intimacy, a warmth and fondness of each for all, spread through the company, and with it a relaxation of manners and a greater informality.

'Like a fairy tale!' Traps exclaimed.

The counsel for the defence raised his napkin to wipe the sweat from his brow. 'You are the fairy tale, my dear Traps,' he said. 'I have never yet met a defendant who made such reckless statements with greater assurance.'

Traps laughed. 'There's nothing to worry about, my friend,' he said. 'Wait till the interrogation begins. I won't lose my head, I assure you.'

This remark was followed by the same deathly silence that had fallen once before. All noise of chewing, of smacking lips, of sipping wine, ceased abruptly.

'You poor fool,' the lawyer groaned. 'What do you mean by "wait till the interrogation begins"?'

'Oh,' said Traps, heaping salad on his plate, 'has it begun already?'

The old men grinned, looked slyly down at their plates, and at last burst into bleats of glee. The silent, equable, bald-headed man sniggered: 'He didn't catch on, he didn't catch on.'

A little disconcerted, Traps paused in his eating. For a moment there seemed something slightly sinister in the roguish merriment of these dignified old men. But the impression quickly passed, and he joined in their laughter.

'I beg your pardon, gentlemen,' he said. 'I imagined the interrogation would be more solemn, dignified and formal – more like a regular court.'

'My dear Traps,' said the judge, 'the expression on your face is priceless. I see our way of holding court strikes you as peculiar and much too frivolous. But, my dear fellow, the four of us here at this table are in retirement, which means that we are free from the needless red tape of forms and verbatim reports and documents and laws which are the burden of our ordinary courts. We dispense justice without regard for weighty tomes and Article This and Article That.'

'Enterprising,' Traps replied, his tongue already beginning to labour over words, 'very enterprising. Gen'lemen, I'm impressed. A court of law without the law books – that's a wonderful idea.'

The defending counsel swayed heavily to his feet. He was going to get a breath of air, he announced. Before they began on the fowl and the rest, it was time for a short stroll and a cigarette. Would Herr Traps care to accompany him?

The two of them stepped down from the veranda into a warm, majestic night, for full darkness had descended. Golden beams of light extended from the windows of the dining-room as far as the rosebeds. The sky was bright with stars, but there was no moon, so that the trees stood out only as masses of denser darkness.

They could barely make out the gravel paths down which they moved, and they clutched each other's arms. Heavy with wine, they staggered and reeled now and again, though they strove to walk straight. Their cigarettes made red dots of light in the darkness.

Traps took a deep breath. 'What a lot of fun we're having in there,' he said, gesturing towards the illuminated window in which loomed the sturdy silhouette of the housekeeper. 'It's splendid, splendid.'

'My dear friend,' the defending counsel said, swaying and leaning on Traps to steady himself. 'Before we return and attack our capon, let me, in all seriousness, give you a word of advice, and beg that you take it to heart. I like you, young man; I feel a tender affection for you, and I want to talk to you like a father. We are well on the way to losing our case all along the line!'

'I'm sorry to hear that,' Traps replied, guiding his lawyer cautiously along the gravel path and around the black pyramid of a shrub. They came to a pool. They came to a stone bench, which they divined rather than saw, and sat down.

Stars glittered in the water and coolness wafted into their faces. From the village came the sounds of an accordion, singing, and then the melancholy blast of an alpenhorn. The Poultry Farmers' Association was celebrating.

'You must pull yourself together,' the lawyer continued. 'The enemy have already taken vital bastions. The death of Gygax – there was no need for that fact to have emerged at all, if you hadn't let your tongue run away with you – the death of Gygax is a serious menace to our case. The situation is so bad that an ordinary lawyer would have to throw in the sponge. But if I stick to it and exploit all opportunities, and above all, if you exercise the utmost prudence and self-discipline, I can still save something from the wreckage.'

Traps laughed. This was an absolutely first-class parlour game, he declared; he would make a point of introducing it at the Utopia Club's next meeting.

'Isn't it, though?' the lawyer agreed, intensely gratified. 'Brings a man to life again. My dear friend, when I retired and was supposed to enjoy my old age here in this village. I began dying by inches. Nothing to do, no chance to practice my profession. Do you think there's anything interesting about this place? Nothing whatever, except that there is no Föhn to give you headaches. And what's the good of a fine climate? No good at all, if the brain has no occupation. The prosecutor was practically on his death-bed; our host was thought to have cancer of the stomach; Pilet was suffering from diabetes; and I was having all kinds of trouble with my blood pressure. That was what our retirement brought us. A dog's life. Now and then we met mournfully, talked nostalgically about our old professions and the successes we had had – that was our sole and rare pleasure. Then the prosecutor invented . . . the game. The judge provided the house. And I placed my resources at the disposal of the company. (After all, I'm a bachelor, and when you've been a lawyer for the upper crust all your life you put aside a tidy little sum, my friend. You can't imagine how generous the robber barons can be when their defending counsel has won them an acquittal – lavish, I can tell you.) . . . Well, the game has become our fountain of youth; hormones, stomachs, gastric juices – everything is in working order again. We are bored no longer; our energy, and youthfulness, and elasticity, and appetites, are entirely restored. Look at this . . .'

In spite of his paunch he performed what Traps in the darkness vaguley recognized as gymnastic exercises.

'We play our game with the judge's guests,' the lawyer continued. 'They function as defendants.' He sat down again. 'Sometimes we have salesmen, sometimes holiday visitors. Two months ago we had the privilege of sentencing a German general to twenty years' hard labour. He was passing through here on a walking tour with his wife. Only my skill saved him from the gallows.'

'Wonderful,' Traps exclaimed. 'What a wonderful game. But you're exaggerating, aren't you, when you speak of the gallows? After all, capital punishment has been abolished in this country.'

'In the official judicial system, yes,' the lawyer replied. 'But we are dispensing our own private brand of justice here, and we have reinstated it. It is precisely the risk of the death penalty that makes our game so exciting and unique.'

'And,' said Traps, chuckling, 'I suppose you have an executioner, too?'

'Of course,' the lawyer declared proudly. 'we certainly have. Pilet.'

'Pilet?'

'Ha, that surprises you, doesn't it?'

Traps swallowed hard several times. But isn't he the proprietor of the Bull and Stirrup? He provides the wines we have been drinking, doesn't he?'

'He always has run a tavern,' the lawyer smirked complacently. 'His work for the State was just a sideline. Almost an honorary office. In his own country he was considered one of the most talented men in his profession. He's been with us for twenty years now, more or less in retirement, but he still keeps up to date in his craft.'

A car passed on the highway, and the glare of its headlights irradiated the smoke of their cigarettes. For a second Traps caught a glimpse of his lawyer, a shapeless figure in a stained frock-coat, with fat, smug, jovial face. Traps shivered. Beads of cold sweat broke out on his brow.

'Pilet.'

'Why, what is the matter with you all of a sudden, my friend? I can feel you trembling. Aren't you well?'

'I don't know,' Traps whispered, breathing heavily. 'I don't know.'

The image of the bald man leapt into his mind – how Pilet had sat at table dumb and unassuming, shovelling in his food. It was an imposition to be asked to dine with a fellow like that . . .

But the warmth of the summer night and the greater warmth of the wine tempered Traps's momentary outrage, inclined him towards feelings of tolerance, of being above prejudice. He reminded himself that he was a man who had seen a good deal – a man who knew the world – a big wheel in the textile industry – not some timorous, strait-laced, small-minded prig. After all, the executioner wasn't to blame for his occupation. In fact, on second thoughts the evening would have been much the poorer without him – far less piquant altogether. What a story this would make for the boys at the Utopia Club. The club might even invite the executioner some day to give a short talk to the members; he would probably be glad to come in return for a small fee and expenses.

Having come to terms with his emotions, Traps laughed heartily.

'That was a bombshell!' he said. 'Gave me quite a turn for a minute. The more I hear about this game, the more it intrigues me.'

'Well now, one confidence deserves another, doesn't it?' the lawyer said. They rose and, arm in arm, blinded by the light from the windows, fumbled their way back towards the house. 'So tell me: how did you do away with Gygax?'

'What makes you think I did away with him?'

'Well, since he's dead.'

'But I had nothing to do with that!'

The lawyer stood still. 'My dear young friend,' he replied sympathetically, 'I quite understand your hesitancy. Murder is the most painful of all crimes to confess. The defendant is ashamed, does not want to recognize his act, forgets it, represses it, drives it from his memory. He becomes touchy about the past altogether, burdens himself with exaggerated guilt feelings, and refuses to trust anyone, even his friend who is like a father to him, his defending counsel. And that, of course, is as wrong-headed as anything could be: for a real defending counsel loves murder – he is absolutely in the seventh heaven if a murder is brought to him. Let's have it, Traps, my boy. I don't really begin to enjoy things until I face a tough problem, like an alpinist before a good ten-thousand-foot ascent. I speak as a regular old mountaineer myself. Give me a tough problem and my brain begins to function, to hum and purr; it's a joy to feel how smoothly it operates. For that reason your distrust of me is your great mistake. Yes, your decisive mistake. So let's have your confession.'

'But I haven't got anything to confess,' the sales manager asserted.

The lawyer stared in astonishment. He gaped at Traps, the planes of his aged face grotesquely lit by the light from the window, through which came the clink of glasses and the old men's shouts of laughter.

'My boy, my boy,' he growled reproachfully, 'what are you up to now? After all I've said, do you still insist on these foolish tactics of yours? Are you determined to go on playing the innocent? Haven't you caught on yet? You have to confess, whether you want to or not, and there is always something to confess – that ought to have dawned on you by now. So let's get at it, my friend. Let's have done with all this playing about. Tell me once for all: How did you kill Gygax? In a sudden rage, wasn't it? In that case we should have to be prepared for a manslaughter indictment. I'll bet the prosecutor is steering that way. I just have a feeling about that – I know the old boy.'

Traps shook his head. 'My dear, devoted counsel for the defence,' he said, 'the particular beauty of this game of ours – if I may be allowed to give my opinion, when this is only the first time I've played it – is the way it gets under one's skin and gives one the shivers. The game threatens to turn into reality. All of a sudden one asks oneself whether one may not be a criminal after all – even if one didn't kill old Gygax. All your talk has been making my brain reel. But as you say, one confidence deserves another, so here you are: I am not guilty of the old bastard's death. Absolutely truthfully, I am not.'

With that, they re-entered the dining-room, where the capon had already been brought to table and a Château Pavie 1921 was glowing in the glasses.

Traps, full of good-humour, went up to the grave, taciturn bald fellow and pressed his hand. The lawyer, he said, had told him about Herr Pilet's former profession, and he wanted to state that he, personally, could imagine no greater pleasure than to have so fine and upstanding a man to dine with. He, Traps, had no prejudices about that sort of thing – quite the contrary.

Pilet, stroking his dyed moustache, flushed, and then murmured, with embarrassment: 'Delighted, delighted, will do my best.'

After this touching exchange of civilities, the capon tasted all the better. The recipe, the judge announced, was a secret of Mlle Simone's. They smacked their lips, ate with their fingers, extolled the masterpiece, drank their wine, toasted one another's health, and while they regaled themselves the trial took its course.

The prosecutor, a napkin tied under his chin, holding the drumstick to his masticating grease-smeared mouth, expressed the hope that the company would have a confession served up along with the fowl. 'Surely, my dearest, my most honourable defendant,' he probed, 'surely you poisoned Gygax?'

Traps laughed. 'No,' he said. 'Nothing of the sort.'

'Then shall we say you shot him?'

'Not that either.'

'Arranged a car crash?'

Everyone laughed except the defending counsel, who whispered sharply once more: 'Watch out, this is a trap.'

'Sorry, friend Prosecutor, sorry,' Traps joked, 'but Gygax died of a heart attack. And it wasn't even his first. He'd had one years before and had to be careful. He let on that he was fit as a fiddle, but there was always the danger that any excitement would bring it on again. I know that for certain.'

'Indeed? Who told you?'

'His wife.'

'For heavens's sake watch your step,' the lawyer urged in his usual audible whisper.

The Château Pavie 1921 surpassed all expectations. Traps was already on his fourth glass, and Mlle Simone had placed an extra bottle near him. Raising his glass to toast the old gentlemen, the sales manager declared that, believe it or not, he had nothing to conceal. Just to prove this to the court, and no matter how unorthodox it seemed, he intended to tell them the truth, the whole truth, and nothing but the truth, despite the fact that his defending counsel had repeatedly urged him to be careful.

The fact was, he said, he'd had a little romance with Frau Gygax. After all, the old bastard was often away on trips, and had cruelly neglected her – and she was certainly a cute little piece. So he, Traps, had undertaken to console her now and then, first on the couch in Gygax's living-room and later on, as he grew more at home, in the Gygax marital bed. Things like that were happening all the time; it was the way of the world.

At these words the old gentlemen froze for a moment, utterly dumbfounded. But when they recovered themselves they screeched with pleasure. Bald-headed old Pilet, who said so little, tossed his white carnation into the air, crying: 'A confession, a confession!' Only the counsel for the defence did not share in the hilarity. He pounded his fists despairingly against his temples. 'Such folly, such folly!' he cried. His client had lost his mind, he protested. They must on no account believe his fabrications. Indignantly, amid renewed applause from the rest of the company, Traps took issue with this. On the contrary, he knew exactly what he was saying. He was simply being frank.

There began a long haggle between the defending counsel and the prosecutor – a stubborn argument, half in jest, half serious, which Traps could hardly understand. It all hinged on the word '*dolus*', and the sales manager did not know what the word meant. The discussion grew steadily louder, more violent and more incomprehensible; the judge intervened, likewise became heated. At the start Traps had made an effort to listen, trying to piece together the substance of the dispute, but his attention soon wandered. He breathed a sigh of relief when the housekeeper served cheese: Camembert, Brie, Emmentaler, Gruyère, Tête de Moine, Vacherin, Limburger, Gorgonzola. Traps turned his attention to these comestibles and let *dolus* be *dolus*; but he drank a glass to the bald man, who alone abstained from the discussion – it seemed to be above his head.

At last the prosecutor turned to Traps again, his leonine mane in disarray, his face flushed, his left hand toying with the monocle. 'Herr Traps,' he asked, 'are you still on friendly terms with Frau Gygax?'

All of them stared at Traps, who had thrust a piece of white bread spread with Camembert into his mouth and was chewing happily. Before making his reply, he took another long swallow of Château Pavie. A clock was ticking somewhere, and from the village there came once more the faint sounds of an accordion and a male chorus.

Traps explained that since Gygax's death he had kept away from there. Naturally he did not want to compromise the reputation of a widow.

To his surprise his explanation was the signal for another outburst of extraordinary, and, to him, baffling, merriment. Everyone – except the defending counsel – shouted with glee. The prosecutor cried: '*Dolo malo, dolo malo*,' and bellowed verse in Greek and Latin, and hurled quotations from Schiller and Goethe. The midget judge blew out all the candles except one; then, bleating, hissing, and growling a wild accompaniment, he held his hands behind the flame of this single candle and deftly threw a shadow-play upon the wall: he crooked his fingers this way and that to make goats, bats, devils and goblins. Pilet drummed on the table until the dishes and glasses danced, chanting: 'We'll have a death sentence, we'll have a death sentence.'

The defending counsel alone held aloof from the general uproar. He pushed the platter of cheese in front of Traps. 'Take some,' he urged. 'We may as well eat hearty. There's nothing left for us to do.'

A Château Margaux was brought in, and the dusty bottle, vintage of 1914, restored quiet. Everyone gazed respectfully at the judge as he cautiously and with great deliberation began removing the cork, employing a curious, old-fashioned corkscrew which enabled him to draw the cork from the bottle as it lay on its side in the basket. They watched in breathless suspense, for the cork had to be removed with the least possible damage, since it was the only proof of the age of the wine. (After more than four decades there was little left of the label.) The cork did not come out quite whole, and the remainder had to be scraped out with delicate care. But enough of the cork was left for the date to be legible. It was handed round the table, sniffed, admired, and finally gravely presented to the sales manager – as a memento, the judge said, of their wonderful evening. The judge now tasted the wine, licked his lips, and filled the other glasses. The rest of the company smelled the wine, sipped it, burst into cries of ecstasy and praise. The cheese was handed round, and the judge requested the prosecutor to make his little speech and present the 'case for the prosecution'.

The prosecutor asked for new candles first, to mark the solemnity of the occasion. The task before him called, he said, for the utmost concentration, reverence, and composure.

Mlle Simone brought the candles, and amid tense silence lit them. The sales manager felt that the atmosphere was slightly sinister, and a chill ran through him; but even so, he thought the whole thing was a first-class adventure, and not for anything in the world would he have missed it.

But his lawyer seemed disgruntled. 'Listen, now,' he said. 'Listen to the prosecutor's charge. You will be startled when you see what you have done with your careless tongue, what a mess you have made of things with your wild tactics. The situation was bad before, but it is catastrophic now. But keep up your courage and I'll get you out of this predicament. Only don't lose your head; you'll need all your wits about you to come through with a whole skin.'

The moment had come. There was a general clearing of throats. Someone coughed. Once more they toasted one another. And then, amid grins and chuckles, the prosecutor began his address.

'The greatest pleasure of our gathering this evening,' he said, raising his glass but remaining seated, 'and its crowning achievement, is that we have uncovered a murder so subtly arranged that of course it has brilliantly escaped the attention of official justice.'

Traps forgot himself for a moment. 'Do you mean to say,' he burst out, 'that I have committed a murder? Now look here, that's going too far. My own lawyer has already got that crazy idea into his head and – ' Then he remembered that it was all in the game, and began to laugh wildly, uncontrollably. Of course – what a wonderful joke! Now he understood it: they wanted to talk him into believing he had committed a crime. It was clever; extremely clever.

The prosecutor, regarding Traps with a dignified air, wiped his monocle and replaced it in his eye.

'The defendant,' he said, 'doubts his own guilt. A human impulse. Who among us knows himself, who knows his own crimes and secret misdeeds? However, I should like to lay stress upon one thing now, before the passions of our game rise once more to high tide. If Traps is a murderer – as I maintain, and as I hope with all my heart – we are about to enter upon an hour of the gravest solemnity. And rightly so: for the discovery of a murder is a joyful event, an event that makes our hearts beat faster, that confronts us with new tasks, decisions, duties. Therefore, before all else I wish to congratulate our dear presumptive culprit – for without a culprit it is scarcely possible to discover a murder or to make justice prevail. A special health to him, then – to our friend, our modest Alfredo Traps, whom a kindly destiny has brought into our midst!'

Shouts of joy greeted this speech. All rose and drank to the sales manager's health. Tears in his eyes, Traps thanked them and assured them that this was the best evening he had ever spent.

The prosecutor likewise had tears in his eyes as he resumed. 'The best evening he has ever spent, our noble friend tells us. Glorious words, gentlemen, deeply moving words. Let us recall the time when we performed our gloomy duties in the interest of the State. Then a defendant stood before us not as a friend but as a foe. We had to thrust him away from us, whereas now we can take him to our hearts.' Leaving his place, he threw his arms around Traps and embraced him fervently.

'Prosecutor, my dear, dear friend,' the sales manager stammered.

'Defendant, my dear, dear Traps,' the prosecutor sobbed. 'Let us drop these formalities. My name is Kurt. To your health, Alfredo!'

'To your health, Kurt!'

They embraced, hugged, patted each other on the back, drank to each other; a tide of emotion washed over them, the joy that accompanies the blossoming of a new friendship.

'How everything has changed!' the prosecutor rejoiced. 'Where once we were harried from case to case, from crime to crime, from verdict to verdict, we now have all the leisure in the world to build our case, to discuss, refute, dispute; we can speak and reply gaily and gladly, come to appreciate the defendant, to love him, to feel the warmth of his sympathy. The two sides are united in bonds of brotherly love. And once that has come into being, crime has no weight, verdict no sting. Let me, then, express my appreciation of the murder which has been committed.'

'Prove it, Kurt, my boy, prove it,' Traps threw in, once again bathed in good humour.

'And it is right that I should express appreciation,' the prosecutor went on, 'for we are dealing here with a beautiful, a perfect murder. Now our delightful culprit may imagine that in using such a term I am being brashly cynical. But far from it; rather, I must characterize his deed as "beautiful" in two respects: philosophically, and by reason of its technical skill.

'Let me assure you, my dear Alfredo, that our company has long since abandoned the narrow and prejudiced point of view that sees crime as ugly and terrible, and justice on the other hand as a thing of beauty. If we are to compare the two, I might say that justice can be the more terrible. But the duality is only apparent: the beauty of crime is indispensable for the beauty of justice – without crime we should have no justice. So much for the philosophical side. Let us now turn to an appreciation of the technical beauty of the act. I believe that "appreciation" is exactly the right word, for my speech for the prosecution is not intended as a terrifying indictment which might embarrass and bewilder our friend, but as an appreciation that will reveal his crime for him, help it to flower, implant it in his consciousness. For the flawless monument of justice can be erected only upon the stainless pedestal of understanding.'

The eighty-six-year-old prosecutor paused in exhaustion. In spite of his age he had spoken in a loud, theatrical voice and with sweeping gestures, all the while eating and drinking copiously. Now he used the greasy napkin tied round his collar to wipe the sweat from his forehead and dry his wrinkled neck.

Traps was touched. He slumped in his chair, sluggish from the meal. He was satiated, but he did not want to be outdone by the four greybeards, though he had to admit to himself that he was hard put to it to match the vast appetite and vaster thirst of these old men. He was a hearty eater himself, but never in his life had he encountered such avidity as theirs. He sat gaping lazily across the table, flattered by the effusiveness of the prosecutor and listening as the bell in the church tower solemnly struck twelve; rumbling in the distance came the chorus of the poultry farmers singing 'Our life is like a voyage . . .'

'Like a fairy tale,' he said. 'Like a fairy tale.'

Then he said: 'So I'm supposed to have committed a murder. Me of all people. Would you kindly tell me how I did it?'

Meanwhile the judge had uncorked another bottle of Château Margaux 1914. The prosecutor, refreshed, began again.

'Now what has happened?' he said. 'How did I discover that our dear friend could justly boast of a murder? And not an ordinary murder – far from it. A masterpiece of a murder, committed without bloodshed, without resort to poison, guns, or anything so crude.'

He cleared his throat. Traps, mouth full of cheese, regarded him in fascination.

It was in the nature of his profession, the prosecutor continued, to cherish the assumption that a crime might lurk behind every event, every person. The first indication that friend Alfredo was one of those favoured by destiny, sanctified by crime, lay in the circumstance that the commercial traveller had driven an old Citroën only a year ago, and now sat proudly at the wheel of a brand-new special-model Studebaker.

'Now I know,' he continued, 'that we live in boom times, so that detail could not be taken by itself as prima facie evidence of anything. It served merely as a clue, feeding the premonition that we were on the verge of a joyous experience – that is to say, the discovery of a murder. That our dear friend had assumed his superior's former position, that he had to force this superior out, and that the superior subsequently departed this life – all these facts were still not proofs, were merely elements confirming my premonition, lending substance to it. Real suspicion, founded upon a logical basis, did not arise until we learned how it was that his superior departed this life. From a heart attack. At this point we had to apply all our skill, utilize all our keenness and subtlety, put two and two together, advance discreetly, creep up on the truth, recognize the extraordinary in the common-place, certainty in uncertainties, outlines in the mist, to believe in a murder precisely because murder seemed ruled out.

'Let us consider the evidence to hand. Let us sketch a picture of the dead man. We know little about him; for what we know we are indebted entirely to our dear friend and guest. Herr Gygax was the sales manager for the company producing Hephaeston, a synthetic textile which we willingly believe possesses all the excellent qualities our dearest Alfredo ascribes to it. Gygax was a man, we may deduce, who was out for all he could get, who ruthlessly exploited his subordinates, who was adept at closing deals, although the methods he used were often more than questionable.'

'You've got him exactly!' cried Traps with animation. 'The old crook – you've hit him off perfectly.'

'We may further conclude,' the prosecutor continued, 'that outwardly he played the part of a vigorous, robust man, a hard-hitting successful businessman bristling with good health, able to cope with any situation, a man who knew his way around. In order to maintain this image, Gygax carefully concealed the fact of his severe heart disease – here too we are quoting Alfredo. We may assume that he took the fact of his illness with a kind of defiant fury, as though it meant an admission of some kind of failure.'

'Amazing!' Traps exclaimed. It was simply uncanny, he went on; he would have bet that Kurt had known the dead man personally.

'Be quiet, be quiet!' the defending counsel whispered sharply.

'But let us complete our portrait of Gygax,' the prosecutor continued. 'There is the additional fact that the deceased neglected his wife, whom we are to imagine as a "cute little piece" – at least that is how our friend has described her. To Gygax only success counted, only business, externals, the façade, and it is safe to guess that he took his wife's fidelity for granted, in that he fancied himself as being far too extraordinary, too overpowering a man, for the thought of adultery ever to occur to his wife. For which reason it would have been a hard blow to him if he had learned of his wife's amusing herself with our Casanova of the Utopia Club.'

All laughed unroariously. Traps slapped his thighs. He beamed all over. 'It certainly was,' he said, confirming the prosecutor's guess. 'It finished him off when he found out.'

The defending counsel moaned. 'You must be mad,' was all he could say.

The prosecutor and judge gazed happily across the table at Traps, who was diligently peeling the rind from the Tête de Moine.

'Ah,' the prosecutor asked, 'how did the old sinner find out? Did his cute little piece of a wife admit to it?'

'She would never have done that, Prosecutor,' Traps replied. 'She was scared stiff of the old bastard.'

'Did Gygax work it out for himself?'

'Him? He was too conceited for that.'

'Did you by any chance spring it on him, my dear friend and Don Juan?'

Involuntarily, Traps flushed. 'Why no, Kurt,' he said. 'What sort of fellow do you think I am? It was one of his fine-feathered business friends who told the old crook.'

'But why should he have done that?'

'It was somebody who wanted to cook my goose – he was always out to get me.'

'What types there are in this world!' the prosecutor exclaimed. 'But how could this honest soul, this business friend of Gygax, have known about your affair?'

'I told him.'

'You told him?'

'Oh well – over a glass of wine. You know how it is, you let things slip when you've had a drop too much.'

'Granted.' The prosecutor nodded agreement. 'But you were just saying that you knew Gygax's business friend to be an enemy of yours. In that case was it not fairly obvious to you that he would go to your boss with the story?'

At this point the counsel for the defence interrupted. He rose to his feet, streaming perspiration, the collar of his frock-coat soaked through. He would like to advise Traps, he declared, that he need not answer this question.

Traps disagreed.

'Why not?' he said. 'There's no harm in the question. After all, I didn't give a damn whether Gygax found out or not. The way the old bastard had always treated me, the way he tried to give me the short end of the stick every time, I really didn't see any reason to be considerate of him.'

For a moment another hush fell over the room, a deathly hush.

Then a deafening tumult broke out, shouts of glee, a hurricane of laughter, a roar of jubilation. The taciturn, bald-headed man embraced Traps, even kissed him on both cheeks. The judge and the prosecutor danced round the room, staggered into the walls, shook hands with each other, clambered on the chairs, smashed bottles, reeled in a delirium of delight.

'A second confession,' the prosecutor bellowed. He had scrambled up on to the arm of his chair and was now balancing on it, first on one leg and then on the other. Hurrah for their guest; he was playing the game beautifully.

Even the defending counsel was doubled up with laughter. It was too rich, he exclaimed. One couldn't even be angry with such a defendant.

'The case is clear, the last link in the chain of evidence has been forged,' the prosecutor continued, rocking on the chair like a weather-beaten baroque statue. 'Behold our noble soul, our dearest Alfredo. We see him under the thumb of that stinker of a boss, and driving his second-hand Citroën about the country. Only a year ago, this was. He must nevertheless have taken pride in his position, our friend, the father of four children, the son of a factory-hand. And rightly so. For during the war he had been a mere door-to-door salesman – not even that, for he was unlicensed, a tramp going about with illegal textiles: a petty black marketeer, travelling by rail from village to village, or trudging on foot over country tracks, making his weary way for miles through dark woods to remote farms, a dirty leather pouch slung over his shoulder, or possibly even a basket, and a battered suitcase in his hand. Now he had bettered himself, had found a foothold for himself in a good firm, was a member of the Liberal Party whereas his father had been a crazy radical. But – if I may be permitted a poetic phrase

– who rests upon the branch to which he has climbed when above his head stretch more branches bearing still finer fruit? Of course, he was earning a good living, flitting about in his Citroën from place to place. The car wasn't bad, but our good Alfredo saw new models bobbing up all round him, roaring towards him, pulling up alongside him, passing him. Prosperity was spreading over the land. Why should he not have a piece of it?'

'That's exactly how it was, Kurt,' Traps beamed. 'Exactly.'

The prosecutor was in his element now: radiant, happy as a child on Christmas morning.

'That was easier said than done,' he continued, straddling the arm of his chair. 'His boss would not let him rise in the world. Spitefully, crassly, openly, his boss exploited him, gave him advances only in order to impose new quotas, fettered him hand and foot, tied him down.'

'That's exactly what he did!' the sales manager cried out. 'You have no idea, gentlemen, how that old bastard put the squeeze on me.'

'And so there was nothing for it but to go out for all you could get,' the prosecutor said.

'Exactly!' Traps agreed.

The defendant's interruptions inspired the prosecutor to further heights of eloquence. He stood up on his chair seat, waving his wine-spotted napkin like a banner, flaunting his waistcoat sprinkled with bits of salad and meat and splashes of tomato sauce.

'Our dear friend set about it first on the business level,' he went on. 'Here his conduct was not entirely ethical, as he himself admits. We can fairly well guess how he went at it. He secretly got in touch with his boss's suppliers, ferreted out what he could, promised better results, confused issues, talked with other salesmen, made alliances and counter-alliances. But then he hit on another way.'

'Another way?' Traps asked in surprise.

The prosecutor nodded. 'A way, gentlemen, which led from the couch in Gygax's apartment directly into his marital bed.'

All laughed, Traps even harder than the others. 'Yes,' he agreed, 'it was a low-down trick I played on the old crook. But when I think back on it, the situation was just too funny. That fact is, I've always felt a little ashamed about it up to now. No one likes to go too deeply into his own actions, and after all, nobody's linen is absolutely spotless. But when I come up against such understanding friends as you, shame seems altogether out of place. It's odd, but I feel that you understand me, and I'm beginning to understand myself, as though I'm meeting a person who happens to be myself and whom I used to know only in a vague sort of way as a sales manager with a Studebaker and a wife and kids somewhere.'

'We observe with pleasure,' the prosecutor replied warmly, cordially, 'that a light is dawning on our friend. Let us lend him our aid until he sees it all in full lucidity. Let us track down his motives with the zeal of archaeologists until we come upon the glory of buried crimes. He began an affair with Frau Gygax. How did this come about? Let us imagine that he saw this "cute little piece" one day. Perhaps it was late one evening, possibly in winter, say about six o'clock . . .'

Traps: 'About seven, Kurt boy, about seven!'

'. . . with night already settled on the city, with the street lamps shedding a golden glow, shop windows and theatres all illuminated, and green and yellow twinkling lights over the awnings. It is the hour of cosy intimacy, of allure and voluptuousness. He had driven his Citroën up the slippery streets to the high-class residential district where his boss lived . . .'

'High-class residential district, that's exactly it,' Traps interjected enthusiastically.

'. . . a briefcase on the car seat beside him, filled with orders, samples of cloth. An important decision had to be made, but Gygax's big limousine was not parked in its usual place at the kerb. All the same, Traps went up the path through the dark garden and rang the bell. Frau Gygax opened the door herself. Her husband would not be home tonight, she said, and her maid was out. She was dressed for an evening at home, or better still, was wearing a dressing-gown. Nevertheless, Traps must come in for a drink; she invited him pressingly, and so they sat together in the drawing-room.'

Traps was thunderstruck. 'How do you know all this, Kurt, my boy? You're a wizard.'

'Practice,' the prosecutor declared. 'People's lives are all much the same. It was not even a case of seduction on Traps's part or the woman's; it was simply an opportunity that came his way. She was alone and bored, had nothing special in mind, was merely glad of the chance to talk to someone. The house was pleasantly warm, and under the flower-printed dressing-gown she was wearing nothing but her nightgown. Traps, seated beside her, saw her white throat and the swell of her breasts, and as she talked in vindictive, disillusioned terms about her husband, the idea came to Traps that it was here he must apply his leverage – and in fact he had already begun by the time it occurred to him. He soon found out everything about Gygax, that the state of his health was shaky, that any disturbance might k.ll him. Traps learned his exact age, learned how coarse and crude he was with his wife, and how completely he took her faithfulness for granted. For you quickly find out everything from a woman who wants to take vengeance on her husband.

'So our friend continued the affair, for now his plan was formed; now he was determined to ruin his boss by any and all means, come what might. At last the moment arrived when he held all the cards. He had won over the suppliers and Gygax's business partners, and at night he held naked in his arms the soft white body of the man's wife. And then he drew his noose tight; created a scandal. Deliberately.

'We can picture this last phase for ourselves. Again the intimate twilight hour. We find our friend in a restaurant, or let us say in one of those typical taverns of the old quarter of the city, somewhat over-heated, the atmosphere in every way consonant with the spirit of our cantonal democracy: patriotic, solid, bull's-eye windows, everything substantial – the prices too, by the way. The bulky proprietor . . .'

Traps: 'It was the Rathauskeller, old boy!'

' . . . pardon, then, we must make a correction – the bulky proprietress sits surrounded by portraits of loyal customers of former years. A newspaper-seller drifts through the place and goes out. Later along comes a detachment of the Salvation Army, singing "Let the sunshine in". Some students are drinking with their professor. Traps at a table, two glasses, a bottle of good stuff in front of him – hang the expense, this once. Opposite him, sallow, fat, drenched in sweat, collar open, as apoplectic a type as the intended victim, sits Gygax's business friend, wondering what this is all about, why Traps has invited him out all of a sudden. He listens attentively, hears from Traps's own lips the admission of adultery. And then, a few hours later, as was inevitable, and as our Alfredo had foreseen, the fellow rushes off to the boss, convinced that duty, friendship and decency demand that he let the unfortunate deceived husband know what he has learned.'

'The hypocrite!' Traps cried. He listened with round, glistening eyes to the prosecutor's description, happy to be learning the truth, his own proud, courageous, unique truth.

The prosecutor continued:

'Thus the fatal moment arrived, the moment so carefully calculated, when Gygax heard the whole story. The old crook was still able to drive home. Let us picture him filled with rage, perspiring profusely as he drives, stabbing pains in the region of his heart, hands shaking on the wheel, traffic policemen whistling angrily after him as he ignores signals. Then the laborious walk from the garage to the front door; collapse, perhaps in the hallway, as the little woman comes towards him, the "cute little piece". It does not take long; the doctor administers morphine, and then it is all over, finished – a brief rattling in the throat, and that is all, while the wife stands by the bed, sobbing. Traps, at home in the bosom of his family, lifts the telephone off the hook. Outward dismay, inner jubilation; the game is won; hurrah. Three months later – the Studebaker.'

This closing note evoked fresh gales of laughter. Traps, who had been batted from one amazement to the next, laughed along with the rest, though with a slight note of embarrassment. He scratched his head and gave the prosecutor an appreciative nod. He was in excellent spirits. It had been a wonderfully successful evening. Of course, the fact that they imputed a murder to him upset him somewhat and made him a bit pensive. But he felt his mood as a pleasant one, for it awakened in him inklings of higher things, of justice, crime and punishment, guilt and atonement, and filled him with amazement at his own capacities. The fear, which he had not yet forgotten, that chill which had swept him in the garden and later during the hilarity at the table, now seemed to him utterly unfounded, part of the joke. It was all so human. He was eager to see what would follow.

The company moved into the parlour for their *demi-tasse*. Staggering, guiding the reeling counsel for the defence, Traps entered a room crammed with knick-knacks and vases. There were enormous engravings on the wall, views of towns and historical subjects: the Rütli Oath, the victory of the Bernese over the Emperor's troops at the Battle of Laupen in 1339, the massacre of the Swiss Guard. Stuccoed ceiling; a grand piano; comfortable armchairs of huge dimensions, their antimacassars embroidered with pious sentiments: *'Blessed be he who walks in the ways of righteousness'; 'A clear conscience makes a soft pillow.'* Through the open window the highway could be sensed – magically present, a sunken path along which the headlights of cars came flaring only occasionally at this hour, for it was approaching two o'clock in the morning.

Traps declared he had never heard anything so true to life as Kurt's account. Hardly anything in it needed revision so far as essentials were concerned, although of course a few minor corrections were called for. For example, Gygax's kind-hearted business friend had been a shrivelled-up little man, and wore a stiff collar not at all soaked with sweat. And Frau Gygax had received him not in a dressing-gown but in a kimono, and one so open that in all decency – if he might be permitted a little joke – he could not very well fail to open it the rest of the way. Also, the super-crook's well-deserved heart attack had struck him down at his warehouse, while the Föhn was blowing; the old boy had not gone home but had been taken to the hospital, where the heart had given out entirely. But as he had said, all these details were unimportant. The chief thing was that the theory of his bosom friend the prosecutor was correct: he had really become involved with Frau Gygax only because he wanted to ruin the old bastard. In fact, he remembered distinctly how, lying in Gygax's bed, on top of his wife, he had stared at the man's portrait photograph which stood on the night table, had looked his fill at that fat, unpleasant face with its owl-like eyes behind horn-rimmed glasses, and how a kind of premonition had come over him, a wild, ecstatic delight at the thought that in what he was doing with such enjoyment and ardour he was really cutting the throat of his bastard of a boss, was cold-bloodedly finishing him off.

When Traps explained this, they were already seated in the soft chairs, reaching out for the coffee, stirring it, and with it drinking an 1893 cognac, Roffignac, out of big brandy-glasses.

It was time now, the prosecutor announced, for him to propose the sentence. He sat sprawled athwart a monstrous reclining chair, his legs in their unmatched socks (one checked in grey and black, the other green) resting over the arm. 'Our friend Alfredo did not act *dola indirecto*, and the ensuing death was not accidental. He is guilty *dolo malo*, of having acted with premeditation, as is clear from the fact that on the one hand he engineered the revelation and that on the other hand after the supercrook's death he ceased to visit the cute little piece in question. Hence it necessarily follows that the wife was only an instrument in his bloodthirsty plans – the delectable murder weapon, as it were. Clearly, then, we have a case of murder, performed by a psychological technique in such a manner that apart from adultery nothing was done contrary to the law – to all appearances, at any rate. Wherefore, now that the guise of innocence has vanished, and our dear defendant has been kind enough to make his confession twice over, I have the pleasure as prosecutor to demand that our high court impose the death penalty upon Alfredo Traps, as reward for a crime that merits admiration, astonishment and respect, and may deservedly be considered one of the most extraordinary crimes of our century.'

They laughed, applauded, and fell upon the cake that Mlle Simone brought in. The highlight of the evening, they all declared.

Outside, as a special attraction, the late moon rose, a thin crescent. The trees rustled softly. Otherwise all was still; only rarely did a car pass on the road now. Occasionally there sounded the hesitant, uncertain footfalls of some belated homecomer.

The sales manager felt secure, happy, sheltered. He sat beside Pilet on an overstuffed sofa whose antimacassar was embroidered with the words 'East and West, Home is Best'. Pilet, still sparing of speech, said no more than an occasional 'Splendid!' uttered with a heavy-voiced, hissing S. Traps pressed close to him with tender, affectionate familiarity, laid his cheek against Pilet's, admired his phlegmatic elegance.

Sluggish and peaceful from the wine, he took a voluptuous pleasure in being himself in this understanding company, in no longer having a secret because secrecy was no longer necessary, in being appreciated, cherished, loved, understood. The idea that he had committed a murder became more and more acceptable to him; it touched him deeply, transformed his life, made everything more complex, more heroic, more precious. He was swept by a current of enthusiasm. He had planned and executed the murder, he told himself. He had done so in order to rise. But not so much to further his career, not so much for financial reasons, for the sake of owning a Studebaker – rather, it was in order to become a more . . . what was the word? . . . a *realer* person – deeper, worthier . . . he fumbled for the thought, having reached the limits of his intellect . . . worthier of the respect and affection of these educated, cultivated men, who now (even Pilet) seemed to him like the ancient Magi he had once read about in the *Reader's Digest* who had known not only the secrets of the stars but the secrets of justice also. Justice – how the word intoxicated him! In his life as a salesman of textiles he had envisaged justice only as abstract pettifoggery; now it rose like a huge, incomprehensible sun over his limited horizon, an idea only vaguely grasped and for that reason all the more able to send shudders of awe through him. So, sipping his cognac and listening to the arguments of the counsel for the defence, he was filled at first with profound astonishment and then with rising outrage, as his fat lawyer strove zealously to fit his crime into the spheres of ordinary life, to reduce it to commonplace.

He had listened with pleasure, said Herr Kummer, to his esteemed opponent's ingenious oration. Herr Kummer lifted his pince-nez from the florid, swollen, shapeless lump of his nose, and made his points with short, precise, geometrical gestures. Granted, the old crook Gygax was dead. Granted, his client had smarted under his domination, had worked up a veritable animosity against the man, had tried to bring about his downfall. No one in his senses would deny this. And where, one might ask, where in the world of business did such things not occur? But it was utterly fantastic to represent as a murder the death of a businessman with a weak heart. ('But I did murder him!' Traps protested valiantly.) Unlike the prosecutor, he considered the defendant not only innocent but even incapable of guilt. (Embittered, insulted, Traps interjected: 'But I *am* guilty, I *am*!')

'On the contrary,' the lawyer continued, 'our sales manager and sole agent for Hephaeston is one example among many. In declaring him incapable of guilt, I do not mean to assert that his is an innocent and stainless soul. Far from it. Traps has committed all the crimes of which he is capable: he has been guilty of adultery; he has swindled his way through life, he has shown a good deal of malignant spite. Not that his life has consisted only of adultery and swindling. Not at all, not at all: it has had its positive sides – our friend Alfredo has his virtues. He is hard-working, hard-headed, loyal to his friends. He is trying to provide well for his children. He has sound political views. Taken all in all we cannot detect more than an unethical taint, a slight spoilage, such as occurs and must occur in so many average lives. But for that very reason, on the other hand, he is not capable of a culpability that is great and pure and proud; he is not capable of a resolute deed, an unequivocal crime.' ('Slander, pure slander!' Traps cried out.) 'He is not a criminal, but a victim of the age, of our Western civilization, which, alas, has fallen farther and farther away from faith, from Christianity, from universals, succumbing more and more to the rule of chaos, so that the individual may no longer look up to a guiding star, and in place of order and true morality disorder and immorality reign, the law of the jungle prevails. Now what has in truth taken place? This average man of ours, this man in the street, has fallen unforewarned into the hands of a crafty prosecutor who has probed, analysed, dissected, his purely instinctive management of his affairs in the textile industry; who has gone muck-raking into his personal life, and cast the harsh light of publicity upon the adventures of a man whose existence was compounded of business trips, the struggle for livelihood, and more or less innocent pleasures; a prosecutor who has tied together unrelated facts, forced a logical plan upon the disorganized whole, seized upon incidents which might as easily have taken quite another turn and given them a causal significance; he has read intention where there was only accident, has twisted thoughtlessness into premeditation, so that in the end the interrogation could have no other outcome but to produce a murderer like a rabbit popping out of a conjurer's hat.' (Traps: 'That isn't so!') 'Let us regard the case of Gygax with sober objectivity, without being misled by the prosecutor's hocus-pocus. We can only conclude that the old crook had himself to thank for his death. His own irregular life destroyed his constitution. We all know only too well the familiar disease of the managerial personality. Its causes are tension, noise, a loveless marriage, and over-strained nerves. As for the heart attack itself, the Föhn that Traps mentioned is the crucial factor. The influence of the Föhn upon cardiac patients is well known . . .'

('Ridiculous!' Traps exclaimed.)

' . . . so that Gygax's death was unquestionably a mere accident. Of course I must admit that there was a certain ruthlessness in my client's behaviour, but ruthlessness is obligatory under the normal laws of commercial life, as he himself repeatedly stressed. Of course he often felt a desire to kill his boss – after all, people will run to anything, venture anything, in thought. But only in thought – and that is precisely the point. It is absurd to assume that this thought was ever carried out in action, especially since my client has now been persuaded that he has actually committed a murder. The fact is that the breakdown of his car has been followed by a nervous breakdown; and therefore, as lawyer for the defence, I propose that Alfredo Traps be acquitted of this charge . . .'

The sales manager was growing more and more indignant as he listened to the well-meaning fog in which his lovely crime was being shrouded, distorted, dissolved, rendered unreal and shadowy, a product of the state of the atmosphere. He felt belittled, and flared up violently almost as soon as his lawyer completed the defence. Rising outraged to his feet, a plate with a fresh piece of cake balanced in his right hand, his glass of Roffignac in his left, he declared that before sentence was pronounced he wanted to insist with the utmost firmness that he agreed whole-heartedly with the prosecutor's speech. Tears filled his eyes. It had been a murder, a deliberate, premeditated murder, he said. He understood that now, and had been profoundly disappointed – horrified, in fact – by the lawyer's defence. He had thought that if anyone would understand him, he could count on understanding from this friend. So now he demanded the verdict, or rather the sentence, not out of any grovelling desire to please, but out of pure idealism; for only in the course of this wonderful night had it dawned on him what it meant to lead a true life, to be true to oneself (at this point our good, honest Traps grew somewhat muddled), for to the true life sublimer ideas of justice, of punishment fitting the crime, were as essential as the chemical elements and compounds which went to make up his synthetic textile, to stick to the field he was at home in. This was a revelation which had resulted in a new birth for him. At any rate – he hoped they would make allowances for the fact that his vocabulary was rather limited outside his own field, so that he found it hard to express what he really meant – at any rate, rebirth seemed to him the proper word for the overwhelming and glorious joy that was now sweeping through him like a typhoon, turning everything upside down inside him, making a new man out of him.

And so there was nothing left but the verdict. Amid the howls of screeching laughter and attempts at yodelling by Pilet, the tiny judge, by now drunk as a lord, announced his decision. It was a matter of some difficulty, not only because he had clambered on to, or rather into, the open grand piano in the corner, but also because his tongue tripped repeatedly. He stumbled over his words, twisted and mutilated them, started sentences he could not finish, continued others whose purport he had already forgotten. But the general sense of it could be guessed. The question at issue was, he declared, whether the prosecutor or the counsel for the defence was right; whether Traps had committed the most extraordinary crime of the century, or whether he was innocent as a lamb. He, the judge, found himself unable to subscribe completely to either view. As the counsel for the defence maintained, Traps had been tricked and trapped by the prosecutor's examination, and consequently had admitted to a good many things which had not happened precisely in the way described. On the other hand he had committed murder, though not out of diabolic premeditation but rather by sharing in the ethical indifference of the world in which he functioned as sales manager for a synthetic textile named Hephaeston. He had killed because it was utterly natural for him to drive another man to the wall, to proceed ruthlessly, come what might. In the world through which he roared at high speed in his Studebaker there would have been no serious consequences for their dear Alfredo; but now he had had the kindness to come to them here, to their quiet little house among the trees (at this point the judge's exposition became rather nebulous, and he brought out the rest of his argument to the accompaniment of joyful sobs, interrupted now and again by a tremendous sneeze of deep emotion, his little head disappearing behind an enormous handkerchief, while the others roared louder and louder with laughter) – to their quiet, white-painted, cosy little home, to four old men who had illumined his world with the pure radiance of justice, which to be sure often bore strange features, he knew, knew, knew very well that the justice grinning out of four weather-beaten faces, reflected in the monocle of a white-haired prosecutor and the pince-nez of an obese counsel for the defence, sniggering out of the toothless mouth of a drunken judge who could barely control his tongue and gleaming with a red glow upon the bald pate of an executioner emeritus (growing impatient over this lapse into poetry, the others howled: 'The verdict, the verdict!') – this justice was indeed a grotesque, crotchety, pensioned-off justice, but as such it was still and nevertheless and in spite of everything *justice* ('The verdict, the verdict!') in whose name he now sentenced their dearest, their best, their noblest Alfredo to death (the lawyer, the prosecutor, the executioner and Mlle Simone shouted huzzas, and Traps, now sobbing with emotion, cried: 'Thank you, dear Judge, thank you!'), although the sole real judicial basis for this verdict was the condemned man's own admission of guilt. But after all, was not that the most important factor?

'I therefore take pleasure in delivering a verdict that the condemned man approves without qualification. Mercy would be incompatible with the dignity of man, and our honoured friend and guest may now joyfully receive the crowning glory of his murder in circumstances which, I may hope, he will regard with no less satisfaction than the murder itself. The fatality which comes to the average man, to the man in the street, as chance will have it, in the form of a car accident, or as a mere imposition of nature, disease, the obstruction of a blood-vessel by an embolism, a malignant growth, here emerges as the moral and indispensable outcome; in our sentence, life is perfected with logical consistency, like a work of art, and the human tragedy is revealed in all its beauty, shines radiantly, is welded into flawless form.' ('Finish, finish!' the others shouted.) 'Indeed, I need not hesitate to declare that only the act of judgment which transforms the defendant into a condemned man truly confers the accolade of justice. There can be nothing nobler, nothing greater, nothing more sublime, than the condemnation of a man to death. Therefore I now pronounce this sentence. Traps perhaps does not entirely deserve his luck, since strictly speaking a straightforward verdict of premeditated murder is not altogether justified, but I will not in any way commute the sentence, for I would not wish to disappoint our dear friend – in short, Alfredo is now one of us, a peer, worthy to be taken into our company and recognized as a master player of the game . . .'

The others roared him down. 'Bring on the champagne!'

The evening had reached its climax. The champagne bubbled; there was no cloud upon their merriment; even the counsel for the defence was taken fraternally to their hearts. The candles had burned down; some had already glimmered out. The first hint of dawn wavered outside the windows; the stars were fading and the air carried a suggestion of cool dew and distant sunrise. Traps was still soaring with exaltation, but also tired out; he asked to be led to his room, and staggered into the arms of each of his friends in turn. All babbled drunkenly, monologues, meaningless speeches; an enormous roar of voices filled the room, since no one was listening to anyone else. Reeking of wine and odorous of cheese, they patted the sales manager's cheeks, ruffled his hair, and embraced him. Happy, exhausted, he submitted to their caresses like a child among a group of grandfathers and uncles.

At last the taciturn, bald-headed man led Traps upstairs. It was a toilsome ascent on all fours; half way up they could go no further and sprawled on the steps, arms and legs entangled. From a window above, a stony dawn light fell upon the whiteness of the plaster walls; from outside came the first noises of a new day – the distant whistling at tiny railway stations, sounds of shunting, vague reminders of a missed opportunity to return home.

Traps was in the seventh heaven, all his desires satiated as they had never been before in his uneventful life. Dim images floated through his mind: the face of a boy, probably his youngest, who was his favourite child; then, mistily, the village in which he had landed as the result of his breakdown; the bright ribbon of the road swinging over a small rise; the hillock on which the church sat; the great rustling oak with the iron rings and props; the wooded hills; the glowing, infinite sky beyond, above, all round.

But then the bald man collapsed. 'Want to sleep, want to sleep – tired, tired,' he murmured, and forthwith dozed off while Traps crawled on up the stairs. The bald man remained conscious just long enough to hear a chair fall over. For brief seconds the noise woke him out of his dreams and memories of dread duties long gone by. Then a tangle of legs passed over the sleeping man as the others climbed the steps.

Croaking and squeaking, the others had scribbled out a death sentence on parchment, choicely worded, filled with witty turns of phrase, with archaic language and academic tags in Latin. Then they had started up to lay the product of their wit upon the bed of the sleeping sales manager, so that when he awoke he would find a pleasant memento of their tremendous drinking bout. Outside, the brightness was growing, and birds were beginning their harsh, impatient cries. They blundered up the stairs, clambering over the bald-headed man in his sleep of innocence.

Clutching one another, each supporting the next, all three staggering, pushing, pulling and crawling, interfering with one another on the landing, so that retreat and a new start were necessary, they arrived at last at the door to the guest-room. The judge opened it – and then the solemn group, the prosecutor still with the napkin tied round his neck, froze to immobility.

In the window frame hung Traps, motionless, a dark silhouette against the dull silver of the sky, amid the heavy fragrance of roses floating in through the open window – hanged so definitely and so finally that the prosecutor, from whose monocle the gathering morning light was reflected with a brightness that increased every second, had to gasp for air before he cried in perplexed helplessness and sadness over the loss of his friend, cried grief-stricken: 'Alfredo, my good Alfredo! For God's sake what were you thinking of? You've ruined the most wonderful evening we've ever had!'

The Pledge

Last March I had to deliver a lecture before the Literary Society in Chur. Subject: the art of writing detective stories. I arrived by train just as night was falling, a night of low-hanging clouds, dismal snow flurries, and icy roads. The lecture was being held in the hall of the Chamber of Commerce. My audience was rather scanty, for at the same hour Emil Staiger was giving a lecture in the school auditorium on the later works of Goethe. Neither I nor any of my listeners could summon up the proper mood, and several local citizens left the hall before I finished. I chatted with some members of the committee, two or three high school teachers who also would have preferred the lecture on Goethe's later works, and a philanthropic lady who occupied the post of Honorary Director of the League of Domestic Employees of Eastern Switzerland. Then, having received my fee and travelling expenses, I withdrew to the Hotel Steinbock, near the railway station, where the committee had chosen to put me up.

But here too all was exceedingly dreary. Except for a German financial newspaper and an old illustrated magazine there was no reading matter to be found. The silence of the hotel was inhuman, sleep unthinkable: the chances of ever waking again seemed slim. Time seemed to be standing still. Outside it had stopped snowing. All movement had ceased; the street lanterns no longer swayed; the wind was still. Not a native or animal was in sight. Only from the railway station came a single clamorous screech. I went into the bar to have another drink. In addition to the elderly barmaid there was a man who introduced himself to me almost as soon as I sat down. He was Herr M., former chief of the cantonal police of Zürich, a tall, heavy-set man, rather old-fashioned in appearance, with a gold watch-chain running across his waistcoat – a rare sight nowadays. In spite of his age his bristly hair was still black, as was his moustache. He sat on a tall bar stool, drank red wine, smoked a cigar, and addressed the barmaid by her first name. His voice was loud and his gestures were lively; altogether, he was an unaffected sort of person who simultaneously attracted and repelled me.

When it was nearing three, and our first whisky had been followed by four more, he offered to drive me to Zürich next morning in his large Opel. Since I did not know Chur or this section of Switzerland well, I accepted the invitation. Herr M. had come to the Grisons as a member of a federal commission. The bad weather had kept him in Chur, and so he had perforce attended my lecture. He did not comment on it, however, beyond remarking: 'You have a rather awkward delivery.'

We set out early in the morning. At dawn, in order to get a little sleep after all, I had taken two sleeping tablets, and now felt numbed. Although the sun must have risen long since, it was still not yet really light. Somewhere a patch of metallic sky gleamed. But everywhere else clouds intervened – sluggish, ponderous clouds still full of snow. Winter seemed unwilling to abandon this part of the country. The city was encircled by mountains, but there was nothing majestic about them. They rather resembled huge dumps of earth, as though an immense grave had been dug here. Chur itself was plainly stony, grey, sown with huge government buildings. It seemed incredible to me that this was a wine-growing region. We tried to penetrate the medieval core of the city, but the big car went astray; we became entangled in narrow blind alleys and one-way streets, and had to execute difficult manoeuvres in reverse in order to escape from the maze of buildings. Moreover, the roads were so icy that we were glad to leave the city behind us at last, although I had really seen nothing of this ancient residence of the bishops of Chur. It was like a flight. I dozed, feeling leaden and weary, vaguely aware of a snow-covered valley moving past me under low-lying clouds. The landscape was rigid with cold. I do not know how long this continued. Then we were driving towards a sizeable village, perhaps a small town. We approached cautiously, until suddenly everything lay before us bathed in sunlight, in such dazzling and overwhelming light that the expanses of snow began visibly to thaw. A white ground mist rose, spreading out over the snowfields and once more veiling the valley from my sight. It was like a bad dream, like witchcraft, as though a spell were upon this region, so that I could never come to know it.

Once more the weariness overcame me. The gravel with which the road had been strewn rattled unpleasantly; as we drove over a bridge we went into a slight skid. We encountered a military convoy. The windscreen became so filthy that the wiper could no longer clean it. M. sat sullenly at the wheel beside me, absorbed in his own thoughts, concentrating on the difficult driving, I regretted having accepted his invitation, cursed the whisky and the tablets. But gradually the going improved. The valley became visible once more, and there were more signs of humanity. Everywhere I saw farms, here and there small factories. Everything was clean and spare. The snow and ice were gone from the road. It glistened with wetness, but it was safe enough for driving at a decent speed. The mountains had given way, no longer closed in all round us.

We stopped at a petrol station. The house looked odd, perhaps because it contrasted so markedly with its shipshape Swiss environment. It was wretchedly built and dripping wet, with streams of water flowing down it. Half the house was of stone, half of it was a wooden shed whose front was daubed with posters. It had evidently long been used for this purpose, for there were many layers of posters overlapping each other: Burrus Tobacco Suits Modern Pipes; Drink Canada Dry; Sport Mints; Vitamins; Lindt Milk Chocolate, and so on. Along the side wall towered a gigantic poster: Pirelli Tyres. The two petrol pumps stood in front of the stone half of the house, on a rough uneven square of worn flagging. Everything gave a run-down impression, in spite of the sun which was now shining with a wicked, almost spiteful harshness.

'Let us get out,' the police chief said. I obeyed without understanding what his intentions were, but glad to step into the fresh air.

On a stone bench beside the open door of the house sat an old man. He was unwashed and unshaven, wore a colourless smock that was crumpled and stained, and dark, grease-spotted trousers which had once been part of a dinner suit. On his feet were worn slippers. He stared blankly, stupidly into space, and I smelt drink when we were still many steps from him. Absinthe. Around the stone bench the flagging was littered with cigarette ends floating in the water from the melting snow.

'Hello,' the chief said. His tone suddenly sounded embarrassed. 'Fill her up, please. Super. And clean the windscreen too.' Then he turned to me. 'Let's go inside.'

Above the single visible window I now noticed a tavern sign, a disc of sheet metal, painted red. Above the door was the name of the place: Zür Rose. We entered a dirty corridor that stank of beer and schnapps. The chief preceded me, and opened a door; obviously, he knew his way about. The bar-room was a dark wretched hole with a few crude tables and chairs, the walls pasted with pictures of film stars cut from illustrated magazines. The Austrian radio station was announcing the prices of stock and produce in the Tyrol. Behind the counter, barely discernible, stood a lean woman in a housedress, smoking a cigarette and washing glasses. She did not greet us.

'Two coffees,' the chief ordered.

Silently the woman began preparing the coffee. From the adjoining room came a slatternly girl whom I at first took for a woman of thirty.

'She is sixteen,' the chief growled.

The girl served us. She was wearing a black skirt and a white blouse, half unbuttoned, with nothing underneath. Her skin was unwashed. Her hair was as blonde as that of the woman behind the counter must once have been, and needed combing.

'Thank you, Annemarie,' the chief said, laying the money on the table. The girl did not reply, did not even thank him. We drank in silence. The coffee was frightful. The chief lit a cigar. The Austrian radio had passed on to flood conditions, and the girl shuffled off into the dark adjoining room. Through the door something whitish could be glimpsed, evidently an unmade bed.

'Let us go,' the chief said.

After a glance at the pump, which registered the price, he paid the old man who had filled the tank and wiped the windscreen.

'Next time,' the chief said in a low, sad voice, and once again his air of haplessness struck me. The old man did not reply this time either; he was already sitting on his bench, staring into space, stupefied, washed out. But as we reached the Opel and started to get in, the old man clenched his fists, shook them, and murmured, the words coming out in violent spurts, his face transfigured by an insuperable faith: 'I'll wait, I'll wait, he will come, he will come.'

To be honest [Herr M. began later] as we were climbing towards the Kerenz Pass [the road was glazed with ice once more, and below us lay Lake Walen, glittering, cold, antagonistic; the leaden weariness from the sleeping tablets had begun again, the recollection of the smoky taste of the whisky, and the feeling of gliding along in an endless, senseless dream] – to be honest I have never thought very highly of mystery stories, and I regret to hear that you too have to do with them. Sheer waste of time. What you had to say in your lecture yesterday was worth hearing, no doubt; since the politicians fail us in so reprehensible a fashion – and I ought to know, since I'm one myself, Federal Deputy, as you probably know [I did not know; I heard his voice as though from a great distance, behind the stockade of my tiredness, but I listened as closely as an animal in a cage] – well, since the politicians are such failures, people hope that at least the police will know how to keep order in the world. I must admit that I myself can conceive of no rottener hope than that. The trouble is that in all these mystery stories an altogether different kind of fraud is perpetrated. I am not even referring to the fact that the criminal has his punishment meted out to him. Such pretty fairy-tales are morally necessary too, I suppose. They are in the same class with the other lies that help preserve the State, like that pious phrase that crime does not pay, whereas anyone has only to look at human society to find out just how much truth there is in that. But I would let all that ride, if only out of strict commercial principles – for every audience and every taxpayer has a right to his heroes and his happy ending, and we of the police and you of the writing profession are equally obliged to supply these. No, what really annoys me is the plot in your novels. Here the fraud becomes too raw and shameless. You build your plots up logically, like a chess game; here the criminal, here the victim, here the accomplice, here the master mind. The detective need only know the rules and play the game over, and he has the criminal trapped, has won a victory for justice. This fiction infuriates me. Reality can be only partially attacked by logic. Granted, we police officials are forced to proceed logically, scientifically, but the factors that muck up the works for us are so common that all too frequently only pure professional luck and chance decide the issue for us. Or against us. But in your novels chance plays no part, and if something looks like chance it's represented as some kind of destiny or divine dispensation. You writers have always sacrificed truth for the sake of your dramatic rules. It's time you threw those rules out of the window. These things can never be equated because we never know all the necessary unknowns. We know only a few, and usually unimportant ones. Chance, the incalculable, the incommensurable, plays too great a part. Our rules are based only on probabilities, on statistics, not causality; they apply only in general and not in particular. The individual stands outside our calculations. Our criminological tools are inadequate, and the more we try to sharpen them the more inadequate they become. But you fellows in the writing game don't worry about that. You don't try to get mixed up with the kind of reality that is always slipping through our fingers. Instead you set up a world that you can manage. That world may be perfect – who knows? – but it's also a lie. Drop the perfection if you want to get anywhere, if you want to get at things, at reality, which is what a man ought to be doing. Otherwise you'll be left behind, fooling around with useless stylistic exercises. But now I must come to the point.

No doubt you were surprised by a number of things this morning. First of all by what I have been saying, I imagine; a former Chief of the Zürich cantonal police should not be holding such views, but I am old and no longer like fooling myself. I know how dubious all our positions are, how little we are capable of doing, how easily we can make mistakes; but I know also that we must nevertheless act, even at the risk of acting wrongly.

Then you must also have wondered why I stopped at that miserable petrol station. I may as well tell you right away: the sad, soused wreck who pumped petrol for us there was once my most capable man. God knows, I knew something about my profession, but Matthäi was a genius, more so than any of your fictional detectives.

The story started just about nine years ago [M. continued after he had passed a Shell Oil lorry]. Matthäi was one of my inspectors, or rather one of my captains, for in the cantonal police force we use military ranks. He was a jurist like myself, a Basler who had taken his doctorate in Basle, and by choice a solitary man. Some of the characters with whom he had 'professional' dealings called him 'Matt the Automat', and after a while we picked up the expression. It became his standard name around headquarters. He was always carefully dressed, formal, impersonal, aloof; he neither smoked nor drank, and had a harsh merciless command of his profession which made him as unpopular as he was successful. I could never quite make him out. I imagine, though, that I was the only one who liked him – because I am fond of single-minded people, even though his lack of humour often got on my nerves. His mind was superb, but because of the all too solid structure of our country he had become emotionless. He was a man for organization who manipulated the police apparatus like a slide rule. Unmarried, he never spoke of his private life, and probably hadn't got any. He thought about nothing but his work, and although he was a first-rate detective he worked without passion. Stubborn and tireless though he was, as he went about his business he seemed bored by it – until the day came when he was involved in a case that suddenly stirred him to passion.

As it happened he had reached the peak of his career just at this time. There had been some difficulties with him in the department. The time for my retirement was approaching, and the cantonal Government had to start thinking about a successor for me. Actually, the only possible person in line for the job was Matthäi. But there were obstacles to the appointment which could not be overlooked. It was not only that he belonged to no political party but that the personnel would probably have raised objections. On the other hand, no one at the top liked the idea of passing over the most capable man. Consequently it was like the answer to a prayer when the Kingdom of Jordan asked our Federal Government to send an expert to Amman to reorganize the Jordanian police. Zürich proposed Matthäi, and both Berne and Amman accepted. Everyone breathed more easily. Matthäi, too, was pleased and not only for professional reasons. He was fifty at that time; he thought a little desert sunlight would do him good; he was looking forward to his departure, to flying over the Alps and the Mediterranean; and probably he was also thinking of making his farewell a final one, for he hinted that afterwards he would move to Denmark to live with a widowed sister there. He was just cleaning up his desk in the cantonal police headquarters on Kasernenstrasse when the call came in.

The report was jumbled and Matthäi had some difficulty making sense out of it [M. continued]. It was one of his old 'clients' who had put in the call from Mägendorf, a tiny place near Zürich. The man was a pedlar named Gunten; and Matthäi felt no particular desire to spend his last afternoon at headquarters with this case. After all, his plane ticket was already bought and he was due to fly to Jordan in three days. But I was away at a conference of police chiefs and was not expected back from Berne until evening. Proper action was called for; inexperience could spoil everything. Matthäi telephoned the police station in Mägendorf. It was towards the latter part of April; outside the rain was pouring down in sheets, for the storm that follows the Föhn had reached the city; but the malignant heat remained, and people could scarcely breathe.

Policeman Riesen answered the telephone.

'Is it raining in Mägendorf too?' Matthäi asked crossly, although he could guess the answer. He frowned more darkly when he heard it. Then he gave orders to keep watch unobtrusively on the pedlar at The Stag in Mägendorf.

He rang off.

'Anything up?' Feller asked curiously. He was helping his superior clean out his office. Over the years Matthäi had amassed a whole library which now had to be packed up.

'It's raining in Mägendorf too,' the inspector answered. 'Wake up the emergency squad.'

'Murder?'

'Damn the rain,' Matthäi murmured, instead of replying; he ignored Feller's hurt feelings.

Before he went out to join the examining magistrate and Lieutenant Henzi, who were waiting impatiently in the car, he leafed through Gunten's file. The man had served a term for a serious offence against a fourteen-year-old girl.

The order to have the pedlar watched proved to be a blunder which could not have been foreseen. Mägendorf was a small community. Most of the people were farmers, although a few worked in factories down in the valley, or in the near-by brick field. There were a few 'city folks' who lived out there – two or three architects and a sculptor, among others – but they played no part in village life. Everyone knew everyone else, and most of the inhabitants were interrelated. The village was at odds with the city, secretly if not officially; for the woods surrounding Mägendorf belonged to the city, a fact which no real Mägendorfer would ever recognize. Their intransigence had caused the Forestry Board some difficulty in the past. It had been the Board which years ago demanded the establishment of a police station in Mägendorf. On Sundays, moreover, the city people overran the village, and at night were apt to converge on The Stag.

Considering all these tensions, the policeman stationed in the village had to know his business. On the other hand it was necessary for him to meet the villagers half-way. Wegmüller, who was assigned to patrol the village, had soon caught on. He came from a peasant family himself, drank heavily, but competently kept his Mägendorfers within bounds – although he made so many concessions that I really should have interfered. But I used to regard him as the lesser evil – especially in view of our personnel shortage. I was not bothered, and I did not bother Wegmüller. But when he was on leave his substitutes had a hard time of it. The Mägendorfers would ride these poor fellows unmercifully. Although the poaching and wood-stealing in the city forests and the brawls in the village had become ancient history, what with the boom and prosperity, the traditional defiance of urban authority smouldered still among the villagers. Riesen, in particular, ran into trouble this time. He was a clumsy fellow, humourless and easily offended, unable to put up with the constant banter of the peasants. As a matter of fact he was too sensitive even for more normal areas. He was so scared of the villagers that he lay low as soon as he had completed his regular rounds. Given these circumstances it was impossible for the police officer to watch the pedlar unobtrusively, since his appearance in The Stag, which he normally avoided like the plague, was in itself virtually equivalent to a public demonstration. Moreover, Riesen so ostentatiously took a seat facing the pedlar that the peasants fell silent, wild with curiosity.

'Coffee?' the innkeeper asked.

'Nothing,' Riesen replied. 'I am here on duty.'

The peasants stared avidly at the pedlar.

'What's he done/' an old man asked.

'That's none of your affair.'

The public room was low and smoke-filled, a wooden cave, oppressively warm and dark. But the innkeeper did not turn on the light. The peasants sat at a long table over beer or white wine, barely visible shapes against the silvery window-panes down which the rain trickled and streamed. From some part of the room came the tinkling and rolling sounds of an American pinball machine.

Cold sweat ran down Gunten's face. He sat hunched in the corner, his right arm propped on the handle of his basket, waiting. It seemed to him that he had been sitting here for hours. The atmosphere was muted, heavy, threatening. The window-panes grew brighter; the rain abated, and suddenly the sun was out again. Only the wind continued to howl and shake the walls. Gunten breathed more easily when at last the car drove up outside.

'Come,' Riesen said, getting up. The two men stepped outside. In front of the tavern stood a dark saloon, behind it the big brake of the emergency squad. The ambulance was still on its way. The village square lay bathed in glaring sunlight. At the fountain stood two children of five or six, a girl and a boy, the girl with a doll in her arms. The boy was holding a small whip.

'Get in beside the driver, Gunten,' Matthäi called from the window of the saloon. And then, when the pedlar had taken his seat with a sigh of relief, as though he were now in safety, and Riesen had got into the brake, Matthäi said; 'All right, now show us what you found in the woods.'

They tramped through wet grass, for the path to the woods had become a single muddy puddle, and shortly afterwards stood round the small body they found lying in dead leaves among the bushes, fairly close to the edge of the woods. The men stood in silence. From the lashing trees great raindrops continued in fall, glittering like diamonds. The magistrate dropped his cigar and stepped on it in embarrassment. Henzi did not dare to look. Matthäi said: 'A police officer never looks away, Henzi.'

The photographers set up their cameras.

'It will be difficult to find tracks after this rain,' Matthäi said.

Suddenly the boy and girl were standing there among the men, staring, the girl still with the doll in her arms and the boy still carrying his whip.

'Take the children away.'

A policeman took them by the hand and led them back to the road. There the children remained.

The first people from the village approached. The owner of The Stag could be recognized from far away by his white apron.

'Cordon!' the inspector ordered. Several of the men posted themselves as guards. Others searched the immediate vicinity. Then the first flashes of lightning darted across the sky.

'Do you know the girl, Riesen?'

'No, sir.'

'Have you seen her around the village?'

'I think so, sir.'

'Have you men finished with the pictures?'

'We're taking one more from above.'

Matthäi waited.

'Tracks?'

'None. It's all mud.'

'Buttons examined? Fingerprints?'

'Hopeless after this cloud-burst.'

Matthäi stooped forward carefully. 'With a razor,' he stated.

He picked up the bready bits lying around and replaced them in the child's small basket.

'Pretzels.'

An officer approached and said that someone from the village wanted to speak to them. Matthäi straightened up. The magistrate looked over towards the edge of the woods. There stood a white-haired man with an umbrella hooked over his left forearm. Henzi was leaning against a beech tree. He had no colour in his face. The pedlar was sitting hunched on his basket, reiterating in a low voice the statement: 'I just happened to come by, I just happened to be by.'

'Bring the man here.'

The white-haired man came towards them through the shrubbery, and froze.

'My God,' he murmured, 'my God!'

'May I ask your name?' Matthäi said.

'I am the schoolmaster, Luginbühl,' the man replied softly, looking away.

'Do you know this girl?'

'The Mosers' Gritli.'

'Where do the parents live?'

'In Moosbach.'

'Far from the village?'

'A fifteen-minute walk.'

Matthäi looked at the murdered child. He was the only one who dared to. No one said a word.

'How did it happen?' the schoolmaster asked.

'A sex crime,' Matthäi replied. 'Did the child go to your school?'

'She was in Fräulein Krumm's class. Class Three.'

'Have the Mosers other children?'

'Gritli was the only one.'

'Someone must tell the parents.'

There was a silence.

'What about you?' Matthäi asked the schoolmaster.

There was a long pause before Luginbühl replied. At last he said falteringly: 'Don't think me cowardly but I would rather not do it. I cannot,' he added softly.

'I understand,' Matthäi said. 'What about the pastor?'

'He is in the city.'

'All right,' Matthäi said quietly. 'You may go, Herr Luginbühl.'

The schoolmaster returned to the road, where more and more of the people of Mägendorf had by now assembled.

Matthäi looked over at Henzi, who was still leaning against the beech tree. 'Please, no, Inspector,' Henzi said softly. The magistrate also shook his head. Matthäi glanced at the body once more, and then at the torn little red skirt lying in the bushes soaked through by blood and rain.

'Then I will go,' he said, picking up the basket of pretzels.

Moosbach was a small marshy dip near Mägendorf. Matthäi had left the police car in the village and gone on foot. He wanted to gain time. He heard footsteps behind him, stopped, and turned round. The little boy and the girl were there again, faces flushed. They must have taken short cuts, otherwise their presence was inexplicable.

Matthäi continued on his way. The house was low, half timbered, with white walls and dark beams, and a slate roof. Behind it grew fruit trees; the soil in the garden was black, in front a man was splitting wood. He looked up as Matthäi approached.

'What can I do for you?' the man asked.

'Inspector Matthäi of the cantonal police,' Matthäi introduced himself and showed his badge. 'Herr Moser?'

'Yes, what do you want?' the man asked again. He approached and stood in front of Matthäi, axe in hand. He looked about forty, a lean man with furrowed brow. His grey eyes studied the inspector. A woman appeared in the doorway; she too wore a red skirt. Matthäi considered what he ought to say. He had been considering this coming along, but still did not know. Moser came to his aid. He had caught sight of the basket in Matthäi's hand.

'Has something happened to Gritli?' he asked, his eyes probing Matthäi's face.

'Did you send Gritli somewhere?' the inspector asked.

'To her grandmother's in Fehren,' the farmer answered. Fehren was the neighbouring village.

'Did Gritli go that way often?' he asked.

'Every Wednesday and Saturday afternoon,' the farmer replied. And then in a sudden access of fear he demanded: 'Why do you want to know? Why are you bringing the basket back?'

Matthäi placed the basket on the stump on which Moser had been splitting wood.

'Gritli has been found dead in the woods near Mägendorf,' he said.

Moser did not move. The woman, too, stood without stirring in the doorway in her red skirt. Matthäi saw the sweat begin to flow down the man's white face, streams of sweat. He wanted to look away, but he was spellbound by the face, by the sweat, and so they stood staring at one another.

'Gritli has been murdered,' Matthäi heard himself saying in a voice that seemed wholly devoid of sympathy. Suddenly he felt a hatred for himself.

'It isn't possible,' Moser whispered. 'There cannot be such devils.' His fist, clenched round the axe handle, quivered.

'There are such devils, Herr Moser,' Matthäi said.

The man stared at him.

'I want to see my child,' he said almost inaudibly.

The inspector shook his head. 'I would not do that, Herr Moser. I know that what I am saying is cruel, but it would be better for you not to go to your Gritli now.'

Moser came up close to Matthäi, so that the two men stood eye to eye.

'Why is it better?' he roared.

'We ourselves scarcely dared to look,' the inspector told him.

For a moment Moser weighed the axe in his hand, as though he wanted to strike out with it; but then he turned and went up to his wife, who still stood in the doorway, still motionless, still mute. Matthäi waited. Nothing escaped his notice, and he suddenly realized that he would never be able to forget this scene. Moser clasped his wife in his arms. He was suddenly shaken by a silent sob. He buried his face against her shoulder, while she stood staring into space.

'Tomorrow evening you may see your Gritli,' the inspector forlornly promised. 'Then there will be nothing horrible – she will look as if she has fallen asleep, believe me.'

Suddenly the woman spoke.

'Who is the murderer?' she asked in a voice so calm and matter of fact that Matthäi was chilled.

'I intend to find that out, Frau Moser.'

The woman looked at him, threateningly, imperiously. 'Do you promise that you will?'

'I promise, Frau Moser,' the inspector said, impelled solely by the desire to leave this place immediately.

'By your soul's salvation?'

The inspector was taken aback. 'By my soul's salvation,' he said at last. What else could he do?

'Then go now,' the woman commanded him. 'You have sworn by your salvation.'

Matthäi wanted to say some consoling last word, but he could think of no consolation.

'I am sorry,' he said softly, and turned away. He walked slowly back the way he had come. Before him lay Mägendorf with the woods beyond. Above, the sky – now cloudless. He caught sight of the two children again, cowering by the side of the road. He passed them spiritlessly, and they trotted along behind. Then, suddenly, he heard from the house behind him a cry like the bellowing of an animal. He quickened his pace, and did not know whether it was the man or the woman who wept so.

Back in Mägendorf, Matthäi found himself confronting his first difficulty. The big emergency squad brake had driven into the village and was waiting there for him. The scene of the crime and the immediate vicinity had been carefully searched and then cordoned off. Three plain-clothes policemen were hiding in the wood. Their job was to observe passers-by. The rest of the squad had to return to the city. The sky had been swept clean by now, but great soft gusts of wind buffeted the village. The Föhn still hung heavily over the villages and woods. The rain had brought no ease; the unnatural clammy heat was making everyone spiteful, irritable, impatient. Street lamps were already alight, although it was still day. The peasants had been gathering in a mob. They had learned that Gunten was somehow implicated and thought him the murderer; pedlars are always suspect. They assumed that he had already been arrested, and were surrounding the emergency squad brake. The pedlar stayed inside, huddling, trembling, between two policemen who sat rigid. The

Mägendorfers moved closer and closer to the brake, pressed their faces against the window-panes. The policemen did not know what to do. In the saloon behind the brake the examining magistrate waited, blockaded by the crowd. Also encircled was the car belonging to the coroner, who had come from Zürich, and the white ambulance in which the small body lay. The men stood in their threatening silence; the women stood pressed against the walls of the houses. They too were silent. The children had clambered on to the rim of the village fountain. A vague, planless fury had brought the peasants together. They wanted vengeance, justice.

Matthäi tried to elbow his way through to the emergency squad, but this proved impossible. He decided to seek out the first local councillor, and asked for him. No one answered; he heard nothing but a few murmured threats. Matthäi considered, and then went into the tavern. He had guessed right; the councillor was sitting in The Stag. He was a small, heavy-bodied man with an unhealthy look. He was drinking one glass of Italian wine after another, and peering through the low windows.

'What can I do, Inspector?' he asked. 'The people are headstrong. They have the feeling that the police are no longer any use, and they must see to justice themselves.' Then he sighed. 'Gritli was a good child. We were fond of her.'

There were tears in the councillor's eyes.

'The pedlar is innocent,' Matthäi said.

'Then you wouldn't have arrested him.'

'We haven't arrested him. We need him as a witness.'

The councillor stared hostilely at Matthäi. 'You're only trying to talk yourself out of this,' he said. 'We know what we know.'

'As local councillor your first duty is to see to it that we are allowed to depart freely.'

The councillor emptied his glass of red wine. He said nothing.

'Well?' Matthäi asked angrily.

The councillor remained stubborn. 'The pedlar is going to swing for it,' he growled.

'Before that happens there will be a fight!'

'You would fight for a sex-murderer?'

'Whether or not he is guilty, the law must be respected.'

The councillor began pacing wrathfully back and forth in the dim tavern room. Since no one was serving he went up to the counter and poured wine for himself. He drank it so fast that great dark streams of it ran down his shirt. The crowd outside was still quiet. But as soon as the driver attempted to start the patrol car the ranks closed more tightly in front of it.

Now the magistrate entered the tavern. He had forced his way with difficulty through the mob. His clothes were in disorder. The councillor started in alarm. The presence of an examining magistrate made him uneasy; like any ordinary citizen he felt that there was something chilling and disturbing about the profession.

'Councillor,' the magistrate said, 'the people of Mägendorf seem interested in a lynching. I see no choice but to send for reinforcements. I imagine that will restore order.'

'Let us try to talk to the people once more,' Matthäi said.

The magistrate tapped the local councillor with the index finger of his right hand. 'You had better bring the people to their senses,' he growled, 'or else!'

Outside the church bells began to peal wildly. The Mägendorfers were receiving new supporters from all directions. Even the firemen arrived and took up positions against the police. A few shrill, isolated shouts of abuse were heard.

The police prepared. They were expecting an attack from the mob, which was growing more and more restive. But they were as helplessly in the grip of the thing as the Mägendorfers. Their regular duties involved routine maintenance of order, and dealing with individual malefactors. Here they were confronting something unknown.

A hush fell over the crowd, and it grew stationary. The magistrate had stepped out of The Stag, along with the councillor and Matthäi. There was a wide step with an iron bannister which flanked the front door of the tavern. Here the three took up their stand.

'People of Mägendorf,' the councillor announced, 'I request you to listen to His Worship, Herr Burkhard.'

There was no visible reaction in the mob. The peasants and labourers stood in threatening silence, without stirring, under a sky brightening with the first glow of evening. Street lamps hung like pale moons over the dark assembly. These people were clearly determined to lay their hands upon the man they thought to be the murderer. The police cars huddled like huge dark beasts in the midst of the human surf. Again and again they tried to break free; their engines whined to a roar and then subsided dispiritedly and were turned off.

It was hopeless. Everything and everyone – the dark gables of the village, the square, the crowd in the street – seemed weighed down by perplexity over the events of the day, as though the murder had poisoned the whole world.

'Fellow citizens,' the magistrate began in a low uncertain voice – but in silence so deep that every word was audible – 'people of Mägendorf, we are shocked by this terrible crime. Gritli Moser has been murdered. We do not know who has committed the crime – '

The magistrate got no further than this.

'Hand him over!'

Fists were raised; boos and hoots made going on impossible. Matthäi contemplated the mob as if spellbound.

'Quick, Matthäi,' the magistrate snapped. 'Telephone for reinforcements.'

'Gunten did it!' a tall raw-boned farmer with tanned, unshaven face shouted. 'I saw him; there was no one else in the dale.'

This was the farmer who had been working in the field near by.

Matthäi considered for a moment, and then stepped forward.

'People,' he called out, 'I am Inspector Matthäi. We are prepared to surrender the pedlar to you.'

The surprise was so great that utter silence followed.

'Have you gone out of your mind!' the magistrate expostulated into the inspector's ear.

'From time immemorial criminals in our country have been convicted by Courts if they were guilty and set free if they were not guilty,' Matthäi went on. 'You have now decided to make yourselves the Court. Whether you have the right to do so is something we will not examine here; you have taken the right for yourselves.'

Matthäi spoke slowly and distinctly. The farmers listened intently, weighing every word. Since Matthäi was taking them seriously they were willing to take him seriously.

'But there is something I must ask of you as I would of any other Court,' Matthäi continued. 'That is justice. For it is clear that we can only surrender the pedlar to you if we are convinced that you want justice.'

'That's what we want!' someone cried.

'Your Court has to meet one condition if it is to be a just Court. That condition is: injustice must be avoided. You must agree to meet this condition.'

'Agreed!' called a foreman from the brick field.

'Therefore you must look into the question of whether the charge of murder against Gunten is a just or unjust charge. How did the suspicion arise?'

'The fellow is a jailbird!' a farmer bawled.

'That adds to the suspicion that Gunten could be the murderer,' Matthäi explained, 'but it is no proof that he really is.'

'I saw him in the dale,' the farmer with the tanned unshaven face called out again.

'Come up here,' the inspector urged.

The farmer hung back.

'Go ahead, Heiri,' someoned called. 'Don't be a coward.'

The farmer came forward uncertainly. The councillor and the magistrate stepped back into the hallway of the tavern so that Matthäi was left alone on the step with the farmer.

'What do you want of me?' the farmer asked. 'My name is Heiri Benz.'

The crowd stared in fascination at the two. The policemen had hung their truncheons at their sides once more. They too were watching the proceedings breathlessly. The boys of the village had clambered on to the half-raised ladder of the fire-engine.

'You say you saw Gunten the pedlar in the dale, Herr Benz,' the inspector said. 'Was he alone there?'

'Alone.'

'What work were you doing, Herr Benz?'

'I was planting potatoes with my wife and kids.'

'Since when had you been at it?'

'Since ten o'clock. I had dinner with my wife and kids there in my field.'

'And you saw nobody but the pedlar?'

'Nobody, I can swear to that,' the farmer declared fervently.

'Why, that's silly, Benz!' a workman called out. 'I passed by your potato field at two.'

Two other workmen spoke up. They too had cycled past the dale at two o'clock.

'And I drove my cart through the dale, you numbskull,' a farmer shouted out. 'But you always work like a horse, you miser, and keep your wife and kids' noses to the grindstone so that they all have crooked backs. A hundred naked women could pass you and you wouldn't even look up.'

Laughter.

'We have established, then, that the pedlar was not alone in the dale,' Matthäi continued. 'But let us continue our investigation. A road to the city runs parallel to the woods. Did anyone pass along this road?'

'Fritz Gerber,' someone called.

'I went that way.' The speaker was a heavy-bodied peasant who sat on the pump of the fire-engine. 'With my cart.'

'When?'

'About two.'

'From this road a path leads through the woods to the scene of the crime,' the inspector declared. 'Did you notice anyone, Herr Gerber?'

'No,' the farmer growled.

'Or did you by any chance see a parked car?'

The farmer looked startled. 'I think so,' he said uncertainly.

'Do you know for sure?'

'There was something there.'

'Possibly a red Mercedes convertible?'

'Could have been.'

'Or a grey Volkswagen?'

'That's possible too.'

'Your answers are pretty vague,' Matthäi said.

'Well, I was half asleep on the cart,' the farmer admitted. 'In this heat it's what everyone does.'

'Then I will take this occasion to remind you that no one is supposed to sleep while driving on a public road,' Matthäi reproved him.

'The horses keep their eyes open,' the farmer retorted.

Everyone laughed.

'You now have some idea of the difficulties you face if you wish to be judges,' Matthäi declared. 'The crime was by no means committed in solitude. It was done only seventy yards from a family working in the potato field. If those people had been alert the thing would never have happened. But they paid no attention because they had not the slightest reason to imagine the possibility of such a crime. They did not see the girl coming, nor the others who took the same road. They happened to notice the pedlar; that is all. Herr Gerber, too, was dozing on his cart and now cannot give any information with the exactness that a court of law requires. That is how the matter stands.

Do you think the pedlar has been proved guilty? You must ask yourself this question. After all, it's a point in his favour that he is the one who called the police. I do not know how you intend to proceed as judges but I will tell you how we, the police, would like to proceed.'

The inspector paused. Once more he was standing alone before the Mägendorfers. Benz had shamefacedly slunk back into the crowd.

'We would proceed as follows. Every suspect, no matter what his position, would be investigated with the greatest care. All imaginable clues would be followed up. Not only this, but the police of other countries would be enlisted if this should prove necessary. As you see, your Court has few means for seeking the truth. We, on the other hand, have a vast apparatus at our disposal. Now decide what you want done.'

Silence. The Mägendorfers had grown thoughtful.

'Will you really surrender the pedlar?'

'I've said I would,' Matthäi replied. 'If you insist on our handing him over.'

The crowd was undecided. The inspector's words had made an impression. The magistrate was nervous. The matter seemed touch and go to him. But then he sighed with relief.

'Take him with you!' a farmer had bellowed.

Silently the Mägendorfers formed a lane.

The magistrate lit a cigar. 'You certainly took a risk, Matthäi,' he remarked. 'Suppose you'd been obliged to keep your word?'

'I had it all worked out,' the inspector replied calmly.

'I hope you never give a promise you have to keep,' the magistrate said. He put a second match to his cigar, bade goodbye to the councillor, and strode towards his now unlocked car.

Matthäi did not ride back with the magistrate. He climbed into the brake with the pedlar. The other policemen made room for him. It was hot in the interior of the big brake. As yet they did not dare to open the windows. Although the farmers had cleared the way for them they were still standing around. Gunten cowered behind the driver. Matthäi sat down beside him.

'I'm innocent,' Gunten protested in a low voice.

'Of course,' Matthäi said.

'Nobody believes me,' Gunten whispered. 'The police don't either.'

The inspector shook his head. 'That's only your imagination.'

The pedlar remained apprehensive. 'You don't believe me either, Inspector.'

The brake started. The policemen sat in silence. Night had fallen. The street lamps cast golden lights upon stony faces. Matthäi sensed the distrust with which all the men regarded the pedlar, the rising suspicion. He was sorry for the man.

'I do believe you, Gunten,' he said, and could feel that he too was not fully convinced. 'I know you had nothing to do with it.'

The first houses of the city were drawing near.

'We have to take you to see the Chief, Gunten,' Matthäi said. 'You are our most important witness.'

'I understand,' the pedlar murmured, and then he whispered again: 'You don't believe me either.'

'Nonsense!'

The pedlar insisted. 'I know,' he said in his almost failing voice, and he stared into the red and green neon lights of street signs which flashed past the moving brake like bizarre constellations.

These were the events that were reported to me at headquarters when I came in from Berne on the seven-thirty express. The case was the third one of this type. Two years before there had been the razor killing of a girl in Schwyz canton, and five years ago of a girl in the canton of St Gall. In both cases not a trace of the criminal had been found.

I sent for the pedlar. The man was forty-eight, small, greasy, unsavoury; in normal circumstances he must have been pert and talkative, but now he was terrified. His testimony was quite clear at first. He had been lying on the edge of the woods, with his shoes off and his pedlar's basket beside him in the grass. His plan had been to visit Mägendorf and go round making door-to-door sales of his brushes, braces, razor blades, shoelaces, and so on. But on the way he had learned from the postman that Wegmüller was on leave and that Riesen was taking his place. That put a different complexion on things and he had sat himself down in the grass to consider. He knew that our young policemen are sometimes attacked by fits of efficiency and insist on the letter of the law. 'I know those boys,' he said. After a while he had dozed off. He described the little dale in the shadow of the woods, cut through by a highway. Not too far from him a family of farmers were working in the field, while a dog kept loping around them. His lunch at The Bear in Fehren had been distinctly on the large side – a 'Berne platter' of sausage, ham, sauerkraut and potatoes, washed down with red wine. He liked a good meal, and could afford it. For although he strayed about the countryside unshaven, unkempt and in rags, his appearance was deceptive; he was a pedlar who earned his living, he said, and had managed to put a few francs aside. He had drunk a good deal of beer after the meal, and eaten two bars of chocolate while lying in the grass. The approaching storm and the gusts of wind had finally lulled him completely to sleep. But a little later it seemed to him that he had been awakened by a cry, the high-pitched cry of a little girl, and he had the impression as he stared up the dale, still sodden with sleep, that the farmers in the field had looked up and listened in surprise for a moment. But then they had returned to their stooping posture, with the dog still circling around them. It must have been a bird, he had thought, possibly an owl – how should he know? This half-explanation had reassured him. He had gone on dozing, but then the sudden utter silence of the woods had roused him, and he had become aware of the threatening sky. He had put on his shoes, taken up his basket, feeling uneasy, for the mysterious cry returned to his mind. Better not risk a brush with Riesen, he decided. He would let Mägendorf be. It had always been an unprofitable little hole, anyhow. He started back towards the city, and chose the forest path as a short cut to the railway station. That was how he came across the body of the murdered girl. Then he ran to the Stag in Mägendorf and telephoned Matthäi; he had said nothing to the farmers, for fear of being suspected.

That was his statement. I had the man taken away, but not released. Perhaps this was not strictly legal. The magistrate had not given orders for him to be held, but we had no time for splitting hairs. His story had the ring of truth to me, but it would have to be checked – and after all, Gunten had a jail record. I was in a bad humour. I had the feeling that this case was fated. Somehow, everything had gone wrong; I didn't know exactly how or why, but I felt it. I withdrew into the 'boutique' as I called it – that was a small smoke-stained room adjoining my office. I sent for a bottle of Châteauneuf-du-Pape from a restaurant near the Sihl Bridge, and drank a few glasses. The room was in a frightful state of disorder, I must admit – books and files everywhere. On principle, however – for in my opinion everyone is duty bound to create little islands of disorder, as it were, in this orderly country, even if he does so only in secret.

I sent for the photographs. They were horrible. Then I studied the map. The scene of the crime could not have been chosen more diabolically. Theoretically it was impossible to say whether the murderer had come from Mägendorf, from the surrounding villages, or from the city; whether he had travelled by foot or by rail. Anything was a possibility.

Matthäi came in.

'I'm sorry you've had such a beastly mess to deal with on your last day,' I said to him.

'That's our job, Chief.'

'When I look at these photographs of the murder I'd like to throw up the damned job,' I replied, and put the pictures back in their envelope.

I was irritable and I suppose not wholly in control of my feelings. Matthäi was my best detective, and at this particular moment his departure could not have been more inconvenient. He seemed to guess my thoughts.

'I think you had best turn the case over to Henzi,' he offered.

I hesitated. That would have been my procedure if this were anything other than a murder case. With other crimes our task is simpler. We have only to consider the motives – money or jealousy, say – and we can light on the suspects. But this method is no use in a sex-murder. A man on a business trip catches sight of a girl or boy; he gets out of his car – no witnesses, no one notices a thing – and in the evening he is back home in Lausanne or Basle or where you will, and there we are without a single clue. I did not underestimate Henzi; he was a capable man, I thought, but he lacked experience.

Matthäi did not look at it in that way.

'He has been working under me for three years now,' he said. 'He's learned the ropes. I cannot imagine a better successor. He'll handle it just as I would. And besides, I shall still be around tomorrow,' he added.

I sent for Henzi and instructed him to take over, with Sergeant Treuler as his assistant. He was overjoyed, for this was his first independent case.

'Thank Matthäi,' I growled, and asked him about the mood among the men. We were up in the air, had nothing to go on and nothing to work with. It wouldn't do for the men to know that we were floundering.

'They are convinced we already have the murderer,' Henzi said.

'The pedlar?'

'The people at Mägendorf actually wanted to lynch him. After all, he has been convicted before of sexual assault.'

'With a fourteen-year-old girl,' Matthäi interjected. 'That's another story entirely.'

'We ought to cross-examine him,' Henzi proposed.

'That can wait,' I decided. 'I don't think the man had anything to do with the murder. He has something nasty about him, it's true. One feels an instinctive distrust for such a person. But that is a subjective reaction, gentlemen, not criminological evidence. We aren't here to work on intuition.'

With that I dismissed the two of them. My humour had not improved.

We assigned all our available men to the case. That very night, and the following day, we called garages to ask whether traces of blood had been observed in any cars; later we also called the laundries. Then we checked on the alibis of all the men who had ever tangled with certain paragraphs of the criminal code. At Mägendorf our men went through the woods with bloodhounds, and even with a mine detector. They ransacked the undergrowth for clues, chiefly in hope of finding the murder weapon. They systematically examined every square yard, went down into the gorge, searched the brook. The woods were combed as far as Mägendorf, and everything found was carefully picked up and saved.

I, too, went down to Mägendorf, although as a regular thing I did not personally take part in investigations. Matthäi, too, seemed uneasy. It was a perfect spring day, the air light, without a trace of Föhn, but our mood remained glum. Henzi established headquarters at The Stag and questioned the peasants and factory workers. Matthäi and I set out to visit the school. We took a short cut through an orchard. Some of the trees were already in full bloom. From the schoolhouse we could hear the voices of children raised in a hymn, 'Then take my hand and lead me'. The yard in front of the school-house was empty. I knocked at the door of the classroom and we entered.

The boys and girls who were singing were children from six to eight – the three lowest classes. The teacher who was conducting dropped her hands and looked apprehensively at us. The song stopped.

'Fräulein Krumm?'

'Yes.'

'You are Gritli Moser's teacher?'

'What is it you want?'

Fräulein Krumm was a thin woman of about forty, with large, elongated, unhappy eyes.

I went up to the front of the room and turned to the children.

'Good moning, children!'

The children stared curiously at me. 'Good morning, sir,' they replied.

'That was a pretty song you were singing.'

'We are practising the hymn for Gritli's funeral,' the teacher explained.

A Robinson Crusoe's island had been built in the sand-box. Children's drawings were tacked on the walls.

'What kind of a child was Gritli?' I asked hesitantly.

'We were all very fond of her,' the teacher said.

'What about her intelligence?'

'She was an extremely imaginative child.'

I hesitated again. 'I would like to ask the children some questions.'

'If you like.'

I stepped closer to the class. Most of the girls were small enough to have their hair in pigtails and wear bright-coloured aprons.

'You have no doubt heard what happened to Gritli Moser,' I said. 'I am from the police – the Commissioner. That is something like a captain among soldiers, and it is my job to find the man who killed Gritli. I want to talk to you now not as if you were children but as if you were grown up. The man we are looking for is ill. All the men who do such things are ill. And because they are ill they try to lure children to a hiding-place to hurt them – to a forest or a cellar or any such hiding-place. These things happen very often; we have had many cases every year in the canton. Sometimes it happens that such men hurt a child so badly that it dies. That is why we must lock up these men. They are too dangerous to be allowed to live in freedom. Now you will ask why we don't lock them up beforehand, before something bad happens, as happened with Gritli. The reason is that there is no way to recognize these ill people. They are ill inside, not outside.'

The children listened with bated breath.

'That is why you must help me now, so that we can find the man who killed Gritli Moser.'

I had walked forward as I spoke, and was now standing among the children.

'Did Gritli ever tell any of you that a strange man spoke to her?'

The children were silent.

'Was there anything about Gritli that struck you as odd, lately?'

The children knew nothing.

'Did Gritli have anything new lately, anything she did not own in the past?'

The children did not reply.

'Who was Gritli's best friend?'

'I was,' a girl whispered.

She was a tiny thing with brown hair and brown eyes.

'What is your name?' I asked.

'Ursula Fehlmann.'

'So you were Gritli's friend, Ursula?'

'We sat together.'

The girl spoke so low that I had to stoop to hear her.

'And you noticed nothing out of the ordinary?'

'No.'

'Gritli did not meet anyone?'

'Yes, she did,' the girl replied.

'Who?'

'Not a person,' the girl said.

I was taken aback by this reply.

'What do you mean by that, Ursula?'

'She met a giant,' the girl whispered.

'A giant?'

'Yes.'

'You mean that she met a big tall man?'

'No, my father is a big man but not a giant.'

'How big was he?' I asked.

'Like a mountain,' the girl replied. 'And all black.'

'And did this giant give Gritli anything?' I asked.

'Yes,' the girl said.

'What did he give her?'

'Little hedgehogs.'

'Hedgehogs? Now what do you mean by that, Ursula?' I asked again, utterly perplexed.

'The whole giant was full of little hedgehogs,' the girl asserted.

'Now that is silly, Ursula,' I objected. 'A giant doesn't have hedgehogs.'

'He was a hedgehog giant.'

The girl insisted on this. I walked back to the teacher's desk.

'You are right,' I said. 'Gritli seems really to have had a great deal of imagination, Fräulein Krumm.'

'She was a poetic child,' the teacher replied, avoiding my eyes. She looked through her rimless glasses somewhere into the distance. 'We really ought to go on practising the hymn now. For the funeral tomorrow. It will need a lot more work.'

She gave the pitch.

'Then take my hand and lead me,' the children piped up anew.

Henzi's systematic questioning of all the villagers at The Stag – where we took over for him – brought nothing new to the surface. Towards evening we drove back to Zürich as empty-handed as we had come. In silence. I had smoked too much and drunk the local red wine. You know these slightly questionable wines. Matthäi, too, sat broodingly beside me in the back of the car, and there was not a word out of him until we were sweeping downhill and were almost at Romerhöf, five minutes from the centre of Zürich.

'I don't think the murderer is a Mägendorfer,' he said. 'This was a job by the same man who is responsible for the St Gall and Schwyz cases. All three murders were alike. I think it probable that the man is operating from Zürich.'

'Possibly,' I replied.

'It's likely to be a man with a car, perhaps a commercial traveller. Gerber, the farmer, said he saw a car parked in the woods.'

'I questioned Gerber myself today,' I said. 'He admitted that he was really too sound asleep to observe anything.'

We fell silent again.

'I'm sorry to have to leave you in the middle of a tough case,' Matthäi began again in a rather edgy voice. 'But I have that contract with the Jordanian Government.'

'You are flying tomorrow?' I asked.

'At three in the afternoon,' he replied. 'By way of Athens.'

'I envy you, Matthäi,' I said, and I meant it. 'I would much rather be police chief among the Arabs than here in Zürich.'

I dropped him off at the Hotel Urban where he had been living as long as I could remember, and went to the Kronenhalle, where I dined under the painting by Míro. That's my regular table. I always sit there and eat 'off the trolley'.

About ten o'clock at night, when I looked in on headquarters once more, I ran into Henzi in the corrdior just as I was passing Matthäi's former office. Henzi had not stayed long in Mägendorf; he had left by noon, which had surprised me. But since I had put the case in his hands it would have been contrary to my principles to interfere. Henzi was Bernese, ambitious but well liked by the men. He had married a girl from one of our most solid Zürich families, had shifted from the Socialist Party to the Liberals, and was well on the way to making a career for himself. I mention this just by the by; he is with the Independents now.

'The fellow still won't confess,' he said.

'Who?' I asked in amazement, stopping in my tracks. 'Who won't confess?'

'Gunten.'

I was taken aback. 'Third degree?'

'All afternoon,' Henzi said. 'And we'll keep it up all night if we have to. Treuler is working on him now. I just came out for a breath of air.'

'I want to have a look at this,' I replied with raised eyebrows, and I stepped into Matthäi's former office.

The pedlar was sitting on an office stool. Treuler had moved his chair over to Matthäi's old desk, which served him as prop for his left arm. The sergeant sat with legs crossed and his head lolling in his left hand. He was smoking a cigarette. Feller was taking down the testimony. Henzi and I halted in the doorway and were not noticed by the pedlar, who had his back to us.

'I did not do it, Officer,' the pedlar murmured.

'I didn't say you did. I only said you could have done it,' Treuler replied. 'Whether I am right or not is what we are trying to find out. Let us start again at the beginning. You say you settled yourself comfortably on the edge of the woods?'

'Yes, sir.'

'And slept?'

'That's right, sir.'

Why? You said you wanted to go to Mägendorf.'

'I was tired, Officer.'

'Then why did you ask the postman about the policeman in Mägendorf?'

'To find out, Officer.'

'What did you want to know?'

'My licence hadn't been renewed. So I wanted to know who was on duty in Mägendorf.'

'And who was on duty?'

'I found out there was a substitute in Mägendorf. That made me scared, Officer.'

'I am a kind of substitute,' the sergeant commented drily. 'Are you scared of me too?'

'Yes, Officer.'

'That is the reason you changed your mind about going to the village?'

'Yes, Officer.'

'That isn't a bad version of the story,' Treuler admitted. 'But maybe there is another version which would have the merit of being true.'

'I have told the truth, Officer.'

'Weren't you really interested in finding out from the postman whether there was a policeman in the vicinity?'

The pedlar looked up warily at Treuler.

'What do you mean by that, Officer?'

'Well,' Treuler replied deliberately, 'I imagine you were chiefly interested in checking with the postman to make sure that no police would be around the little dale?'

'Why should that interest me?' Gunten asked.

'Because you were waiting for the girl.'

The pedlar stared in horror at Treuler. 'I did not know she was coming, Officer,' he cried desperately, 'and I wasn't alone there in the dale. The farmers were working in the field. You've got to believe me!'

'I believe you,' Treuler placated him, 'but I have to check your story – and you understand that. You say that after you had your nap you went into the woods in order to return to Zürich?'

'There was a storm coming up,' the pedlar explained. 'So I wanted to take the short cut.'

'And that is how you came across the body?'

'Yes.'

'And you did not touch the body?'

'That's right, Officer.'

Treuler paused. Although I could not see the pedlar's face I sensed his fear. I felt sorry for him. But I was beginning to believe in his guilt, perhaps only because I was in a hurry to find the criminal.

'We have taken your clothes away and given you these clothes, Gunten. Can you guess why?' Treuler asked.

'I don't know, sir.'

'To make a benzidine test. Do you know what a benzidine test is?'

'No, Officer,' the pedlar gasped.

'It is a chemical test for traces of blood,' Treuler declared with weird friendliness. 'We discovered traces of blood on your shirt, Gunten. It is the girl's blood.'

'Because ... because I stumbled over the body, Officer,' Gunten said, aghast. 'It was frightful.'

Then he covered his face with his hands.

'And of course the only reason you did not mention that was that you were scared?'

'Yes, Officer.'

'And now we are supposed to believe you are telling the truth?'

'I didn't do it, Officer,' the pedlar pleaded desperately. 'Please believe me. Send for Inspector Matthäi. He knows I'm telling the truth. He knows.'

'Inspector Matthäi no longer has anything to do with this case,' Treuler replied. 'He is flying to Jordan tomorrow.'

'To Jordan,' Gunten muttered. 'I didn't know that.'

He stared at the floor in silence. There was utter stillness in the room; you could hear the clock ticking, and now and then a car outside in the street.

At this point Henzi took over. First he closed the window. Then he sat down at Matthäi's desk with an air of goodwill and consideration. But he placed the desk lamp so that the cone of light fell full upon the pedlar's face.

'There is no need to be upset, Gunten,' the lieutenant said with exaggerated politeness. 'We aren't out to get you; we only want to find out the truth. That is why we must appeal to you. You are our most important witness. You must help us.'

'Yes, Inspector,' the pedlar replied. He seemed to regain his courage.

Henzi packed his pipe. 'What do you smoke, Gunten?'

'Cigarettes, Inspector.'

'Give him one, Treuler.'

The pedlar shook his head. He stared down at the floor. The light was dazzling him.

'Does the light bother you?' Henzi asked amiably.

'It is shining right in my eyes.'

Henzi tilted the lampshade somewhat. 'Is that better?'

'Better,' Gunten murmured. He sounded grateful.

'Tell me, Gunten, what sort of things do you sell?' Henzi began anew. 'Dish-cloths?'

'Yes, dish-cloths too.' The pedlar spoke hesitantly. He did not know what the question was leading to.

'What else?'

'Shoelaces, Inspector. Toothbrushes, toothpaste, soap, shaving cream.'

'Razor blades?'

'Those too, Inspector.'

'What brand?'

'Gillette.'

'Is that all, Gunten?'

'I think so, Inspector.'

'Good. But I think you have forgotten a few things.' Henzi probed at his pipe. 'It won't draw,' he said, and then went on in a casual tone: 'Go on, don't worry, count up the rest of your little toys. We have looked your basket over.'

The pedlar did not answer.

'Well?'

'Kitchen knives, Inspector,' the pedlar said in a low, sad voice. Beads of sweat glistened on the back of his neck. Henzi puffed out billow upon billow of smoke, calmly, deliberately – a friendly well-disposed fellow.

'Go on, Gunten. What else besides kitchen knives?'

'Razors.'

'Why did you put that last?'

The pedlar remained silent. Henzi put out his hand as though intending to aim the light in Gunten's face again, but he withdrew it with a casual air when Gunten twitched. The sergeant stared fixedly at the pedlar. He was smoking one cigarette after the other. To that was added the smoke of Henzi's pipe. The air in the room was choking. I would have liked to open the windows. But closed windows were part of the method.

'The girl was killed with a razor,' Henzi commented casually, as if the observation had dropped from him by sheer chance. Silence followed. The pedlar sat hunched, lifeless, in his chair.

'My dear Gunten,' Henzi went on, leaning back in his chair, 'let us talk as man to man. There is no sense pretending. I know that you committed the murder. But I also know that you are just as shocked by the act as I am, as we all are. It was something that simply came over you. All at once you became like an animal; you attacked and killed the girl without wanting to, and without being able to stop yourself. Something was stronger than you. And when you came to yourself, Gunten, you were horrified. You rushed to Mägendorf because you wanted to give yourself up, and then you lost your nerve. Lost the nerve to confess. You must find your nerve again, Gunten. And we want to help you.'

Henzi fell silent. The pedlar swayed slightly on his stool. He seemed on the point of collapse.

'I am your friend, Gunten,' Henzi asserted. 'We're giving you this chance – why not take it?'

'I'm tired,' the pedlar moaned.

'So are we all,' Henzi replied. 'Sergeant Treuler, get us some coffee, and some beer. For our guest Gunten too. We are fair here.'

'I am innocent, Inspector,' the pedlar whispered hoarsely. 'I am innocent.'

The telephone rang. Henzi answered it, listened attentively, rang off, smiled.

'Tell me, Gunten, what exactly did you eat for lunch yesterday?' he asked easily.

'Berne platter.'

'Good, and what else?'

'Cheese.'

'Emmentaler, Gruyère?'

'Tilsiter and Gorgonzola,' Gunter answered, wiping the sweat from his eyes.

'Pedlars eat well these days,' Henzi commented. 'Was that all you ate?'

'Yes.'

'I would think that over carefully,' Henzi admonished him.

'Chocolate,' Gunten recalled.

'Well, so there was something else,' our lieutenant said, giving him an encouraging nod. 'Where did you eat that?'

'By the edge of the woods,' the pedlar said, throwing a wary and fatigued glance at Henzi.

Henzi switched off the lamp. Only the ceiling light feebly illuminated the smoky air of the room.

'I have just received the report from the coroner's office, Gunten,' Henzi declared triumphantly. 'The autopsy on the girl is complete. Chocolate has been found in her stomach.'

Now I too was convinced of the pedlar's guilt. His confession was only a question of time. I nodded to Henzi and left the room.

I was not mistaken. Next morning – it was a Saturday – Henzi telephoned me at seven o'clock. The pedlar had confessed. I arrived at the office at eight. Henzi was still in Matthäi's former room. He sat looking out of the open window, and turned tiredly to greet me. Beer bottles were all over the floor, the ash-trays were overflowing. There was no one else in the room.

'A detailed confession?' I asked.

'He will give one later,' Henzi answered. 'The main thing is that he confessed to the murder.'

'I hope you kept your hands clean,' I growled. The interrogation had lasted more than twenty hours. That was not legal, of course; but in the police force, after all, we cannot observe regulations to the letter.

'No shady methods were used, Chief,' Henzi declared.

I went into the 'boutique' and had the pedlar shown in. He could hardly stand on his feet and had to be supported by the policeman who brought him; but he did not sit down when I invited him to do so.

'Gunten,' I said, and there was a friendly note in my voice, I don't know why, 'I hear you have confessed to the murder of little Gritli Moser.'

'I killed the girl,' the pedlar murmured so low that I could scarcely understand him. He stared down at the floor as he spoke. 'Let me alone now.'

'Go and get some sleep, Gunten,' I said. 'We'll talk about the rest later on.'

He was taken out. At the door he encountered Matthäi. Gunten stopped, breathing heavily. His mouth opened as though he wanted to say something, but then he remained silent. He only looked at Matthäi, who stood somewhat discomposed in front of the wretched figure.

'Come on,' the policeman said, leading Gunten away.

Matthäi stepped into the 'boutique' and closed the door behind him. I lit a cigar.

'Well, Mattäi, what do you say?'

'Wasn't the poor fellow interrogated for more than twenty hours?'

'Henzi has only been imitating your method,' I replied. 'You were always great at interrogations. But he seems to have handled his first independent case very well, wouldn't you say?'

Matthäi did not answer me.

I sent for two coffees and croissants. The two of us were both depressed. The hot coffee did not improve our mood.

'I have the feeling that Gunten will retract his confession,' Matthäi said at last.

'Possibly,' I replied glumly. 'Then we'll just have to work him over again.'

'Do you think he's guilty?' he asked.

'Don't you?' I retorted.

Matthäi hesitated. 'Yes, I suppose I do,' he answered without conviction.

Morning light flooded in through the window. A dull silver. From Sihlquai came the noises of the street, and soliders marched out of the barracks.

Then Henzi appeared. He came in without knocking.

'Gunten has hanged himself,' he said blackly, and stuck a cigarette into his mouth.

The cell was at the end of the long corridor. We raced down it. Two men were already busy with the pedlar. He lay on the floor. They had ripped open his shirt; his hairy chest did not stir. His braces were still dangling from the window-bars.

'Gunten!' Matthäi cried out, kneeling down beside him.

'No use,' one of the two policemen commented. 'The man is dead.'
Matthäi stood up.

'I expect that ends the case of Gritli Moser,' I said as we walked
wearily down the endless corridor back to my office. 'I hope you'll
have a pleasant flight to Jordan, Matthäi.'

Towards two o'clock in the afternoon Feller brought the official car
round to the Hotel Urban for the last time, in order to take Matthäi
to his plane. But when the suitcases were already loaded the inspector
remarked that they had time and might as well drive out to the airport
through Mägendorf, which was only a little out of the way. Feller
reached the village square just as the funeral procession approached
it, a long line of silent people. A large crowd from the surrounding
villages, and from the city as well, had poured into Mägendorf to
attend the funeral. The newspapers had already reported Gunten's
death, and there was a general feeling of vindication. Justice had
prevailed. Matthäi left the car, and he and Feller stood among the
children opposite the church. The coffin had been placed on a cart
drawn by two horses, and was heaped with white roses. Behind the
coffin came the children of the village, two by two, each pair carrying
a wreath, led by Fräulein Krumm and the principal. There was a sea
of flowers, a sea of children. Then came Gritli Moser's parents, two
figures in black. The woman stopped and looked at the inspector.
Her face was expressionless, her eyes empty.

'You have kept your promise,' she said in a whisper, but speaking
with such precision that the inspector heard every word. 'Thank you.'
Then she walked on, unbowed, proud, beside her husband, a broken
man who had suddenly become fearfully old.

The inspector waited until the whole procession had passed – the
local councillor, the representatives of the canton Government, the
farmers, workmen, housewives, village girls – all in their best and
most solemn dress. Silence lowered over everything under the afternoon sun; among the spectators, too, no one made a sound; only the
resonant peal of the church bells could be heard, the grinding sound
of the cart-wheels, and the footfalls of the procession on the hard
pavement of the village street.

'To the airport,' Matthäi said, and got back into the car.

*

After he had bid Feller goodbye and had his passport checked, Matthäi bought a *Neue Züricher Zeitung* in the waiting-room. There was a picture of Gunten in it; the caption named him as the murderer of Gritli Moser. There were also a picture of the inspector and a news story about his latest appointment to Jordan. Here was a man who was clearly on the way up. But when he stepped on to the runway, raincoat over his arm, Matthäi noticed that the terrace of the airport building was crowded with children. There were whole classes from schools, being taken to see the airport. There were girls and boys in pretty, summery clothes; they were waving little banners and handkerchiefs, shouting with excitement and exclaiming over the ascents and descents of the gigantic silver craft. The inspector started and lingered for a moment, but then he walked on to the waiting Swissair plane. By the time he reached it the other passengers had already entered. The stewardess who had led the group to the plane held out her hand to take Matthäi's ticket. But the inspector turned round once more. He looked at the crowd of children who were waving, joyfully and enviously, at the plane which was about to start.

'Stewardess,' he said, 'I am not taking this flight.' And he turned back to the terminal building, walked under the terrace with its masses of children, and continued on towards the exit.

I did not receive Matthäi until Sunday morning, and when I saw him it was not in the 'boutique' but in my official office with its equally official view out to the street along the Sihl. On the walls were Gublers, Morgenthalers, and Hunzikers – reputable Zürich painters. I was distinctly annoyed. There had been quite a fuss. I had had a telephone call from some gentleman at the Political Department who insisted on talking nothing but French; the Jordanian Government had protested and the Federal Council had requested information which I could not give because I did not understand my former subordinate's action.

'Sit down, Herr Matthäi,' I said. I suppose my formality rather daunted him. We sat down. I did not smoke, and gave no indication that I intended to. That, too, disturbed him.

'The Federal Government,' I continued, 'concluded a treaty with the Kingdom of Jordan. You, Captain Matthäi, likewise signed a contract with Jordan. Your failure to depart violated these agreements.

Speaking as one man of the law to another I need not make myself plainer.'

'No need,' Matthäi said.

'I must therefore ask you to leave for Jordan just as soon as you possibly can.'

'I am not going,' Matthäi said.

'Why?'

'The murderer of little Gritli Moser has not yet been found.'

'You don't think it was the pedlar?'

'No, I don't.'

'After all, we have his confession.'

'He must have lost his nerve. The long third degree, despair, the feeling of being abandoned. And I was partly to blame,' he added softly. 'The man was depending on me, and I did not help him. I wanted to be off to Jordan.'

The situation was peculiar. Only the day before we had talked to one another without any sense of strain, and now we sat stiff and formal, both of us in our Sunday clothes.

'I want to ask you to turn the case over to me once more, Chief,' Matthäi said.

'I cannot do that,' I replied. 'Besides, you are no longer with us, Herr Matthäi.'

He stared at me in surprise.

'I am dismissed?'

'You resigned from the cantonal police force to take the post in Jordan,' I explained quietly. 'If you have broken your contract that is your affair. But if we employ you again it would mean that we endorse your action. You will understand that this is impossible.'

'Oh, I see,' Matthäi said.

'Unfortunately there is nothing to be done about,' I said.

We sat for a while in silence.

'When I passed through Mägendorf on my way to the airport there were many children there,' Matthäi said softly.

'What do you mean?'

'So many children in the funeral procession.'

'Naturally,' I said.

'And at the airport there were many children, too. Whole classes from the schools.'

'Well?' I looked at Matthäi in perplexity.

'Assuming that I am right, assuming that the murderer of Gritli Moser is still around, would not other children be in danger?' Matthäi asked.

'Certainly,' I said calmly.

'If there is this danger,' Matthäi went on insistently, 'it is the duty of the police to protect the children and prevent another crime.'

'So that is why you did not take your plane,' I said slowly. 'To protect the children.'

'That is why,' Matthäi replied.

I saw the whole thing more clearly now, and began to understand Matthäi. But finally I said that the possibility of danger to other children must simply be accepted. If Matthäi were right we could only hope that the real murderer would betray himself at some time; or that, assuming the worst, he would leave some substantial clues when he committed his next crime. That sounded cynical, I admitted, but it was not: it was only terrible to think of. The power of the police had limits and must have limits. Certainly everything was possible, I went on, even the most improbable things, but we had to go on probabilities. We could not say that Gunten was guilty beyond all doubt – we never really could make such statements about guilt. But we could say that he was probably guilty. Unless we wished to construct some fictional unknown the pedlar was the only plausible choice. He had already been convicted of one assault, carried razors and chocolate with him, had had blood on his clothing. Moreover, it had developed that he likewise plied his trade in Schwyz and St Gall – that is, in the cantons where the two other murders had taken place. Moreover, he had made a confession and committed suicide. To doubt his guilt now would be most unprofessional. Common sense told us that Gunten had been the murderer. Common sense could err, of course – we were only human; but we had to take that risk. We had to face the possibility. Moreover, the murder of Gritli Moser was unfortunately not the only crime we had to deal with. The emergency squad had just been sent out to Schlieren where there had been four serious burglaries the previous night. For purely technical reasons we could not afford the luxury of re-examining a closed case. We could only do what lay within our means, and that we had done. Children, I went on, were always in danger. There were more than two hundred sex-crimes involving children every year in the canton of Zürich alone. We could instruct the parents and warn the children, and we had done all that, but we could not weave our police network so close that no crimes at all would be committed. Crimes always happened, not because there were too few policemen but because there were policemen at all. If *we* were unnecessary there would be no crimes either. We must keep that fact in mind. We had to do our duty – Matthäi was right about that, I conceded – but our first duty was to remain within our limits. Otherwise we would only find ourselves setting up a police state.

I made this long speech and then fell silent. Outside the church bells were beginning to ring.

'I can understand that your personal situation has become rather difficult,' I said by way of concluding our interview. 'You have got yourself into a jam.'

'Thank you, Commissioner,' Matthäi replied. 'For the present I shall look into the case of Gritli Moser. Privately.'

'I would let this matter rest,' I said.

'I have no such intention,' he replied.

I did not show my vexation.

'Then may I request you not to trouble us with the affair,' I said, standing up.

'If you wish,' Matthäi said.

We parted without shaking hands.

It was hard for Matthäi to walk past his former office and leave the almost deserted headquarters. The name-plate on his door had already been changed, and when he ran into Feller, who often hung round the office on Sundays, the man avoided his eyes. He barely murmured a greeting. Matthäi felt like a ghost. But what bothered him most was that he no longer had an official car at his disposal. He had made up his mind to return to Mägendorf as quickly as possible, but it was not easy to carry out this intention. The village was not far, but transport was complicated without a car. He had to take tram No. 8, and then change to the bus. In the tram he met Treuler who was on his way, with his wife, to see his wife's parents. Treuler stared in astonishment at the inspector, but asked no questions. In fact Matthäi kept running into acquaintances – a teacher at the Federal Technical School, and a painter-friend. He gave only vague answers to their questions about his reasons for not leaving. Every such encounter was embarrassing, for his 'promotion' and departure had already been celebrated. He felt like someone resurrected from the dead.

In Mägendorf the church bells had finished ringing. The farmers were standing about the village square in their Sunday clothes, or drifting by groups into The Stag. It was chillier than it had been during the last few days; hordes of clouds were moving in from the west. At Moosbach the youths were already playing soccer; there was nothing to suggest that a few days ago a crime had been committed near the village. Everything was gay. Somewhere people were singing, 'Am Brunnen vor dem Tore'. In front of a large farmhouse with half-timbered walls and a huge roof children were playing hide-and-seek. A boy counted loudly up to ten, and the others scurried off. Matthäi watched them.

'Mister,' a low voice said beside him. He looked round. Between a pile of logs and a garden wall stood a small girl in a blue skirt. Brown eyes and brown hair. It was Ursula Fehlmann.

'What do you want?' the inspector asked.

'Stand in front of me,' the girl whispered, 'so they don't find me.'

The inspector placed himself in front of the girl.

'Ursula – ' he said.

'You mustn't talk so loud,' the girl whispered. 'Or else they'll hear that you're talking to someone.'

'Ursula,' the inspector whispered back, 'I don't believe that about the giant.'

'What don't you believe?'

'That Gritli Moser met a giant as big as a mountain.'

'But there are such giants.'

Have you ever seen one?'

'No, but Gritli did. Hush, be still now.'

A red-haired, freckled boy came creeping round the corner of the house. He was the seeker. He paused in front of the inspector, then stole round to the other side of the house. The girl giggled softly. 'He didn't see me.'

'Gritli told you a fairy-tale,' the inspector whispered.

'No,' the girl said. 'Every week the giant waited for Gritli and gave her hedgehogs.'

'Where was that?'

'In Robin Dale,' Ursula answered. 'And she made a picture of him. So there must be one. And the little hedgehogs, too.'

Matthäi was startled.

'She made a picture of the giant?'

'The picture is hung up in the schoolroom,' the girl said. 'Move out of my way.' Before he could say another word she had squeezed between the pile of logs and Matthäi, sprinted towards the house, and with a cry of joy reached the door-jamb which was 'home' before she could be caught by the boy who came rushing out from behind the house.

The news I received on Monday morning was unusual and disturbing. First the Mägendorf councillor telephoned to complain that Matthäi had forced his way into the schoolhouse and stolen a drawing by the murdered girl; he wanted no more snooping around by the cantonal police in his village; things should be allowed to settle down now, after all the commotion. In fact, he blurted out, he was going to chase Matthäi out of the village with dogs if he turned up there again. Next Henzi came in to report that he had had an argument with Matthäi, and to add to his discomfort it had been in the Kronenhalle; his former superior had been plainly intoxicated, had polished off a whole bottle of Reserve du Patron and then sent for cognac, had reeled up to Henzi's table and accused him of causing a miscarriage of justice. Henzi's wife, a girl from a nose-in-air family, had been both outraged and revolted.

But that was not all. After the morning briefing Feller told me that one of those birds from the municipal police – it would be one of them, of course – had passed on word that Matthäi had been seen in various bars and was now living at the Hotel Rex. Moreover, and this struck an odd note, they had news that Matthäi had taken to smoking cigarettes, and these the cheapest brand on the market. In short, the man was completely changed; he seemed to have become a different person overnight. To me, the whole thing sounded like an impending nervous breakdown, and I rang up a psychiatrist who often helped us out with psychiatric opinions.

To my surprise the doctor answered that Matthäi himself had made an appointment with him for that very afternoon. I told him a bit of the story. Then I wrote a letter of explanation to the Jordanian Legation. I said Matthäi was ill and asked for a stay of two months before he would have to assume his new post.

The psychiatrist's private clinic was far out of town, near the village

of Röthen. Matthäi had taken the train, but the clinic was a good walk
from the station. He had been too impatient to wait for the bus, which
soon caught up with him and passed him, so that he was left staring
irritably after it. He passed through a number of tiny hamlets. Children
were playing by the roadside and farmers working in the fields. The
sky was clouded over, a silvery grey. It had turned cold once more;
the temperature had dropped towards freezing point, although happily
stopping short of it.

Matthäi walked along the line of hills, and after passing Röthen
turned into the path across the flat which led to the sanatorium. The
first thing that caught his eye was a yellow building with a tall chimney,
which might have been a gloomy old factory. But soon the scene
became somewhat more attractive. The main building was still hidden
by beeches and poplars, but he noticed cedars and an immense
sequoia. Finally he was walking through the grounds. The path
branched. Matthäi followed a sign reading: OFFICE. Through the trees
and shrubs a small lake gleamed, but perhaps it was only a patch of
mist. Deathly silence everywhere. Matthäi heard nothing but his footsteps crunching on the gravel. A little later he heard the sound of a
rake. A young man was raking the gravel path. He performed the
motions slowly and evenly. Matthäi paused indecisively. He did not
know which way to turn, and saw no other sign. 'Can you tell me the
way to the office?' he asked the young man. There was no answer.
The young man went on raking evenly, quietly, mechanically, as
though no one had spoken to him, as though no one were there. His
face was entirely expressionless, and since his delicate movements
contrasted so oddly with his powerful frame, the inspector felt an
obscure sense of threatening danger: as though the young man might
suddenly strike out at him with the rake. With some trepidation he
walked on and came to a courtyard. This led into a second, larger
yard. Both sides of the yard were colonnaded, as in a cloister; but the
third side was bounded by a building that appeared to be a country
house. Here, too, there was no one in sight, although a plaintive voice,
high and feverish, came from somewhere. The voice kept repeating
a single word again and again, without stopping. Matthäi paused
doubtfully once more. An inexplicable sadness overcame him, and a
discouragement greater than he had ever felt before. He pressed down
the latch of the old portal striated with cracks, but it did not yield.
Still he heard the voice, that unending lament. In a kind of trance he

went down one colonnade. In some of the huge stone vases were red tulips, in others yellow. Now at last he heard footsteps. A tall old gentleman minced daintily across the yard with a distant, faintly astonished air. A nurse was leading him.

'How do you do,' the inspector said. 'I should like to see Dr Locher.'

'Have you an appointment?' the nurse asked.

'I am expected.'

'Go straight into the salon,' the nurse said, pointing to a double door. 'Someone will come for you.' Then she went on, the old man leaning his weight on her arm, his expression vague. She unlocked a door and vanished with the man. The voice could still be heard. Matthäi entered the salon. It was a large room furnished with antique pieces, capacious easy chairs and an enormous sofa. Above the sofa hung the portrait of a man, in a heavy gold frame. This must be the founder of the hospital, Matthäi thought. The other pictures on the walls were of tropical landscapes, perhaps places in Brazil. Matthäi thought he recognized the vicinity of Rio de Janeiro. He went to a french window and stepped out on a terrace. Large cacti stood on the stone flagging. But he could no longer see the park; the mist had thickened. He vaguely made out a spacious, rolling expanse with some monument or tomb standing in it, and the shadowy, menacingly pale trunk of a poplar. The inspector was growing impatient. He lit a cigarette; this new vice of his calmed him. He returned to the room and sat on the sofa. In front of it stood an antique round table with old books. He leafed through *Flore Complète de France, Suisse et Belgique*, by Gaston Bonnier. There were carefully drawn plates of flowers and grasses – certainly very beautiful and tranquillizing, but the inspector felt utterly at a loss with them. He smoked another cigarette. At last a nurse entered, a small energetic person with rimless glasses.

'Herr Matthäi?' she asked.

'Yes.'

The nurse looked round. 'Have you no luggage?'

Matthäi shook his head, wondering for a moment at the question.

'I only wish to ask the doctor a few questions,' he replied.

'Follow me, please,' the nurse said, and led him through a door.

He entered a small and, to his surprise, rather unprepossessing room. Nothing about it suggested a medical atmosphere. On the walls were pictures similar to those in the salon. There were also photographs, of sober men with beards and rimless glasses: monstrous visages – obviously predecessors of the present incumbent. The desk and chairs were heaped with books; only an old leather armchair was unoccupied. The doctor, in a white coat, sat behind piles of documents. He was small, lean, birdlike, and wore rimless glasses, like the nurse and the bearded men in the portraits. Rimless glasses seemed to be obligatory here, as if they were the insignia of a secret order, like the tonsure of monks, Matthäi reflected, and then shrugged the thought away. The nurse withdrew. Locher rose and greeted Matthäi.

'Welcome,' he said with a note of embarrrassment in his voice. 'Make yourself comfortable. Everything's rather shabby here. We're supported by private endowment; funds are always rather tight.'

Matthäi sat down in the leather armchair. It was so dark in the room that the doctor switched on his desk lamp.

'May I smoke?' Matthäi asked.

Locher seemed taken aback. 'Go ahead,' he said, regarding Matthäi keenly through his dusty glasses. 'But you used not to smoke?'

'Never.'

The doctor took a sheet of paper and began scribbling some sort of notation. Matthäi waited.

'You were born on November the eleventh, 1903, weren't you?' the doctor asked as he wrote.

'Yes.'

'Your address is still the Hotal Urban?'

'It's the Rex now.'

'Oh, it's the Rex now. On Weinbergstrasse. So you are still living in hotel rooms, my dear Matthäi?'

'Does that surprise you?'

The doctor looked up from his papers.

'Look here,' he said, 'you have been living in Zürich for thirteen years now. Other men establish families, beget children, build for the future. Haven't you any private life at all? Excuse me for asking so bluntly.'

'I see,' Matthäi replied, suddenly understanding it all, including the nurse's question about his luggage. 'I suppose the Commissioner has been in touch with you.'

The doctor laid down his pen with some deliberation. 'What do you mean by that, Inspector?'

'You have been asked to examine me,' Matthäi stated, crushing out his cigarette. 'Because the cantonal police do not think I am entirely – normal.'

The two men sat in silence. Outside the fog pushed sluggishly against the window, a faceless duskiness that crept greyly into the small room cluttered with books and piles of papers. Still worse was the cold and the stale air, mingled with the smell of some medicament.

Matthäi rose, went to the door and opened it. Outside stood two men in white smocks, their arms folded. Matthäi closed the door again.

'Two attendants. In case I make a fuss.'

Locher remained imperturbable.

'Listen to me, Matthäi,' he said. 'I want to talk to you as a doctor.'

'As you like,' Matthäi replied, sitting down again.

Locher picked up his fountain pen once more. He had been informed, he said, that Matthäi had recently committed acts that could not be described as normal. He wanted to speak frankly to him. Matthäi practised a hard profession and was often faced with the necessity of dealing harshly with people who crossed his path. He should therefore be prepared to excuse a doctor for plain speaking, for his profession had also made him hard. Hard and hard-headed. After all, when he considered Matthäi's conduct it was peculiar that he should so abruptly have dropped a unique chance like this post in Jordan, simply flung it to the winds. And then this obsession that he must seek a murderer who had already been found. Moreover this sudden decision to smoke, this equally unusual tendency towards dipsomania – four double brandies after a bottle of Reserve – why, damn it all, taken all together that certainly looked like abrupt person- ality disintegration, like the symptoms of an incipient illness. It would be only to Matthäi's own advantage to submit to a thorough examin- ation, so that they could round out the clinical and psychological picture. He therefore suggested that Matthäi spend a few days in Röthen.

The doctor fell silent, and crouching behind his papers began scribbling anew. 'Do you have occasional fevers?' he asked.

'No.'

'Speech defects?'

'Of course not.'

'Voices?'

'Nonsense.'

'Sudden perspiration?'

Matthäi shook his head. The deepening twilight and the doctor's foolish questions were trying his patience. He fumbled for his cigarettes, and at last found them. His hand trembled as he took the lighted match the doctor held out to him. Trembled with irritation. The situation was too silly; he should have foreseen it and chosen another psychiatrist. But he was partial to this doctor, whom they picked for their professional consultations down at headquarters primarily as an act of kindness; Matthäi inclined towards this doctor because other medical men in the city were contemptuous of him, regarding him as an eccentric.

'You are agitated,' the doctor pointed out, almost with delight. 'Shall I call the nurse? If you would go to your room now – '

'I have no such intention,' Matthäi replied. 'Have you any cognac?'

'I'll give you a sedative,' the doctor offered, rising.

'I don't need a sedative, I need cognac,' the inspector answered roughly.

The doctor must have touched a concealed button, for one of the attendants appeared in the doorway.

'Bring a bottle of cognac and two glasses from my room,' the doctor ordered, rubbing his hands – probably they were cold. 'And make it snappy.'

The attendant trotted off.

'Really, Matthäi,' the doctor said, 'it seems to me urgently necessary for you to sign in here. Otherwise we will wake up to a classic psychological and physical breakdown. We do want to avoid that, don't we? With a little effort we could do so.'

Matthäi did not respond. The doctor, too, fell silent. The telephone rang once. Locher picked it up and said: 'I'm engaged.' It was almost black outside the window – so complete had the evening suddenly become.

'Shall I switch on the ceiling light?' the doctor asked, merely to find something to say.

'No.'

Matthäi had now regained his composure. When the attendant came with the cognac, he poured himself a glass, drank it and poured another.

'Locher,' he said, 'will you kindly drop this man-to-man and make-it-snappy rot and all the rest of it. You are a doctor. Has it ever happened in your profession that you could not solve a case?'

The doctor looked at Matthäi in astonishment. He was discountenanced by the question, did not know what the inspector was aiming at.

'Most of my cases cannot be solved,' he answered honestly, although even as he spoke he knew that he should never have given such a reply to a man he regarded as a patient.

'I can well imagine that would be so in your profession,' Matthäi replied with a degree of sarcasm that saddened the doctor.

'Did you come here only to ask me this question?'

'Among other things.'

'For heaven's sake what is the matter with you?' the doctor asked uncomfortably. 'You have always been one of the most rational men I have ever known.'

'I don't know,' Matthäi replied uncertainly. 'The murdered child.'

'Gritli Moser?'

'I can't stop thinking about this child.'

'It is preying on your mind?'

'Have you any children?' Matthäi asked.

'Like you, I am unmarried,' the doctor replied softly, once more ill at ease.

'So, you too.' Matthäi sat frowning. 'You see, Locher,' he explained. 'I looked straight at what lay before me, and did not funk it like my successor Henzi – solid, normal Henzi. A mutilated corpse lay there in the leaves. Only the face was untouched, a child's face. I stared at it: in the bushes lay a red skirt and bits of pretzel. But that was not the real horror.'

Matthäi lapsed into silence again, as if he were frightened. He was a person who never spoke of himself and was now being forced to do so because he needed this short, birdlike doctor with the ridiculous glasses who alone could help him pursue his case, and whom he had to repay by confidences.

'You rightly wondered,' he went on at last with an effort that was almost an act of violence, 'that I have lived in an hotel all these years. But I did not want to face the world. I wanted to master it like an automaton, but not suffer with it. I wanted to remain indifferent to it, not lose my head, control things like a technician. So I was able to look at that murdered body of the child, but when I faced the parents

I suddenly could stand it no longer; all at once I found myself wanting to run away from that damned house, away from those agonized parents. And so I gave them a promise I could not keep because I was ready to fly to Jordan – I would have promised them anything just to escape seeing their suffering. And then I let the old indifference come over me again, Locher. That was the horror. I did not fight for the pedlar. I let everything take its course. I retreated into the impersonality I'm noted for. "Matt the Automat", as the boys in the backroom call me. I dropped everything, slipped back into the calm, the superiority, the formality, the inhumanity that I have always used as armour. Until I saw the children at the airport.'

The doctor laid his notes aside.

'Then I turned back,' Matthäi said. 'You know the rest.'

'And now?' the doctor asked.

'I want to keep my promise. I want to find the man who murdered Gritli Moser.'

The doctor rose and went to the window.

One of the attendants came in, followed by the other.

'You can go back to the ward,' the doctor said. 'I won't need you any longer.'

Matthäi poured himself another glass of cognac, and laughed. 'Good, this Remy Martin.'

The doctor still stood at the window, staring out.

'How can I help you?' he asked rather forlornly. 'I am not a criminologist.' He turned to face Matthäi. 'Why are you so set on believing it was not the pedlar?'

'Look at this.'

Matthäi brought out a sheet of paper and carefully unfolded it. It was a child's drawing. At the lower right, in clumsy script, it was signed *Gritli Moser*. It was a crayon drawing of a man. He was tall, taller than the fir trees which surrounded him like a fantastic sort of grass. The drawing was characteristically childlike – dot, dot, comma, dash, circle, and the face was done. He wore a black hat and black clothes, and from his right hand, which was an oval pierced with five dashes, a number of tiny circlets with many fine hairlines, looking like little stars, fell towards a tiny girl who was even smaller than the trees. At the top of the drawing, in what was actually the sky, stood a black motor car and beside it a queer animal with strange horns.

'This drawing was done by Gritli Moser,' Matthäi explained. 'I took it from the schoolroom.'

'What is it supposed to represent?' the doctor asked, staring at the drawing in puzzlement.

'The hedgehog giant.'

'How am I supposed to interpret that?'

'Gritli said that a giant in the woods gave her little hedgehogs, and then she drew this scene,' Matthäi explained, pointing to the little circles.

'And now you think – '

'The hedgehog giant may well have been the murderer,' Matthäi replied. 'It is possible that Gritli Moser made a drawing of her murderer.'

'Nonsense, Matthäi,' the doctor retorted angrily. 'This drawing is a pure product of the imagination. Don't base any theories on it.'

'Probably it is,' Matthäi answered. 'On the other hand the car is pretty well observed. It looks to me like an old American model. And the drawing of the giant comes to life, too.'

'Giants are imaginary,' the doctor snapped impatiently. 'Kindly spare me the fairy-tales.'

'A tall, heavy-bodied man might easily seem like a giant to a little girl.'

The doctor looked at Matthäi with an air of surprise.

'You think the murderer was a big man?'

'Naturally that is only a guess,' the inspector said evasively. 'If my assumption is right, the murderer was driving around in an old black American car.'

Locher pushed his glasses up on his forehead. He picked up the drawing and studied it closely.

'Why did you bring this to me?' he asked uncertainly.

'Assuming that the only clue I have to the murderer in this drawing,' Matthäi explained, 'all I can do is follow up this clue. But I am like a layman confronted with an X-ray photograph. I do not know how to read it. I need your help in interpreting this drawing.'

The doctor shook his head.

'A child's drawing like this one would tell you nothing about the murderer,' he anwered, laying the drawing back on the desk. 'It is only possible to say something about the girl who made the drawing. Gritli must have been an intelligent, wide-awake and gay child. Children do not only draw what they see but also the feelings that are

aroused in them by what they see. Fantasy and reality mingle. Thus
there are some real things in this drawing: the big man, the car, the
girl. Other things seem to be a code, such as the hedgehogs, the
animal with the big horns. Sheer riddles. And, unfortunately, Gritli
has taken the answers to the grave with her. I am a doctor, not a
medium. Put away your drawing. It is ridiculous to go on thinking
about it.'

'It's just that you haven't the nerve.'

'I hate sheer waste of time.'

'What you call waste of time may be nothing but an old, tried-and-
true method,' Matthäi declared. 'You are a scientist and know what
a working hypothesis is. Take my assumption that this is a drawing
of the murderer as a working hypothesis. Fall in with my fiction for
a while and let's see what comes of it.'

Locher studied the inspector thoughtfully for a moment, and then
examined the drawing once more.

'Just what did the pedlar look like?' he asked finally.

'Insignificant.'

'Intelligent?'

'Not stupid, but lazy-minded.'

'Was he not convicted once of sexual assault?'

'He seduced a fourteen-year-old girl.'

'Relations with other females?'

'Well – yes – as a pedlar. He was pretty notorious around the
countryside,' Matthäi answered.

Locher put his questions briskly. Evidently the story had piqued
his professional curiosity.

'A shame this Don Juan confessed and hanged himself,' he said.
'Otherwise I would not put him down for a sex-maniac at all. But
now let us take a stab at your hypothesis. The hedgehog giant in the
drawing is quite conceivable as a sex-murderer. He looks tall and
massive. Men who commit such crimes against children are usually
primitive, more or less feeble-minded, imbeciles or morons, robust,
inclined towards violence, impotent and displaying inferiority feelings
towards women.'

He stopped and leaned forward as though he had discovered something. 'That's odd.'

'What is?'

'The date on the drawing.'

'What about it?'

'More than a week before the murder. Gritli Moser must have met her murderer before, if your hypothesis is acceptable, Matthäi. What is strange, if that were so, is that she then recounted the meeting in the form of a fairy-tale.'

'Just a child's way.'

Locher shook his head. 'Children never do anything without a reason,' he said. 'That would probably mean that the big black man forbade Gritli to say anything about the mysterious meeting. And the poor little girl obeyed and told a fairy-tale instead of the truth. Otherwise someone might have been suspicious and she could have been saved. You see, on that assumption the whole story takes a really horrible turn. . . . Was the girl actually raped?' he asked abruptly.

'No,' Matthäi answered.

'Was it the same with the girls who were killed years ago in St Gall and Schwyz?'

'Exactly the same.'

'With a razor too?'

'Yes.'

Now the doctor also poured a glass of cognac for himself.

'Then it is not properly speaking a sex-murder,' he commented, 'but an act of revenge. The criminal's intention in committing these murders was to avenge himself on women, no matter whether he was the pedlar or your fictional hedgehog giant.'

'But a little girl is not a woman.'

Locher went on undeterred: 'But to a sick man a little girl can serve as substitute for a woman. Because the murderer does not dare to attack women he attacks little girls. He kills them instead of the specific woman he has in mind. For that reason he will always pursue the same type of girl. I would wager that all his victims resemble one another. Do not forget that we are dealing here with a thoroughly primitive person. It does not matter whether the feeblemindedness is inborn or develops later; such persons have no control over their impulses. The resistance they can oppose to these impulses is abnormally small; it takes damnably little – altered metabolism or a few degenerated cells – and such a human being becomes a beast.'

'What would be the reason for this revenge?'

The doctor shrugged. 'Possibly sexual conflicts,' he explained. 'Perhaps the man was repressed, or exploited by a woman. Perhaps his wife was rich and he was poor. Perhaps she held a higher social position than he.'

'None of this would apply to the pedlar,' Matthäi commented.

The doctor shrugged again.

'Then some other possible factors will apply to him. The utmost absurdities are possible between man and woman.'

'Assuming that the pedlar was not the murderer, would there be continuing danger of more murders?' Matthäi asked.

'When did the murder in St Gall canton take place?'

'Five years ago.'

'And in Schwyz canton?'

'Two years ago.'

'Then, as you see, the intervals are diminishing,' the doctor pointed out. 'That might suggest accentuation of a morbid condition. Resistance to these impulses would obviously be growing increasingly feeble, and the chances are that the sick man might commit murder within a few months, even weeks if the opportunity offered.'

'How would he behave in the interval?'

'To begin with he would feel relief,' the doctor stated rather hesitantly. 'But soon new emotions of hatred would accumulate, a new craving for revenge would demand outlet. At first he would merely loiter about in the vicinity of children. In front of schools, say, or in public squares. Then he would gradually begin driving around in his car, seeking a new victim; and when he had found the girl he would strike up a friendship with her, as he had done before, until you would have another murder.'

Locher fell silent.

Matthäi took the drawing, folded it, and tucked it into his breast pocket. He stared at the window. It was now deep night outside.

'Wish me luck in my search for the hedgehog giant, Locher,' he said.

The doctor gaped at him for a moment, then suddenly grasped his meaning. 'So the hedgehog giant is more to you than a mere working hypothesis, isn't he, Matthäi?'

'He is utterly real to me,' Matthäi agreed. 'I do not doubt for a moment that he exists.'

But everything he had just said had been mere speculation, an intellectual concept without scientific validity, the doctor cried out, irritated that he had been hoodwinked and had failed to see what

Matthäi was leading up to. He had only pointed out one among a thousand different possibilities. By the same method it could be proved that anyone you named might have been the murderer. Why not? – after all, any sort of nonsense was conceivable and could somehow be logically supported. Matthäi knew that just as well as he. 'I was merely being co-operative in falling in with this hypothesis of yours. But you should be man enough to regard reality without benefit of hypotheses, and have the courage to accept the factors which plainly point to the pedlar's guilt. The child's drawing may just as well be a pure product of her imagination, or represent a meeting with someone who was not the murderer at all, could not possibly have been the murderer.'

'Please allow me to decide what degree of probability should be assigned to your deductions,' Matthäi replied, finishing off his glass of cognac.

The doctor did not respond at once. He had again taken his seat behind his battered old desk, surrounded by his books and files; he was once more the director of a hopelessly antiquated hospital, lacking in funds, personnel, the barest necessities, and wearing himself out trying to keep the creaking institution running. 'Matthäi,' he said at last, his voice weary and bitter, 'you are attempting the impossible. I don't want to be sentimental now. A man has his will, his ambition, his pride, and does not like to surrender them. I understand that; I am the same myself. But if you want to seek a murderer who in all probability does not exist, and whom you will never find even if he does exist, because there are too many of his kind who fail to commit murder only by sheer chance, you are putting yourself in a grave situation. It may be courageous of you to choose madness as a method. I'll gladly pay tribute to your bravery – extremist attitudes command respect nowadays. But if this method does not lead to its goal I am afraid that in the end nothing but the madness will remain for you.'

'Goodbye, Dr Locher,' Matthäi said. 'Thank you.'

This conversation was reported to me by Locher. As usual his minute German handwriting, spidery and fine as if engraved, could barely be read. I sent for Henzi and got him to look over the letter. He commented that the doctor himself spoke of untenable hypotheses. I was not so sure; it seemed to me that the doctor had gone out on a limb and then become afraid of his own courage. He was now inventing counter-arguments which had not occurred to him before. After all, we possessed no detailed confession by the pedlar, nothing we could check, just a general statement that he had committed the crime. Moreover the murder weapon had not yet been found. None of the razors in the pedlar's basked showed traces of blood. That again made me wonder. Certainly this one fact did not posthumously clear Gunten; the circumstantial evidence still weighed heavily. But I was disturbed. Moreover, I was more impressed than I admitted by Matthäi's actions. To the examining magistrate's annoyance I went so far as to have the woods around Mägendorf searched once more; but again we found nothing. The murder weapon could not be found. It probably lay at the bottom of the gorge, Henzi said.

'Well,' Henzi said, taking one of his execrable perfumed cigarettes from its box, 'we really can't do anything more about the case. Either Matthäi is crazy or we are. That is what we have to decide now.'

I pointed to the photographs I had sent for. There was a clear resemblance among the three murdered girls.

'That supports the hedgehog giant idea,' I said.

'Why should it?' Henzi replied cold-bloodedly. 'The girls simply fit the type the pedlar went for.' Then he laughed. 'I just wonder what Matthäi is up to. I wouldn't like to be inside his skin.'

'Don't underestimate him,' I growled. 'He is capable of anything.'

'Even finding a murderer who does not exist, Chief?'

'Perhaps,' I said, and slipped the three photographs back into their files. 'I know one thing – that Matthäi won't give up.'

I was right about that. The first report came from the chief of the municipal police, after a conference. We had had another of those situations of overlapping authority to settle. As the damn fool was leaving he brought the conversation round to Matthäi. Just to upset me, I imagine. I learned that Matthäi had frequently been seen hanging around the zoo; and that he had also bought an old car from a garage on Escher-Wyss Platz. Shortly afterwards I received another report that completely baffled me. I can still remember exactly how it came to my ears; it was in the Kronenhalle on a Saturday night. The dining-room was full – everybody who counted for anything in Zürich and did not count his calories was there, as usual. Waitresses bustled about; steam rose from the trolley; and from the street outside sounded the rumble of traffic. I was sitting under the Miro, having liver-dumpling soup and feeling at peace with the world when the salesman of a large fuel company came over to me. Without more ado he sat down at my table. He was slightly tipsy and in high spirits, ordered a Marc and told me, laughing heartily, that my former captain had changed his profession. Matthäi, he said, had taken over a filling-station in the Grisons, near Chur – a station that the firm had been on the point of closing down because it was so unprofitable.

At first I refused to believe the story. It struck me as utterly out of character, a ridiculous and idiotic rumour. But the salesman stuck to his tale. He asserted that Matthäi was making his mark in his new work as he had in the old. The petrol station was flourishing. Matthäi had a great many customers – almost all of them people he had dealt with formerly, although on a different basis. Word must have got round that 'Matt the Automat' had been promoted to filling-station attendant, and the result was that the 'old-timers' came parading and tooting up to his station in everything on wheels, from old crocks to the most expensive Mercedes. Matthäi's service station had become a Mecca for the underworld of all eastern Switzerland. The sale of petrol had climbed tremendously; in fact the company had just installed a new pump of super grade for him. They had also offered to put up a modern building instead of the old shack Matthläi was now occupying. But he had refused with thanks, and had also refused to hire an assistant. Sometimes cars and motor-cycles stood in long lines, but no one ever seemed to be impatient. Apparently it was too great an honour to be served by a former captain of the cantonal police.

I could not say a word. The salesman took himself off, and when the trolley came steaming towards me I no longer had any appetite. I chose a few snacks and then ordered beer. Later Henzi came in as usual, accompanied by his classy wife; he was in a black mood because a referendum had not gone according to his wishes. I told him the news. He commented that Matthäi must have really gone out of his mind, just as he had always predicted. Suddenly he was in high good humour, and gobbled down two steaks while his ladylike wife chattered away endlessly about the Schauspielhaus – she knew several of the actors there.

A few days later the telephone rang in the middle of a conference. A conference with the municipal police, of course. It was the directress of an orphanage. The old spinster told me in high excitement that Matthäi had called upon her, solemnly dressed all in black – obviously to cut an earnest figure – and had asked whether he might have a particular girl for adoption from among her protégées, as he called them. This girl was the only one he wanted; he had always longed to have a child, and now that he was managing a garage in the Grisons he was in a position to take care of one. Naturally she had refused his request, politely referring to the regulations of the orphanage. But my former Captain had made so strange an impression upon her that she considered it her duty to inform me. Whereupon she hung up.

This certainly was a strange development. I puffed away at my Bahianos, trying to figure it out.

But an entirely different affair really set us back on our heels at headquarters, and convinced me that Matthäi's conduct was becoming something more than an acute embarrassment for us. We had a highly questionable character on the carpet. He was officially a hairdresser and unofficially a pimp who had set himself up very comfortably in a handsome villa in one of our lakeside suburbs where many men of letters lived. At any rate, the taxicab and private car traffic round the house was extraordinarily lively. I had scarcely begun the interrogation when he came out with the news. Beaming with pleasure he flourished the story under our noses. Matthäi at his filling-station was now living with a former streetwalker. The Heller girl. I immediately rang police headquarters in Chur, and asked to be connected with the station house nearest to Matthäi's new place of business. The story was true. I was stunned. The ladies' hairdresser lolled triumphantly in front of my desk, munching away at his chewing-gum. I capitulated and gave orders to let the old pimp go. He had trumped all our aces.

This was really alarming. I was perplexed, Henzi outraged, the examining magistrate disgusted, while the Federal Councillor, who had also heard the story, talked of public disgrace. Liesel Heller had once been our guest at headquarters. A chum of hers – a lady equally notorious – had been murdered; we had suspected that Liesel knew more about the affair than she was willing to tell us. Later she had been summmarily expelled from the canton of Zürich although, apart from her profession, there was no real evidence against her. But there are always people in the administration who do things on principle.

I decided that the time had come to intervene, to go out there personally and see what was going on. I sensed that Matthäi's antics had some connection with Gritli Moser, but I could not see what it might be. My ignorance infuriated and disturbed me. Moreover, I might say, I was also activated by a detective's curiosity. I wanted to know what was going on.

I set out alone in my car. It was a Sunday again. It seems to me, now that I look back upon it, as though a great many of the key events in this story took place on Sundays. Bells chiming everywhere: the whole country seemed to be ringing and clanging. Moreover, somewhere in Schwyz canton I ran into a procession. On the road one car after another; on the radio one sermon after the next. Later on in the morning the guns started banging, popping, rat-tatting, and cracking at the firing-ranges near every village. Everywhere there was monstrous, senseless tumult. The whole of eastern Switzerland seemed to be on the move. Somewhere a motor race was being held, and a swarm of cars from Western Switzerland streamed towards it. Families, whole clans, were out for a drive, and when I finally reached the service station – which you've seen – I was worn out by all the turmoil of this noisy day of rest.

I looked round. At the time the station did not look as run-down as it does today. It was rather pleasant, everything clean, and geraniums in the windows. The house had not yet been turned into a tavern, either; it had a self-respecting, lower middle class air. I noticed, too, that everywhere, strewn all along the highway frontage, various objects proclaimed the presence of a child. There was a swing, a large doll's house set up on a bench, a doll's pram, a rocking-horse. Matthäi himself was just attending to a customer who hastily sped off in his Volkswagen when I stepped out of my Opel. Next to Matthäi stood a little girl of seven or eight, with her arms about a doll. She had blonde plaits and a red skirt. The child reminded me of someone, but I did not know why, for she did not really resemble the Heller woman.

'That was Red Meier, wasn't it?' I said, pointing to the Volkswagen which was making off. 'He's been out just a year now.'

'Regular?' Matthäi asked indifferently. He was wearing a pair of blue mechanic's overalls.

'Super.'

Matthäi filled the tank and cleaned the windscreen.

'Fourteen francs thirty.'

I gave him a ten and a five. 'Keep the change,' I said, as he started counting it out, and immediately afterwards I flushed. 'Forgive me, Matthäi; that just slipped out.'

'I don't mind,' he replied, pocketing the money. 'I'm used to it.'

Embarrassed, I looked down to the girl again. 'A pretty little thing,' I said.

Matthäi opened the door of my car. 'Have a pleasant trip.'

'Come now,' I growled, 'I wanted to have a talk with you. Damn it all, Matthäi, what is the meaning of all this?'

'I promised not to bother you any more with the case of Gritli Moser, Chief. Fair's fair: don't bother me with it either,' he replied, turning his back on me.

'Matthäi,' I said, 'let's stop being childish.'

He did not answer. A crackling, roaring and whistling began. Evidently there was a firing-range near here, too. It was approaching eleven o'clock. I watched as he attended to an Alfa Romeo.

'He did time for three and a half years,' I commented as the car drove off. 'Hadn't we better go in? All this shooting is making me nervous. I never could stand rifle practice.'

He showed me into the house. In the hall we met Liesel Heller, coming up from the cellar with potatoes. She was still a fine-looking woman, and as a police official I was somewhat embarrassed – guilty conscience. She looked questioningly at us, and seemed for a moment somewhat disturbed, but greeted me agreeably; altogether, she made a rather good impression.

'Is the kid hers?' I asked after she had vanished into the kitchen.

Matthäi nodded.

'Where did you pick Liesel up, anyway?' I asked.

'Near here. She was working in a factory.'

'And why have her here?'

'Well,' Matthäi replied, 'after all, I needed somebody to keep house for me.'

I shook my head.

'I'd like to talk to you privately,' I said.

'Annemarie, go into the kitchen,' Matthäi ordered the child.

The girl went out.

The room was bare but clean. We sat down at a table near the window. Outside the marksmen were firing away, one salvo after another.

'Matthäi,' I asked again, 'what is all this about?'

'Very simple, Chief,' my former captain answered. 'I am fishing.'

'What do you mean by that?'

'Detective work, Chief.'

Irritably, I lit a cigar. 'I am not a beginner, but I really do not understand.'

'Let me have one of those.'

'Please.' I held out the cigar-case to him.

'I suppose Locher has sent a memo on our conversation,' Matthäi said after he had carefully lit the Bahianos.

'We made nothing of the whole thing.'

'But I did.'

Matthäi set a bottle of kirschwasser on the table. We were sitting in the sun; the window was half open, and outside it was mild June weather. The firing-range ... but I've mentioned that. When a car stopped – there were fewer of them now, because it was approaching noon – Liesel attended to it.

'In what way?' I asked.

'The child's drawing represented the truth.'

'Did it? Then how do you interpret the hedgehogs?'

'I don't know yet,' Matthäi answered. 'But I have figured out the animal with the strange horns.'

'Well?'

'It's an ibex,' Matthäi said deliberately. He drew on his cigar and puffed the smoke forcefully out into the room.

'Is that why you went to the zoo?'

'I spent days there,' he replied. 'I also got children to sketch ibexes for me. All their drawings were like Gritli Moser's picture of the animal.'

I saw the light. 'The ibex, or Steinbock as it is called locally, is the cantonal emblem of the Grisons,' I said. 'The emblem of this region.'

Matthäi nodded. 'The cantonal emblem on the car's licence plate caught Gritli's attention, and so she drew the ibex.'

'We should have been able to think of that right away,' I said.

Matthäi attentively studied his cigar, the faint curl of smoke, the growing ash. He said quietly:

'The mistake we made, you, Henzi and I, was to assume that the murderer was acting from Zürich as a centre. In reality he comes from the Grisons. I traced back the scenes of the other crimes; all of them lie on the route from the Grisons to Zürich.'

I considered the matter. 'Matthäi, there may be something in that.'

He regarded me mockingly.

'That isn't all,' he declared.

'What else?'

'I met some fishermen.'

'Fishermen?'

'Well, boys who were fishing, to be more exact.'

I gaped at him.

'You see,' he explained, 'after my discovery about the ibex I drove to the Grisons straight off. Logical enough. But I soon realized the foolishness of it. The canton of the Grisons is so large that it would be sheer luck to find a man in it when you know nothing about him except that he must be tall and that he drives an old black American car. More than twenty-seven hundred square miles; more than one hundred and thirty thousand people scattered through innumerable small valleys. The thing is plainly impossible. One cold day I was sitting in hopeless perplexity by the Inn, in the Engadine, watching some boys at the bank of the river. I was about to turn away when I noticed that the boys had become aware of me. They looked frightened, and were standing about with an air of constraint. One of them was carrying a home-made fishing-rod. "Go ahead and fish," I said. The boys scowled at me. "Are you from the police?" up and asked a red-haired freckled boy of about twelve. "Do I look it?" I replied; "Well, I don't know," he answered. "I'm not from the police," I said.

'Then I watched as they cast their hooks into the water. There were five of them, all absorbed in their fishing. After a while the freckled boy said resignedly, "They're not biting today." He trudged up the bank and came over to me. "Have you got a cigarette?" he asked. "I like that!" I said. "You at your age." "But you look as though you'd give me one," the boy said. "Then I suppose I must," I answered, and held out my packet of Parisiennes to him. "Thanks," he said. "I have matches." He puffed the smoke out through his nose. "That sets you up when the fishing's been such a dead loss," he said with a swaggering air. "Well," I said, "your friends seem to have more perseverance than you. They're going on with the fishing and are bound to catch something soon." "No they won't," the boy said. "Or at most a grayling." "I suppose you want a pike," I teased him. "Pike don't interest me," the boy answered. "Trout are the thing. But that's a question of money." "Why is that?" I wondered. As a child I used to catch them in my hand. Young trout, of course. But just try to catch a veteran trout in your hand. "Trout are a lot finer than pike and much harder to catch," the boy answered. "But you need a licence to get one, and that costs money." 'Oh well, you get along without a licence," I laughed. "The trouble is," the boy explained, "that we can't go to the right places. The people with licences fish there."

' "What do you mean by a right place?" I asked. "I see you know nothing about fishing," the boy observed. "I see that too," I replied. Both of us had moved down and were sitting on the embankment now. "I suppose you think a fellow just has to drop the hook into the water anywhere?" he said. I wondered a little, and asked what was wrong about that idea. "Just what an amateur would think," the freckled kid said, again puffing the smoke through his nose. "For fishing you have to know two things first of all: the place and the bait." I listened attentively to him. 'Suppose," the boy went on, "you want to catch a trout, a full-grown old veteran. You have to think out where the fish is most likely to stay. Naturally in some place where he is protected against the current, and at the same time where there is a strong current, so that more of his prey will come swimming by. That means somewhere downstream behind a boulder; or even better, behind a bridge pier. The trouble is, of course, that such places are always taken by the licensed fishermen." "I see, the current has to be interrupted," I said. "You've got the idea," he nodded proudly. "And what about the bait?" I asked. "That depends on whether you want to catch a predatory fish, or a grayling, or burbot, which are vegetarians," he replied. "You can catch a burbot with a cherry, for instance. But predatory fish like trout or perch have to be caught with something living. With an insect or a smal fish."

"With something living," I repeated thoughtfully, and stood up. "Here," I said, giving the boy the rest of the cigarettes. "You've earned these. Now I know how to catch my fish. First I must look for the place, and then the bait." '

Matthäi fell silent. I said nothing for a long while, drank my kirsch, stared out into the lovely summer day with the rifles ripping away outside, and relit my cigar. 'Matthäi,' I spoke at last, 'now I understand what you meant by saying that you were fishing. This service station is the favourable spot, and this road is the river. Is that it?'

'Anyone who wants to go from the Grisons to Zürich must use this road unless he wants to make a big detour through the Oberalp Pass,' Matthäi replied quietly.

'And the girl is your bait?' I shuddered as I said this.

'Her name is Annemarie,' Matthäi said.

'And now I realize whom she reminded me of,' I added. 'That poor child, Gritli Moser.'

We both fell silent again. It had grown warmer outside; the mountains were shimmering in rising mists, and the guns were still blasting away. Evidently there was a marksman's meet. 'Isn't there something diabolic about your plan?' I asked timidly after a long silence.

'Probably,' he retorted.

'You intend to wait here until the murderer passes by, sees Annemarie, and falls into the trap you have set for him?'

'The murderer *must* pass by here,' he answered.

I thought about that. 'Good,' I said finally, 'let us assume you are right. Assume this murderer exists. It's not one of the question, after all. Anything is possible in our profession. But don't you think that your method is too risky?'

'There is no other method,' he said, tossing the cigar stump out of the window. 'I know nothing about the murderer. I cannot hunt for him. Therefore I had to pick out his next victim, a girl, and use the child as bait.'

'Very well,' I said. 'But you have adopted this method from the technique of fishing. Unfortunately the parallel is not perfect. You cannot keep a child near the road as bait all the time. She must go to school after all, and there will be times when she wants to get away from your damned road.'

'The summer holidays start soon,' Matthäi replied stubbornly.

I shook my head.

'I am afraid you are becoming obsessed with a single idea,' I said. 'You can't simply sit here until something happens that may never happen. Even granting that the murderer is likely to pass by here, that still doesn't mean he will take your bait – to stick to your horrible comparison. And so you'll wait and wait . . .'

'An angler has to wait too,' Matthäi insisted.

I peered through the window and caught a glimpse of Liesel filling the tank for young Oberholzer. A total of six years inside, counting all his short sentences.

'Does Liesel know why you are here, Matthäi?' I asked.

'No,' he replied. 'I only told her that I needed a housekeeper.'

I did not feel easy in my mind. The man impressed me, certainly, and there was something magnificent about his unusual method. I found myself admiring him and wishing him success, though perhaps only in order to humble that insufferable Henzi. Nevertheless I really thought his undertaking hopeless, the risk too great and the chances of winning too small.

'Matthäi,' I tried once more to make him see reason, 'there is still time for you to accept that post in Jordan. Otherwise Berne is going to send Schafroth.'

'Let them send him.'

Still I did not give up. 'Wouldn't you rather like to come back with us?'

'No.'

'We would keep you on headquarters work for the time being, at your old pay.'

'I don't want to.'

'You might also switch to the municipal police. You really ought to think it over, if only from a purely financial point of view.'

'As proprietor of a filling-station I am making as much if not more than I did working for the Government,' Matthäi replied mockingly. 'But here comes a customer, and Liesel ought to be getting on with the dinner now.'

He rose and went out. Then another customer drove up. Pretty-boy Leo. By the time Matthäi was finished with him I had got into my car.

'Matthäi,' I said, as I took my leave, 'there really is no helping you.'

'That's how it is,' he replied, and signalled to me that the road was clear. Beside him stood the little girl in her red skirt; and in the doorway Liesel, wearing an apron, again threw me a look full of suspicion. I drove back to Zürich.

And so he waited. Waited obstinately, inflexibly, passionately. He served his customers, did his work, always the same mechanical motions of pumping petrol, checking oil, adding water to radiators, wiping windscreens. The child stayed at his side or in the doll's house when she returned home from school; she went tripping and hopping about, dreaming, talking to herself, or sat singing on the swing, plaits and red skirt flying. He waited and waited. The cars drove by – cars of all colours and makes, old cars and new cars. He waited. He wrote down the number of the cars with Grisons licence plates, looking up their owners to the official list, telephoned to town clerks to inquire about them. Liesel Heller worked in a small factory near the village at the foot of the mountains, and would return in the evening over the small rise behind the house, her string shopping-bag full of bread. At night there were often footsteps around the house, and low whistles, but she did not open the door.

Summer came, oppressively hot, endless, the air shimmering, the heat venting itself sometimes in tremendous downpours. And so the long summer holiday began. His chance had come. Now Annemarie always stayed with him, and thus by the road, visible to everyone who drove past. He waited and waited. He played with the girl, told her fairy-tales, went through all of Grimm, all of Andersen, through the *Arabian Nights*, invented stories of his own – desperately did all in his power to keep the girl by him, in sight of the road where he had to have her. The child stayed, content with the stories and fairy-tales. The drivers regarded the pair in astonishment, or were touched by this idyll of father and child. They gave the little girl chocolate and chatted with her, while Matthäi watched them tensely. Was this big heavy man the murderer? His car had Grisons plates. Or that tall, lean one who had been bent down to say a few words to the girl? Owner of a sweet-shop in Disentis, as Matthäi had long before found out. Check your oil sir? Very well, sir. Could do with a quart. Twenty-three ten. Have a pleasant trip, sir. He waited and waited. Annemarie loved him, was content with him; he had only one thing in mind: the murderer. Nothing existed for him but this faith that the murderer would turn up; nothing but this hope, this longing. This alone could be fulfilment. He pictured the man's coming, powerful, clumsy, child-like, full of tenderness and murderous cravings; how he would come again and again to the station, grinning amiably, stiffly dressed, a pensioned-off-railway conductor or Customs guard; how he would lure the child away, gradually, and how he, Matthäi, then, would follow the two into the woods, crouching, creeping; how he would leap forward at the crucial moment, and there would ensue a wild, bloody, man-to-man struggle; the terrible grip, the final release, and then the murderer would lie before him, beaten, whimpering, confessing. But then Matthäi had to tell himself again that this was all impossible because he was guarding the child too obviously; that he must allow the girl more freedom if he wanted to see results. And after such thoughts he would let Annemarie wander where she liked, but would secretly follow her, leaving the pumps untended with drivers grumpily blowing their horns. At such times Annemarie would skip to the village half an hour or so away, would play with the farmers' children or on the edge of the woods, and shortly afterwards return. She was accustomed to solitude and became shy of others. And the other children rather avoided her.

Then Matthäi would change his tactics again, would invent new games, new stories, would again cajole Annemarie to stay with him. He waited and waited, undeterred, determined, though not always undismayed. And he made no explanations. For Liesel Heller had long since noticed how much attention he paid to the child. She had never believed that Matthäi had taken her as his housekeeper out of sheer kindness. She sensed that he had some hidden intention but she was safe and sheltered with him, perhaps for the first time in her life, and so she preferred not to think about it. Perhaps too, she had certain hopes; who knows what goes on in the mind of a poor woman like that? In any case, after a while she ascribed Matthäi's interest in her child to genuine affection, although occasionally her old wariness, her old bitter realism, came to the fore.

'Captain Matthäi,' she said once, 'it's none of my business, I know, but did the Chief of Police come here on my account?'

'Why no,' Matthäi replied. 'Why should he'

'People in the village are talking about us.'

'Who cares about that?'

'Captain Matthäi,' she began again, 'is the reason for your staying here something that has to do with Annemarie?'

'Nonsense,' he laughed, 'I'm just fond of the child, that's all.'

'You're good to me and Annemarie,' she replied thoughtfully. 'I wish I knew why.'

Then the summer holidays came to an end. Autumn descended; the countryside turned all reds and yellows, with everything excessively distinct, as under a tremendous magnifying glass. Matthäi felt as though a great opportunity had slipped away. Nevertheless he continued to wait, tenaciously, intently. The child walked to school; Matthäi usually went to meet her at noon and at the end of the day, fetching her home in his car. His plan appeared daily more and more senseless, more and more impossible, the chances of winning slimmer and slimmer. He knew this perfectly well. How often the murderer must have passed his service station, he considered – perhaps daily, certainly once a week; and still nothing happened, still he was groping in the dark; still he had not fastened on the slightest clue, not a hint or a trace, nothing but drivers who came and went, occasionally had a few words with the girl, talked innocently, haphazardly, impenetrably. Which of them was the man he sought? Was it any one of them at all? Perhaps he was having no luck because his old profession was known to so many people; that was an unavoidable factor which he had not reckoned on at the beginning.

Nevertheless he stuck it out, waited and waited. He could no longer turn back; waiting was his only method, even though it wore him out, even though he was often on the point of packing his bags, and leaving, taking flight, going somewhere, anywhere – even to Jordan, perhaps. He stuck it out though he often feared he would go out of his mind. Then there were hours, days, when he became indifferent, apathetic, cynical, let matters take their course, sat on the bench in front of the service station drinking glass after glass of schnapps, staring into space, cigarette ends accumulating on the ground at his feet. Then he would pull himself together again. But more and more he relapsed into his lethargic state, dozed away the days and weeks in cruel, absurd waiting. Lost, tormented, hopeless and yet full of hope. Until one day, as he sat there unshaven, dull, grease-smeared, he started. It suddenly occurred to him that Annemarie was not yet back from school. He set out to meet her, on foot. The dusty, unmade country road climbed slightly behind the house, then dropped down and over a patched level field and crossed through the woods, from the brink of which the village could be seen, old houses huddling round a church, bluish smoke rising from chimneys. From this point the whole road along which Annemarie had to come could be surveyed. But there was no sign of her. Matthäi turned towards the woods again, filled with a new tension, wide awake now. Under the small fir trees and hardwood saplings the ground was blanketed with rustling red and brown leaves. A woodpecker hammered away some-where deeper in, where large firs blocked off the sky and the sun's rays slanted down between their trunks. Matthäi left the road and forced his way through the briers and undergrowth. Branches lashed back into his face. He reached a clearing and looked around in astonishment; he had never known it was here. From the other side of the clearing a broad path cut through the woods; it was no doubt the road by which the villagers brought their refuse to the dump, for a mound of ashes was heaped up in the clearing. Along its flanks lay

tin cans, rusty wire and similar rubbish – a huge collection of junk
sloping down to a small brook which trickled through the centre of
the clearing. Then Matthäi caught sight of the girl. She was sitting
on the bank of the small silvery stream, her doll and school-bag beside
her.

'Annemarie,' Matthäi called.

'I'm coming,' the girl replied, but remained where she was.

Matthäi picked his way over the refuse heap to the child's side.

'What are you doing here?' he asked.

'Waiting.'

'For whom?'

'For the wizard.'

The girl had nothing but fairy-tales in her head. Sometimes she
would be waiting for a fairy, at others for a wizard. It was like a
mockery of his own waiting. Despair swept him again, realization of
the futility of his actions and the paralysing knowledge that he must
nevertheless wait because there was no longer anything he could do
but wait, wait and wait.

'Come along now,' he said listlessly. Taking the child's hand he
walked back through the woods with her. Then he sat down on the
bench once more, and stared into space. Twilight came, then the
night. He had become indifferent to everything. He sat there, smoked,
waited and waited, stubborn, inflexible, though sometimes whispering
to himself, conjuring his enemy without knowing it: Come, come,
come, come. Motionless, he sat in the white moonlight, suddenly fell
asleep, awoke stiff and frozen at dawn, and crawled into bed.

But next day Annemarie came home from school somewhat earlier
than usual. Matthäi had just risen from his bench to go to fetch her
when she came tripping along, school-bag strapped on her back,
singing 'Marie sat upon a stone' softly to herself and hopping from
one leg to the other. The doll dangled from her hand, its small feet
dragging over the ground.

'Have you any homework?' Matthäi asked.

Annemarie shook her head and went on singing. Then she went
into the house. He let her go; he was too apathetic, too hopeless, too
weary to tell her new fairy-tales, to lure her with new games.

But when Liesel came home she asked: 'Has Annemarie been good
all day?'

'Why, she was at school,' Matthäi answered.

Liesel looked at him in astonishment. 'At school? She had the day off. Teachers' conference, or something.'

Matthäi came to life. The disappointment of the past week vanished immediately. He sensed that fulfilment of his hope, of his insane expectations, was approaching. With difficulty he controlled himself and asked Liesel no more questions. Nor did he try to probe the girl. But the following afternoon he drove into the village and left the car in a side street. He wanted to watch the child secretly. It was nearly four o'clock. From the windows came singing, then shouts; the school-children came rushing wildly out of the building, the boys brawling, tossing stones, the girls arm in arm. But Annemarie was not among them. The teacher came out, reserved, scrutinizing Matthäi sternly. From this lady he learned that Annemarie had not been to school; she had also not been the day before yesterday, in the afternoon, and had brought no excuse; the teacher wanted to know whether she was ill. Matthäi replied that the child was in fact ill, apologized for not having informed her sooner, and drove like a madman back to the woods. He stormed through the woods to the clearing, and found nothing. Exhausted, breathing heavily, scratched and bleeding from the thorns, he returned to his car and drove back to the service station. Before he reached it he saw the girl skipping along the road. He stopped.

'Get in, Annemarie,' he said pleasantly, opening the door. He extended his hand to her, and she climbed into the car. Then he started. The child's hand was sticky. And when he looked at his own hand he saw traces of chocolate on it.

'Who gave you the chocolate?' he asked.

'A girl,' Annemarie replied.

'At school?'

Annemarie nodded. Matthäi made no comment. He drove back home. Annemarie got out and sat down on the bench near the pump. Matthäi unobtrusively watched her. The child was putting something into her mouth and chewing. Slowly he went up to her.

'Let me see,' he said, and carefully opened the clenched little hand. In her palm lay a prickly ball of chocolate, half bitten off. The kind called toffees.

'Have you any more of them?' Matthäi asked.

The girl shook her head.

He reached into the pockets of her skirt, took out her handkerchief and unfolded it. There were two more truffles in it. Annemarie said nothing.

Matthäi, too, was silent. He was overcome by a tremendous feeling of joy. He sat down on the bench beside the girl.

'Annemarie,' he asked at last, his voice trembling, the two prickly chocolate balls cupped carefully in his hand, 'did the wizard give these to you?'

The girl did not reply.

'Did he forbid you to tell anyone about the two of you?' Matthäi asked.

No answer.

'You don't have to keep it a secret,' Matthäi said pleasantly. 'He's a nice wizard. You go along and see him tomorrow.'

All at once the girl beamed, as if overwhelmed by a great gladness; she reached up her little arms and hugged Matthäi, ardent with happiness, and then ran up to her room.

Next morning at eight o'clock – I had just arrived at my office – Matthäi laid the chocolate truffles on my desk. He was in such a state of excitement that he barely bothered to greet me. He was dressed in his town clothes, but without a tie and unshaven. I pushed the box of cigars towards him. He took one and lit it.

'What are these chocolates for?' I asked in bewilderment.

'The hedgehogs,' Matthäi replied.

I stared at him, turning the little spheres of chocolate round and round. 'What do you mean?'

'It's very simple,' he explained. 'The murderer gave Gritli Moser truffles, and she interpreted them as hedgehogs. That is the solution of the child's drawing.'

'I laughed. 'How do you expect to prove that?'

'Because the same thing has happened with Annemarie,' Matthäi replied. And he told me the train of events.

I was instantly convinced. I sent for Henzi and four policemen, gave them my instructions, and informed the examining magistrate. Then we set out. The service station was deserted. Liesel had taken the child to school and then gone on to her factory.

'Does Liesel know what has happened?' I asked.

Matthäi shook his head. 'She has no idea.'

We went to the clearing and searched it carefully, but found nothing. Then we scattered. It was approaching noon. Matthäi returned to his service station in order not to arouse suspicion. The day was a favourable one – Thursday; the child had no school in the afternoon. Gritli Moser had also been murdered on a Thursday, it suddenly occurred to me. It was a brilliant autumn day, hot, dry; bees, wasps and other insects were humming everywhere, birds screeching, and from far away came the echo of axe blows. At two o'clock we heard the bells of the village, and then the girl appeared. She broke through the shrubbery opposite me, effortlessly, hopping and jumping, ran to the little brook with her doll, sat down and looked steadily toward the woods. She was tense, attentive; her eyes shone; she was obviously waiting for someone, but could not see us. We were well hidden behind trees and shrubs. Then Matthäi returned cautiously, and leaned his body against a tree-trunk near me, as I was doing.

'I think he will come in half an hour,' he whispered.

I nodded.

Everything had been organized with the greatest care. We kept watch where the road through the woods intersected with the highway; we even had radios. All of us were armed. The child sat by the brook, almost without stirring, full of anxious, wondering, keyed-up expectation, the refuse heap at her back, now in the sunlight, now in the shade of one of the tall dark firs. Not a sound could be heard except the hum of the insects and the trilling of the birds. Only now and then the girl sang to herself in her thin voice, 'Maria sat upon a stone', singing it again and again, the same words and verses. And around the stone on which she sat the tin cans made a rusty heap, interlaced with wires. Now and then, but only in unexpected gusts, the wind rushed across the clearing; leaves leaped up and crackled, and then silence fell again. We waited. Nothing existed for us any longer but this autumnally enchanted wood with the little girl in the red skirt in the clearing. We waited for the murderer, resolute, craving justice, settlement, punishment. The half-hour had long since passed – two whole hours, in fact. We waited and waited; we ourselves now waited as Matthäi had for weeks and months. Five o'clock came; the first shadows fell, then twilight; everything paled, all the glowing colours faded. The girl skipped away. Not one of us said a word, not even Henzi.

'We'll come back tomorrow,' I decided. 'We'll spend the night in Chur. At the Steinbock.'

And so we waited there on Friday and Saturday also. Strictly speaking I should have enlisted the Grisons police. But this was our affair. I did not want to have to make explanations, did not want any interference. The examinining magistrate telephoned me that Thursday evening, simmered, protested, threatened, called it all nonsense, raged, insisted we return. I remained firm, refused to leave, consented only to the return of one policeman. We waited and waited. We were no longer really concerned about the child now, or the murderer; we were concerned about Matthäi. The man had to be confirmed, had to win his point; otherwise there would be a disaster. We all felt that, even Henzi, who admitted that he was convinced at last. On Friday night he declared firmly that the unknown murderer would certainly come on Saturday. After all, we had incontrovertible proof – the hedgehogs, and the fact that the child came again and again, sat motionless in the same spot; it was perfectly plain that she was waiting for someone.

And so we stood in our hiding-places, behind our trees and bushes, stood unmoving for hours, staring at the child, at the tin cans, at the tangled wire, at the mound of ashes, smoking mutely, without talking to one another, listening to the eternal singing of 'Maria sat upon a stone'. On Sunday the situation was more difficult for us. The woods suddenly became filled with hikers, because of the long period of fair weather. At one point a mixed chorus with musical director tramped into the clearing, noisy, perspiring, shirt-sleeved, and planted themselves in rows. The woods rang with 'To wander is the miller's joy, to wander'. Luckily we were not in uniform behind our shrubs and trees. 'The Heavens praise the Glory of th' Eternal . . .' but the longer it went on the worse it became for us. Later a pair of lovers strolled along, and carried on shamelessly in spite of the child's presence. Through it all the girl simply sat there, with incomprehensible patience, in incredible anticipation. She had been doing this now for four afternoons in a row. We waited and waited. The three policemen had also gone back to Zürich, taking the radio apparatus with them. There were only four of us left: Henzi and Feller in addition to Matthäi and myself. Strictly speaking the effort could no longer be justified. But when you really considered it only three of the afternoons we had waited should actually count. For, as Henzi pointed out, on Sunday the area would have been again too full of people for the murderer to dare put in an appearance. And so we also waited through Monday.

On Tuesday morning Henzi, too, went back to Zürich. Someone had to look after things at headquarters, after all. But when he left Henzi was still convinced that we would nab our man.

We waited and waited and waited, lying in wait, lurking in the bushes, each of us independent of the others, for there were too few of us now to set up a proper cordon. Feller had posted himself behind a bush near the wood road, where he lay in the shade, dozing the summery heat of these autumn days and once snoring so heavily that the wind carried his snores over the clearing. That was on Wednesday. Matthäi, for his part, stood on the side of the clearing opposite the service station; and I observed the scene from the other side, opposite him. So we lay in wait, lay in wait expecting the murderer, the hedgehog giant, starting at each passing car that we heard coming from the main road, the child between us. Every afternoon she came to the clearing and sat by the little brook singing 'Maria sat upon a stone', persistent, bemused, incomprehensible. We began to despise the child, to hate her. Sometimes, of course, she did not come for a long while; she straggled about near the village with her doll. But she did not go too close to the village, since she was playing truant from school. That had not been managed without difficulties: I had had to have a private conversation with the teacher in order to prevent the school from investigating. I circumspectly hinted at the situation, identified myself, and obtained tremulous consent.

The child would often circle about the woods; we watched her with binoculars. But she always returned to the clearing, except on Thursday, when to our despair she stayed near the service station. There was nothing for it but to keep hoping that Friday would bring some developments. For I now had to make up my mind. For days now there had not been a word out of Matthäi; he was at his post behind his tree next day when the child came skipping up again, in her red dress, carrying her doll, and sat down once more as she had done all the previous days. It was still glorious autumn weather, vibrant, colourful, confiding, melting with sweetness before the quietus of winter. But the examining magistrate could not endure it for more than half an hour. He had come towards five in the afternoon, driving down with Henzi. He turned up entirely unexpectedly, came over to me who had been at my post since one o'clock in the afternoon, shifting my weight from one foot to the other; he came over and stared at the child, flushed with anger. 'Maria sat upon a stone', the thin voice floated over to us. But now I could not stand the song, could no longer endure looking at the child, that ugly gap-toothed mouth, those skimpy plaits, that nondescript red dress. The girl now seemed to me repulsive, vulgar, common, stupid; I could have strangled her, killed her, torn her to pieces just to stop hearing that idiotic 'Maria sat upon a stone.' It was maddening. Everything was the same, the same as it had been all along – moronic, senseless, dreary – except that the dry leaves were piling higher and higher, the gusts of wind came perhaps more frequently, and the sun glowed a still deeper gold upon the damned heaps of rubbish. It was unbearable, unbearable – and suddenly the magistrate stalked forward – it was like a release from prison – stalked forward, broke through the under- growth, went straight up to the child, ignoring the fact that he sank to his ankles into the ashes. And as we saw him marching towards the girl, we too burst out of our hiding-places. There had to be an end to this, right away.

'Whom are you waiting for?' the magistrate roared at the girl, who stared terrified at him, sitting on her stone, clutching the doll. 'Whom are you waiting for? – answer me, do you hear, you damned brat!'

Now we had all reached the girl; we surrounded her, and she stared at us, filled with horror, terror, incomprehension.

'Annemarie,' I said, my voice quivering with rage, 'a week ago someone gave you chocolate. You remember, chocolates like little hedgehogs. Did a man in black clothes give you those choclates?'

The girl did not answer; she only looked at me, eyes welling with tears.

Now Matthäi knelt down before the child, grasped her thin shoul- ders. 'Listen, Annemarie,' he explained, 'you must tell us who gave you the chocolates. You must tell us exactly what the man looked like. I once knew a girl,' he went on urgently, for now everything was at stake, 'a girl who also wore a red skirt like yours, who was given chocolates by a big man in black clothes. The same kind of prickly little balls you ate. And then the girl went into the woods with the big man, and the big man killed the girl with a knife.'

He fell silent. Still the child did not reply; she stared mutely at him, eyes wide.

'Annemarie,' Matthäi screamed, 'you must tell me. I only want to see that nothing happens to you.'

'You're lying,' the girl answered softly. 'You're lying.'

Then the magistrate lost his patience for the second time. 'You stupid brat,' he yelled, gripping the child's arm and shaking her, 'will you tell us what you know, this minute!' And we others yelled too, wildly, senselessly, because we had lost control of ourselves; likewise shook the girl and began to hit her, rained blows upon the little body that lay in the ashes among the tin cans and the red leaves, beat her cruelly, furiously, screaming and yelling.

The girl let our rage pass over her, lay mute for an eternity, though it must have lasted only a few seconds. And then suddenly she shrieked out in so uncanny and so inhuman a voice that we were all numbed. 'You're lying, lying, lying.' Horrified, we let her go; her screams brought us back to our senses, filled us with horror and shame at our own behaviour.

'We're beasts, beasts,' I gasped. The child was running now across the clearing towavds the edge of the woods. 'You're lying, lying, lying!' she shrieked again, so horribly that we all thought she had gone out of her mind. But she ran straight into her mother's arms – for Liesel, to make matters worse, appeared in the clearing at just this moment. that was all we needed. Liesel knew the whole story; the teacher had talked after all, when the girl's mother passed by the school; I knew just what had happened without having to ask. And now the wretched woman stood there, pressing the sobbing child to her, and staring at us with the same look we had just seen in her daughter's eyes. Worse still, she knew every one of us – Feller, Henzi and the magistrate too. The situation was grotesquely painful; we were all embarrassed and all felt ridiculous. The whole thing was nothing more than a lousy, miserable farce. 'Lies, lies, lies,' the child was still shrieking, beside herself. 'Lies, lies, lies.' Then Matthäi went up to the two of them, crushed, uncertain.

'Liesel,' he said politely, in fact humbly – which was altogether silly, for now there was only one thing to do and that was put an end to the whole affair – finish it, finish it for good, drop the case, be done once and for all with our speculating and puzzleing whether or not the murderer existed. 'Liesel, I have discovered that Annemarie has been given chocolate by an unknown person. I have sound reasons for suspecting that it is the same person who lured a child into a forest some time ago and killed her.'

He spoke precisely, and in so official a tone that I almost burst into laughter. The woman gazed quietly straight into his eyes. Then she spoke as formally and politely as Matthäi himself. 'Captain Matthäi,' she said softly, 'did you take in Annemarie and me solely in order to find this person?'

'There was no other way, Liesel,' Matthäi replied.

'You are a swine,' the woman said calmly, without change of expression. She took her child by the hand and went off through the woods towards the service station.

We stood there in the clearing, the shadows already dense, surrounded by old tin cans and tangled rusty wire, our feet deep in ashes and leaves. It was all over; the whole thing had become senseless, ridiculous. A fiasco, a catastrophe. Matthäi alone had regained his composure. He stood straight, stiff and dignified in his blue mechanic's overalls. Then he bowed – I could scarcely believe my eyes and ears – bowed to the magistrate and said: 'Herr Burkhard, all we can do now is to go on waiting. there is no choice. We must wait, wait and wait. If you could let me have another six men and the radio apparatus, that would suffice.'

The magistrate stared in shocked alarm at my former subordinate. He had expected anything but this. He had just been on the point of giving us a good ticking off; but now he swallowed hollowly several times, wiped his brow, then turned abruptly on his heel and tramped off with Henzi through the leaves. He vanished in the woods. At a sign from me, Feller also left.

Matthäi and I were alone.

'Now listen to me,' I shouted, determined to bring the man to reason at last, furious that I myself had lent support to this nonsense, had made the whole thing possible. 'The operation has failed; we have to admit it. We have waited more than a week and no one has come.'

Matthäi did not answer. He only looked around, attentive, peering. Then he went to the edge of the woods, circled the clearing and returned to me. I was still standing on the refuse heap, ankle-deep in ancient ash.

'The child was waiting for him,' Matthäi said.

I shook my head. 'The child came here to be alone, to sit by the brook, dream with her doll, and sing 'Maria sat upon a stone'. *We* read a story into this.'

Matthäi listened attentively to me.

'Annemarie was given the hedgehogs,' he said stubbornly, still clinging to his theory.

'Annemarie was given chocolate by someone,' I said. 'That is true. But anyone can give a child chocolate. That the truffles are the hedgehogs on the child's drawing is only your interpretation, Matthäi, and there is nothing to prove that it was really so.'

Again there was no anwer from Matthäi. Once again he paced about the clearing, examined the spot where the leaves had heaped up, looked at something, then gave up and returned to me.

'This is a place for murder,' he said. 'You can feel it. I intend to go on waiting.'

'It's sheer nonsense,' I replied. All at once I was filled with horror, with disgust, with weariness. I shivered.

'He will come here,' Matthäi said.

Beside myself, I shouted at him: 'Rot, nonsense, idiocy!'

He seemed to pay no attention. 'Let's go back to the service station,' he said.

I was glad to be leaving this accursed spot at last. The sun hung low now; the shadows were gigantic, and the broad valley glowed a violent gold. The sky above was purest blue, but I hated it all. I felt as though I had been exiled in the heart of an unspeakably trashy picture postcard. Then we came out on to the main road – the stream of traffic, convertibles with smartly dressed people, the wealth of life roaring past. It was absurd. We reached the service station. Beside the pumps Feller sat waiting in my car; he had already half dozed off. Annemarie perched on the swing singing again in her tinny if now tearful voice 'Maria sat upon a stone'. Against the door-jamb some man stood leaning, probably a worker from the brick field, his open shirt showing a hairy chest, cigarette dangling from his lips, grinning. Matthäi paid no attention to him. He went directly into the room with the window where we had sat before, and I followed. He placed a bottle of schnapps on the table, and poured himself glass after glass. I could not drink, I was too disgusted by it all. Liesel Heller was nowhere in sight.

'It will be difficult – what I have in mind,' he commented. 'But the clearing isn't far, really. Or do you think I would do better to wait here at the station?'

I made no reply. Matthäi paced back and forth, taking no account of my silence.

'It's a pity that Liesel and Annemarie know the story now,' he said. 'But we'll manage, anyhow.'

From outside came the road noise, the child blubbering 'Maria sat upon a stone'.

'I am going now, Matthäi,' I said.

He went on drinking, did not even look up at me.

'I shall wait here some of the time, at the clearing some of the time,' he decided.

'Goodbye,' I said, and left the room, went outside, passed by the man and the little girl, beckoned to Feller who started out of his snooze, drove up and opened the door of the car for me.

'Back to Zürich,' I ordered.

This is the story as far as poor Matthäi really figures in it [the former chief of the cantonal police continued his tale]. [This is as good a place as any to mention that the old chief and I had long since finished our drive from Chur to Zürich and were now sitting in the Kronenhalle which he had so often mentioned and extolled in his story, being served by Emma of course, and under a painting by Gubler which had replaced Miro's – all this in strict accordance with the old fellow's habits. Furthermore we had already eaten – from the trolley – *bollito milanese*; this too was one of his traditions, and why should I not follow suit? It was nearing four o'clock, and after the 'coffee and', as the chief referred to his passion for smoking a Havana along with his Espresso, followed by Reserve du Patron, he suggested a second charlotte. Moreover I should also add, as a purely technical point, for the sake of literary honesty and in due homage to the craft, that I have of course not always reproduced the story exactly as it was told to me by the loquacious chief. When I say this I am thinking of those parts of his story which he did not relate from his own point of view, as his own experiences, but described objectively as happenings in themselves – for example the scene in which Matthäi made his pledge. At such points I had to interfere, to shape and reshape, although I took the greatest pains not to falsify the events but simply to rework the material that the old man supplied to me, according to certain laws of the writer's craft.]

Naturally [he continued], I returned to see Matthäi several times, more and more convinced that it had been the pedlar after all, and the rest was Matthäi's imagination. For in the following months and then years there were no new murders of the same type. Well, I need not go into detail; the man degenerated mentally, physically, morally, became a sot. There was no helping him, no changing him. At night the fellows of the neighbourhood no longer whistled and sneaked about the service station in vain; things went from bad to worse; the local police made a number of raids. I had to tell my colleagues in Chur the whole story, and after that they looked the other way. They have always been more sagacious than we are in such matters. And so everything took its fatal course; you yourself have seen the results, on our trip. It's dreary enough, especially since the child Annemarie has turned out as bad as the mother. Perhaps only because a number of welfare organizations pounced on her. The child was put into foster homes, but always ran away and back to the service station where Liesel set up that shabby tavern two years ago. The devil know how she wangled a licence; at any rate, that finished the kid. She helped out – in every respect. Four months ago she came back from a year in the reformatory, but don't think that taught the girl a lesson. Well, you saw it all for yourself; we needn't talk about it.

But you must be asking yourself what my story has to do with the criticism I made of your lecture, and why I should have called Matthäi a genius. A valid question. You may object that a wild inspiration need not necessarily be a correct one, or the inspiration of a genius. That is true, too. I can even imagine how you are working this thing out in your writer's mind. You are probably cleverly saying to yourself that you need only make it turn out that Matthäi is right in the end and catches the murderer and then you'll have a wonderful plot for a novel or a film, that after all the writer's job is to make things translucent by giving them a certain twist, so that the higher idea shines through them, can be glimpsed or inferred. That by such a twist, by showing Matthäi as a success, you would not only be making my degenerate detective interesting but in fact transforming him into a Biblical figure, a kind of modern Abraham in the greatness of his hope and faith – and thus a senseless story, of someone who searches for a non-existent murderer because he believes in the innocence of a guilty man, would become a meaningful parable; the guilty pedlar would then be innocent in the realm of the higher imagination, the non-existent murderer existent, and an affair which tends to make mock of man's faith and reason would be transformed into one that rather glorifies these powers. It would not matter whether the facts

were what they were, since the main thing is to show this version of
the story as equally possible. This, I imagine, is more or less your
train of thought, and I can predict that this variant of my story is so
edifying and so affirmative that it will inevitably be made public before
too long, either as a novel or a film. You will tell the whole thing
more or less as I have tried to do, only of course much better. You
are, after all, a professional in storytelling, and only at the end will the
murderer really appear, will hope meet its reward and faith triumph, so
that the narrative will in the end be acceptable to this Christian world
of ours. I can think of a few more alterations that are in order. I
would suggest, say, that as soon as Matthäi discovers the truffles and
becomes aware of the risk Annemarie is running he can no longer
continue with his plan of using the child as bait – either out of
humanitarianism or out of his newly awakened love for the child,
whereupon he makes sure that Annemarie and her mother are in
safety and then sets up a big doll by the brook in the clearing. Then,
portentously, the murderer, Annemarie's wizard, comes striding out
of the woods towards sunset, approaches the supposed child, filled
with lustful bliss at the kill that awaits him. Seeing that he has fallen
into a diabolic trap he is thrown into a rage, into a fit of madness,
battles with Matthäi and the police, and then perhaps at the end – you
must forgive me my dabbling in fiction – comes a moving conversation
between the wounded inspector and the child: not long, just a few
fragments of sentences, why not? – the girl would simply have run
away from her mother in order to meet her beloved wizard, to hasten
to her happiness, and so at the end there would be a chance for a
moment of luminous calm, of gentle loving-kindness, renunciation,
and sweet poesy after all the horrors. Or else, and this is no doubt
more likely, you will fabricate something entirely different. I have read
a little of your stuff, you know, although in strict honesty there are
some other authors I prefer. The very illogicality of this tale will attract
you, the fact that here is someone who believes in the innocence of
a guilty man and seeks a murderer who cannot exist, as we have
defined the situation accurately enough. But now let's suppose you
choose to be crueller than reality, out of sheer sportiveness and in
order to put us policemen in an utterly ridiculous light. You'll decide
that Matthäi actually finds a murderer, one of your comical saints, a
kind-hearted preacher of some sect who of course is in reality innocent
and simply incapable of doing harm to anyone, and for that very

reason in one of your nasty inspirations you'll arrange that all the evidence points to him. Matthäi will then kill this pure-hearted simple soul; all the proofs will fit like a glove; whereupon the happy detective will be hailed as a genius and taken back on the force. That, too, would be like you. You see, I am on to your tricks. But you certainly are not going to ascribe all my babbling to the Reserve du Patron – I grant you we're on the second bottle. On the contrary you no doubt feel that I still have the end of the story to tell, even though I'm taking uncommonly long to come to it. For I don't have to hide from you the fact that this story unfortunately has a point, and you must suspect by now that this is a thoroughly shabby point, so shabby that it simply cannot be put to use in any decent novel or film. It is so ridiculous, stupid and trivial that it would have to be suppressed if this story were to be set down on paper. Yet in all honesty it must be admitted that this point is thoroughly in Matthäi's favour, puts him in the proper light, shows him as a genius, as a person who fathomed the factors of reality which were hidden to the rest of us, fathomed them to such an extent that he broke through the theories and assumptions which tripped us up and penetrated close to those laws we never ordinarily get at, and which keep the world in motion. Only close to them, of course. For the very fact that this gruesome point unfortunately does exist, that there is this element of incalculability – of chance, if you will – exposes his genius, his plans and actions as all the more painfully absurd in hindsight than was the case when in the opinion of everyone at headquarters he was mistaken. Nothing is grimmer than a genius stumbling over something idiotic. But when such a thing does happen everything depends upon the attitude that the genius takes towards the ridiculous thing that has brought him to a fall, whether or not he accepts it. Matthäi could not accept it. He wanted his calculations to accord with reality. Therefore he had to deny reality and end in a void. And so my story comes to its conclusion, in a peculiarly dreary fashion, because what happened was the most banal of all possible 'solutions'. Well, now and then that is how things turn out. The worst *does* sometimes happen. As men we have to count on that possibility, have to arm ourselves against it, and above all we have to realize that since absurdities necessarily occur, and nowadays manifest themselves with more and more forcefulness, we can prevent ourselves from being destroyed by them and can make ourselves relatively comfortable upon this earth only if we humbly include these absurdities in our thinking, reckon with the inevitable fractures and distortions of human reason when it attempts honestly to deal with reality. We have to realize that without this knowledge we are in danger of making an absolute of absurdity, of taking it 'in itself', as though it were established somewhere outside the human mind; that we would then be forced to regard the absurd as an error which it was within our power to avoid; on the basis of which illusion we might find ourselves executing the whole world out of a kind of defiant morality once we undertook to try to establish a flawless rational structure, for its very flawless perfection would be its deadly mendacity and a sign of the most frightful blindness. But forgive me for introducing this commentary in the midst of my pretty little tale; I know that it is logically not quite watertight; still, you must allow an old man like me to have a few thoughts about his experiences, unpolished though these thoughts may be. In spite of the fact that I come from the police I do make an effort, after all, to be a man and not an ox.

Well, it was just last year, and on a Sunday again, of course, when I received a telephone call from a Catholic priest and had to pay a visit to the cantonal hospital. This was just shortly before my retirement, in the very last days of my term in office, in fact, and my successor was actually already taking over – not Henzi, who fortunately did not make it, in spite of his fine wife – but a man of stature and punctiliousness, also endowed with decency and kindliness, which are qualities badly needed in that post. The telephone call reached me at my home. I went to the hospital only because there seemed to be something important that a dying woman wished to tell me. That sort of thing happens now and then. It was a sunny but cold December day – everything bare, sad, melancholy. At such times our city can be a mournful place. So it was rather a trial to see a dying woman on such a day. The result was that I walked several times around Aschbacher's 'Harp' in the park, in a pretty downcast frame of mind, but finally screwed up my resolution and tramped into the building. I had to see a Frau Schrott, medical section, private room. The room looked out on the park. There were vases of flowers everywhere, roses and gladioli. The curtains were half drawn, slanting rays of light falling on the floor. At the window sat a massive priest with a rough, florid face and a grey untended beard, and in the bed lay a little old woman, all delicately wrinkled, hair thin and snow white, enormously gentle, obviously very rich, to judge by the sumptuousness of the room. Beside the bed stood a complicated apparatus, some sort of medical business, to which ran a number of tubes that emerged from under the blanket. The machine had to be constantly checked by a nurse. The nurse entered the room at regular intervals, silent and conscientious, so that the conversation was interrupted at these same regular intervals – I want to mention this circumstance right at the beginning.

I greeted them and introduced myself. The old woman gazed attentively at me, with the utmost calmness. Her face was waxen, unreal, and yet still curiously animated. In her yellow wrinkled hands she was holding a small black gilt-edged book, evidently a Bible. Yet it seemed scarcely credible that this woman was about to die; the force which emanated from her, in spite of all the tubes that crawled from under her blanket, seemed so vital, so unbroken. The priest remained in his seat. With a gesture as majestic as it was awkward he indicated a chair beside the bed.

'Sit down,' he invited me, and when I had taken the seat his deep voice rumbled from the window, against which he loomed in vast silhouette: 'Frau Schrott, tell the Commissioner what you have to tell him. At eleven o'clock we must proceed with Extreme Unction.'

Frau Schrott smiled. She was sorry to put me to this trouble, she twittered in a ladylike manner, and although her voice was low it was extremely distinct and even lively.

No trouble at all, I lied, convinced now that the old grandmother was going to inform me of a bequest she wished to make for needy policemen, or something of the sort.

It was really an unimportant and harmless story she had to tell me, the old woman continued, a thing that probably happened in all families once or several times, and that was why she had forgotten about it; but now, this was just how things happened, because eternity was approaching she had mentioned the matter during her general confession, purely by chance because a moment before a granddaughter of her only godchild had come to bring her some flowers and had been wearing a red skirt, and Father Beck had become all worked up and said she ought to tell the story to me: she really didn't know why – after all it was all over now, but if the reverend Father thought –

'Tell the story, Frau Schrott,' the deep voice spoke from the window, 'tell the story.' And in the city the church bells began ringing the end of the sermons, changing low and far away.

Well, she would try to, the old woman began again, and started rattling on. It was a long time since she'd told any stories – she only used to tell them to Emil, her son by her first husband; but then dear Emil had died of consumption, there was nothing anyone could do about it. He would have been as old as I by now, or rather as old as Reverend Father Beck; but she would try to imagine now that I was her son and Reverend Father Beck also, for immediately after Emil she had had Mark, but he had died after only three days – premature really, he'd come into the world after only six months and Doctor Hoble had said it was best for the poor little fellow ... and so the woman's muddled mind ran on.

'Tell the story, Frau Schrott, tell the story,' the priest admonished her in his bass voice, still sitting immobile at the window except for an occasional gesture of drawing his right hand Moses-like through his wild grey beard and sending forth in gentle waves a strong odour of garlic. 'We must soon proceed with Extreme Unction.'

At this point she suddenly became proud, quite aristocratic; she even found strength to raise her small head slightly, and her tiny eyes flashed. She was a Stänzli, she said, and her grandfather had been Colonel Stänzli who led the retreat to Eschholzmatt in 1847; and her sister had married Colonel Stüssi, member of the Zürich General Staff during the First World War, who had been an intimate friend of General Ulrich Wille and had known Kaiser Wilhelm personally, as I no doubt was aware.

'Of course,' I replied wearily, 'naturally.' What did I care about old Willie and Kaiser Wilhelm? I thought. Come out with your request now, old woman. If only I could smoke, a little cigarillo would be the thing to bring a touch of jungle air into this hospital atmosphere and offset the smell of garlic. And the priest droned stubbornly, inexorably: 'Tell your story, Frau Schrott, tell your story.'

She would have me know, the old lady continued, and her face now took on a curiously bitter, really hate-filled expression, that her sister with her Colonel Stüssi was to blame for it all. Her sister was ten years older than she, ninety-nine now, and had been a widow for almost forty years, had a villa on the Zürichberg, a good number of Brown-Boveri stocks, owned plenty of property on Bahnhofstrasse. And then suddenly a dreary stream, or rather a filthy torrent of vituperation, burst from the mouth of this dying old grandmother, such filth that I dare not reproduce it. At the same time the old woman sat up a little and her ancient head with the snow white hair waggled vigorously back and forth, as though she were insane with joy over her outburst of rage. But then she quietened down again, for fortunately the nurse came to her bedside – now, now, Frau Schrott, let's not have any excitement, let's lie nice and still. The old crone obeyed. When we were left alone again she waved her hand in a feeble gesture. All these flowers, she said, had been sent by her sister just to annoy her; her sister knew perfectly well that she didn't like flowers and hated seeing money wasted on useless things; but they had never quarrelled, as I was no doubt thinking; they had always been sweet and affectionate to one another – out of sheer spitefulness, of course; all the Stänzlis had the same way of being polite although they could never endure one other, and their politeness was only their method of getting at one another and tormenting one another to death – fortunately, she must say, because how otherwise could they have remained the souls of propriety?

'Tell your story, Frau Schrott,' the priest said again. 'Extreme Unction is waiting.' And I began wishing that instead of a little cigarillo I had one of my big Bahianos.

In 1895 she had married her dear departed Dr Galuser, the torrent rippled endlessly on, a physician in Chur. Her sister with her colonel had even taken that amiss and thought the marriage not fine enough, she had made that perfectly plain, and when the colonel died of influenza immediately after the First World War the sister had become more and more impossible and had practically set up altars to her soldier husband.

'Tell your story, Frau Schrott, tell your story,' the priest kept after her, but by no means impatiently; he seemed at most faintly sad at how her mind was wandering, while I dozed and now and then started into wakefulness. 'Think of Extreme Unction, tell your story.' There was nothing to be done; the shrunken little woman babbled on and on upon her death-bed, endlessly loquacious in spite of her chirping voice and the tubes emerging from under the blanket. One thing led to another, she could not come to the point. In so far as I was still able to think at all I vaguely expected some story about a helpful policeman, then the announcement of a bequest of several thousand francs in order to infuriate her ninety-nine-year-old sister; I prepared a little speech of thanks and longed, resolutely repressing my unrealistic dreams of smoking, longed, in order not to give way entirely to despair, for my customary aperitif and the traditional Sunday dinner in the Kronenhalle with my wife and daughter.

Then, the old woman was meanwhile continuing in a more or less straight line, after the death of her husband, her dear departed Galuser, she had married her dear departed Schrott, who had been a sort of chauffeur and gardener for her and undertaken all the work that can best be done by a man in a big old house, like heating, repairing shutters, and so on; and although her sister had made no comment about it, and even come to Chur for the wedding, she had still been irked by the marriage, the old woman was certain of that, even though the sister, just to annoy her, of course, had concealed her feelings. And that was how she had become Frau Schrott.

She sighed. Somewhere in the corridor outside the nurses were singing Christmas carols 'Well, it was a really harmonious marriage with my dear departed,' the old crone went on after she had listened to a few bars of the song, 'even though it may have been harder for him than I could imagine. My dear departed Albert was twenty-three when we married, since he had been born just in 1900, and I was already fifty-five. But I know it was best for him, he was an orphan, you see, and his mother was – I don't want to say what she was – and nobody knew his father, not even the name. My first husband had taken the boy in when he was sixteen; he had quite a bit of trouble in school, you see, and never did get on very well with writing and reading. Marriage was simply the most decent solution; it's so easy for a widow to be talked about, even though I never did have anything to do that way with my dear departed Albert, not even after we were married; that's quite understandable with such a difference in age. But my means were limited; I had to budget carefully to manage with my houses in Zürich and Chur; and what would my dear departed Albert have done, seeing he was a little short of brains, in the hard struggle for existence out in the world? He would have been lost, and after all a Christian has obligations. And so we lived honourably together; he busied himself about the house and garden – a fine figure of a man, I must say, big and strong, always dressed in a dignified formal way. I had no need to be ashamed of him, even though he hardly ever talked except perhaps to say 'Yes, Mummy; of course, Mummy.' But he was obedient and temperate about drinking – only he liked to eat, especially noodles, all sorts of starches in fact, and chocolate. He really was crazy about chocolate. But otherwise he was a good sober man and he stayed like that all his life, very much nicer and better behaved than the chauffeur my sister married four years later, in spite of her late colonel, and he too was only thirty.'

'Tell your story, Frau Schrott,' the priest's voice wafted from the window, indifferently inexorable, when the old woman now paused for a while, probably somewhat exhausted after all – and I sat in my simplicity still waiting for the bequest for needy policemen.

Frau Schrott nodded. 'You see, Commissioner,' she said, 'during the 'forties my dear departed Albert started drifting downhill. I really don't know exactly what was wrong with him, but something must have been damaged inside his head. He became duller and quieter than ever, would stare into space and sometimes not talk for days, only did his work as he should so that I didn't have any real reason for scolding him, but he also rode around for hours on his cycle. Perhaps the war upset him, or the fact that the Army wouldn't take him; how are we to know what goes on inside a man's mind? Besides that, he became more and more of a glutton – luckily we had our chickens and some rabbits too. And then the thing happened with my dear departed Albert that I'm supposed to tell you about. The first time was towards the end of the war.'

She fell silent because the nurse and a doctor entered the room again. They busied themselves behind the apparatus and then behind the old woman. The doctor was a German, blond as though he had stepped out of a picture-book, cheerful and brash, doing his routine. Sunday round – how do you feel, Frau Schrott, keep the chin up, we're getting excellent results, marvellous, marvellous, don't let it get you down. Then he trotted off, the nurse followed him, and the priest admonished: 'Tell your story, Frau Schrott, tell your story; Extreme Unction at eleven.' A prospect which did not seem to disturb the old creature in the least.

'Every week he had to take eggs to my sister in Zürich,' the old woman made a fresh start. 'Poor dear departed Albert would fasten the basket on the back of his cycle and come back towards evening, because he started out very early in the morning, about five or six o'clock, always neatly dressed in black, with a black bowler. Everybody gave him a friendly greeting when he pedalled through Chur and out into the country, whistling to himself his favourite song: 'I am a Switzer lad and love my country dear.' This time it was a hot midsummer day, just two days before August the first – I remember everyone was preparing bunting for the national holiday – and this time it was after midnight before he came home. I heard him fussing and washing for a long time in the bathroom and I went in and saw that there was blood all over my dear departed Albert, over his clothes too. 'My goodness, Albert dear,' I said, 'what has happened to you?' He just stared goggled-eyed at me and then he said, 'An accident, Mummy, I'll be all right, go to sleep, Mummy,' and so I went to sleep, though I wondered because I hadn't seen any wounds on him. But in the morning when we were at breakfast and he was eating his eggs – he always ate four at a time and his slices of bread and jam – I read in the newspaper that someone had murdered a little girl in the St Gall canton, probably with a razor, and then I remembered that last night in the bathroom he had been cleaning his razor although he always shaved in the morning, and then it suddenly dawned on me like a revelation and I became very stern with my dear departed Albert and said, "Albert dear, you killed that girl in St Gall canton, didn't you?" Then he stopped eating his eggs and bread and jam and pickles and said, "Yes I did, Mummy, it had to be; it was a voice from Heaven," and then he went on eating. I was very worried to think he was so ill; I was sorry for the girl and I thought of telephoning Sichler – not the old doctor but his son who is also a very good doctor and sympathetic. But then I thought of my sister, how she would gloat – it would have been the finest day in her life; and so I was just very stern and firm with my dear departed Albert and told him plainly that this must never, never, never happen again, and he said "Yes, Mummy." "How did it happen?" I asked. "Mummy," he said "I kept meeting a little girl with a red skirt and blonde plaits when I rode to Zürich by way of Wattwil. It was a long distance out of my way, but ever since I met the girl near a little clump of woods I've had to go that way – the voice from Heaven, Mummy – and the voice ordered me to play with the girl, and then the voice from Heaven told me to give her chocolate, and then I had to kill the girl; it was the voice from Heaven, Mummy, and then I went into the nearest woods and lay under a bush until night and then I came back to you, Mummy." "Albert dear," I said, "you're not going to pedal your cycle to my sister any more; we'll send the eggs by post." "Yes, Mummy," he said, and smeared another slice of bread with jam and went out to the yard. Now I really must go to Father Beck, I thought, so that he can give Albert a good talking to; but when I looked out of the window and saw my dear departed Albert out there in the sun doing his duty so faithfully and quietly, and working a little sadly around the rabbit hutch, patching it up, and I saw how spick and span the whole place was, I thought: what's done is done, Albert is a good soul, a dear good boy at heart and it will never happen again, of course.'

The nurse came into the room once more, examined the apparatus, rearranged the tubes, and the little old woman in the bed seemed exhausted once more. I scarcely dared to breathe; the sweat was running down my face and I paid it no heed. Suddenly I shivered, and felt doubly ridiculous because I had been imagining the old woman was going to make some bequest to the police force. And then those bunches of flowers, all the red and white roses, the flaming gladioli, asters, zinnias, carnations, obtained from God know where, and a whole vase full of orchids, idiotically ostentatious; and then the sun behind the curtains; the motionless, massive figure of the priest; the smell of garlic. I should have been able to fly into a rage, to arrest the woman – but there was no point in it any longer; she was about to receive Extreme Unction, and there I sat in my Sunday clothes, solemn, formal and useless.

'Go on with your story, Frau Schrott,' the priest patiently admonished, 'go on with your story.' And she went on. 'And my dear departed Albert did really get better,' she explained in her calm gentle voice, and it was really as if she were telling two children a fairy-tale in which evil and absurdity simply happened and were just as wonderful as good. 'He no longer went to Zürich. But when the Second World War was over we were able to use our car again, the one I had bought in 'thirty-eight because the car that belonged to my departed Galuser was really out of fashion by then, and so my dear departed Albert used to drive me about in our Buick. Once we even went to Ascona, and then I thought, since he gets so much pleasure out of driving he really can start going to Zürich again – after all it won't be dangerous in the Buick because he has to pay attention to driving and can't hear any voices from Heaven; and so he took to driving to my sister and faithfully delivering the eggs again like a good boy, and every so often a rabbit. But then unfortunately he suddenly came home after midnight once more. I went to the garage straight away – I sensed it at once because all of a sudden he had been taking truffles from the sweet dish, and sure enough I found my dear departed Albert washing the inside of the car, and everything was covered in blood. "Have you killed a girl again, Albert dear?" I said, and I was very serious with him. "Mummy," he said, "don't worry, not in St Gall canton but in Schwyz canton, that's how the voice from Heaven wanted it, and this girl had a red skirt and yellow plaits too." But I was not satisfied; I was even sterner with him than the first time, almost angry. For a week I wouldn't allow him to use the car, and I wanted to go to Father Beck about it – I was really determined. But my sister would have been just too overjoyed, I couldn't allow that, and so I watched my dear departed Albert closer than ever, and for two years everything went along well until he did it once more because he had to obey the voice from Heaven, poor dear departed Albert; he was all broken up and cried, but I caught on to it at once because of the truffles missing from the sweet dish. It was a girl in Zürich canton, and she had a red skirt and yellow plaits too – it's unbelievable how dangerously mothers will dress their daughters.'

'Was the girl Griti Moser?' I asked.

Her name was Griti, and the others were Sonya and Eveli,' the old lady answered. 'I noted all the names. But then my dear departed Albert began getting worse and worse; he started running away, and I had to tell him everything ten times over, I had to scold him all day long like a little boy; and in 1949 or 50, I don't remember exactly any more, but a few months after Griti, anyhow, he started getting restless and nervous again; even the chicken coop was untidy and the hens kept up a frightful cackle because he did not feed them properly, and he started riding about in our Buick again and would be gone whole afternoons, though he would only say "I'm going for a little ride"; and all of a sudden I noticed the truffles were missing from the sweet dish again. Then I kept my eye on him, and when he stole into the living-room again, poor dear departed Albert, with his razor tucked into his pocket like a fountain pen, I went up to him and said: "Albert dear, you've found a girl again." "The voice from Heaven, Mummy," he answered; "please let me do it just this time; the command of Heaven is the command of Heaven, and she has a red skirt too and yellow plaits." "Albert," I said sternly, "I cannot permit it. Where is the girl?" "Not far from here, at a service station," my dear departed Albert said. "Please, please, Mummy, let me obey." Then I became really firm. "It won't do, Albert," I said; "you've promised me; clean the chicken coop at once and give the hens a decent feeding." Then my dear departed Albert flew into a rage; for the first time in our marriage, which was so harmonious otherwise, he actually screamed at me, "I'm only your servant" – that was how ill the poor fellow was – and he ran out with the truffles and the razor and jumped into the Buick, and only fifteen minutes later they telephoned me that he'd had a collision with a van and was killed. Father Beck came and Police Sergeant Bühler – he was wonderfully tactful, and that is why I've remembered the police of Chur in my will and left them five thousand francs, and five thousand francs I've left to the Zürich police because I have houses here on Freiestrasse, you know; and of course my sister came with her chauffeur, just to vex me, and spoiled the whole funeral for me.'

I stared down at the old woman. So now the bequest too had come, the bequest I had been expecting all along It was as though an especially refined mockery of me had been conceived.

But now the senior doctor and an assistant and two nurses came in; we were sent out, and I bade Frau Schrott goodbye.

'Goodbye, keep well,' I said in empty-headed embarrassment, the only thought in my mind being to get away as quickly as possible – whereupon she began to snigger and the senior doctor threw me a peculiar look. The scene was embarrassing beyond belief; I was enormously relieved to leave the old woman, the priest, the whole assembly of them behind me at last, and step out into the corridor.

Everywhere there were flocks of visitors with parcels and flowers, the place reeked of hospital. I fled. The exit was close by; in a moment I would be safely in the park. But then a tall man came down the corridor pushing a wheelchair in which sat a wrinkled, trembling old woman in a mink coat, holding armfuls of flowers, monstrous bouquets. Perhaps this was the ninety-nine-year-old sister with her chauffeur-husband – how should I know? I glanced back at them in horror until they disappeared into the private section. Then I began almost to run; I rushed out of the building and through the park, past patients in wheelchairs, past convalescents and visitors, and did not really begin to calm down a little until I was seated in the Kronenhalle. Over liver-dumpling soup.

From the Kronenhalle I drove straight to Chur. Unfortunately I had to take my wife and daughter along; it was Sunday and I had promised to spend the afternoon with them, and did not want to become involved in explanations. I said not a word, drove like mad; perhaps there was still a chance to save the situation. But my family did not have to wait long outside the service station. Inside the tavern a crowd of pretty tough characters were having a roaring time; Annemarie had just come back from reform school. Cold though it was, Matthäi was sitting in his mechanic's overalls on his bench, smoking a cheroot, reeking of absinthe. I sat down beside him and told him the story briefly. But there was nothing to be done. He seemed not even to listen to me. For a moment I was undecided; then I went back to my Opel and drove on to Chur. The family was impatient and hungry.

'Wasn't that Matthäi?' my wife asked; as usual she never knew what had been going on.

'Yes.'

'Why, I thought he was in Jordan,' she said.

'He did not go, my dear.'

In Chur we had trouble finding a parking place. The pastry-shop was overcrowded, but we managed to find a table and ordered tea and pastries. Then my wife called the waitress back again.

'Please bring us half a pound of truffles,' she said.

She was only a little surprised when I refused to eat any truffles. Not for the world.

And now, my dear sir, you can do whatever you like with this story. Emma, the bill.

Picador

☐	**Burning Leaves**	Don Bannister	£2.50p
☐	**Making Love: The Picador Book of Erotic Verse**	edited by Alan Bold	£1.95p
☐	**Bury My Heart at Wounded Knee**	Dee Brown	£4.50p
☐	**Cities of the Red Night**	William Burroughs	£2.50p
☐	**The Road to Oxiana**	Robert Byron	£2.95p
☐	**If on a Winter's Night a Traveller**	Italo Calvino	£2.95p
☐	**Auto Da Fé**	Elias Canetti	£3.95p
☐	**Exotic Pleasures**	Peter Carey	£1.95p
☐	**Chandler Collection Vol. 1**	Raymond Chandler	£4.95p
☐	**In Patagonia**	Bruce Chatwin	£2.75p
☐	**Crown Jewel**	Ralph de Boissiere	£2.75p
☐	**Letters from Africa 1914—1931**	Isak Dinesen (Karen Blixen)	£3.95p
☐	**The Book of Daniel**	E. L. Doctorow	£2.95p
☐	**Debts of Honour**	Michael Foot	£2.50p
☐	**One Hundred Years of Solitude**	Gabriel García Márquez	£3.50p
☐	**Nothing, Doting, Blindness**	Henry Green	£2.95p
☐	**The Obstacle Race**	Germaine Greer	£6.95p
☐	**Roots**	Alex Haley	£4.95p
☐	**The Four Great Novels**	Dashiel Hammett	£5.95p
☐	**When the Tree Sings**	Stratis Haviaras	£1.95p
☐	**Dispatches**	Michael Herr	£2.75p
☐	**Riddley Walker**	Russell Hoban	£2.75p
☐	**Three Trapped Tigers**	C. Cabrera Infante	£2.95p
☐	**Unreliable Memoirs**	Clive James	£2.50p
☐	**Man and His Symbols**	Carl Jung	£3.95p
☐	**China Men**	Maxine Hong Kingston	£2.95p
☐	**Janus: A Summing Up**	Arthur Koestler	£3.50p
☐	**Memoirs of a Survivor**	Doris Lessing	£2.95p
☐	**Albert Camus**	Herbert Lottman	£3.95p
☐	**Zany Afternoons**	Bruce McCall	£4.95p
☐	**The Cement Garden**	Ian McEwan	£2.50p
☐	**The Serial**	Cyra McFadden	£1.75p
☐	**McCarthy's List**	Mary Mackey	£1.95p
☐	**Daddyji/Mamaji**	Ved Mehta	£3.50p
☐	**Slowly Down the Ganges**	Eric Newby	£2.95p
☐	**The Snow Leopard**	Peter Matthiessen	£3.50p

☐	**Lectures on Literature**	Vladimir Nabokov	£3.95p
☐	**The Best of Myles**	Flann O' Brien	£3.50p
☐	**Autobiography**	John Cowper Powys	£3.50p
☐	**Hadrian the Seventh**	Fr. Rolfe (Baron Corvo)	£1.25p
☐	**On Broadway**	Damon Runyon	£3.95p
☐	**Midnight's Children**	Salman Rushdie	£3.95p
☐	**Awakenings**	Oliver Sacks	£3.95p
☐	**The Fate of the Earth**	Jonathan Schell	£2.50p
☐	**Street of Crocodiles**	Bruno Schultz	£1.25p
☐	**Poets in their Youth**	Eileen Simpson	£2.95p
☐	**Miss Silver's Past**	Josef Skvorecky	£2.50p
☐	**A Flag for Sunrise**	Robert Stone	£2.50p
☐	**Visitants**	Randolph Stow	£2.50p
☐	**Alice Fell**	Emma Tennant	£1.95p
☐	**The Flute-Player**	D. M. Thomas	£2.50p
☐	**The Great Shark Hunt**	Hunter S. Thompson	£4.95p
☐	**The Longest War**	Jacob Timerman	£2.50p
☐	**Aunt Julia and the Scriptwriter**	Mario Vargas Llosa	£2.95p
☐	**Female Friends**	Fay Weldon	£2.95p
☐	**No Particular Place To Go**	Hugo Williams	£1.95p
☐	**The Outsider**	Colin Wilson	£3.50p
☐	**Mars**	Fritz Zorn	£1.95p

All these books are available at your local bookshop or newsagent, or can be ordered direct from the publisher. Indicate the number of copies required and fill in the form below   12
....

Name_____
(Block letters please)

Address_____

_____

Send to CS Department, Pan Books Ltd, PO Box 40, Basingstoke, Hants
Please enclose remittance to the value of the cover price plus:
35p for the first book plus 15p per copy for each additional book ordered
to a maximum charge of £1.25 to cover postage and packing
Applicable only in the UK

While every effort is made to keep prices low, it is sometimes
necessary to increase prices at short notice. Pan Books reserve
the right to show on covers and charge new retail prices which
may differ from those advertised in the text or elsewhere